RISE FROM RUIN

BAEN BOOKS by MELISSA OLTHOFF

Rise from Ruin

RISE FROM RUIN

BOOK 1 OF THE GRIFFIN CORPS

MELISSA OLTHOFF

A Baen Books Original

Baen Publishing Enterprises
P.O. Box 1403
Riverdale, NY 10471
www.baen.com

ISBN: 978-1-6680-7267-7

Cover art by Pierluigi Abbondanza

First printing, June 2025

Distributed by Simon & Schuster
1230 Avenue of the Americas
New York, NY 10020

Library of Congress Cataloging-in-Publication Data

Names: Olthoff, Melissa, author.
Title: Rise from ruin / Melissa Olthoff.
Description: Riverdale, NY : Baen Publishing Enterprises, 2025.
Identifiers: LCCN 2025001275 (print) | LCCN 2025001276 (ebook) | ISBN
    9781668072677 (trade paperback) | ISBN 9781964856254 (ebook)
Subjects: LCGFT: Fantasy fiction. | Novels.
Classification: LCC PS3615.L85 R57 2025 (print) | LCC PS3615.L85 (ebook)
    | DDC 813/.6—dc23/eng/20250212
LC record available at https://lccn.loc.gov/2025001275
LC ebook record available at https://lccn.loc.gov/2025001276

Printed in the United States of America

10 9 8 7 6 5 4 3 2 1

DEDICATION
To my dad. My real life superhero.
and
For Howard.

PART I
FALL FROM GRACE

CHAPTER 1

Every cadet wanted to be a dragon rider right up until they were hanging upside down from the saddle a thousand feet in the air—but I just tightened my grip and grinned.

Silver wings flared wide an instant before the instructor dragon threw himself into another snap roll. The sky and ground spun in a dizzying whirl. Without pause, wings tucked in tight, a gray nose pointed straight down, and we flipped into a dive toward the ground so very far below. The wind was in my face, my heart was pounding, and I was fairly certain I'd left my stomach several hundred feet up in the air.

And I loved every second of it.

We leveled off barely two hundred feet above the ground and were blazing along so fast the trees were nothing more than a green blur. Seated directly behind me, the instructor dragon rider shouted something lost to the wind and tapped my leg to confirm I was able to continue with the next phase of maneuvering. Just as I had every time, I tapped his leg in immediate acknowledgment, slightly harder than necessary in my enthusiasm.

I wanted to scream *go, go, go*, but that wouldn't be professional. As a third-year military cadet at the Tennessan Bonded Training Academy, I'd have to keep my excited screaming internal. It helped that I truly had no breath for screaming anything. The saddle and leather straps wrapped around legs and hips did a lot to secure us, but it wasn't enough. Legs had to grip, core muscles constantly flexed, and proper body position was critical. Flying was a whole-body workout at the easiest of times—a defensive aerobatics checkride was not one of those times.

Great wings beat hard to increase our speed, and I sharpened my focus. While I knew and had trained to every maneuver, the order was entirely up to the instructor. From this low of an altitude, there were two types of simulated threats Gregor, the instructor dragon, could react to—one from above, or one from below. Since Savinia's anti-air artillery had taken out more Tennessan dragons than anything else, and we'd already covered an airborne threat response...

Sure enough, Gregor abruptly pulled up and arched back, turning all that speed into an inverted loop. For two seconds, for an eternity, those leather straps were the only thing keeping us in the saddle, because legs could only do so much. And then Gregor rolled upright facing the opposite direction in a textbook Immelmann turn, and I remembered how to breathe.

Without giving my heartrate a chance to slow, the gray dragon dipped and swerved in an unpredictable pattern, sometimes dropping low enough that the wind of our passage tossed the treetops, other times catching thermals to balloon several hundred feet higher in seconds. My spine flexed, and my hands rested lightly on leathery gray hide, every bit of my skill needed to move with the dragon.

The next time the instructor tapped my leg, it was just a little harder. A subtle warning that the next phase was the final—and hardest—of the checkride.

I'd proven I could ride. Now I had to prove I could ride *and* maintain situational awareness. That meant I had to keep my head on a swivel, calling the threats our dragon couldn't see, all while keeping my seat in the most physically demanding phase of flight.

Without hesitation, I tapped the instructor's leg back and scanned for threats. Left, clear. Right, clear. Up, as clear as I could tell with the sun directly overhead, half blinding me.

Left and down—a flash of light in the trees.

"Contact, nine o'clock low!" I bellowed.

In response, Gregor unleashed a harsh roar-scream. I felt as much as heard the ear-piercing cry, and if I hadn't known it was part of the checkride, I would've thought the alarm in his voice real. I clamped my legs tight an instant before he jinked to the right to avoid the simulated ground fire.

Gregor jinked again, and the breath exploded from my lungs as my core tightened to compensate. Another dodge, another lost breath, but I didn't falter. Not even when he slipped sideways and we dropped down to just above the treetops.

Suddenly, we were the last place a dragon rider wanted to be—low and slow. Gregor could either go for speed or altitude to escape the "shoot me, fuck me" zone. Not both.

Wings flared wide an instant before he pitched his nose up and fought for altitude. It wasn't smooth, or graceful. The big dragon beat the sky into submission through sheer determination on fragile wings. It was like trying to ride a bucking horse going straight up, but three years at the academy had conditioned my muscles to handle it. I leaned forward, my seat balanced and my body hugged tight to his neck, and caught his rhythm.

A friendly thermal boosted us higher, and our flight smoothed out. Now several thousand feet above ground level and out of range of even the biggest dragon lance, Gregor relaxed. The tension eased from my shoulders, and I waited for the instructor to tap my leg a final time, signaling the end of the checkride.

Except, he didn't.

Oh. *Shit.*

Almost frantically, I scanned the skies and the ground below. When I found nothing, my gut twisted. I should've looked up first. Squinting against the brilliant sunlight and wishing my goggles were tinted, I searched the flawless blue skies above—and caught a flash of red where there shouldn't be any.

"Contact, twelve o'clock high!"

My screamed warning gave Gregor just enough time to react. As the red dragon dropped down on us from out of the sun, the gray tilted on one wing and side-slipped out of his path. Red wings flashed past, the world tilted sideways, and all of my weight went to my right leg. Leather straps creaked, but I managed to keep my boot tucked into the indentation that served as a stirrup and held my position despite the strain.

The "enemy" dragon spiraled up on a thermal with a friendly roar and was quickly out of sight, either returning to the academy or getting ready to ambush another student. I certainly wasn't the only cadet out on a checkride today—and then came the final tap on the leg I'd been waiting for.

My checkride was over. The only question was whether I'd passed.

As Gregor looped back toward the academy in a wide turn, the sunlight played across my face. For all that I hadn't paid much attention, the early autumn day really was gorgeous. Warm, sunny, with small puffy clouds scattered across the sky. It was absolutely perfect flying weather, but I was far too distracted replaying the checkride to get lost in the wind.

Every maneuver, every time my seat wasn't flawless, my near failure to spot the final threat. It all played on an endless loop in my mind. I had to pass to advance, had to score well to keep my ranking high, but it wasn't just about academy bullshit.

The Savinians had dragons of their own—and worse—and we had to train to meet that threat. The fact that it was fun as hell was irrelevant, because after I bonded a dragon of my own and graduated to active duty, those defensive maneuvers I'd just been graded on would mean the difference between surviving . . . or not.

In an effort to distract myself, I leaned over slightly and picked out ground reference points as we flew along at a leisurely pace. The refresher would be useful since I was double-turning today and would be back out on a different dragon this evening.

There to the north, the griffin rider training grounds where they practiced scouting and patrol riding. Cadets who weren't quite as good in their first two years at the academy bonded to griffins instead of dragons. A flash of feathers drew my gaze to a pair of griffins spiraling higher above the training grounds. It looked like they were playing.

Dismissing them, I turned to the right and picked out the strange tower spearing into the sky, an easy waypoint on any of the southern routes. Unlike our current materials, whatever the tower was made of didn't rust. A pre-War relic from another time, when we had the power to do amazing things.

A glint of sunlight on metal, a lot of metal, drew my gaze east. The last reference point until the academy itself—anti-air emplacements, placed at every cardinal point around the academy grounds. Great, crew-served ballistae armed with dragon lances and flechette rounds, because when the enemy had dragons of their own, no place was truly safe, no matter how far from the front lines.

Gregor beat his wings, and my core tightened as he side-slipped into another thermal. We rose several hundred feet higher in a matter of seconds, and a grin pulled at my lips as the academy finally came into sight. Three years a cadet, and I never got tired of seeing it from the air.

Nestled in the verdant foothills of western Tennessan, the academy's chaotic mix of ancient gray duracrete, white stone, and wooden buildings stood out from all the green like a beacon. All of it encircled by protective stone walls. All of it home to hundreds of bond-capable cadets, bonded riders, instructors, and support personnel.

The skies above the academy were busy, gray and green and red wings flashing as dragons flew, with the occasional feathered wings catching my eye as griffins darted in and around the bigger dragons. No black or blue dragons were out today, but they were so rare I wasn't surprised.

As we banked left and slipped into the landing pattern, another gray dragon, slightly larger than Gregor, joined on our wing. Close enough for me to identify the cadet riding in the student position—Dimitri, my best friend and rival for the top spot in our class.

A broad smile creased my face, and I lifted one hand in a wave. Dimitri didn't return it. I couldn't quite make out his expression, but he didn't look happy. Either his own checkride hadn't gone well, or he was still mad at me for the latest volley in our ongoing prank war.

Possibly both.

I was still feeling pretty smug about the itching powder I'd gotten into his leathers just before a training sortie last week. The fact that I'd managed to get our friends Zayne and Callum at the same time was a definite bonus. Zayne, ever the peacemaker, had taken the prank in stride. Callum had looked as if he wanted to stab me. And not in a fun way.

Too bad, because that dick had deserved every miserable second on his flight after what he'd done to me.

Gregor dropped his right wing, and the shift in gravity pulled my wandering thoughts back where they belonged—landing. The big dragon turned on short final before spiraling down to the landing field within the dragon campus walls. Silver wings flared and beat hard a final time just before his back legs touched the ground. Front legs followed, wings folded, and our flight was over.

Which meant debrief was next.

My hands shook with nerves as I undid the straps, carefully rolled them up, and secured them to the saddle for the next student. I glanced down at the ground, but Gregor snorted and helpfully cocked his front leg, giving me an easy path that didn't involve sliding down his side or jumping straight to the ground.

I murmured my gratitude once my boots were firmly in the dirt again and twisted to face my instructor. Captain Durant's expression was impassive, and my gut tightened to the point where I worried I was going to throw up on his leather boots.

And then he smiled.

"Excellent ride, Cadet Tavros."

With those simple words, the instructor told me everything I needed to know.

I'd passed.

Not just passed. I'd passed the hardest checkride of the semester with an *excellent*. No way to know who held the top ranking until the instructors posted official scores at the end of the week, but an excellent was enough to keep me in the top five. Relief loosened the tension knotting my shoulders, and I bit the insides of my cheeks to keep my grin from breaking free.

"Thank you, sir."

"Just remember to look up a little sooner when scanning for threats. Always think three-dimensionally."

"Yes, sir," I said with a solemn nod.

The big gray snorted again and nudged his rider pointedly. Captain Durant grinned up at his bondmate.

"Gregor says your seat was damn near perfect the entire flight, no matter what he did to throw you off balance. I think he's a little miffed." The instructor's smile faded into a thoughtful frown. "Have you considered switching to grays, Tavros? I know your green is due to hatch soon, but it's not too late."

"Thank you, sir," I said carefully. "But I'm happy with my choice."

"Well, if you have any doubts at all, come see me before you bond. A rider like you would be wasted on rescue."

Stunned at the magnitude of the compliment, I held onto my

bearing by the skin of my teeth. Before I could embarrass myself, Gregor nudged his rider again and grumbled. This time, Captain Durant laughed.

"Yes, it's time to eat, you bottomless pit." He tilted his head toward the center of the academy. "Debrief over, Cadet. Go enjoy a little free time before your next event."

"Yes, sir!"

No longer able to contain my grin, I turned away from instructor and dragon and tugged my flight cap off. Some of my long, copper hair had escaped my braid and immediately drifted into my eyes, but we were given leeway on dress and appearance regulations directly after a flight.

"Hey, Harper!"

My heart jumped at that familiar voice, but I took my time tucking my flight cap and goggles into my belt and smoothed out my expression into a blank mask before I turned. Dimitri strode across the grassy landing field, his short brown hair sticking up in sweaty spikes, flight cap clenched tight in one hand. He looked torn between annoyance and concern, a little furrow in his brow as his gaze searched mine.

"How'd you do?"

My lips twitched as I fought back a smile. "Oh, are you talking to me again?"

Annoyance won. So did my smile.

"Excellent," I said with just a touch of smugness. "You?"

"Same." His eyes narrowed. "What'd you mess up?"

"You first." I stared a challenge up into his stupid brown eyes. He stepped close enough I had to tilt my head back to hold his gaze. I barely noticed when the two gray dragons cleared the landing field and moved past us, though I felt the ground shiver beneath my boots. It wasn't until a griffin playfully buzzed us, flying so low over our heads the fan of feathers on his tail nearly brushed skin, that Dimitri broke with an irritated sigh.

"Slid out of position on the Immelmann by this much." He held his fingers apart by a fraction of an inch. Not horrible, but I knew my best friend. He was beating himself up about it, so I admitted my own fuckup.

"I almost didn't spot the ambush."

Dimitri rolled his eyes. "How many times do I have to tell you to look up, hotshot?"

I scowled and crossed my arms. "How many times do I have to tell you to look through your turns, asshole?"

We glared at each other for a handful of heartbeats before we both broke into grins. Together, we marched toward the busy campus, and just in time, too. One of the irritable reds flared serrated wings and landed, taking up far more space than necessary. We walked just a little faster as an annoyed hiss chased after us, but before we could clear the field, a harsh voice called out.

"Cadets!"

Dimitri and I spun in unison and snapped off crisp salutes to the brawny captain striding toward us. I didn't recognize the rider—and I knew all of the academy instructors by sight if not by name—but I *did* recognize the red dragon looming over his shoulder. They had been the ambushers on my checkride.

The captain casually returned our salutes, fiery orange eyes flicking between us. "Which one of you flew with Durant?"

I lifted my chin slightly. "I did, sir."

"Nero and I almost had you." The corner of his mouth curled up in a predatory smile. "A few seconds slower, and we would have. A few seconds faster, and you *might* have matched my old score."

"Matched, not beat, sir?" I asked, emboldened by the amusement in his eyes.

"Can't beat perfection, Cadet." He turned his attention to Dimitri. "As for you, her seat was better, but your situational awareness was top notch. Both of you keep it up, and maybe one day you'll be as good as me."

"Thank you, sir," Dimitri said with quiet pride.

"Captain Westbrook!" One of the academy's support staffers jogged up, a leather messenger satchel under one arm. "Dispatches are ready for you, sir."

That explained why I didn't recognize him—he was an active duty rider on a messenger relay. Sometimes, our instructors pulled them in as observers, and in this case, ambushers.

"Looks like playtime's over for us." Westbrook secured the satchel and leaped up into the saddle, tightening his straps with practiced efficiency. He glanced down at us with those fierce orange eyes.

"Study hard and bond well. You both have the potential to do a lot of good, and we need every dragon rider we can get out on the Savinian border."

Westbrook waved a sharp dismissal as Nero snapped his wings out in preparation to take off. As the red dragon sprang into the air, we jogged clear of the field and didn't slow until we were in the middle of the busy campus.

Cadets hustled across the courtyard to their next class or training flight, shouts and banter and conversations blending into an overwhelming wave of sound that hit all the harder after the relative quiet of the skies. Before heading our separate ways, we paused next to an out of the way bench beneath the dappled shade of an ornamental maple tree.

Excitement bubbled up, and my smile broke free as I looked up at Dimitri. Not only had we both scored an excellent on our checkrides, we'd gotten one hell of a compliment from an active duty rider. And with the fear of failure a distant memory, I was suddenly very much looking forward to that evening's sunset orientation flight. Even better, we'd get to fly it *together*.

"See you at pre-brief?"

Dimitri smirked. "Wouldn't miss that flight for the world. Oh, and Harper?" He reached out and tucked a loose strand of hair behind my ear. His voice dropped low and teasing. "You're out of regs."

I ignored the shiver that arose when his fingertips brushed my cheek and swatted his hand away. "I'll fix it after I check on my egg, asshole."

"Just make sure you do it before an instructor dings you, hotshot." His smirk deepened into a wicked grin. "Have fun at the hatchery."

"I will," I shot back, but suspicion unfurled deep in my gut as I stalked away from him. I knew that grin. That asshole was up to something. Running into Zayne and Callum loitering under the gates separating the dragon rider campus from the academy proper confirmed it.

"Hey, Harper." Zayne shifted his weight as I drew near, apprehension and pride warring on his intelligent face.

"Zayne!" I called out brightly. "So weird that you guys are just standing here for no obvious reason."

"Happy coincidence." The bigger cadet smiled easily enough, but his gaze skipped away from mine, a dead giveaway he was involved in whatever prank was heading my way. There was no question about Callum.

"Brat," he said casually, smug anticipation burning bright in his eyes.

"Cal. Are those your second-best flying leathers?" My voice dripped with false sympathy. "It must *burn* that your best set isn't clean yet."

Instead of anger, that lean bastard gave me a mischievous grin. The one that said he thought he'd gotten one over on me.

"You may have won a battle, brat . . ." He leaned closer and crooned, "But I'm gonna win the war."

"*We*." Zayne tilted his chin up, pride winning out over apprehension. "*We're* going to win the war."

"You boys keep thinking that." I smiled as if I hadn't a care in the world and sauntered away.

As I followed the paved path toward the hatchery, I felt their eyes on my back and kept on smiling. Let them watch. There was nothing between me and the hatchery, and the Mavens who ruled that precious building wouldn't tolerate unprofessional behavior of any sort.

I was safe enough for now. Later though? Game on.

Halfway across the grassy quad, I ran into Bethany. My roommate was all muscle and focus, an unstoppable force of nature. She'd excelled in combat training and was one of the few female cadets entrusted with one of the fierce reds. They were the heart of our shock troops, but I didn't envy her.

I'd joined the academy because I wanted to *fly*. Both of my parents were dragon riders, and I'd grown up in a border town surrounded by dozens of other dragon riders—and their dragons. Before I came to the academy, I'd never traveled further than twenty miles from my home, but I knew my situation wasn't unique. Tennessan's borders were dotted with towns just like mine, full of retired dragon and griffin riders.

Tennessan's ready reserve force, guardians of our less contentious borders.

During my first year at the academy, everything changed. After twenty years of raids and minor skirmishes, our border clash with Savinia erupted into open war. Many unbonded cadets dropped out, wanting no part in frontline combat against the Savinians and their monsters. I'd stayed, but not because I wanted to fight.

The Savinian bastards did terrible things to captured riders, things to break them and twist them. Search and Rescue was instrumental in keeping downed riders out of enemy hands, and a green's strength, camouflage, and hover capabilities made them perfect for that mission.

We were going to *save* people.

Bethany gave me an absent wave as I strolled up, most of her attention on her best friend Katie Bex, one of the unbonded griffin riders. The shorter girl bounced on her toes, warm brown eyes more than a little wild. I didn't know her well enough to tease, or even to ask outright, but Bethany accurately interpreted my side-eye.

"It's almost time," she said quietly.

Understanding hit. Bex's griffin was hatching soon. I smiled and wished her luck, but her whispered thanks was absent at best. Too anxious and excited and impatient to meet her bondmate. An echoing flutter rushed through me. My green wouldn't hatch that soon, but soon enough.

A dark-haired cadet jogged around to the front of the hatchery and waved at her urgently. Bex took off like a shot.

"You've got this, Katie!" Bethany called after her in a battlefield bellow that would do any commanding officer proud. We followed at a slower pace. "So?"

"Passed."

"Never doubted it for a second, girl." She held out a fist, and I gently tapped it with my own. She eyed my thick flying leathers as she hauled open the reinforced steel hatchery door. "You sure you don't want to change first?"

"Not enough time." I braced myself as the outer door shut behind us, enclosing us in the dimly lit atrium, and pulled open the inner door. A wall of dense, humid air rolled over us, and I wasn't the only one who faltered. As my lungs struggled to adjust, I gasped out, "You know all those stories we were raised on about the brave dragon riders who defend our country from the evil Savinians?"

"Yeah?" One blonde eyebrow rose high at my sarcastic tone.

"Did any of them mention the horrors of wearing thick leather in high humidity?" I tugged at the front of my flight jacket.

"Nope."

"Didn't think so."

We exchanged a rueful grin and stepped into the heat.

A long central hallway stretched out before us. Built-in lights were evenly spaced along the ceiling, bathing the metal walls in a dim, yellow glow. Metal doors lined either side of the hall, each with a small glass panel at eye level. Griffin hatcheries, griffin crèches, dragon hatcheries, and at the far end of the hall, the dragon crèche. We only had to go halfway down the hall to reach the main dragon hatchery.

This time, I didn't falter when Bethany pulled open the door. I stopped in my tracks.

At a sharp glance from one of the Mavens, I stepped onto the warm sands and closed the door behind me. The dragon hatchery was always the warmest chamber, but today the heat took my breath away. Bethany, looking almost comfortable in her lightweight mottled-green uniform, rolled her eyes and passed me a canteen.

"I'm not going to say I told you so."

"Pretty sure you just did," I muttered before I drained half the water and handed it back.

My gaze landed on my designated nest, and I grinned as I hustled across the sands. I might be the only idiot suffering in flying leathers out of dozens of uniformed cadets scattered across the orderly rows of nests, but I couldn't bring myself to regret it. Not even when sweat popped up on my brow and gathered under my leathers. Because the dragon's egg—*my* dragon's egg—was just as beautiful as the last time I'd laid eyes on it.

I knelt in front of my nest, reached a hand out to caress the smooth shell half buried in sand—and froze.

"Oh gods, I know that look. What's wrong this time?" Bethany asked in exasperation.

"I thought I heard a squeak," I muttered as I brushed the sand away.

"And last week you thought the egg had a crack, but it was just a stray hair." She glanced over from her significantly larger egg. "Would you relax? Your future bondmate is fine."

I threw my hand up in a demand for silence. There it was again! Another squeak, louder this time, though that might be because I'd pressed my ear against the warm shell. Carefully, I picked up the heavy egg.

It felt *different*.

A wet crack echoed through the hatchery as the warm shell vibrated in my hands. Alarm whipped through me. It was too soon. My dragon wasn't supposed to hatch for another two weeks.

My head snapped up, frantic gaze searching for one of the Mavens. The women who ruled the hatchery would know what to do. My eyes landed on Maven Naomi, clear across the vast chamber.

"I need help!"

My anxious shout cut across the quiet murmur of other cadets, and the older woman immediately set off across the sands in a long-legged stride. Before she could reach me, the hatchling gave a mighty squeak even Bethany could hear. She shot to her feet and gripped my shoulder to steady me when I swayed in a mix of sheer terror and excitement. I was about to meet my bondmate, the dragon I'd spend the rest of my life with!

My heart pounded so loudly I was amazed I could hear anything over its frantic beat, and I had to force my hands to relax on that precious egg. The lesson had been hammered home. No matter how much we wanted to help our dragons, they had to break free on their own. It was important to their development . . . but mine was hatching early. I held my breath as the smooth perfection of the egg distorted and a wing pushed up and out of its warm haven.

A *feathered* wing.

A sharp beak flung another piece of shell out of the way, and an avian head rose up, wobbling unsteadily as he blindly searched. The egg flexed in my hands as he struggled to get free, and he let out a frustrated growl. Back legs kicked out hard, and I scrambled to keep the hatchling from tumbling to the floor along with his discarded shell.

His adorable little roar sounded equal parts hungry and triumphant, and he extended feline limbs in a luxurious stretch. Damp fur tickled my hands, and delicate nails that would one day be fearsome claws flicked out from soft paws and pricked the thin skin of my forearms. The tufted ears were still flattened to his skull, and it was impossible to tell what color the feathers or fur were, soaked as they were from the amniotic fluids.

"What?" I gasped as a feline tail wrapped around my arm, the spray of feathers at the end a wet clump against my elbow. "A griffin?"

Shock held me immobile for vital seconds. Where was my dragon?

The Maven shouted in alarm as she broke into a sprint. "Close your eyes *now*, Cadet Tavros!"

Too late. The cub opened his eyes ... and found mine.

I couldn't look away, couldn't blink, not even when my eyes stung and watered uncontrollably. Tears poured down my face, but I wasn't crying. My blue eyes were changing, shifting, and so were the griffin's—a visible manifestation of the forming bond. The magic of bonding was an entanglement of two souls and demanded like for like. How else were you supposed to see through your bondmate's eyes if they didn't match?

Even as I watched, blue crept into his crimson gaze, the colors blending in a hypnotic swirl. A second, an eternity later, the burning faded away as if it had never been. I didn't need a mirror to know my eyes were now a perfect match to the brilliant purple of the tiny griffin in my arms.

"No," I moaned, on the verge of actually crying. This couldn't be happening. I was supposed to be a dragon rider. I was supposed to *fly*, to save people ... to ... the baby griffin nuzzled my chest and a wave of undeniable love washed through the nascent bond.

My knees hit the warm sands, and I cradled him close to my chest. Mine. He was mine now. And I was his.

Only death could tear us apart.

CHAPTER 2

Word traveled fast.

Before I'd even had time to wrap my mind around what happened, I had orders to report to Commandant Iverson as soon as I'd seen to my bondmate. Bethany stayed with me as long as she could, but eventually she had to leave for a training flight, and then it was just me, a hangry griffin cub, and one of the griffin Mavens. The woman was incredibly patient with me, given that I was suffering from shock and had very little idea of how to care for a newborn griffin.

Her brisk practicality and complete lack of sympathy were exactly what I needed to compartmentalize and function, and soon enough my griffin had been cleaned and fed. The moment his belly was full, he promptly passed out. Affectionately, I nuzzled the top of his head with my cheek, and he let out a faint, whistling snore. Being born was hard.

Despite everything, a fond smile tugged at my lips. Every second we spent together, breathing the same air, hearts beating the same rhythm, deepened our bond. Already, I loved him with my whole heart. I stroked a hand down his spine and never wanted to leave the warmth of the hatchery . . . but my reluctance to move was only partly due to the bundle of fur and feathers sprawled across my lap.

If I moved, it'd be real, but I'd delayed as long as I dared.

With a heavy sigh, I gathered up my sleeping griffin and stood on legs that had gone numb. As I stomped my feet to get the blood flowing, I absently wished I could steal all that numb and use it to armor my heart, because I was feeling raw and more than a little broken.

I knew what was coming.

Hiding in the hatchery wouldn't change a damn thing though, so I put some steel in my spine and declined the Maven's offer to leave my griffin in the crèche while I answered my summons. I wasn't ready to let him go, and the woman's serene smile was at once approving and full of understanding. That smile said she thought I needed him right now, probably more than he needed me. She was right.

His limp body was a comforting weight in my arms as I strode out of the humid warmth of the hatchery and into the cooler fall air. My steps slowed, and I stumbled to a halt only a few paces beyond the doors. The brilliant sunlight was a shock to more than my eyes. It felt as if days had passed since my morning flight, but it was only early afternoon, and the academy grounds were bustling. Cadets rushed past on their way to classes, training flights, and combat lessons, and the familiar cacophony washed over me in a wave of white noise.

My griffin made a sleepy noise of protest and snuggled deeper into my chest, though whether he was protesting the cold, the light, or the racket was unclear. His sleepy baby thoughts were a muddle of impressions and emotions. Words would come later. I tightened my hold on him, drew in a deep breath, and strode across the quad.

After the third dragon rider cadet I knew avoided my gaze, I kept my eyes focused on my destination, refusing to look at anyone. I didn't need their pity, and I sure as hell didn't need to see their relief that it hadn't happened to them, or worse, the *satisfaction* on some of their faces.

They'd *wanted* to see me fall. Well, fuck them.

I marched across the quad with my head held high and my face expressionless. I'd be damned before I let them see me break, and the only one who could tell it was nothing more than a flimsy mask was snoring in my arms.

The worst part was I understood the reactions. Dragon rider cadets were a competitive, arrogant bunch. We *had* to be to fly dragons in combat, and I was no different. I hadn't even let my friendships with . . . my mind skittered away from the thought.

I didn't want to think about *them*. Not now, not when my griffin was sleeping and my building rage might wake him. Because I knew *exactly* who was responsible for my dragon egg being swapped for a griffin, and so did the officers who ran the academy. Not that it mattered, not really. What was done was done, and all that was left was the administrative cleanup.

Dread sank through my stomach like a rock as I pushed open the doors to the dragon rider admin building with my foot. I knew what was coming. I'd bonded a griffin. Intentional or not, I couldn't stay with the dragon riders. I wasn't one of them.

Not anymore.

The sergeant manning the front desk swept a cool, professional gaze over me as my steps dragged across the lobby. At her expectant look, I forced my feet to move faster until I stood before the desk. I opened my mouth to report in, but I couldn't get any words past the knot constricting my throat.

A frown drifted across the sergeant's face, but then her stern expression softened as recognition flared in her eyes. Her normal, brown, perfectly ordinary eyes. She wasn't one of the bonded. The older woman was one of the many support staff who kept the academy running, someone most cadets never thought about.

"He's beautiful," she said, something not quite sympathy in her voice. Longing maybe, mixed with genuine appreciation. "Forest or mountain breed?"

My eyes dropped to my sleeping griffin of their own volition, and I found my voice. "Forest."

Bred to blend in, to sneak, to scout. Not to fight. Soft feline paws instead of eagle talons, and dappled fur and wings, lighter and darker spots to break up the golden brown. The spray of feathers at the end of his long tail tickled my side as it idly flicked back and forth. His beak gaped just a little as he snored, and his tufted ears twitched as he dreamed griffin dreams.

He wasn't just beautiful. He was utterly adorable.

I forced my gaze back up to the sergeant's and cleared my throat. "Cadet Tavros reporting."

Her professional expression settled into place. "Commandant Iverson is expecting you. You can wait outside his office. He's just finishing up with his . . . prior appointment."

My brow furrowed at the odd hesitation, but I nodded and strode deeper into the building. I knew the way. I'd been there just a few weeks and a lifetime ago for a one-on-one counseling session about my choice in dragon specialization. Just like Captain Durant, Commandant Iverson had urged me to switch to a gray, the backbone of our fighting forces. When I'd respectfully declined, he'd shocked me by offering up the sole black dragon egg in the hatchery.

It was the first one the Mavens had been able to produce in years. Again, I'd respectfully declined, but *damn* it had been a near thing. The riders of black dragons tended to become Dragon Corps commanders, and not just because their dragons were nigh-unstoppable tanks. From the commandant, that had been one hell of a vote of confidence, but I'd stood by my decision.

I'd wanted a green.

My arms tightened around my griffin, a subconscious reaction to the yearning the thought engendered. When he grumbled, I forced my grip to relax. I'd never have a green, but I had him. It was enough. *He* was enough.

As I marched down the main hallway, I could hear Iverson bellowing even though half a building separated us. Anticipation curled with the dread circling my belly, slowing my steps again as I turned the corner toward his office. His *closed* office.

So that was why the sergeant had hesitated. Commandant Iverson wasn't in a prior appointment—he was in the middle of delivering an epic ass-chewing. And I knew *exactly* which cadets were on the other side of that door. Even better, I didn't even have to try to eavesdrop. Despite the fact that the thick wooden door was firmly shut, I had no problem hearing every word as the commandant ripped into the cadets who'd destroyed my life.

I leaned against the wall across from his office, adjusted my griffin's limp weight so some of it rested on my hip, and settled in to enjoy the show.

"One of our best dragon rider cadets reduced to a griffin's bondmate! You'll be cleaning latrines with your personal toothbrushes for the rest of your time here! That's *if* we don't drum you out for deliberate sabotage of a cadet's future and robbing the Tennessan military of a promising young rider!"

"It was just a joke!" Callum's defiant voice grated on my nerves, and my fingers itched to curl up into a fist. "She's so obsessed with her egg, we figured she'd notice in seconds! Maybe she's not as good as you thought, *sir*, if she couldn't tell the difference between a griffin and dragon egg."

My lip curled up into a snarl. *Thank you, Cal, for being the first to volunteer to get punched in the face.*

"Or maybe she was distracted because the damn thing started to hatch the moment she picked it up!" Commandant Iverson roared as something—probably his fist—cracked against his desk. "You morons not only deprived Cadet Tavros of her chance to bond with her dragon, you deprived a griffin cadet of his intended bondmate!"

I . . . hadn't thought of that. I'd been so wrapped up in my own problems, I'd forgotten about the griffin cadet whose place I'd inadvertently taken. At least he could just wait for the next clutch. His future hadn't been destroyed, only delayed.

A tiny snore drew my gaze down to my griffin, who somehow managed to remain asleep throughout the tirade. I sighed and adjusted his weight again, my arms beginning to feel the strain of carrying him. A nest could've magically appeared at my feet in that moment and I still would've carried him. No matter how much I resented the circumstances, I couldn't resent *him*. He was perfect, and completely oblivious to the upheaval he'd caused in my perfectly planned life.

I blinked rapidly to clear my eyes. I'd been *so* close to my dream . . .

"We didn't know the griffin clutch was supposed to hatch today," Zayne said carefully. "I didn't think—"

"That's obvious, Cadet Serrano! If you don't start using your brains, I'll have you out on your ass faster than you can whine about who your daddy is." Dead silence fell but for the nervous shuffling of feet and the squeak of a desk chair. Iverson broke it with a growl that sounded more like it came from his red dragon's maw than a human throat. "Cadet Thompson! You've been remarkably quiet. Anything you'd like to say in your defense?"

Despite myself, I held my breath and leaned closer to the door. More than anything, I wanted to know what Dimitri had to say.

"No, sir," he said flatly. "I have nothing to say."

I froze. My best friend, the person I trusted more than anyone else in the world, had *nothing* to say?

My heart cracked.

A rumble from deep in my griffin's chest jerked my tear-filled gaze down. It wasn't a growl. Even though he was still sleeping, my little bondmate had sensed my distress and was *purring*. The soothing sound was far louder than I'd expected from a baby fluffball, and I cuddled him closer, finally able to breathe again.

"What will happen to Harper?" Zayne asked quietly.

"Cadet Tavros will be transferred to the griffin riders." Iverson's tone of voice made it clear what he thought of griffin riders. As if they were lesser because they weren't *dragon* riders. The fact that I'd shared that opinion until an hour ago was irrelevant. "She'll never be the asset she should've been thanks to you three." After a long moment of uncomfortable silence, he growled, "You're all to report to Sergeant Spencer for punishment detail."

Recognizing the signs of impending dismissal, I hurriedly wiped away my tears and straightened up. I would show them *nothing*.

"For how long?" Callum asked cautiously before he hurriedly tacked on a "sir."

He'd always found verbal discipline the hardest of the four of us. A born smartass, but one hell of a fighter.

"As long as I feel like, *Cadet*, which as of right now is until you graduate. Assuming Cadet Tavros doesn't convince me to boot all of you out on your asses! Now get the hell out of my office."

The door opened, and three cadets in pristine dress uniforms tumbled out into the hall. I was suddenly very aware of my sweaty flying leathers and the strands of hair plastered to my face. I looked and felt like a mess in comparison, but I lifted my chin and refused to show it.

For an instant, they froze. Time slowed as I stared at them. My best friends, my rivals, my betrayers.

Callum glared at me in a mix of defiance and guilt though his complexion turned ashen, while Zayne couldn't even look me in the eye as he mumbled a miserable apology at his boots. Dimitri just stared back at me, expressionless, eyes blank.

My jaw flexed, and if it weren't for the griffin in my arms, I might've punched him right then and there, if only to get some kind of reaction out of him. Mentally, I moved him above Callum on my "to be punched" list.

"Cadet Tavros!"

I tore my gaze off my former friends and marched into the commandant's office with my head held high. Unfortunately, I had no way to close the door unless I wanted to use my foot. Somehow, I didn't think Commandant Iverson would react well if I kicked his door shut.

Zayne glanced back, saw the problem, and carefully pulled it closed for me with another mumbled apology. He was definitely at the bottom of my list. Then again, with how apologetic he was acting, it wouldn't shock me in the least if he was the one who'd figured out how to switch the eggs. With as closely as the Mavens watched the hatcheries, it would've taken a lot of planning—something he excelled in.

To my shock, Commandant Iverson came out from around his desk and pulled out a chair. "Sit, Cadet. I know that furball's got to be getting heavy."

His voice was just as brusque as ever, but there was no animosity or anger in his tone. Struggling to hide my relief, I sat, arranging my griffin across my legs and covertly stretching my arms.

"Thank you, sir." As ridiculously difficult as it was to remain professional with a snoring griffin cub in my lap, I did my best to maintain proper military bearing. "Cadet Tavros reporting as ordered."

A faint smile creased his weathered face, there and gone in an instant as he sat in the opposite chair. "At ease, Cadet. You're not in trouble, and this meeting is more of a formality than anything else. The paperwork to transfer you over to the Griffin Corps is already complete, effective immediately." He sighed when I wasn't quite able to suppress my flinch. "For what it's worth, you have my sympathies."

My jaw flexed again, but I managed to keep my tone even. "Respectfully, sir, I don't want sympathy."

He studied me for a moment before he dipped his head in a short nod. "Neither would I." His eyes narrowed. "If I were in your boots, I'd want revenge."

For just a moment, I thought about it, *really* thought about it. Iverson had just heavily implied that if I truly wanted to, I could destroy the cadets who'd destroyed me. Utterly, without the risk of retaliation. The temptation faded as quickly as it had flared up. That wasn't who I wanted to be . . . and deep down, I knew they hadn't meant for this to happen.

It didn't mean I was ever going to forgive them, but it also didn't give me the right to ruin their careers. Tennessan *needed* every dragon rider it could get.

Slowly, I shook my head. "I don't want that either, sir."

Approval shone in his eyes. "You don't think it was deliberate sabotage then? I know the four of you were competing for the top slot."

I swallowed hard.

"No, sir. It . . . it wasn't malicious, no more than any other prank we played on each other in the past year." A laugh that was only slightly bitter escaped my control. "Though if you want to have them scrubbing latrines with toothbrushes for the rest of the year, I wouldn't be sad about it."

There was a flicker of amusement on Iverson's face, shocking because the only emotions I'd ever seen were anger, fury, and rage, in that order.

"I'll see what I can do." He stood and pulled open the door. "Commandant Pulaski is expecting you."

My jaw clenched as I hauled my griffin into my arms and slowly stood up. Pulaski was over the griffin riders ... and my new commander. I was proud when my voice came out steady.

"Thank you, sir."

"You're welcome, Cadet Tavros." Iverson hesitated, as if he wanted to say more, but in the end, he just gave me a brisk nod. "Dismissed."

My steps started out even, steady, but by the time I reached the front doors, I was practically sprinting. As if I could escape my new reality if I just ran fast enough. I burst out of the admin building, lungs heaving for air, and ran halfway across the grounds before I stumbled to a stop. Thankfully, unlike last time, classes were in session and there weren't any witnesses around as I tried not to completely lose it.

Tremors shook my frame, and I hunched over slightly, curling around my pain—and my griffin. One shuddering breath turned into another and another. My eyes burned, and I teetered on the edge of fully breaking down in the center of campus.

A rumbling purr thrummed against my chest as my griffin stirred in my arms. Once again, he was responding to my distress. Determined not to let anything else spill over onto him, I compartmentalized everything and promised myself later. Later, I could break down. Right now I needed to function. I soothed my griffin back to sleep with a hand that only shook a little and straightened up.

Drawing in a deep breath, I walked out of the dragon gate for the last time and marched across the quad to the griffin side of the academy.

And froze.

I stared up at the open gates, nothing stopping me but my own shattered dreams. As if stepping over that threshold would make everything real. As if it weren't already as real as the snoring griffin cub in my arms.

Commandant Iverson's words echoed in my mind. *She'll never be the asset she should've been . . .*

Resolve burned through the last of my shock. I'd show Iverson. I'd show my classmates, I'd show them *all*. I could still make a difference— even if I shared a soul with a griffin instead of a dragon.

"Hey, little one," I crooned as I stroked my bondmate's dappled fur possessively. His tiny wings fluttered and his purple eyes opened. There was so much love, so much trust in those eyes, that a genuine smile pulled at my lips. "Let's show them what a dragon rider can do in the Griffin Corps."

Lifting my chin, I strode through the gate with a griffin in my arms.

My newfound determination died a swift death at the hands of my new commander. My ego was the next thing to take a hit, because a dragon rider in the Griffin Corps was apparently the next best thing to useless. I tried not to let my panic show as Commandant Pulaski gave me an incredibly detailed, incredibly fast overview of my new training schedule, her expectations for me, and all the ways I was behind the curve when it came to my training in general, and griffin care in particular.

And I had to endure all of it without the comfort of my griffin. The griffin I really needed to name soon, so I could stop thinking about him as "my griffin."

Commandant Pulaski had taken one look at the fidgeting cub, recognized the signs of impending hunger—which explained the curious red haze coating his baby thoughts—and kicked me right back out of her office with orders to get him fed and leave him to nap in the crèche with the other newborns. The rest of his clutch had hatched just before he burst out of his egg and into my life, and while it was important for bondmates to spend time together, it was also important for him to socialize with his clutchmates.

Unlike most dragons, griffins were social creatures. Something I'd belatedly remembered from the introductory classes all cadets went through their first year at the academy. Still, it had been so hard to let him go, even knowing it was only temporary. I'd delayed for long minutes, just watching him sleep, but orders were orders, so I'd forced myself away.

". . . any questions, Cadet Tavros?"

I blinked and wrestled my focus back where it belonged. Again. "No, ma'am."

Iron—that was all I could think of when I'd first laid eyes on the older woman. Iron-gray hair, iron-straight spine, and an unyielding iron spirit lurking behind a pair of brilliant green eyes. She looked like she would break long before she ever bent.

And then she snorted a laugh and grinned, effectively destroying the illusion. "You look like I just slapped you across the face with the manual, Cadet."

My mouth opened and closed, but I wasn't quite sure how to respond. The dragon rider instructors were a strict, disciplined bunch— at least around their cadets. It took every bit of control I possessed not to let my jaw hit the floor when the Griffin Commandant of the Tennessan Bonded Training Academy leaned back in her chair, crossed her arms, and propped her boots up on the desk.

A shower of dirt rained on the manual in question. It looked like it wasn't the first time that had happened.

"Um, yes, ma'am? I mean, no, ma'am, I don't have any questions." I shook off my shock and stiffened to attention. "I know I'm behind where I need to be, but I'll work hard to catch up to the rest of my flight."

Her grin softened into a genuine smile and she waved a casual hand. "At ease, Cadet. And it's clutch." When I frowned in confusion, she took pity on me and explained. "Dragons are organized by flight, griffins by clutch."

I wanted to find a convenient hole in the ground to throw myself into. Here I was promising to catch up, and I couldn't even remember the right terms.

"Right, I knew that."

"Give yourself some grace," she said kindly. "Today did not go like anyone expected, least of all you." She eyed me for a long moment before she nodded to herself, dropped her boots to the floor, and leaned forward. "Cadet Tavros, I'm going to add one more item to my list of expectations for you—you are not allowed to drive yourself into the ground."

My brow furrowed. "Ma'am?"

"I'll be blunt with you, Cadet. There is no way for you to graduate on time."

Dismay sank through my gut, and I bit back an automatic protest. The amusement had faded from her expression, and I was looking at the commandant once more, all unbending iron.

"You'll need to catch up on a year's worth of griffin-oriented classes, as well as train with your clutch. And while you're catching up on last year's classes, you'll be missing this year's." She shook her head, already anticipating my response. "Please refer to my expectation for you. No driving yourself—or your griffin—into the ground."

That stopped me cold. I was willing to work as hard as it took, but I had to remember that I was now responsible for and permanently attached to another soul, one who was still very much a baby. My fingers twitched as longing to stroke his fur momentarily distracted me.

"We'll work out a schedule for you that is healthy and *sane*. Remember, nothing is more important right now than solidifying your bond with your griffin and learning how to be *more* than you were when you woke up today."

I blinked. *Oh gods, is it still the same day?*

Sympathy softened her stern expression, and I fought to keep my face impassive. I didn't want sympathy, I wanted . . . I didn't know what I wanted.

My fingers twitched again.

No, I knew exactly what I wanted. I wanted my griffin, because I didn't feel whole, or safe, or balanced without him. My weight shifted toward the door as impatience to return to his side momentarily overrode my discipline.

Pulaski's eyes narrowed slightly, but she slid a single sheet of paper across her desk. "Here's your initial schedule, we'll adjust as needed. We won't hold you back, Tavros, but we won't break you, either."

My spine stiffened. *I'd like to see you try.*

The commandant paused and regarded me silently.

"There she is," she finally said in a voice soft as steel. "There's the hotshot dragon rider cadet I heard so much about."

I held her stare without flinching. No matter how friendly she acted, she wasn't my friend. She didn't get to see me break either. After a long moment, the corner of her mouth kicked up in what looked like approval.

"Hold on to that fire, Cadet," Pulaski said quietly. "You're going to need it."

Well, if that wasn't ominous. In the next instant, she was all business again. I was getting emotional whiplash.

"Unfortunately, we can't allow you to stay in the dragon rider dorms. You've been reassigned to Echo Barracks with the rest of your clutch."

My stomach tightened. I'd thought I'd at least be able to keep one part of my life unchanged. It wasn't even the cushy double room I'd miss. It was Bethany. I shoved my sorrow behind the same wall where I'd compartmentalized everything else and maintained my bearing.

"We had the bulk of your belongings already moved over, you just need to pack your personal effects."

I straightened my shoulders. "Yes, ma'am. I'll see to it as soon as I get my griffin—"

Pulaski arched a brow. "And how exactly are you planning to carry your belongings *and* a griffin cub?" She shook her head. "Leave him in the crèche and handle your business, Cadet. He'll be waiting for you when you're done."

Panic tightened my throat, constricting my airway even as my lungs heaved for breath. No, I needed to get him now. It had been too long and I *needed* him. My vision tunneled, and gray sparks danced along the edges.

"Tavros? Tavros!" Pulaski was suddenly just *there*, weathered hands gripping my upper arms. "Deep breath in, girl." She mimed taking a deep breath, and my body listened, automatically following the nonverbal cue. "Good, now out. Come on, Cadet. Keep taking those deep breaths for me."

"Sorry," I gasped out, mortified and unsure where that surge of sheer panic had come from—or how to make it stop. I was holding on by my fingertips, and if it weren't for Pulaski's iron grip, I would've already taken off running for the crèche. "I'm sorry, I don't know what's wrong with me."

"For fuck's sake, *what* is Iverson teaching you people?" When I flinched at her deep scowl, she immediately shook her head. "No, it's okay, this is part of it. The bond turns us all into a codependent mess, especially in the beginning. Your body still thinks that you have to physically touch him to feel him, but you don't. You *can* feel him. Your griffin is still there."

I dragged in air, searching but not finding, my belly twisting to the point of nausea. "I can't, I can't—"

"Yes, you can," she said sharply enough to shock me out of my panic. "Close your eyes."

My eyes slammed shut, desperation and years of training making me latch onto her command.

"Reach for that bundle of emotion that isn't yours," she said firmly, her tone losing its sharpness without sacrificing an ounce of authority. It gave me something to hold onto as panic threatened to drown me. "He's right there, you just have to *feel* for him."

My shoulders relaxed inch by inch. She was right, I *could* feel him, all warm and content, curled up in the back of my mind and in my heart like a warm knot of energy, a part of me but not. My griffin. Mine.

"Find him yet?"

"I found him," I breathed out, relief making my voice shake. Mentally, I curled around that warm ball of griffin and rubbed at my chest, where it felt like the bond had sunk its hooks deep, tugging and binding us together.

"Good," she said briskly as her grip tightened to just shy of painful. "Remember this—he'll always be with you. He'll never leave you. There is nowhere in this world you can go that will be far enough to break that bond. And whether he's sleeping in the crèche or he goes beyond your reach on a scouting mission, there is *nowhere* he can go that you can't go too." She gave me a little shake, her fingers wrapped around my upper arms like bands of steel. "That is what it means to be bonded. You will *never* be alone again."

Rather than scary, it was so damn comforting. I was able to take a deeper breath, then another, always keeping a mental hand on my griffin. My panic faltered and faded, leaving staggering relief and overwhelming embarrassment behind.

Heat washed over my face, but I forced my eyes open and looked my commander in the eye. "I'm so sorry, ma'am. We were taught about this, but I didn't think..."

Pulaski released my arms with a wry grin. "You didn't think it would feel like you'd die if you couldn't touch your bondmate? Like you couldn't breathe, or think, or that your heart might refuse to beat without him?" She snorted. "Trust me, every last one of your clutchmates just went through the same panic attack under the supervision of an instructor."

I paused, mentally repeated her words, and could only come to one conclusion. "You separated us on purpose."

"Yes."

"*Why?*"

She met my outrage with a calm expression. Once again, that iron will shone through in the implacable steadiness of her gaze. "Because that first separation is a bitch, but it's also unavoidable."

Her raised brows said she was waiting for me to contribute something other than outrage to the discussion. It occurred to me that I would never have gotten away with this behavior if this were *Iverson's* office, but she didn't look angry. Just expectant.

So I let out a slow breath and turned the situation over in my mind, trying to look at it from all angles. One word jumped out at me. "Supervision. You separate us on purpose so you can control it . . . so you can help us."

She nodded sharply. "Just like our instructors did for us when we were newly bonded. I wanted to handle yours because a griffin bond feels different than a dragon bond. Dragons are heavy, they spread out, impossible to miss. But griffins? They're sneakier."

Absently, I rubbed my chest again. She was right. Part of the reason I'd panicked when I'd reached for him was because I couldn't find him. Oh, I could feel the bond itself, but not *him*. Now that I knew how to look, I'd never lose him again.

"Well?" Pulaski arched a brow and tilted her head toward her door. "What are you standing around for? The sooner you square away your gear, the sooner you can get back to your griffin."

I couldn't get out of her office fast enough.

As I rushed out of the Griffin Corps admin building, a trio of gray dragons flashed by overhead, leathery hides shining silver in the light of the setting sun and their formation so tight their wings practically overlapped. My feet stopped of their own accord, rooting me in place, and I couldn't stop my gaze from tracking their graceful flight until they were out of visual range. My stomach tightened at the sight of two riders on each dragon's back.

Formation flying 101, sunset orientation.

I was supposed to be on that flight.

And then I couldn't stop the thought that followed as naturally as breathing. *I wonder who took my spot?*

CHAPTER 3

I trudged out of the griffin gates and headed down one of the paths that wound through the extensive quad. The main academy formed an irregular square, with the dragon rider campus holding the northern quadrant, griffins the southern, untracked cadets to the east, and the myriad dorms, barracks, support buildings, and a small chapel to the west. An auxiliary section held the livestock pens and produce gardens, while a restricted section held the warm sands where dragons and griffins laid their eggs before they gave them over to the Mavens.

Until now, I'd never noticed that the dragon rider campus was situated at the highest point, placing it firmly above the rest. Even the dragon rider dorms were higher up on the western slope, though supposedly that was to place the cadets closer to the dragon eyries occupying the upper half of that diminutive mountain.

The academy wasn't as large as the conventional military or civilian colleges, but then again, it didn't need to be. Not everyone who was bond capable chose to serve, and unlike Savinia, the Tennessan government gave its citizens that choice. Even then, there were plenty of bond capable soldiers who chose the conventional military rather than a life bound to a dragon or griffin.

My path eventually took me near the long, low building placed in the protected center of that irregular square. The hatchery's plain exterior belied the fact that it was the single most important building at the academy.

I longed to veer off my chosen path and turn toward the hatchery, toward my griffin, but I managed to keep walking. And while my feet behaved, my eyes latched onto the plain gray walls, as if I could see *through* the duracrete and to the crèche inside.

Before I knew it, the *crunch* of boots on dried leaves hit my ears as I stumbled off the paved path and onto the leaf-strewn lawn, halfway to the sidewalk that would lead directly to the hatchery's front entrance. Growling in annoyance, I shook my head sharply and forced myself back on my original path through sheer determination alone.

In a desperate bid to distract myself, I studied the innocuous building as I marched past.

While it was more than large enough to hold the separate dragon and griffin hatcheries as well as the crèches, there were rumors of a massive underground facility beneath that supposedly spanned most of the academy grounds, where the Mavens did whatever it was they did to the fertilized eggs to spawn the different dragon and griffin specializations. The instructors always scoffed at the stories, claiming the sublevel below the hatchery held nothing more than the equipment necessary to maintain the ideal temperature and humidity levels for hatching baby dragons and griffins.

And while it was true that the sands were kept warm even throughout the worst winters due to some mysterious process involving underground hot springs and a clever assortment of pumps and pipes, that wasn't nearly exciting enough for a bunch of bored cadets with too much time for gossip and ghost stories on their hands. Every year, cadets would sneak out after curfew, determined to find the secret entrance.

As far as I knew, no one had ever actually succeeded, though there were always those rumors about that one group of cadets who were never seen again . . .

The three morons and I had certainly failed spectacularly, and we'd been caught to boot. But only because Callum was incapable of keeping his smartass remarks under control. He—

Again, I shied away from thinking about my former friends, and I sped up until I was jogging along the path. I wasn't going to waste *any* time on them when I had gear to square away and a sleeping griffin calling to my soul. My thighs burned as the path wound into a series of switchbacks as it climbed up the terraced slope, and I passed by the basic cadet barracks, then the griffin rider barracks, and finally made it to the dragon rider dorms.

The only thing above this level were the dragons themselves.

My palms hit the door to my former dorm, slamming it open with barely a hitch in my stride. The door hit the wall with a sharp, echoing *bang*, and for just an instant, I faltered, but the dorm was empty. The cramped, empty feeling in my belly said everyone was probably at evening chow. Or on that sunset orientation flight.

Without further hesitation, I sprinted up the stairs to the third level and down the hall to the room I'd shared with Bethany for the past two years.

I stumbled to a halt at the threshold.

I really shouldn't have been surprised another cadet had already taken my place. The war with Savinia didn't stop just because my life had exploded in spectacular fashion, and my displacement would've meant a reshuffling of the ranks. I stared at the unfamiliar items lying on what had been *my* shelves, the blue-striped blanket covering what had been *my* bed, and let out a slow breath.

At least Bethany wouldn't be alone.

With that comforting thought, I yanked the standard issue green canvas bag from the closet and shoved my tiny assortment of civilian clothes, my battered books, and the few keepsakes I'd collected during my years as a cadet. My breath caught as I picked up the small dragon Dimitri had carved for me sophomore year. The sinuous lines perfectly captured the graceful nature of the greens, as if even then he'd known what I would choose given even the smallest chance.

I trailed a finger along the dragon's back, the wood worn smooth by the countless times I'd done exactly that, and for one, awful moment, I had to fight the urge to smash it to splinters and light the remains on fire. My jaw trembled before I carefully packed the tiny dragon away. She was mine. Dimitri didn't get to ruin that, too.

Just like Commandant Pulaski had promised, all of my issued gear had been packed away and supposedly delivered to my new barracks. Even my flying leathers were gone, though I imagined they'd been returned to the supply depot to be reissued to another cadet. All except the leathers I'd been wearing all day. The leathers I'd worn on my checkride.

If I'd known it would be my last flight, I might have paid more attention, might have seared the feeling of the wind on my face into my memory.

If I'd known…

As loss whipped through me, my hands balled up into fists—and brushed against the flying cap and goggles I'd absently tucked into my belt and promptly forgot about all day. With a snarl, I tugged them free and tossed them to the floor.

It wasn't like I needed them anymore.

Griffins weren't big enough to carry their bonded in flight.

I slung the canvas bag on my shoulder and took one last look around the room before I walked out without a second glance and headed for the griffin rider barracks. Again, I got lucky. Echo Barracks was empty, my new clutchmates eating dinner or possibly already at the hatchery, where I desperately wanted to be.

Urgency drove my steps as I marched down the center aisle of the high-ceilinged open bay, small human-sized beds next to griffin-sized nests lining both sides with battered metal lockers between. My bunk was all the way at the rear on the left, the locker marked with a handwritten nametag that read TAVROS, HARPER, though the familiar gear dumped on the bed had been a dead giveaway.

I spared the not-so-familiar riding leathers that had appeared in place of my flying sets a single glance before I dropped my bag on top of them, turned on my heel, and strode back out into the cool evening air. It was later than I'd thought, with the moon already over the horizon and the stars sweeping across the sky in a brilliant display that I couldn't care less about. My stomach grumbled a complaint, and I briefly considered swinging by the chow hall for food, but just as quickly dismissed it in favor of inhaling a ration bar as I jogged down the slope. The emergency food might as well have been ashes for all I tasted it. The one thing, the only thing, that mattered was waiting for me in the duracrete building at the end of the path.

Finally, *finally*, I could get back to my griffin.

As I burst into the humid warmth of the hatchery, I felt the beginnings of panic stirring again, but this time I knew how to find him. Even as I rushed through the atrium, my mental fingers wrapped around the bond like it was a security blanket, and I brushed against my griffin's mind with a fond, desperate yearning that felt at once absolutely normal and completely insane. We'd been bonded for less than a day, and already I felt like I couldn't live without him.

The fact that I *literally* couldn't live without him was irrelevant.

My griffin's sleepy mind stirred within mine, all affection and love-drenched drowsiness, and I was able to regain a semblance of control as I trotted down the long hallway to the griffin crèche. Apparently, my clutchmates had beat me to the hatchery, because my griffin was alone. The same Maven who'd helped me that morning sat with him as he sprawled out on his back, wings spread to either side, all four paws in the air and his tail lazily flicking back and forth as he napped in the warm sand.

The second I drew near, purple eyes flew open, and my griffin cub let out an adorably squeaky little roar of delight. He rolled to his feet and leaped, tiny wings fluttering and beak gaping wide. I caught him, pulled him close, and tried very hard not to bawl like a baby at the warmth of his fur against my skin and the clean scent of his feathers in my nose.

Something tight in my chest eased, and it felt like I could finally breathe again.

He yawned and snuggled deeper into my chest, purring softly in utter contentment. For long moments I just held him close, but eventually I remembered my manners and dipped my head respectfully to the Maven.

"Thank you for caring for him."

"It's my duty," she replied simply as she stood up and brushed the sand from her lightweight uniform. She turned to leave but paused. "What did you decide to name him?"

I'd planned to name my green Cassia, but I'd had a male backup name picked out. Just in case.

A smile tugged at my lips as I gazed fondly at my sleepy griffin. "Atticus."

Out of all the imagined reactions of my new clutchmates, somehow, outright hostility had never crossed my mind.

Echo Barracks was filled to capacity, every bed and nest occupied. A pair of guys wrestled in the middle of the open room, mocking and taunting each other in a way I wasn't sure was exactly playful, while a third tried to break them apart with a long-suffering expression on his face. Two girls sat at the long table near the entrance, gear scattered across the surface as they cleaned and repaired their leathers with the neat stitches we were all taught in year one. The rest were spread out across their beds, and the walls echoed with laughing cadets and trilling griffins.

It was chaotic and messy and so far removed from the quiet discipline of the dragon rider dorms that I froze in the doorway for a long moment. When I stepped inside, still wearing my sweat-stained flying leathers and carrying a sleepy griffin in my arms, heads snapped around and everyone fell silent. All that was left was the echo of comradery as every last cadet glared at me. Their griffins shifted uneasily, tiny wings rustling in the silence.

My jaw tightened as shock and dismay and anger ricocheted through me. It wasn't enough that I didn't belong with the dragon riders anymore, I couldn't even belong with my flight ... my *clutch*. Atticus lifted his head and snapped his beak in response to the hostility, and I stroked a soothing hand down his back and across his little wings.

Damn it, I've got to get this right.

Drawing in a deep breath for courage, I strode forward with as pleasant a smile as I could manage, though it probably looked more like a pained grimace than anything else. "Um, hi. I'm Harper Tavros—"

"We know who you are." A young man stepped into the aisle, blocking my path. He was easily twice my size, and I couldn't stop my muscles from tensing up as he glared down at me. "The dragon rider bitch who stole Marcos' griffin."

Outrage whipped through me, and I glared right back at him even as guilt bubbled up. "I did *not*. I'm sorry Marcos has to wait for the next clutch—"

"The next clutch?" Katie Bex called out from where she lounged on her bed with her snowy gray-and-white mountain griffin cub. Any hope I'd had for an ally died at the hard look in her new topaz eyes. "Try next year."

I gritted my teeth. "I'm sorry he has to wait, but I'm just as much a victim as he is."

It was the wrong thing to say.

The two guys who'd been wrestling when I walked in popped to their feet. While they looked nothing alike—one tall and lanky with brown hair, the other short and muscular with black hair—they acted like brothers as they moved to confront me.

"Victim, huh?" the black-haired guy growled. "Says the girl who got Marcos' griffin, the best of the clutch." He paused, his red eyes narrowing. "Oh, that's right. I forgot. Dragon riders think we're worthless shit. I guess to you, even the best of the griffins would be a letdown, huh?"

The lanky guy snorted a laugh. "You should've seen the look on Marcos' face when he went to the hatching, expecting to meet his bondmate—and found a dragon egg in its place." All traces of levity fell away, leaving a hard expression in its place as he leaned closer to me. "But it's not like Marcos got to keep your dragon egg, did he? Oh no, that'll go to another dragon rider cadet. Meanwhile, our team leader, the best in our class, got kicked to the back of the line. He'll have to wait for another chance to bond. Meanwhile you have *his* griffin, and you walk in here trying to play the victim?"

My mouth hung open, and all the words I wanted to say got tangled up in a ball of rage and hurt and frustration. It wasn't *fair*. I hadn't asked for this, hadn't done anything wrong, but they still blamed me for taking Marcos' place. My jaw clenched. I longed to lash out, to tell them exactly how I felt about the situation . . . but I didn't. There was no way I could say anything without hurting my griffin.

So I shielded my spiteful, toxic, swirling, angry thoughts from my tiny bondmate . . . and shut my mouth.

The lanky guy's purple eyes, a shade bluer than mine, gleamed in satisfaction. "Nothing to say, hotshot?"

Bile rose up in the back of my throat. Dimitri might've called me hotshot, but never with that mix of scorn and loathing.

The lanky guy leaned close enough I could feel the hot wash of his breath across my cheek and smiled. "Yeah, that's what I thought."

Atticus screeched a warning, and my griffin beat his tiny wings so hard I had to scramble to keep hold of him. Lanky backed off, remorse flickering across his face so fast if I'd blinked I would've missed it. Surprise flashed through me until I realized his remorse was only directed at Atticus. He didn't give a shit about upsetting me, but he was decent enough to care that he'd upset my griffin.

"All right, guys, that's enough," a calm voice cut through the background murmur without any apparent effort.

Not quite as large as the big guy who'd first blocked my path, the young man who pushed his way through the cadets was bigger than the two knuckleheads currently blocking the aisle, and they reluctantly moved aside at his firm stare. Recognition rocked through me. This was the cadet who'd waved for Bex earlier today at the hatchery.

My eyes latched onto the small lightning bolt insignia pinned to his uniform collar. He couldn't have been wearing the badge of a team leader for more than a few hours, but he carried himself with an unmistakable air of command that reminded me so much of Dimitri that I couldn't quite hold back a flinch.

His stern expression softened when his eyes rested on mine. "Give Tavros some space and stop acting like a pair of dickheads without an ounce of empathy."

The grouchy black-haired cadet winced. "Sorry, Keaton."

Keaton arched a brow. "And you're apologizing to *me* because?"

When Grouchy frowned in confusion, Lanky elbowed him hard and cleared his throat. "Uh, we're sorry, Tavros. We're just upset over Marcos."

He sounded as sincere as Callum did when forced to apologize for being a smartass, which was to say, not at all . . . and I *had* to stop thinking about those morons. I forced another ghastly smile on my face and lied through my teeth.

"Don't sweat it. It's been a long day."

"For all of us," Keaton said with a nod of agreement. "Come on, Tavros, let's get you and your griffin settled."

As I followed him down the aisle, my shoulders tensed at the hostile stares from either side. When we finally reached my bunk at the very end, Keaton nodded across the aisle. Unlike the hasty scrawl on my locker, his locker had an actual name tag that read KEATON, TYLER in neat lettering.

"That's me," he said gruffly. "If you have any questions or issues, come to me first."

While he said it loudly enough for the others to hear, I wasn't stupid enough to mistake his offer for kindness. There was a distinct lack of friendliness in his amber gaze, and I had no doubt he was just as pissed as the others over Marcos' setback. Even though it wasn't my fault. It *wasn't*. Atticus shifted in my arms, and again, I bit back anything I might have said in my defense.

"Thanks," I said quietly.

He regarded me for an uncomfortably long moment before he gave me the smallest nod of acknowledgment. "I know it's been a long day, Tavros, but get your shit squared away."

With that brusque order, he turned on his heel and walked back to Grouchy and Lanky, snagging the big guy on his way. It looked like he was lecturing them, but for all I knew he was conspiring with them to make my life miserable.

Sighing, I turned my back on the whole barracks and stared at the disorganized mess lying across my bunk and on the floor. I was so damn tired. Only the feeling of all those eyes on my back gave me the strength to keep my spine straight. They were watching me, waiting to see me break.

Well, fuck them too. They could keep waiting, because I wasn't about to break in front of people who hated my guts.

My arms ached from carrying Atticus, so I set him down in his new nest and got to work. While it was tempting to just throw everything in the locker and call it good, instructors liked to spring surprise inspections, and I didn't want to look like more of an idiot than necessary. By the time I'd squared away my gear, the rest of the cadets had started to settle down for the night.

And I was still in sweat-stained, stinking leathers.

It didn't truly hit me how dirty I was until a pair of cadets walked out of the back where the attached bathrooms were located. Steam and the fresh scent of soap swirled inside with them, and I suddenly, desperately wanted to peel my skin off. There was sand in places sand had no business being, and my skin *itched*. I had to get clean.

Atticus had curled up in his nest, but he hadn't gone back to sleep. Instead, his purple gaze followed me, and his baby thoughts were bright with curiosity.

I smiled as I knelt and scratched behind his tufted ears. "I'm going to get cleaned up. I'll be back soon."

He trilled softly and angled his head, eyes drifting closed with a hum of pleasure as my fingers found a particularly itchy spot. Only my driving need to get clean tore me away from him.

Exhaustion crept around the edges of my thoughts, coating everything in a soft haze, but I forced myself back to my feet. Yawning, I grabbed my bath supplies and a clean set of PT gear to sleep in, and shuffled off to the attached bathrooms. While the open barracks curtailed any *extracurricular* activities, a shared shower would do the exact opposite, so they were segregated by gender. Small mercies. It was still a far cry from the private bathroom I'd shared with Bethany in the dragon rider dorms.

Fine tremors shivered throughout every muscle by the time I was clean, and I staggered back to my bunk in the dark. As quick as I'd tried to be, it was still past lights out, and more than one cadet was out cold. Several snored in a loud, discordant symphony that was going to make sleeping on the nights where I wasn't quite so exhausted... interesting.

Bethany had never snored.

Before anything else, I checked on Atticus, but his baby thoughts were sleepy again, and his eyes were closed. Moving quietly, I secured my supplies in my locker and crawled into bed. My bunk had a small shelf built into the headboard, but I very deliberately didn't look at the dragon figurine I'd reluctantly placed in the darkest corner, as if I couldn't decide whether to proudly display it or hide it away forever.

For long minutes, I lay rigidly under the blankets and tried to resist the habit. I failed. With a defeated sigh, I twisted around and caressed the little wooden dragon with a single finger just like I did every night, and then curled up in a tight ball and huddled under my blanket.

With a shuddering breath, every wall I'd put in place to get through the day came crashing down. Every bit of despair, of *loss*, ricocheted through my soul, and it took everything I had to keep my tears silent.

I'd never felt so alone.

Until Atticus woke up and leaped from his nest to my bed in an uncoordinated tangle of limbs and wings and tail. Purring in a soft but steady vibration I could feel in my bones, he rubbed his downy cheek against mine in an affectionate caress before he collapsed in a sleepy pile of fur and feathers. The clean, slightly spicy scent of griffin cub filled my nose. A faint smile tugged at my lips. He smelled like sun-warmed cinnamon. He smelled like *home*.

I fell into a deep, dreamless sleep with my griffin curled up against my belly.

The next two weeks passed in a blur of emotional whiplash hell. Outside of Keaton, who remained cool but professional, my clutchmates either ignored me or outright hated me. Nobody bothered to mess with me though, not even during afternoon group training. They didn't need to. I'd gone from being the top dragon rider cadet to the bottom-ranked griffin cadet.

Mornings were spent in the classroom surrounded by younger cadets who didn't know me and who never bothered to speak to me directly. But they knew *of* me, and they whispered plenty when I walked past in the halls. Hushed voices full of relief, pity, and scorn filled my ears for hours every day, pricking holes in my self-confidence. The holes were tiny but many—there was *so much* I didn't know about griffins in general, or being a griffin rider in particular, and I was struggling.

As I rushed out of my last class of the morning into a crowded hallway, another cadet rammed his shoulder into mine, knocking me into the wall. He didn't even seem to notice, he just strode away like I was invisible . . . but for a split second, his eyes had connected with mine, and I saw hatred. I flexed my shoulder with a grimace. Dragon and griffin cadets had always maintained a less than friendly rivalry, but a dragon rider cadet who'd "stolen" a griffin seemed to bring out the worst in some people.

Shaking it off, I dove back into the nonstop moving flow of cadets and out into the chill day. I needed to get back to Atticus.

It felt like I was drowning, and I didn't have anyone to help keep my head above the waves—except for my griffin, who loved me unconditionally. What he did not love was his name.

"Atticus stupid name."

They were practically his first words. It should have been an indication of how things were going to go. His growth, both physical and mental, had been explosive. He'd almost doubled in size, and he'd quickly progressed from formless baby thoughts to having an opinion on *everything*.

Sometimes I missed those brief days where he couldn't talk.

"It's not stupid, it's the name of one of the first dragons," I protested as we ambled along the path to the hatchery after lunch.

"Stupid name," he muttered, his tufted ears flicking back in disapproval. I might have thought it was for the chill breeze sweeping through campus, sending dried leaves swirling up into the sky . . . except for the fact that I could *feel* his irritation, like an itch deep

within my mind, a discordant note that sang with his displeasure. And then a thoughtful *hum* permeated his thoughts. *"Felix better name."*

I blinked. My two-week-old, incredibly gangly, opinionated-as-fuck griffin cub had just *named* himself? That was precocious, even with as quickly as griffins matured. From what I'd gleaned from snatches of overheard conversation, my clutchmates' griffins were barely forming words—meanwhile, mine wouldn't shut up. Pride welled up and obliterated any irritation I felt over his dislike for the name I'd chosen.

He really was the best of his clutch.

And then he promptly tripped over his own paws and fell beak-first onto the ground. His wings snapped out and his tail lashed with embarrassment as he popped back to his feet. His narrowed eyes dared me to comment, and I pressed my lips tightly together to hold back a grin. Not that it mattered when he could feel my amusement.

Atticus snapped his beak at me and stalked along the path, his paws far too big for his body and his wings far too small. Still, it was possible to see the graceful creature he would become in the way he moved when he wasn't tripping all over himself. Already, he had the beginnings of sleek muscle, and he was by far the largest forest griffin in the clutch, almost as tall as the mountain griffins though not nearly as stocky.

I arched a brow down at him. "Somebody's hangry. Let's get you fed, and then I need to drop you off in the crèche so I can get to PT."

"Don't wanna go."

"Atticus—"

"Felix," he replied with a decisive clack of his beak.

My jaw clenched. *"Atticus,* you need to stay in the crèche with the others. You're not allowed to go to PT with me."

Silence.

"What's wrong?"

More silence.

I stopped in my tracks. It took Atticus a few steps to notice I was no longer walking with him. He turned back to me with an inquisitive look, but another gust of wind tore through the campus, and his purple eyes latched onto a particularly large leaf tumbling past. He crouched down low, rear end sticking up high, and launched himself. Little wings snapped out, beak gaped wide, and claws sprang out from front paws as he snatched the leaf out of the air and landed in a surprisingly coordinated tumble.

His little roar of triumph brought a grin to my face. When he was done shredding the leaf, he bounced to his feet before leaping for another pile of leaves, batting them this way and that with his oversized paws.

This time, I realized what he was doing.

"You know," I said casually even as my eyes narrowed, "I can *feel* you trying to distract me with adorable antics. Avoidance isn't going to work on me."

Atticus froze for an instant before he raised guilty eyes, fragments of leaves falling from his beak. *"It was."*

He was entirely too smart for his own good.

I knelt in the leaves, ignored the damp that immediately seeped into my pants, and held open my arms. Blowing out a sharp huff of air, he slunk over and butted his head against my chest.

Carefully, I asked, "Do you not like being with your clutchmates?"

"I like being with Tavi." A tawny brown forest griffin much like Atticus flashed in my mind. He grumbled and twisted around so his side pressed against mine in a griffin hug. *"Rest of clutchmates as stupid as name."*

Protective rage roared up. It was one thing for the other griffin cadets to shun me. I would bite my tongue until it bled if it protected my little griffin, but if their shitty attitude was spilling over onto him, I would make *them* bleed.

Atticus angled his head so he was looking at me from the corner of one eye. *"Not mean to me."*

Oh.

I tilted my face up to the overcast sky and blinked back stupid, useless tears. No dragons flew overhead today... or if they did, they flew high above the clouds.

A purr rumbled in my griffin's throat, drawing my gaze back down. *"Love Harpy, love Tavi, rest of clutchmates stupid."*

At his fierce declaration, a smile tugged at my lips. "Harper," I corrected gently before I sighed. "It's okay—"

"No." He snapped his beak, tufted ears flattened to his rounded skull. *"Not nice."*

I gave in to the burning need and wrapped my arms around him, burying my face against his feathered neck. "It's *okay*. Just . . . give them time."

I wasn't sure if I was talking to him or me.

Atticus leaned into the embrace for a few moments before he wiggled free and pounced on another tumbling leaf with a piercing shriek. His thoughts took on a red tinge, different from when he was hungry, as he viciously shredded it.

He snapped his head up and glared at me. *"Don't wanna."*

His petulant tone destroyed the last of my melancholy, and I snorted a laugh as I climbed back to my feet. Absently, I brushed a handful of wet leaves off my knees and strode out of the griffin campus and toward the hatchery. "Tough."

After a beat, he scrambled after me, his tail lashing in annoyance and his mind churning with bloodthirsty images. *Loud* bloodthirsty images. Despite his incessant chatter, he didn't always think in words. A lot of it was emotion-tinged impressions. Sometimes, my brain translated those flashes into words, other times, I got a visual of what he was thinking or imagining.

As he growled and slashed another innocent leaf to shreds, I was treated to an impressively detailed image as he imagined the leaf was another griffin in his clutch. Judging by the dark brown ear tufts, I was fairly certain she was Langston's—the big guy who had been the first to confront me in the barracks.

"Vicious little monster," I said fondly. As another gust swept across the grounds, depositing the chill straight into my bones, I tucked a loose strand of hair behind my ear and glanced down at him. "Behave."

"No." Atticus said with a trilling laugh as we walked into the hatchery. His beak dropped open in a griffin grin before he stalked down the hallway on silent paws. Groaning, I darted after him just as he shouldered the crèche door open. The rest of his clutch had already been dropped off, their bondmates on a different class schedule than mine. As Atticus stepped out onto the warm sands, avian heads snapped around, and a chorus of trills and roars rose up in friendly greeting. A tawny brown forest griffin who must be Tavi brushed against Atticus, and my griffin nuzzled his neck affectionately.

One sleek forest griffin ignored him in favor of narrowing muddy green eyes at me. In the next instant, Atticus let out a fierce war cry and pounced on the other cub. I winced as they tumbled across the sands in a tangle of limbs and wings, but at least it looked like they were keeping their claws sheathed.

The Maven tasked with their care for the day didn't seem concerned, so I left Atticus to work out his issues with his clutchmate. I had my own problems to solve.

Striding back into the crisp fall afternoon, I made it halfway to the physical fitness area before I ran into trouble. Specifically, a trio of morons heading down the same path I was on. The way they sped up told me they'd not only spotted me, they'd been looking for me.

My jaw clenched, and I spun on my heel, intending to take the long way around. I had nothing to say to them—until Callum opened his mouth.

"Did bonding a griffin turn you into a coward, Harper?" he called after me mockingly.

Oh, hell no. *He did not just say that to me.*

I spun back around and marched up the path to confront the assholes who'd blown up my life. My baleful glare rested solely on Callum, who'd just moved back to the top of my list.

The corner of his mouth kicked up in a humorless smirk as he planted his feet and let me come to him. While Callum was shorter than the other two, he was still taller than me, and all lean, whipcord muscle. It made him deadly fast in a fight, and he'd kicked my ass more times than I could count on the training mat. Before the end of our first semester, I'd learned not to underestimate him—that didn't mean I wasn't going to punch him in the face.

Zayne stepped between us. Tall, broad shouldered, and muscular without being bulky, he had the physical presence to break up most of our fights but usually relied on his words. He'd always been the strategic thinker of our group, the one who had bullied the four of us into working together more often than not that first year until the bonds of friendship took hold.

Or at least, I thought we'd been friends.

I sucked in a sharp breath as I stared up at Zayne's eyes. The last time I'd seen him two short weeks ago, they were a dark brown. Now, they were a warm green shot through with gold. He'd bonded a dragon.

My hands balled up as rage flashed through me, setting fire to my heart and eating away at my restraint. I lifted my chin and glared at the taller boy. "Get out of my way, Zayne."

"Not happening," he said with quiet authority, but his eyes...his beautiful, stupid eyes begged for understanding. "We're not here to fight, Harper. We're here to *apologize*."

That last was tossed over his shoulder, though I couldn't tell if it was meant for Callum, Dimitri, or both.

Zayne turned back to me with a determined glint in his eyes. "I'm so fucking sorry, Harper—"

"Skulls up," Callum muttered.

All four of us stepped off the path, stiffened to attention, and saluted as an instructor walked past. He absently returned the salute without breaking stride, clearly in a hurry. It was a sorely needed splash of cold reality, dampening my rage. Fighting was against the rules, and I had enough trouble right now without adding an administrative punishment detail to the list.

Drawing in a deep breath, I decided focusing on Zayne was the best course of action. Possibly the *only* course of action that would get me through this without bloody knuckles.

"From where I'm standing, the only cowards are you three," I said with barely controlled venom. "You assholes could've apologized days ago, *weeks* ago, but you didn't. So why bother now?"

I couldn't keep my gaze from flicking to Dimitri. He stood just behind Zayne's left shoulder, slightly shorter, slightly more muscular. The first to come up with pranks, the first to take the top rank of our class...the first to befriend me, to fight with me, to fight *for* me. His jaw tightened, but his gaze didn't waver from mine. I couldn't read his expression, couldn't tell what he was thinking at all. And he didn't say a damn word.

It pissed me off.

Zayne held up his hands in an attempt to redirect my attention to him. "We were confined to campus the last two weeks on punishment detail. We couldn't risk breaking the rules."

"Hasn't stopped you before," I snapped.

Zayne winced. "One toe out of line, and they would've held us all back from bonding for a year."

"Oh, no," I muttered. "Not that."

"You wouldn't have anything to do with that, would you?" Callum sidestepped around Zayne, glaring at me like *I* was the bad guy. "We know you talked with Iverson after we left his office that day. What the hell did you say, Harper?"

Fury whipped through me, obliterating the last shreds of my control. I didn't think, I just lunged forward with my fist leading the way. Zayne caught me around the waist and pulled me back before I could connect with Callum's face.

The bastard had the audacity to smirk. "Looks like bonding a griffin made you slow, too."

For an instant, I hung in Zayne's grip, unable to react—because my griffin had felt my anger and surged forward in alarm. His presence, normally curled up in a tight ball, spread out across my mind as if he'd just flared his wings and soared forward until he was all I could feel.

"Harpy okay?"

My eyes burned as he looked through them for the first time, even as I tried to reassure him.

"Harper, are you okay?" Zayne asked cautiously in an unintentional echo of Atticus.

"I'm *fine.*"

Irritably, I tore myself out of Zayne's hold and bowed my head, struggling to adjust to the new sensation of an additional soul looking out through my eyes. They felt . . . heavy. A blink, and the burn faded. A slow breath, and the weight felt normal. When I looked up, I knew my eyes shone brighter, an unmistakable sign that I wasn't alone.

I shifted to mindspeak and softly repeated, *"I'm fine."*

I could feel Atticus' concern mingle with delight at his accomplishment. We hadn't been taught how to look through our bonded's eyes yet, and I honestly wasn't sure how he'd done it. Precocious indeed.

"Harpy sure?"

"I'm sure. Go back to playing with the others." I snorted a laugh. *"Or beating up that other griffin."* A warm smile graced my lips, and I didn't care that the guys could see. It wasn't for them. *"Love you, Atticus."*

"Felix," he said firmly. He laughed when I rolled my eyes. *"Love too, Harpy."*

"Harper," I shot back just as firmly, but his attention was already elsewhere, and my eyes were my own again. I blinked a few times to adjust before I glared at the morons. "Your weak-ass apologies aren't

accepted. Oh, wait. The only one who actually apologized was Zayne."
I shifted my glare to Callum. "You can take your accusations and shove
them. After everything, if you really think I'd do that to you—"

I broke off, unable to force the words out past the knot of rage in
my throat, and drew in a deep, calming breath. Judging by the way my
hands shook, it wasn't enough, so I took another deep breath, and
another. One more, and I finally turned to the silent Dimitri. My
former best friend.

"And you've apparently turned mute in the past few weeks. Nothing
to say?" I waited for him to say something, *anything*, but he didn't.
Curling my lip in disgust, I stepped past them. "I don't have time for
this crap. I'm late for PT."

Dimitri's hand shot out as I brushed past him and wrapped around
my upper arm. The warmth of his fingers burned through my sleeve
like a brand. "Hotshot, wait—".

Again, I didn't think. I just reacted, whipping around and slamming
my fist into his nose. Blood spurted in a highly satisfying arc, and he
stumbled back, clutching his face.

"Damn it," he mumbled, blood oozing through his fingers.
"Hotshot—"

"Don't call me that." I leaned closer to him, my voice a hoarse rasp
that revealed far more pain and vulnerability than I wanted. "Ever
again."

Zayne lurched forward, one hand up. "Harper, *wait*."

"No," I said coldly and walked away from them.

"*Harper!*"

My heart bled at the desperation in his voice, but I kept walking,
and I didn't look back . . . no matter how much I wanted to.

As I stalked into the PT area, late enough to earn extra pushups
and two extra laps, I cast a rueful grimace at my throbbing hand. *So
much for not getting bloody knuckles.*

Still, I didn't regret the pain. Not when the shocked look on
Dimitri's face danced in my memory. My griffin didn't have to tell me
he approved of my actions, not when I could feel his satisfaction as a
warm glow in the back of my mind.

Keaton frowned at my hand as I fell into the back row of the
formation. "You good?"

A small smile crossed my face at the gruff question. He still didn't like me very much, but he'd cared enough to ask. It was a start.

"I'm good," I said as I began warming up. "Just a minor disagreement."

Grouchy and Lanky, whose names were actually Asher Reese and Sam Elias, exchanged smirks as they jogged in place.

"Oh no," Elias said mockingly. "Did the little hotshot get into a fight?"

This time, I didn't hesitate. I pushed past Reese, fisted my hand in Elias' shirt, and dragged his face down to mine. "Call me hotshot again, and you'll find out."

Elias clenched his jaw, but I just glared a challenge at him and didn't back down. For once, he didn't seem to know what to say. And then Reese roared a laugh and clapped him on the shoulder hard enough to stagger the lanky cadet sideways, tearing his shirt from my grip.

"Tavros has some claws. I like it."

When Elias whirled on the shorter cadet, Garrett Hawthorne, the stocky guy who'd tried to break up their wrestling match on my first night in the barracks, heaved a sigh and placed himself between them. It seemed like he had to do that a lot.

"You only like it because she sharpened them on Elias," he told Reese with a roll of his eyes.

Reese grinned, a surprisingly bright expression that transformed his typically grumpy face into something approaching friendly. "Maybe."

"Yeah, yeah," Elias muttered as he straightened his shirt. He glanced at me. "Whatever, Tavros."

Before he turned away, I caught the barest glimmer of amusement in his eyes. Maybe I'd been going about this all wrong. What was it that Commandant Pulaski had told me? A slow smile spread across my face as the memory snapped into place.

Hold on to that fire.

I could do that.

CHAPTER 4

The academy wasn't all work and no play. Besides regular rest days, there were also "mandatory fun" events, where the attendance was mandatory and the fun entirely optional. Some events like the griffin relay race and dragon war games were annual traditions, but most were games designed to foster healthy competition and improve teamwork. Any of which were preferable to the mass briefings. Mostly because those briefings usually only happened when we'd screwed something up.

There had been one from the head Maven after my egg was swapped, reminding everyone of the rules and regulations governing the hatchery. Sitting through that had been an experience in misery and an exercise in control, because every last cadet had stared at me at some point during that never-ending lecture.

Another time, we'd gotten the safe sex and consent talk from the medical staff. The academy instructors weren't stupid enough to think we wouldn't have a little fun, and the Mavens were smart enough to produce a preventative measure to ensure it wasn't an issue. Nobody who'd volunteered for the academy had any intention of losing their spot to an unplanned pregnancy.

Then there was the briefing just for female cadets. Without the power of pre-War weapons, we had no place in the infantry. Instead, we served Tennessan as messengers, light cavalry, and bonded riders. But that didn't mean we wouldn't see combat or have to deal with the potential consequences of being captured by enemy soldiers.

That had been fun.

Today's briefing was different. With the ongoing threat of the Savinian invasion, the academy had started bringing in combat veterans to give us declassified reports from the front lines—or hijacking active duty riders whenever they swung through the academy on a messenger run. This particular briefing was only for third- and fourth-year bonded griffin riders, and we'd started our morning in the only place large enough on academy grounds for mass briefings—the amphitheater. Surrounded by curved stone walls and set in a manmade depression in the untracked cadet campus, the amphitheater was partially open to the elements, with narrow terraces carved in a stepping-stone descent to the covered stage at the front.

We'd filled the front half of the terraces, with the senior clutches getting the terraces closest to the stage. A pair of dragon riders from Fort Ashfall, one of the major forts on the eastern border, were our guest lecturers for the day. Captain Franklin, a rangy blonde with a deep scar cutting through one cheek that did nothing to detract from her beauty, stood at the center of the stage, her posture relaxed as she concluded her briefing on how forest griffin riders positively contributed to air strikes.

There was nothing relaxed about the brawny captain who took her place center stage. He didn't bother to introduce himself. I remembered him though. I remembered everything from that never-ending day when I lost my chance to fly.

This version of Captain Westbrook was a far cry from the arrogant but amused rider who had bragged about nearly ambushing me on my checkride. Impatience was reflected in every flex of his shoulders, every grimace barely restrained, and his harsh voice rang out across the amphitheater.

"Stand up if you're a mountain griffin rider."

There was the barest hesitation before dozens stood, including Bex and Volakis, Echo Clutch's mountain griffin riders. Westbrook pointed to his massive red dragon perched on the curving stone wall of the amphitheater as Nero spread his wings with a rippling snarl. The morning sun shone through the membranes and cast a red-tinged shadow across the terraces.

"Protecting those wings is your primary duty as a mountain griffin rider." Westbrook's fiery orange gaze swept across the standing cadets. "When you ride with us into battle, you need to be prepared to sacrifice your griffin, to sacrifice *yourself*, without hesitation. The entire reason for your existence is to be our shields."

There wasn't a hint of softness in the dragon rider's voice as he continued. He didn't sugarcoat anything, didn't shy away from the purpose of the mountain griffins—to fight the Savinian monsters that could and *would* take down an unprotected dragon, to die in the dragon's defense if necessary. But while his tone was all brisk practicality, there was an underlying edge of callousness, almost cruelty. We all knew what the mountain griffins' mission was, but I'd never heard it stated with such a lack of empathy before.

Maybe that was the point.

I'd ended up seated next to Bex, and while she remained impassive throughout the briefing, I caught the faintest tremor in her fingers before she tightened them into fists. The hard glint in her topaz eyes could be anger, but her carefully expressionless face argued for fear. I chanced a quick glance around and noted the rest of the mountain griffin riders were almost exclusively male, and even the handful of female cadets were much larger than the tiny Bex.

"Never forget you are the Talons of the Dragon Corps. Your service and sacrifice are vital to the survival of our dragons, and the defense of our nation."

Commandant Pulaski stood next to Captain Franklin on the left of the stage, her brilliant green eyes focused with unwavering intensity on the red dragon rider. She stepped forward into the ringing silence.

"Thank you both for your inspiring words—"

"With all due respect, ma'am, I'm not finished," Westbrook interrupted in that harsh voice. "All the training in the world won't prepare you cadets for active duty if you don't understand the harsh realities of this war. You *will* lose friends. You *will* get hurt. Many of you won't survive until retirement. The Savinians have more conventional soldiers than us, more artillery and ammo stockpiles than us, they have their wyverns and their broken beasts. The one advantage we have is more dragons, and that advantage could be lost in a single battle."

Once again, that fiery orange gaze swept over all of us.

"Without our dragons, we will lose this war. Remember that."

"*Thank you*, Captain Westbrook." The commandant's jaw flexed once before she addressed us. "Dismissed."

The red dragon rider gave an impatient tug on his flying leathers and strode off the stage before we'd even stood to attention. *Wow, what an ass.*

Elias smirked as we filed out of the amphitheater. "Man, I don't know about you guys, but *I'm* inspired."

"Shut up, Eli," Reese growled as he marched next to a stone-faced Bex. "Or I'll pick *you* for my sparring partner today."

"Shutting up," Elias said with a sarcastic salute, but he fell back a few paces as if he wanted to distance himself from even the possibility of sparring with Reese.

"Holy shit, Tavros." Reese stared down at me in genuine confusion, his typical belligerence completely absent. "It's like you've never done this before."

I gritted my teeth as my lungs struggled to remember how to draw in air. "I haven't."

Griffin rider training was so utterly at odds with dragon rider training that most of what I'd learned, what I'd *excelled* at, no longer applied. I'd been trained in aerial combat—to support a dragon in flight and fight, to protect my partner's vulnerable wings, to *fly*.

But griffin riders didn't fly in battle, or at least, forest griffin riders didn't. We were the scouts. Our duties sent us far from civilization, from supply depots, from backup. We needed to learn land navigation, survival skills, memorization, attention to detail. We needed to learn to work in tandem with our griffin partners, to see through their eyes when they went places we couldn't, to build a complete intelligence picture. Every last bit of our training was designed to turn us into the eyes and ears of the Tennessan military.

Part of that training was ensuring we were capable of defending ourselves so we could get that information back to those who needed it most. Which was why I was flat on my back with the freezing ground nipping at my skin, struggling to remember how to breathe after Reese effortlessly put me on my ass in hand-to-hand combat training.

Just like Callum used to—nope. Not going there.

"We get basic combat training," I added when Reese's confusion didn't clear up. "Not whatever the hell martial arts crap you just pulled on me."

Reese grimaced and rubbed the back of his neck as if embarrassed.

I was fairly certain he was embarrassed *for* me though, which was somehow worse than the expected scorn.

"Oh," he muttered. "That explains why you're so bad at it."

I let my head fall back to the cold ground. "Gee, thanks."

Keaton leaned over my prone position, sweat running down his face despite the winter chill. "Problem, Tavros?"

Yes, there was a problem. Everything hurt and I was failing *spectacularly.*

"Nope." Groaning, I pushed myself up onto my elbows. "No problem."

At the flare of pain, Atticus brushed against my mind, but he was getting better at gleaning when I was actually hurt. A faint, trilling laugh echoed along our bond along with a burst of encouragement to "do better," and then he went back to whatever game he was playing with his clutchmates.

A grin flashed across my face as I leveraged myself into a sitting position. My back felt like one long bruise, and my wrist twinged when I flexed it, but nothing was broken. *I* wasn't broken. For all that Reese hadn't held back, he also hadn't deliberately tried to hurt me.

Neither of my clutchmates offered a hand up. Even with the faint glimmers of comradery, everyone in Echo had made it clear from the beginning I had no friends here, that I was alone but for Atticus. That was fine. I could stand on my own.

Despite my best efforts, a hiss of pain escaped as I climbed to my feet.

"Dragon rider pussy," Langston muttered *loudly* as he sparred with Hawthorne. The two biggest cadets had been paired up at the beginning of the class, and what I'd caught of their matches told the story of their personalities. Langston was all attack and aggression, while the stockier Hawthorne was a mix of defense, offense, and most importantly, patience.

"What did you just say?" Hawthorne's expression hardened. "That is *not* how we talk about ladies, you fucking prick."

In the next instant, he caught the bigger cadet in a nasty armlock, decisively ending their current match.

"Fuck!" Langston went up onto his tiptoes and arched his back, grunting at the strain. Another inch, and Hawthorne would dislocate his elbow. "Ease up, man, I just meant she was being a wimp, not *that.*"

Hawthorne held him for another few seconds before he released him and stepped back. His eyes flicked to mine for a brief instant before he refocused on Langston. "I don't see any wimps here."

With that, the big guy stomped over to the water station. I blinked a few times. That had been . . . unexpected.

With a curl of his lip, Langston leveled a glare at me. He made it exactly a single step in my direction before Elias casually sidestepped—and stuck his foot out. When the asshole tripped, Elias pretended to catch him, but in reality, he just redirected his momentum and put the bigger cadet on his ass. It was remarkably similar to the move Reese had used on me.

"Oops, sorry about that, Langy." Elias' smirk said he wasn't sorry in the least. "Gotta watch your footing."

I stared. Had Elias just *helped* me? Or was it just an opportunity to mess with Langston, who hadn't exactly been making any friends either? Elias was such a troublemaker, it was impossible for me to guess. And then the lanky bastard glanced over his shoulder at me . . . and winked.

Langston scrambled to his feet, fists clenched tight. "What'd you just call me?"

Elias' smirk widened. "Langy—it's your griffin name."

"*What?*" His face turned a brilliant shade of red that contrasted horribly with his muddy green eyes. "How'd you know Bailey calls me that?"

"Your griffin told my griffin, and now you're stuck with it."

Oh hells, I'd forgotten about the Griffin Corps naming tradition. If it got out that Feli—*Atticus* called me Harpy, I'd never escape it. It was a miracle he hadn't told the other griffins already.

"*Waiting,*" he purred into my mind. Apprehension shivered down my spine at the sly mischief in his tone.

"*Waiting for what?*"

"*The perfect moment.*"

My brow furrowed before understanding hit. "*You're waiting for the perfect moment to tell everyone you call me Harpy?*"

"*Yes.*" He trilled a laugh. "*Live in fear.*"

My griffin was evil.

Elias spread his hands and affected an innocent look that fooled exactly nobody. "Sorry, *Langy*, I don't make the rules."

Reese snickered, and even Keaton cracked a smile before his eyes abruptly hardened. "Lock it down."

Even a first-year cadet knew what that meant. Langston snapped his jaw shut, and Elias' expression carefully blanked as he sidled back to Rodriguez, his original sparring partner.

The winter wind gusted sharply, and the sweat plastering my PT gear to my skin turned to ice as the rest of us straightened up. Unfortunately, I wasn't tall enough to see past the others. In fact, the only person smaller than me in Echo was Bex. But even though I couldn't see why Keaton had called knock it off, I didn't need to. Our instructor, or sabeo, was more than capable of making herself heard.

"Excuse me," Sabeo Taylin said from behind Langston, her soft voice somehow cutting straight through the background noise of the training field. "Did I call for a break?"

Langston leaped aside as if he'd been goosed, and our diminutive instructor marched through where he'd been standing. Her demeanor conveyed that she'd fully expected him to move—and would have moved him if he'd declined. Despite being less than half Langston's size, I had no doubt she was more than capable.

While the rest of us snapped to attention, Keaton stepped forward, chin up, shoulders back, and professional mask firmly in place. "No, Sabeo."

Her dark eyes took in everything in an instant and landed on me. If it were possible to stand more at attention than I already was, I'd have done it. As it was, my belly tightened with nervous anticipation.

She shifted her dark gaze to Reese. "Assessment?"

To my shock, a flash of what might have been respect crossed the grumpy cadet's face. "She got up."

"Very well." Sabeo Taylin's serene expression never faltered as she dipped her head in a nod. A single finger pointed at my chest. "With me, Tavros."

I'd thought the sabeo had hated me when she'd paired me with Reese. While he wasn't much larger than me, he was all wiry muscle and speed. The mismatch in our training was painfully obvious from the moment we'd first sparred, and I could see why Elias hadn't wanted to partner with him. It turned out she'd done me a favor by not sparring with me personally until now.

For the third time in as many minutes, I stared up at the gray skies.

The tiny woman was equal parts terrifying and unstoppable. I wanted to be her when I grew up. Assuming I survived until the end of class.

My eyes idly tracked a pair of dragons as they flew past overhead, dancing across the wintry skies while I lay in the dirt. It almost didn't hurt this time. Of course, that might have been because of the high-pitched whine in my ears. With a sharp shake of my head, the world snapped back into focus, and I got back up.

Slowly, painfully . . . but I did it.

Sabeo Taylin dipped her head in a gesture of respect. "Again."

I mirrored her gesture. "Yes, Sabeo."

By the time the lesson concluded, my gray PT shirt was closer to brown with all the dirt ground into it. But I'd gotten back up, every time.

Periodically, I'd felt Keaton's gaze on me. Watching me. Judging me. Waiting for me to break. He'd be watching for a long time, because I refused to give up. I might be the worst griffin rider cadet now, but I wouldn't stay that way. I'd get better at this.

Commandant Pulaski's voice floated in my memory. *Give yourself some grace . . . no driving yourself into the ground.*

I snorted a laugh as I got back up for the last time and bowed to my tiny, brutal instructor. Good thing the commandant hadn't meant that last part literally, because I was well acquainted with the ground at this point. Everything hurt, but I refused to limp as we jogged in formation to the next event on our afternoon schedule—the obstacle course.

Not just any obstacle course. The griffin rider course. The course we had to master to graduate. Located well outside the academy walls, it covered miles of terrain and a variety of challenges meant to simulate a scouting mission. When our griffins were big enough, we'd have to get through it together. Until then, we were here to learn how to survive it.

Instructor Anton Bayard, a burly ex-ranger with more muscles than a black dragon, cast an unimpressed look over the lot of us before he launched into an overview of the safety rules, the course rules, and finally, his expectations. The temperature steadily dropped throughout his lecture, and dark clouds built on the western horizon. Snow was an exceedingly rare event, but based on the hint of clean frost in the brisk wind, we might actually get some this time.

As inconspicuously as possible, I flexed cold-numbed fingers behind my back and hoped we'd be able to move soon. Preferably before I *couldn't*.

"Well, go on." Instructor Bayard concluded his lecture with a flick of his hand toward the start of the course, a trail leading into a thickly wooded stretch of rolling hills. "Impress me."

In the time he'd spent briefing us, my muscles had stiffened horribly, and I couldn't quite suppress my limp from hitting the ground hip first earlier. My clutchmates left me so far behind, I might as well have been on that trail alone. Before I'd made it even a fraction of the way through the first section, it felt like a dragon sat on my chest, and I struggled to suck in enough air. Why had I thought moving was preferable again?

My boot caught on a branch hidden in a pile of leaves, and I faceplanted in the middle of the trail. Growling, I smacked one fist on the ground and staggered to my feet—and froze.

Keaton stood further up the trail, his amber gaze fixed on me and his expression unreadable. I tried to resist the urge, but when his lips twitched as if suppressing a smirk, I gave in and held up my middle finger. His lips twitched again, and then he arched a brow and tapped a finger against his cheek . . . where I had mud clinging to my skin.

With a grimace, I wiped the chill mud off my face. When I opened my eyes again, he was gone. Forcing rubbery legs to cooperate, I jogged down the trail. Only four more days until rest day.

"*Harper Tavros!*"

So much for my rest day.

BAM!

The doors to Echo Barracks slammed open, silencing every last human and griffin as an enraged dragon rider cadet marched inside.

"Harper Tavros!" my old roommate roared again. "Front and center!"

"Hey!" Langston's face turned red and he planted himself in the aisle. "No dragon cadet assholes allowed—"

"Piss off."

Bethany slipped around him without breaking stride. When he spun around and caught her arm, she put him on his ass without breaking a sweat. She bent down, still holding his arm in a painful lock, and whispered in his ear. Whatever she told him was enough to make him simultaneously pale and back down with a mumbled apology. The glare he shot me promised retribution, but I didn't care—my friend was such a badass.

Unfortunately, my badass friend seemed *pissed*, and not at Langston. Sighing, I tucked my book away and slipped off my bunk. Atticus didn't bother to uncurl from his nest, but he lifted his head and watched, his gaze bright and full of mischief.

"You're enjoying my apprehension a little much, don't you think?" I muttered.

"No."

"Traitor."

Atticus trilled a laugh as Bethany stalked toward me with fire in her eyes. I braced myself.

"Harper Tavros," she snarled. "I gave you space because I thought you needed it, but I think I've let you sulk long enough." She slammed to a halt in front of me and jabbed a finger at my chest. "No more hiding!"

"I wasn't hiding!" I shot back in automatic protest. "I was . . . busy."

At her exasperated glare, I winced. Okay, maybe I'd been hiding from her a little. Then I took a good look at her face, and a gasp tore itself from my throat.

"Your eyes!"

Her exasperation drained away as she blinked fiery orange eyes at me, pride and joy shining bright in her gaze. But all the way in the back, buried so deep I almost missed it, was guilt. Oh, *hells* no. My girl was not allowed to feel even a speck of guilt on today of all days.

I grinned, so broadly it hurt my cheeks, and grabbed her by the shoulders. "He hatched?"

A grin that seemed born from relief as much as joy spread across her face. "He hatched!"

I squealed, not giving two shits about the show I was putting on for my clutchmates, and pulled her into a wild, spinning dance right there in the aisle. It ended in a tight hug that lasted only until Atticus butted in with a squawk, forcing his way into the embrace.

Bethany immediately let me go to drop down to one knee. "Hello there, little one. You've grown so much since I saw you hatch."

Atticus tilted his head, purple eyes studying my former roommate intently. *"She was there when I hatched?"*

"Yeah," I said softly. "She was there."

He clacked his beak in irritation. *"Don't remember."*

I snorted a laugh and grinned at Bethany. "Atticus is miffed he doesn't remember you."

Our bondmates couldn't talk to other humans. Their souls weren't entangled, so there was no way for them to be heard. It left us playing translator, but none of us minded.

"May I?" Bethany lifted one hand toward my griffin but stopped short of touching him. Atticus answered by practically shoving his neck into her fingers, trilling happily when she scratched beneath the feathers. Her eyes flicked to mine. "He's beautiful."

"He knows," I replied dryly as he preened under her attention.

After a long moment—though not nearly long enough based on Atticus' surge of outrage when she stopped scratching behind his tufted ears—she stood back up, her fiery orange eyes sparkling. "Want to meet Jasper?"

"Yes!" I hesitated, because red dragons were notoriously cranky, antisocial assholes, even as hatchlings. "Atticus too?"

Her nod was firm. "Atticus too."

As we strode down the aisle with my griffin bouncing between us, my clutchmates eyed us in silent hostility. It seemed like any ground I'd gained in the past three weeks was gone. Bex, the only one who might not have had a problem, was off somewhere with Reese.

When Keaton stepped into my path, I gritted my teeth and glared at him. He might be the team leader, but his authority only went so far, and we were free to do as we pleased on rest days. Within limits. Going with Bethany to the hatchery was well within those limits, and I was sick of being on the defensive. So I attacked.

"Would you respect me more if I turned my friend away just because she's a dragon rider?" I demanded in a low voice.

The fact that I'd been hiding from her the past few weeks was irrelevant. I wasn't hiding anymore, and I wasn't going to ruin my friendship with Bethany over stupid academy rivalries. I'd already lost enough friends. Surprise flickered in Keaton's eyes, and he snapped his mouth closed on whatever he'd planned to say.

"That's what I thought." I lifted my chin. "I'll be back before curfew."

He held my stare for an uncomfortably long moment before he tilted his head, a griffin-like gesture many of us were picking up from our bondmates. "Don't be late, Tavros."

As we stepped out into the weak winter sunlight, Bethany rolled her shoulders. "Tough crowd. Have they been dicks this whole time?"

I avoided her piercing stare in favor of watching my cavorting griffin. He wouldn't be considered a cub for much longer. He was growing so fast.

"Damn it," Bethany muttered when I refused to answer. She whipped an angry glare over her shoulder at the barracks as her steps slowed. She looked seconds away from waging war on my entire clutch, and I'd never loved her more.

I grinned. "Damn, I missed you."

Bethany turned that fiery orange glare on me before her gaze softened. The new color was definitely going to take some getting used to, but it really suited her.

"Well, if you hadn't been hiding with a bunch of rude assholes the past few weeks like a stubborn bitch, you wouldn't have missed me," she said flatly. But then her lips twitched into a smirk. "Missed you too, girl."

When she still looked like she wanted to charge back into the barracks, I started walking again, leaving her the choice to go back alone or follow. She growled under her breath and quickly caught up.

"Don't think too badly of them," I said quietly, thinking back on how very little sympathy I'd felt toward Echo's displaced team leader, Marcos. I'd been so wrapped up in my own pain that day, but it was no excuse. "I didn't exactly make the best first impression."

Bethany scoffed. "You had a rough day, they should've made allowances."

I rolled my shoulders in a shrug, as if shedding my past mistakes was that easy. A playful smirk crossed her face.

"At least some of them are nice to look at." She wrinkled her nose. "There's definitely no hotties in Alpha Flight, that's for damn sure."

My gut tightened. I should've been in Alpha with her. I pushed the thought away, determined not to wallow on my friend's day.

"Poor baby," I teased. "Feel free to go hunting in Echo. I certainly don't want any of those assholes."

Bethany snickered as we made a beeline straight for the hatchery—

or as much of a beeline as possible with a griffin who didn't feel like hurrying. My newly bonded dragon rider friend had to be impatient to get back to her hatchling, but she'd always been the most disciplined in our class, and not a trace of it showed in her expression as she watched my griffin play.

With a trilling cry, Atticus spread his wings and leaped into the slightly warmer than usual breeze. The anticipated snow had never materialized, which was a shame. It would've been fun to watch him play in the snow. Regardless, I loved watching him try to fly, though his wings were still far too small for him to do much more than extended jumps. He actually managed to stick the landing on this one, and he preened at the burst of pride I sent his way before he leaped again— and faceplanted.

When I couldn't hold back my laugh, he snapped his beak in annoyance and flounced toward the hatchery in a huff.

"Named him after one of the first dragons, huh?" Bethany murmured with a straight face, but barely suppressed laughter suffused her tone.

"Yeah." I sighed as Atticus flattened his ears and sped up his pace, as if he could escape the name if he just walked fast enough. "He hates it."

"Atticus stupid." He flared his wings, accidentally-on-purpose smacking me in the side before he shoved the door to the hatchery open with one oversized paw. Sly amusement threaded through his mental voice when he added, *"Harpy not stupid. Harpy good name for you."*

I rolled my eyes as we followed him into the humid warmth of the hatchery. Bethany and I had to pause in the atrium to allow our eyes to adjust to the dim interior lighting, but my griffin just ambled down the central hallway, his eyes automatically adjusting in a fraction of an instant. When I learned how to share his eyes, I'd be able to do that too.

Bethany's patience finally snapped at my griffin's slow pace. With an explosive huff only slightly tinged with desperation, she hustled around him and all the way down to the heavily reinforced steel door at the end. There was a small, square panel to the right, a relic from a different time when we had the power to do magical things.

Without that power, the locks built into the door wouldn't engage, but the academy had improvised. Instead of the inert panel, Bethany rapped sharply on the door, triggering a call and response with the Maven inside. Only when she'd given the correct responses did the Maven unbar the door. The griffin crèche didn't have that level of security.

The door swung inward silently, and I stepped into the dragon crèche for the first time. The differences were immediately apparent. It was larger for one, the sands hotter, the air a touch less humid. And there was a green dragon hatchling sleeping in the sands, her graceful tail tip curled in front of her muzzle.

My heart stopped.

She looked about a week old. There had only been one green due to hatch in that time frame.

"*Shit*," Bethany snarled before she whirled to me with wide eyes. "I'm so sorry, Harper. I thought he would've picked her up by now."

"Who," I said, my voice little more than a harsh rasp of acidic pain. My griffin leaned against my leg, purring, but the quiet rumble didn't soothe me this time. "Who bonded her?"

I couldn't tear my gaze off that perfect little green. It wasn't like I hadn't known someone else would bond her, wasn't like I hadn't understood she'd share her soul with another. It still hurt far more than I'd thought it would.

"Harper…" Her voice gentled. "Is knowing going to help? Really help?"

"No," I said in a ragged whisper. "But not knowing will be so much worse."

Bethany was silent for so long I didn't think she would answer. So I watched the little green while my heart bled and my griffin purred. She shifted in her sleep, wings rustling as she stretched the membranes out before furling them tight against her back.

Bethany's heavy sigh broke the heartbroken spell I was under. "Zayne."

The bottom dropped out of my stomach. I snapped my head around, certain I'd misheard. One look at her expression was enough. Outrage joined the toxic swirl of jealousy and loss. After everything he'd done, for him to get rewarded with *my* dragon—

A bitter, disbelieving laugh ripped its way out of my throat, and I couldn't stop my gaze from shifting back to the sleeping green again. Mine. She was supposed to be *mine*.

"How could he do this?" I barely recognized the shredded voice as my own. "That *bastard*. How could he do this!"

Possessive jealous rage roared. My hands shook, and for just an instant, I wanted nothing more than to burn the world down. Atticus let out a distressed cry, but it was muffled, as if he were very far away.

Shock allowed me to tamp the rage back down, compartmentalize it where it wouldn't hurt my bonded. Shame quickly followed. I'd forgotten him. How could I forget my griffin—the literal other half of my *soul*—was standing at my side, purring in a desperate attempt to make me feel better?

I was a terrible bondmate.

"Harpy okay?" Atticus asked in a tentative voice that threatened to shatter what was left of my broken heart. Trembling, I reached out and stroked a hand down his head and neck in an attempt to soothe him. It wasn't enough.

"Oh, gods." I dropped to my knees so I could look him in the eye, so shaken I couldn't even manage mindspeech. "I'm so sorry."

"Why sorry? Harpy hurt." He sounded puzzled as he inspected me, as if he were looking for physical wounds. Understanding lit up his gaze before he dipped his head and tapped his beak against my chest, right over my heart. *"Harpy hurt here."*

I thought about lying to him, but I'd already shielded what I could. Besides, lying to the other half of your soul was stupid, even when your other half was still so very young.

"Harpy hurt," I said in agreement and gently wrapped my arms around his neck. "But I'll be okay. Promise."

Bethany did us the courtesy of pretending she couldn't hear my half of the conversation and waited patiently. Almost of its own volition, my gaze tracked back to the green. She wasn't mine. Even though I'd tended her egg, even though she was supposed to be mine, she wasn't. Unshed tears burned the back of my eyes.

"He didn't tell me," I whispered as I carded my fingers through Atticus' feathers. This . . . this might be the moment I finally broke. At least Bethany was the only one present to witness it. I tore my gaze from the green who wasn't mine, who would *never* be mine, and looked at my friend. "He didn't say a word."

She gripped my shoulder, the touch at once comforting and grounding. "Maybe he couldn't. Maybe he didn't know how." Her voice turned wry. "Maybe somebody wouldn't stop walking away from him long enough for him to get the words out."

I froze for a moment before my shoulders slumped.

"Damn it."

Groaning, I buried my face in my griffin's feathers in embarrassment while he trilled a soft, relieved laugh. I breathed in his clean, spicy scent, then I stood up, rolled my shoulders back, and looked at the green dragon.

"Zayne will be a good rider for her," I said as resolutely as I could. It helped that it was true. His personality would be a good fit for a green, though it was a little puzzling—he'd always claimed he wanted an active combat role. "If it had to be anyone, I'm glad it was him."

Bethany gave me a little side-eye. "You want to drench all his clothes and leave them out overnight to freeze again, don't you?"

"Maybe."

She bumped her shoulder to mine. "Just say the word, and Operation Popsicle is a go."

"I love you so much." A tentative smile spread across my face. "Introduce me to your bondmate?"

She grinned broadly. "Thought you'd never ask."

To my chagrin, when we'd first walked into the crèche, my attention had been so riveted to my—to *Zayne's* green, I hadn't even noticed the other dragons. And while the crèche wasn't crowded, there were a decent number of hatchlings in the low-ceilinged room.

A pair of grays who could only be a day or two old at best were curled up together in the middle of the sands, with a quartet of slightly older grays to the right, a black hatchling twice the size of the others to the left, and even a rare blue peeking out from behind one of the Mavens. A flash of red in the far corner behind the hulking black caught my eye as Bethany led us across the hot sands.

The black dragon hatchling tilted his head and watched as we drew near. He couldn't have been more than a few days old. One day, he would be an unstoppable tank on the battlefield, but right now he was downright adorable. Beautiful black-ringed amber eyes regarded me solemnly, and my steps slowed, caught in the intensity of his gaze. And then the hatchling yawned, showing off an impressive number of fangs, and flopped onto his side with a huff, his eyes already drifting closed.

As we skirted around the sleepy-eyed black, I finally got my first look at Bethany's new bondmate, Jasper. Only a day old, and the fierce red raised his head on a wobbling neck and bared his fangs at us. Bethany grinned fondly, I kept my distance, and my idiot griffin took it as an invitation to play.

Atticus bowed and pranced around the hatchling, trilling in delight while Jasper snapped his jaws and hissed in warning. Griffins and dragons couldn't talk to each other, but even a young griffin couldn't mistake that kind of body language.

"Atticus, *no!*" My heart skipped several beats, because reds were lethal from the moment they broke their shell. Bethany's eyes went vague for a moment before she waved a reassuring hand.

"He won't hurt him, but he says 'stupid bird annoying.'"

I gaped at her. "He's already talking?"

Pride shone bright in Bethany's fiery orange eyes, but she shook her head. "Not in words, no, but the imagery and emotion came through loud and clear."

"Precocious." I grinned as my griffin dropped low on his front legs, leaving his tail waving in the air. "Just like someone else I know."

When Jasper made no move to get up and play no matter how Atticus teased him, my griffin stretched out on the sand next to him and crossed one paw over the other. His head tilted as he studied the irritable hatchling through narrowed purple eyes.

"*I like him,*" he announced as he tucked his wings against his back. "*Her too. Bethany good for Harpy.*"

My eyes narrowed. "Oh, so you can say *her* name right, but not mine?"

"*I am saying your name right.*" Atticus trilled a laugh. "*You're saying mine wrong.*"

"What's he saying?" Bethany asked with a grin. "You look like steam is going to burst out of your ears."

I rolled my eyes. "He wants to be called Felix, not Atticus."

"He *named* himself?" Astonishment stamped her features before she shook her head in admiration. "Whoever started the rumor that griffins are stupid is a moron."

Atticus raised his head proudly. "*Griffins sneaky and smart.*"

A smile pulled at my lips, and my shattered heart knit together a little more. I'd wanted a dragon. Instead, I'd ended up with an incredibly smart, incredibly *stubborn* griffin.

"If he bites your tail, I'm going to say I told you so," I said in warning as my wonderful idiot spread the wide fan of feathers at the tip of his tail and dangled it in front of Jasper's muzzle like a lure. The red hatchling eyed the feathers with predatory interest. In the next instant, his head darted forward teeth first, but Atticus snapped his tail out of his reach, and his fangs only closed on air.

As the red grumbled in annoyance, Atticus dropped his beak open in a griffin grin and waggled his tufted ears. *"Gonna be friends. Can tell."*

We stayed for a little longer, but it was getting close to curfew, and we needed to head back. Bethany insisted on walking with us after giving Jasper a loving caress. The fierce little red seemed indifferent to her touch, almost haughty, until his eyes slipped closed in unmistakable contentment.

Outside, the brilliant reds and oranges of sunset splashed across the sky, while a crescent moon hung on the eastern horizon, shining bright amid the cool purples and blues of approaching twilight. It was the kind of sky that made you stop and take notice, the kind that had made me long to soar in the first place.

As I turned to watch Atticus attempt to fly again, the small hairs on the back of my neck stood up. A shiver that had nothing to do with the cold air crawled down my spine, and unease settled in my gut. Bethany noticed my reaction.

"What's wrong?" she asked quietly, her eyes scanning the quad for threats.

"Nothing." The crawling sensation of unfriendly eyes quickly faded, and I shrugged my shoulders to shed the tension. I tilted my head toward the gaggle of unbonded griffin cadets heading up the slope toward their barracks. "I'll just be happy when they forget about me and stop watching me all the time."

Bethany grimaced. "That can't be fun."

"Nope," I said, but a slow smile crossed my face. I'd come so close to breaking this afternoon...but I hadn't. "They can watch all they want. They'll never see me break."

"Damn right they won't." She waited until we were alone in the quad before she spoke again. "So. Harpy, huh?"

I shoved her sideways. "Shut up."

She snickered. "I could not think of a better griffin name for you, girl."

"Don't you dare breathe a word of it to anyone," I said with a growl, but she just gave me a grin that meant nothing but trouble.

We fell back into our friendship as if no time had passed since Atticus hatched and changed my life forever. We bantered and bickered while my griffin leaped and pounced and stretched his wings, gamboling around us as we tromped up to Echo barracks. Just outside the double doors, an enthusiastic roar split the air.

"Harpy catch!"

Startled at the demand in his tone, I turned just in time to see Atticus leap toward me, wings flared wide and beak dropped open in a grin. He slammed into my chest, and I suddenly had an armful of griffin.

"Oof." Completely blinded by tawny feathers, I staggered back a step as his momentum threatened to bowl me over. Only Bethany's swift reaction kept me from falling backward, her arm a solid counterbalance across my back. He trilled a joyous laugh as he hooked his paws over my shoulders and shifted his head back. I spat out a feather and gave him an exasperated look. "Don't you think you're getting a little big for this?"

Atticus tilted his head. *"No."*

Contentment and sleepiness accompanied that decisive remark, along with a less than pleasant ache in his wings. He'd overdone it. My arms already burned from the strain, but I hitched him a little higher to rebalance his weight without further complaint. One day soon, he'd be big enough to carry me. I only had so much time to return the favor.

"Looks like you've got your hands full," Bethany said with a grin.

She reached for the door, but it opened before she could grasp the handle. Elias paused in the opening, slowly dragged his gaze over my friend, and gave her a first-class leer.

"Any time you want to put me on my ass like you did Langston, you just let me know, pretty lady," he said smoothly before stepping aside and holding the door for us.

I stared. Elias was *flirting* with her. To my utter shock, Bethany flirted back.

"You like it rough, pretty boy?" she purred as a smile danced on her lips.

He winked. "Try me and find out."

"I think I might vomit," I muttered.

"What?" Bethany grinned. "You said your clutchmates were fair game."

I wrinkled my nose and walked past Elias. "That doesn't mean I want to witness it."

"Rude." She let out a low chuckle and waved. "See you later... *Harpy!*"

She'd raised her voice back to that battlefield bellow she'd used before, and the damning nickname echoed throughout the barracks. Heads snapped around, more than a few of my clutchmates snickered, and a truly evil glow lit up Elias' eyes.

"Aw, she ruined my game," Atticus grumbled as I shot a glare over my shoulder.

"I hate you."

Bethany smirked. "Consider this payback for the hair incident."

"Oh, come *on*," I muttered. "The pink washed out... eventually. Now I'm stuck with Harpy forever."

My griffin's annoyance vanished and he rumbled happily, his eyes bright with mischief. *"Good."*

After the way I'd treated him earlier, I'd rather die than ruin his happiness, though I couldn't stop my defeated sigh from escaping. "Harpy it is."

CHAPTER 5

Despite the many differences between dragon and griffin rider training, there was one commonality. We were *riders*. Whether through the air on the back of a dragon, or through the forests on the back of a griffin, we all needed to know how to ride. And since there were only so many instructor dragons and griffins to go around, the Tennessan Bonded Training Academy compensated with horses. From year one, every cadet was expected to learn how to ride and ride well. While it wasn't a direct correlation to flying, many of the basic principles translated, and it was part of the core curriculum for everyone regardless of tracked status.

It was the one thing I'd always been good at.

No, not just good—I was a natural, and I'd worked hard to hone that natural talent into something great. In the three years I'd been at the academy, riding had become my strength, my peace, my gods damned *happy place*.

Today was the first day it had been added back to our schedule after bonding our griffins, and I couldn't wait to get back in the saddle. Almost a month out was going to hurt, but the burn would be worth it. The stable hands were a familiar sight, and I'd spent so many extra hours in the barn that they remembered me—and my preferred mount.

"Renegade is in his stall if you want to get him groomed and tacked up," George called out in his whiskey-rough voice from the back of the barn.

The old man was my favorite stable hand, and I'd spent long hours of my free time learning everything about horse care I could from him. He hadn't taught me everything *he* knew, but he'd certainly taught me almost everything *I* knew. His most important lesson—never let fear stop you from getting back in the saddle.

"Thanks!" I called back as George limped out of the shadows with a bridle looped over one stooped shoulder. His right leg might be twisted from a bad break that had never healed right, but he was still a better rider than half the instructors.

"Good to see you again, girl," he said, wrinkled face breaking into a warm smile before he turned to help one of my clutchmates.

The bay gelding stuck his head over the stall door and nickered as I strode down the aisle. He wasn't mine, and I wasn't his only rider by a long shot, but he was typically reserved for the more experienced riders and was usually available when I wanted or *needed* to ride. I should've come here sooner after bonding with Atticus, but my schedule had been so full that I'd been too tired on the handful of rest days I'd had.

And I'd wanted to spend the time with my griffin.

The familiar scents of hay, horse, and manure filled my nose as I quickly brushed and tacked up Renegade. The rest of my clutch were still getting their mounts ready, but I was too excited to wait, and I led the gelding outside. The sky was achingly blue, the sunlight was blinding, and the wind was chilly, and none of that mattered the instant I swung up into the saddle.

Renegade pranced and tossed his head, but it was a simple matter to collect him and channel all that energy into a brisk warmup. The big gelding was a different breed than most of the lesson horses, with an extra gait between his regular trot and canter, where his already smooth stride turned smooth as silk. Riding him was as close to flying as I'd ever gotten outside of a dragon's back. My spine flexed with every step, and I swayed to the rhythm of his stride, comfortable in the saddle and confident in my skills in a way I hadn't been in weeks.

By the time the rest of my clutch had gathered outside, I'd thoroughly warmed the gelding up and was ready for the day's lesson. Of course, I had to wait for them to warm up their mounts, but that was fine. More time in the saddle for me.

Like all border-town kids, I'd been taught basic survival, but my father had also trained me to ride and to shoot. He'd wanted me to have skills that would serve me well regardless of what path my life took. Even though I'd wanted nothing more than to be a dragon rider, there'd been no guarantee my blood would carry the recessive trait.

It helped that my mother wasn't just bond capable, but a *rider*. Bonding increased the odds of carrying a bond-capable child, which was one of the reasons women served as riders—the other being that there simply weren't enough bond-capable men to match the number of dragons and griffins.

But even if I *was* bond capable, there was no legal requirement to bond. Not in Tennessan. One of my older cousins had tested positive, but she'd decided that life wasn't for her. Instead, she managed one of the farms supporting Royal Oak, our border town, and had a whole brood of kids with her retired griffin rider husband.

It wasn't any different for the men. If they tested positive, they could volunteer for the academy or not—nobody should be forced to share their soul with another—but either way they were expected to contribute to society, marry, and have kids.

That wasn't the life I'd wanted. Not yet. I'd wanted to fly.

My excitement momentarily dimmed, but I shook it off. *Nope, not going there. Not today. Today is going to be a* good *day.*

I breathed deep and took Renegade through increasingly difficult warmup patterns until our horseback riding instructor, Lauren Loffler, decided everyone was ready. My excitement returned full force when she led us out of the warm-up arena to the practice range.

Riding was amazing. Riding while shooting targets? Pure fucking joy.

Instructions and safety briefs were given, compact recurve bows and quivers were distributed, and when Instructor Loffler asked for a volunteer to go first, my hand shot into the air. Being able to shoot from horseback translated to both close-quarters aerial combat and scouting deep into enemy territory. It was why my father had spent so many extra hours with me on Royal Oak's training range after I'd tested bond capable. The skill was vital to our graduation rankings, which in turn determined our active duty postings.

This wasn't just academy rivalries, or games—this directly impacted my future, my ability to *make a difference* in our war with Savinia, and I was determined to do well. While this was only the beginner course, a straight shot across an open field with evenly spaced targets and no fancy riding required, it still took practice. I eyed the course and grinned.

My clutchmates would see I wasn't a complete idiot or an embarrassment.

Renegade sensed my rising excitement and tossed his head, prancing in place in matching eagerness. I easily rode out his little dance and patted his neck with a laugh.

"Ready, huh?"

The rest of my clutch pulled back, Instructor Loffler gave the signal to start, and finally, *finally* I was turned loose to do something I was good at.

A little inside leg and outside rein, and the bay gelding broke into a fast jog, but at a gentle correction he settled into a perfectly collected canter. A few strides to catch his rhythm, a few more to loop the reins over the saddle pommel and nock the bow.

A deep breath, a slow exhale. Three, two, one, *release.*

Thwack!

Another arrow, another deep breath. Three, two, one, *release.*

Thwack!

A slight rise in the ground, a squeeze of the thighs to maintain balance as Renegade pushed slightly harder with his hindquarters.

Last arrow, last deep breath. Three, two, one, *release.*

Thwack!

Three targets. Three arrows. Three hits.

A wide grin split my face as I slung the bow across my back and picked up the reins. Renegade didn't want to stop, and I let him stride out a little past the final target before bringing him back in a wide loop toward the start of the course and my waiting clutchmates.

Instead of the expected approval or acceptance, all I saw on their faces was scorn and disgust. My heart sank, and I snapped my head around as we cantered past the line of targets. I'd thought I'd hit them all, but maybe I'd missed one? Relief gusted through me. Only one arrow had found the small red center, but the other two shots weren't horrible, especially with nearly a month out of practice. So why—

"Show off!"

My smile died and I sat back in the saddle, an unconscious reaction to the disdain in the remark. I wasn't even sure which of the guys had said it, but another girl, Matthews, shook her head and turned to Foster, the girl next to her. I couldn't hear what she said, but it definitely wasn't complimentary.

Renegade slowed to a trot in response to my weight shift, and I leaned forward and patted his neck. "Good boy."

And if my voice shook a little, nobody was close enough to hear.

"Now *that*, boys and girls, is how it's done," Instructor Loffler called out as I reluctantly rejoined my clutch. "Did you see how she rebalanced her weight without losing sight of the final target? That's how you need to ride. You need to *feel* your mount and *react*, not think."

The older woman was notoriously stingy with praise. Rather than bask in it, I wanted to sink into the ground. My shoulders hunched defensively, and I felt heat wash across my cheeks as more than one of my clutchmates shot me an irritated glare.

"Why?" Matthews demanded. "When we're riding our griffins, the bond will let us feel what they're doing."

"Because being able to feel your bondmate won't do shit for you if your body doesn't know how to react," Instructor Loffler said. "Training and building that muscle memory is the only way to hone those reactions. And thank you, by the way, for volunteering to go next." She raised a brow when Matthews just sat on her horse, staring at her. "Well? Get to it, Cadet."

Grumbling under her breath, Matthews kicked her horse into a lumbering trot and bounced down the range. She missed every shot. So did Elias, and Bex, and Hawthorne. Keaton and Langston did better. In fact, Langston was nearly as good a rider as I was, and while Keaton was arguably a better shot than either of us, his course time dropped his score.

They were the only two to get a passing score.

One by one, the rest of the cadets ran through the target course. One by one, they failed to hit all three targets. With every failure, my shoulders hunched a little further and my face burned a little hotter. While my score would've been considered above average among the dragon rider cadets, it was far and away the best out of Echo.

No wonder they thought I was showing off.

"Cadet Tavros, I want you to give the intermediate course a try," Instructor Loffler said once everyone had a turn. "Everyone else, run through the beginner course until you can hit at least one target or until our time is up. I don't care if you have to drop back to a walk to do it. Same order as before, minus Tavros, and go." She glanced at me. "What are you waiting for? An engraved invitation?"

"Sorry, ma'am." I swallowed hard and guided Renegade away from my sullen clutchmates and toward the trail to the left of the open field, where the intermediate course wound through the trees. I felt eyes on me the whole way, though when I glanced back, the only person still watching me was Keaton. Once again, his expression was unreadable.

Atticus sensed my distress as he woke from his nap, his sleepy contentment falling away in a heartbeat. *"Harpy okay?"*

"I'm fine, buddy. Just some training stuff I'm working through."

"Harpy sure?"

At his concern, I compartmentalized every last bit of my dismay. I didn't want it touching him.

"I'm sure." I forced a smile, not just for my griffin, but for anyone still watching—like Keaton. "I just got a little too excited. Go play."

Blowing out a bracing breath, I urged Renegade into a canter and rode into the trees. Any pride I'd felt in finally doing something *right* was long gone. Even my happiness at getting back in the saddle had drained away. All that was left was determination to finish the training session without giving in to the burning in the back of my eyes.

The first target flashed into view.

A deep breath, a slow exhale. Three, two, one, *release.*

Thwack!

That evening, we had the late shift for dinner. The chow hall was brightly lit, coated in layers of grease, and packed full of long tables. A low hum permeated the open space, with roughly half the tables occupied, a full buffet table at the rear, and a half wall separating the kitchen area.

I just picked at my food, because while it was usually somewhat edible, it currently tasted like crap. I wasn't the only cadet barely eating though, so it probably really was the food rather than my shitty mood. Honestly, it looked like the kitchen staff had taken leftovers from breakfast and turned it into an unholy casserole of overcooked potatoes, soggy vegetables, and sadness.

So much sadness. There wasn't even cheese, let alone bacon.

With a sigh, Keaton pushed back from the long bench running along the scuffed, heavily graffitied metal table.

"I don't know about you guys, but I think I'm done." Our team leader picked up his tray and tilted his head toward the door. "Let's go get our griffins and call it a night."

For once, Echo Clutch was in complete agreement. We all dumped our trays and headed outside without argument. The lingering daylight was long gone, and a harsh wind whistled through the hills and cut through my riding leathers. Goosebumps raced across my skin as I breathed in the night and exhaled frost, my breath vaporous like the ice-breathing dragons of children's bedtime stories.

A faint smile creased my face. I drew in a deep breath to do it again—and an ear-piercing wail shattered the quiet. The air-raid siren, impossible to ignore, impossible to miss. For a breathless moment, we all froze, waiting for the split tone that would tell us it was yet another training exercise.

It never came.

Training kicked in, and I ran for my assigned fire brigade—only to be pulled up short by Keaton. He gave my arm an urgent shake, but his eyes were focused on Reese.

"Not our place, not anymore," he barked out loudly enough to be heard by the entire clutch.

Reese was held back by Hawthorne, and Langston had frozen midstep. They'd also tried to run to help, but Keaton was right. The unbonded cadets were primary on fire-brigade duty for a reason. As cruel as it was, they were easier to replace than the griffins or dragons who would die with us if we fell to the flames. And there would be flames. Deep raids like this were rare, but whenever enemy dragons managed to slip through our lines, they always carried firebombs in their talons.

A shudder wracked my frame. The instructors had demonstrated what white phosphorous and napalm could do earlier that year.

The academy's lone blue dragon rose into the sky with an eerie cry, riderless. Where she was going, her bonded couldn't follow. High, too high for humans to breathe, high enough to see what was coming for us through strange, multifaceted eyes that could see better than even the sharpest-eyed griffin. The intel she gleaned would be relayed through her rider, safely on the ground.

Or as safe as the ground could be when we were under attack.

"Move!" Keaton bellowed, and we all took off running for the hatchery, where our bonded griffins slept off their dinners in the crèche...though the air-raid siren was loud enough to stir even meat-drunk cubs.

"Harpy?" Atticus mumbled. Sleepy confusion weighed down his normally quick mind, and the first yellow tinges of alarm colored his thoughts.

"Stay where you are, we're coming to you," I said hurriedly, too busy running and scanning the night sky for incoming threats to spare him more than a moment's comfort.

The previously quiet academy grounds erupted with personnel as everyone moved with a sense of purpose, reactions well-honed thanks to countless drills. The majority ran for their assigned fire-brigade sectors, while others sprinted for the hatchery, just like us. It was the safest, most heavily reinforced building at the academy, and as much as it sucked, it was where we needed to go. A much smaller group, seniors all on the cusp of graduating, raced for their bonded, dragon or griffin, and prepared to defend us along with the instructors and staff.

Frustration simmered, and I wasn't the only one to clench jaws or fists as we ran, not to help, but to *hide*, to stay safe while others fought. We were right in the middle of the most vulnerable part of bonding— our griffins too young to fight, too valuable to lose. Understanding didn't make it gall any less, and for once, I completely related to Langston as he growled a steady stream of vicious curses.

A deep, booming roar that was felt as much as heard cut through the piercing sirens. Red wings spread wide atop the highest eyrie. Backlit by the dim nighttime lights, they were nearly translucent, a reminder of just how fragile the membranes between the wing spines could be. The dragon they belonged to was far from fragile, a massive beast of war and veteran of countless aerial combat missions with the scars to prove it. His deep, booming roar sounded again.

Commandant Iverson's dragon, Tiberius, calling the other dragons to battle.

In a matter of seconds, his call was answered by the thunder of wings as every combat-capable dragon and rider ascended into the night sky. The softer beat of feathered wings quickly followed as mountain griffins shot into the air to support, and a handful of forest griffins flew low and fast in all directions to scout. The deep *thrum* of the anti-air battery to the south of the academy added to the growing cacophony.

With the element of surprise gone, the enemy dragons made themselves heard. I picked out everything from the booming roars of reds, to the harsh roar-screams of grays, and even the deep, wailing cries of coppers. Any hope that this was a training exercise vanished in a burst of fear. Coppers were a bastardized crossbreed born from red males and green females. Lithe and strong like a green, bad-tempered and ruthless like a red, the spiky assholes were deadly little fighters—and the Savinians were the only ones who'd ever managed to successfully breed them.

Ice shivered down my spine as the enemy dragons roared again.

That was no small raiding team bearing down on us—that was an entire wing. Twenty dragons at a minimum.

Fire bloomed in the distance. Men screamed, and the ballistae in the southern quadrant fell silent. Our first line of defense was gone. Shadowy shapes swept across the sky in a staggered line, blocking out the stars, and the first bombs fell across the academy. Shouts rose as flames splashed across the walls and raced across the winter-dry grass, the detonations felt as much as heard. A burst of fiery destruction engulfed the supply shed next to the chow hall, and a fire brigade team rushed to contain the damage.

A hysterical laugh bubbled up beneath the terror—if they'd given it a few more seconds to spread, the Savinians could've done us the favor of destroying what was left of that gods awful casserole. *Missed opportunities.*

Another round of bombs dropped, and I couldn't help my violent flinch as the explosions reached out and punched me in the chest. Keaton steadied me, both of us coughing violently as the breeze whipped blackened clouds of smoke and ash over us. The instant my legs steadied, he let go, and we ran faster. An outraged shriek snared my attention, and I whipped a glance backward as Reese slung Bex over his shoulder.

"Put me down!" the shorter girl howled, her legs kicking ineffectively at the grumpy cadet's chest.

"You're too slow!" Reese grunted as he wrapped an arm around her legs. Elias steadied Reese when he staggered, and then he slapped Bex on the ass *hard.*

"Quit struggling, damn it!" the lanky cadet roared. Bex's curses put Langston's to shame, but she stopped trying to break free, and the trio quickly caught up.

Our dragons finally gained enough height to engage the enemy, and the orderly row of shadows deteriorated into the chaotic swirl of aerial combat. Roars and cries of pain drifted down from the night sky, and more than one firebomb tumbled from talons prematurely or without a proper release trajectory.

"*Watch out!*" Keaton yanked me backward so hard I slammed into Langston.

The bigger cadet's snarl of annoyance shifted to a snarl of rage as a poorly aimed bomb skipped off the high walls and detonated in front of us, splashing fire and ruin across the grassy lawn and cutting between us and the rest of our clutch. We were so close to the flames my skin prickled from the heat, and I didn't object when Langston pulled us back toward Elias, Reese, and Bex. Cries of shock and fear rose up from the rest of our clutchmates, and for an instant, I couldn't breathe. But then the breeze blew the smoke aside and we saw they were safe on the other side of the flames, if a little singed.

"Keep going!" Keaton bellowed to them. "Hawthorne has lead!"

The burly cadet glanced back, flames highlighting the determination etched into his face. He nodded sharply and got his half of the clutch moving.

"Langy, rearguard," Keaton snapped as he led us around the rapidly spreading fires.

Langston grimaced at the griffin name but obediently fell back behind the others, while I ran at Keaton's heels. Another bomb bounced across the quad, and we were forced further from our path. Smoke grew thick in the air, and my throat burned in irritation as we wove a jagged line between the flames.

A triumphant roar shook the skies, and a shattered scream followed on its heels. There was so much soul-rending anguish and pain and *loss* in that terrible cry that we all stumbled, the echo of grief reverberating down our own bonds. A red dragon spiraled out of the sky and crashed to the ground in front of the dragon gates, not a mark on him ... but his rider was missing his head, his gore-streaked body still strapped to the saddle.

Kill one, kill both, and riders were always the softer target.

"Fuck," I breathed out as my steps slowed, caught in the horror of it all. From a distance, I couldn't tell if it was a Savinian or Tennessan dragon, and in that moment, I couldn't say if it mattered. At a low *thrum* just at the edge of my hearing, my eyes widened. "Everyone down!"

We all hit the ground as silvery-gray wings flashed by directly over our heads, that low *thrum* the sound of wind over membranes stretched taut as the dragon hit the low point of his dive and pulled up, his wings precisely angled to gain height as rapidly as possible. The dragon's neck arched back and his back legs swung forward, releasing the firebomb clutched in his talons in a perfectly timed release. The *boom* rattled my bones as fresh flames raged across the academy—and then the gray's tail snapped out to balance his flight as he shot back into the sky, so close overhead we felt the wind of its passage.

Adrenaline flooded my system. If we'd been standing, we would've been hit. Keaton darted a glance at me, his amber eyes wide as he gave me a little nod. Then we were back on our feet and running hard. Another dragon dove low and arced up in a bombing dive, then another. The flames and the smoke thickened until we were all coughing and hacking, desperately trying to suck in enough oxygen to keep running.

"They're aiming for the barracks," someone cried out in horror.

But if they had meant to hit the dragon rider dorms or eyries, they missed, whether through luck or interference from our own dragons. Instead, the bombs hit the empty griffin barracks, most slamming into Alpha and Bravo. None came near the hatchery itself.

And then there were no more diving dragons, no more low *thrums* of wind over wings, no more explosions.

The sounds of aerial combat drifted further afield as our dragons drove the enemy away, and the grass fires were burning themselves out as they hit the paved paths cutting across the quad. We still had to skirt around the blackened patches, as the heat rising off them was considerable, but our path to the hatchery was finally clear.

Relief whispered through me until one last gray dragon vented a roar-scream, almost a warning cry, as she cut through the air in a fast dive. She smoothly released her bomb with perfect timing but horrible aim. Flames splashed uselessly over an already scorched section of the quad, and she swiftly rose back into the star-speckled night sky.

Shadowy shapes converged on her before she could complete her escape and tore into her in a frenzy. Moments later, a blood-streaked gray dragon crashed to the ground between us and safety with a sickening *crack* of breaking bones and an agonized cry, wings little more than shreds of membrane clinging to shattered spines.

We drew up short, barely fifty yards from the hatchery, as the dragon thrashed and moaned in agony. Grays weren't the largest of dragons, but she was more than large enough to pose a real threat to us.

My eyes quickly took in the details. Savinian harness, but no saddle. New injuries overlaid on top of still-healing wounds and old scars. She rolled slightly, just enough for the gaping wound in her gut to show the slippery shine of exposed intestines, and I fought back a surge of nausea even as pity and sadness rose up to take its place.

She was dying. Alone and afraid and abandoned by her wingmates.

"Where's her rider?" Bex mumbled as Reese finally let her slide off his shoulder and onto the ground. Her elfin features drew taut with horror and reluctant sympathy as she crept up to stand next to me. Savinian or not, none of us liked to see the bonded suffer.

At the sound of Bex's voice, the dragon's eyes flew open, and everything stopped—because her eyes were the color of a sunset before a storm, a swirling mix of purples and oranges and reds. They were unique, and I knew *exactly* who she was.

"Zathrid," I gasped, stumbling forward a step toward the dying dragon before Keaton yanked me to a halt. I glared up at him. "She's one of ours!"

"How do you *know* that?" he demanded with an air of frustrated bafflement.

"Captain Chance Mikkelsen, middle-aged male, blond, scar on left side of face. Bonded partner Zathrid, gray dragon female, average sized, missing a talon on right wing. Eyes the color of sunset." I recited it all from memory as if it were a damn classroom test before I glared up at my team leader. "They were on the last MIA dispatch I saw when I was still in the dragon rider classes. They went down over enemy lines a few months back."

Keaton stared for a heartbeat. His grip loosened as he turned back to the dragon.

"Look at her legs," Elias whispered, the color washed from his face. Raw, weeping sores banded her legs just above her clawed feet.

Horror sank icy claws into my soul. She'd been chained. I shook off Keaton's hand and stepped closer to the gray, who had gone very still, her eyes focused on mine with unmistakable desperation.

"Zathrid?" She dipped her head in a nod. I took another step. "Where is your rider?"

Zathrid moaned, the sound full of pain and heartbreak, but of course she couldn't answer me. Even as I cursed our inability to directly communicate, I snapped my gaze to the sky, searching for friendly wings and finding nothing but stars peeking through the smoke. All of our dragons were occupied driving off the invading force, and none of them were near enough to *hear* Zathrid. My eyes drifted past the suffering dragon to the hatchery behind her, but the current crop of dragon hatchlings were all too young to speak. Except for maybe—

"Jasper!" I spun back to Keaton. "We need Bethany."

"Why?" Langston muscled forward and shot a pointed glare around the academy, at the scorch marks and flames, the destruction and death wrought by the attack. Shouts and screams drifted through the haze, human and dragon and griffin voices melding into a symphony of pain and rage. "Why should we help her?"

"Because she has intel we need, and without her rider, another dragon is the only way to get it." I bit back the "moron" but I'm sure it came through loud and clear regardless. "Also, she's *Tennessan*."

"Then she's a traitor," Reese said as he tugged Bex behind him, his eyes hard.

"No, she did what our griffins would do for us if we were in enemy hands—anything," Keaton said grimly. "Tavros is right. She has intel we need. Elias, you're fastest, get Bethany and her hatchling."

Elias shifted on his feet, the air-raid siren still screaming its unrelenting warning, louder now that the sounds of battle were further away.

"The Mavens will never let her out with—"

"Tell them we have a dragon down and we need Jasper," I said quickly, feeling time slipping away with every gasping breath Zathrid took. "They won't stop her. Dragon Down protocols supersede everything else."

"Go," Keaton barked, and Elias took off at a dead sprint. I knelt next to Zathrid and slowly held out my hand.

"Can I...?" The dying dragon blinked at me before she shifted her head to lean against my side with a pained sigh. My eyes burned from more than the smoke as I stroked a comforting hand over the top of her wide skull and along the ridges over her eyes.

"You guys get to your griffins and hunker down," Keaton said firmly.

Langston jogged off without comment, his large form quickly disappearing in the thick haze. Bex let out a muffled protest, but Reese nudged her into a run, and the sound of their boots quickly faded under the wailing drone of the sirens.

"Tavros—"

"*No.*" I didn't even bother to look up at my team leader. I just kept stroking Zathrid's head, ignoring the blood trickling from the side of her mouth, soaking into my pants and the ground equally. "I'm not leaving her."

To my shock, he dropped down into the dirt and blood and sat next to me.

"Wasn't going to make you." His jaw tightened as he glanced at me sidelong before redirecting his amber gaze up to the sky. "I was just going to say, keep your eyes up. This isn't over until the all clear has sounded."

"...oh."

"Yeah, *oh.* Dragon Down protocols are clear. It's our *duty* to get whatever intel we can out of her before she dies." His words were stern, almost cold, but his voice had softened into something barely audible over the sirens and the dying dragon's labored breaths, and he stretched out a hand to stroke Zathrid's neck.

"I don't understand you at all," I admitted quietly, darting my gaze between the impassive expression on his face and the kindness in his eyes. He took his gaze off the sky long enough to frown at me.

"I'm beginning to think the same—"

THUD.

We both snapped our heads around. Keaton's hand dropped to the long knife strapped to his hip before he stilled...because what good was a knife against a *dragon.* Fear shot through me, leaving me frozen in panic. Atticus surged forward in response, his terror adding to my own until it felt like I'd drown under the icy waves.

"*Harpy!*"

"Not now," I said, my mental voice a shaking whisper and my eyes burning as they adjusted to the weight of his soul.

"Help Harpy," he shot back, determination pushing aside his fear. No. He *shielded* his fear from me and helped me control my own. The panic receded, freeing my limbs, though my hands still trembled in reaction.

"Get ready to run," Keaton breathed out, his amber eyes just as bright from the presence of his griffin, Tavi. Slowly, I braced my shaking hands on the ground and tensed my legs, as ready as I could get from a kneeling position. Keaton shifted his weight slightly so his shoulder pressed against mine in silent support, and together, we stared up at the copper dragon crouched on the roof of the hatchery. "On three. One."

The copper bared fangs easily the length of Keaton's knife, gleaming in the light of the spluttering fires, mantled his wings, and roared. His deep, wailing cry rattled the deadly spikes running down the length of his spine and lashing tail, sending a fresh wave of terror through my soul.

"Two."

The copper, enraged blue eyes focused on the dying gray, dropped his head low—revealing his rider, strapped securely to the saddle just in front of the wings. The Savinian dragon rider eyed us with cool detachment as he whipped up his short recurve bow, arrow already nocked.

"Son of a *bitch*," Keaton snarled.

Three things happened nearly simultaneously, so fast I had to replay what happened in my mind to sort out the blurred impressions.

Keaton threw himself over me, shielding me like the stupid team leader he was.

Zathrid jerked her head up, her eyes unnaturally bright with the presence of her rider's soul, and swept what was left of her wings in front of us, shielding us both with a defiant roar.

And Tiberius swooped out of the darkness like a silent red wraith and slammed into the copper talons-first, saving us all.

The much larger red carried both dragon and rider off the hatchery roof, crushed them into the unforgiving ground, and proceeded to mercilessly rip them apart.

"Tavros."

I couldn't look away.

"*Tavros.*"

The copper and his rider died together. Horribly. Painfully. *Messily.*

"Look at me, damn it," Keaton snarled and forcibly wrenched my head away. "Harpy, look at me!"

Wide-eyed and shaking, it took me a long moment to focus on him, and an even longer one to realize he was just as wide-eyed, just as shaky. I flinched when Tiberius let out a bloodthirsty roar of triumph, and cursed at the unmistakable sound of massive wings launching the red dragon back into the air, but I didn't try to look again.

"Should've asked Commandant Iverson for help," I mumbled.

"I don't think he would've heard us over . . . that," Keaton replied, swallowing hard.

We both froze as a deep sigh whispered behind us, the sound laden with so much relief it was painful to hear. With a rustle of torn membrane, the gray dragon's wings went limp with an awful sort of finality. I didn't want to look, but when Keaton turned his head, I slowly followed suit.

Zathrid's glorious sunset eyes had slipped closed.

She was gone.

A wordless growl made up of equal parts rage, denial, and sorrow escaped Keaton as he dropped to one knee to rest a hand on her head. Hot tears born from anger as much as grief spilled over onto my cheeks. Somewhere in Savinia, a Tennessan rider had drawn his last breath—but for a brief moment, Captain Chance Mikkelsen had been here, with his bonded, with us. He'd helped Zathrid save us.

My hands clenched into fists as recrimination and anger won out over the grief. Dragon and rider had given everything they had left, for *us*, and now they were lost.

And whatever intel they'd possessed was lost with them.

CHAPTER 6

Keaton and I both knew damn well we should've retreated to the hatchery after Zathrid died, but the air-raid sirens abruptly stopped, the quiet so loud my ears rang with it. Seconds later, the hatchery door slammed against the wall and rebounded as Bethany charged outside with Jasper.

"Harper!"

"Harpy!"

My head snapped around. For an instant, my vision doubled as a blur of fur and feathers followed Bethany out, but then Atticus retreated from my mind as he ran for me.

"Over here," I called out to them as I blinked my eyes clear.

Keaton stood abruptly as my griffin raced around Zathrid's hindquarters. No, not Atticus. *Tavi.* Until that moment, I hadn't realized how similar our griffins were in appearance. Atticus was there in the next instant, and I braced myself to catch him as he flung himself at my chest. I wrapped him up in my arms and buried my face in his neck, downy feathers tickling my nose and absorbing my tears.

Footsteps slowed to a stop in front of me, and I reluctantly raised my soot and tear-stained face, though I didn't release my griffin. Not even when my arms began to burn from the strain.

"We're too late," Bethany whispered as Jasper leaned against her leg with a mournful grumble. "I'm so sorry."

I wasn't sure if she was talking to me or Zathrid. What I was sure of was my relief that she hadn't been here *sooner.*

"Trust me," I said in a hoarse rasp. "I'm not."

Despite my best intentions, my gaze drifted to the left of the hatchery, where pieces of the copper dragon and his rider were scattered across the quad. If Bethany and Jasper had been any quicker, they would've emerged right under the vicious gaze of the copper, who wouldn't have hesitated to take out a baby red. A shudder ran through my body, and Atticus let out a deep, rumbling purr I felt all the way down in my bones.

"I'm not sorry, either, to be clear," Keaton said in grim understanding. "But I wish we could've gotten some intel from her."

Bethany nodded agreement as I sat in the dirt next to Zathrid's head again with Atticus in my lap. It was either that or drop him, and that would never happen. Together, we kept silent watch over the gray dragon's body until Captain Amines, one of the instructors, landed in the quad on her green. She took our report and firmly sent us to the hatchery to care for our tired griffins.

It was a long night, with little sleep as reports and rumors trickled in from other cadets.

We'd gotten lucky. Lucky we'd had at least a little warning. Lucky the academy hadn't suffered damage that couldn't be repaired. Lucky more hadn't died in the attack. Even one death was too many, and there were more far more than one when the final tally was posted.

Five seniors and their bonded were on that death roll. Cadets who would never graduate, cadets who saw combat before the rest of us. The war had never felt so real, or so close. It was no longer an abstract thing, and I couldn't help but recall that asshole Captain Westbrook's words. *You* will *lose friends . . .*

I'd come so close to losing Bethany that night. Because I was a moron.

The next day, Keaton and I were summoned to Commandant Pulaski's office. We exchanged a silent grimace. Neither of us thought we were about to get praised. Reluctantly, we left our griffins and clutchmates behind in the warmth and safety of the crèche and headed out into the chill early spring morning.

The sun was shining, birds were singing. After the horror of last night, it seemed . . . wrong. Like the day should be gray and dismal, not beautiful. Unease and fear hung over the academy in a nearly perceptible cloud, as thick as the residual smoke in the air. While this wasn't the first time the academy had been attacked, the Savinians shouldn't have been able to penetrate this deeply into our country in those numbers. Something had shifted in the war, but if our instructors knew anything, they weren't sharing.

My eyes strayed to the blackened and bloodstained ground where Zathrid had died. It turned out she *had* tried to get Tiberius' attention after he killed the copper, but her mind had been too fragmented by agony. The great red had only received a confusing impression of starvation, and pain, and unforgiving gray walls that could be anywhere in Savinia.

Regret and recrimination swirled in a toxic mess in my belly as we marched across the blackened quad. If we hadn't stayed with her, if Captain Mikkelsen and Zathrid hadn't had to give everything they had left to protect us, her mind might have been clearer. She might have been able to tell Tiberius *exactly* where more Tennessan POWs were being held.

As we passed onto the griffin campus and turned toward the admin building, Keaton spoke out of the corner of his mouth.

"I'll take full responsibility for our actions last night. Just keep your mouth shut, Tavros."

"Not happening," I replied calmly.

"Quit being so damn stubborn," he growled quietly as he held the admin building door open for me. "I'm the team leader. It was my call, *my* responsibility."

"You can shove your responsibility up your ass sideways." I gave him a pleasant smile and stalked down the hall toward the commandant's office.

Keaton quick marched after me, darting ahead to knock on the door. At a sharp "Enter," he hauled it open. This time he didn't hold it for me. Instead, he strode inside and tried to take up as much space in front of Pulaski's desk as possible. Still trying to shield me, still trying to be the responsible team leader. He was turning out to be an annoyingly decent person beneath the gruff exterior.

That didn't mean I was going to let him take the blame. Despite his not-so-subtle maneuvering, I managed to stand shoulder to shoulder with him in front of our commandant. It had been my idea to get Bethany and Jasper, my idea that had almost gotten them killed. If Jasper hadn't been soundly sleeping and *highly* reluctant to wake up, they probably would've been.

Commandant Pulaski let us stew at attention for several long, highly uncomfortable minutes while she ostensibly worked on paperwork. A smudge of soot high on one cheekbone, fresh tears in her riding leathers, and bloodshot eyes suggested she'd gone straight from battle to admin duties. The sharpness of her voice when she finally deigned to acknowledge our presence suggested she had little time or patience for our bullshit.

"Cadets Keaton and Tavros. Just the idiots I wanted to start my day with . . ."

Things went downhill from there.

Officially, we received a letter of commendation for our actions during the raid. Unofficially, we got a thorough ass-chewing for risking both ourselves, our griffins, and a dragon rider cadet and her hatchling. As a bonus, that ass-chewing came with a week-long punishment detail clearing rubble so the incoming Engineers Corps team could rebuild.

Throughout that endless, backbreaking, exhausting week, I caught Keaton periodically watching me. No, not watching me. *Studying me*, as if I were a puzzle he wanted to solve.

When the academy recovered enough for training to resume, Keaton continued to watch me. He watched me get my ass handed to me in hand-to-hand. He watched me not-limp to the obstacle course. He watched me ride, he watched as I cared for Atticus. He watched me struggle and fall and fail and get back up again and again.

Even when the scorched and bloodstained patch of earth haunted me every time we went to the hatchery. Even when the guilt of my mistake threatened to pull me under. Even when the weight of his stare seemed to follow me everywhere.

I got back up again.

Because I'd be damned if I did less than my best. Not when it would impact my future—and my griffin's.

The day before our rest day was particularly brutal. Freezing rain sheeted from the gray skies in an unrelenting downpour all morning. While it had tapered off by early afternoon, a persistent drizzle soaked us all to the skin before we'd even jogged halfway to the dreaded obstacle course. The entire course was a muddy mess, so of course Instructor Bayard directed us to run the lowland section.

Ditches had been dug through the open valley nestled between the hills, where thick mud remained throughout the heart of even the driest season. After all the rain, the ditches were more freezing slurry than mud. Crisscrossed with logs and netting to force us to keep as low as possible, there were points where we were practically swimming. Others where the only way to get through was to hold our breaths and fully submerge.

The bigger guys like Langston and Hawthorne had the most trouble with those chokepoints, but we all eventually made it through. By that point, Echo Clutch looked identical—every last one of us coated in mud from head to toe and miserable. Instructor Bayard eyed us as we huddled together in a shaking mess and mercilessly directed us to the next section of the course. When there were muttered complaints, he shot us an impatient look.

"You won't always get the chance to dry off and warm up in the field," he said with a snap to his voice. "Best you learn now that sometimes you have to push through the discomfort and pain, because it's better than dying. Now get to it! Last cadet through has to do another ditch run."

Atticus brushed against my mind, at once both entirely sympathetic and laughing his feathered head off.

"Harpy look ridiculous!"

I scowled and would've grumped back at him, but then our bond flared with heat . . . and tendrils of warmth bloomed within my cold muscles. Shock held me immobile as he withdrew with a smug laugh. Once again, Atticus had done something instinctively that I didn't know how to do yet. He'd sent me a quick surge of his own energy—just like Captain Mikkelsen had done for Zathrid before they died.

"Cadet Tavros, *move your ass!*"

At Bayard's bellow in my ear, I leaped straight up like a startled rabbit and slipped in the muck. The ex-ranger gave me an unimpressed look as I scrambled to catch up to my clutchmates, who were already making their way through the first of a series of wooden obstacles.

Bolstered by my griffin, I easily caught up to the stragglers and passed them, leapfrogging from post to post across a manmade pond. At the opposite bank, a series of ropes were strung low over the ground, because we hadn't low crawled enough today. By the time I made it through, my elbows ached, and my second wind was long gone. I was squarely in the middle of the pack for once though, so I forced my lungs to keep dragging in air and my trembling legs to keep moving.

Langston, Hawthorne, and Elias—who while not as bulky as the other two was just as tall—took a decisive lead at the log hurdles. It would've been an easy matter to duck under them, but we had to go over, and I knocked the wind out of myself on the last when I misjudged my leap and slammed belly-first into the log.

Wheezing, I slid down the far side and staggered to the next obstacle as a chill wind whistled between the hills. On the plus side, the wind also shepherded the clouds away, and the first sunlight we'd seen in two days broke through the jagged overcast skies. It didn't provide any real warmth, but it was better than all the gray, and I swarmed up the ladder to the zigzagged set of monkey bars with slightly more enthusiasm.

The wooden bars, worn smooth from countess cadets, were wide enough for two abreast, and I managed to catch up to Hawthorne as he swung his way along with dogged perseverance. Midway through, the soft calluses on my palms began to rub raw. Near the end, they tore open, and my hands became so slippery with blood and sweat that my grip slipped off the last bar. I landed awkwardly on one knee and sucked in a sharp breath at the burning agony in my hands. For a second, I knelt in the mud, just breathing through the pain.

Hawthorne passed me again, then Matthews landed next to me and took off with a huffed laugh. "Pathetic."

Growling, I shoved myself to my feet and took off after her. An inclined wall rose up in front of us with three evenly spaced ropes to help us climb to the top. Hawthorne took a running jump and hit the wall hard, but he managed to snag the rope three quarters of the way up and quickly hauled himself over and disappeared down the far side. Matthews slid to a stop at the bottom, grabbed the rope, leaned back, and walked her way up. A glance back showed the last three cadets quickly catching up, so I didn't stop at the bottom—I ran halfway up the wall before my momentum died and I was forced to snatch the rope. Gritting my teeth against the pain as my palms tore further, I slowly hauled myself up, using my legs more than my arms. Matthews still beat me to the top, but I wasn't far behind her.

Panting, I slung one leg over the apex of the wall and glanced down.

The far side was a sheer drop into a mud pit, because *of course* it was. As I slung my other leg over and prepared to jump, a playful roar ricocheted through the valley. My head snapped up. Silvery-gray wings filled my vision as a dragon flashed by low overhead, so close it felt as if I could stretch my arm out and tweak his trailing tail. I caught a glimpse of a double saddle and two riders. Instructor and cadet returning from a training flight and blowing off steam by buzzing the griffin cadets struggling through the muck. Just like I'd done not too long ago.

Unable to stop myself, my head tilted back as I watched their flight—and lost my balance.

I didn't even have time to scream before I hit the ground, or rather the muddy pit and *then* the solid ground beneath all the mud and water. My right side took the worst of it, but there was enough water to cushion the impact, and nothing broke. It still hurt like a bitch.

"Harpy!"

Atticus surged back into my head in alarm as I rolled up onto my hands and knees. Dirty water streamed off my body in a freezing deluge, and I coughed miserably as my lungs struggled to remember how to breathe. Unable to manage a coherent thought, I sent my griffin a burst of wordless reassurance, but my eyes burned from more than the muddy water as he looked through them.

Before I could adjust to the weight of his soul, the last three cadets crested the wall and dropped down into the pit on either side, sending more water and mud cascading over me.

"You should've kept your eyes off the sky and on the dirt with the rest of us, dragon girl," Sansing called out as he splashed his way out of the pit with Rodriguez and Foster. Grimacing, I watched through watering eyes as they casually jogged toward the last obstacle. None of them were worried about coming in last. Not anymore.

A hand appeared in my face. I glanced up, expecting to see Instructor Bayard's disapproving face—and found Keaton frowning down at me instead.

"You okay, Tavros? That was one hell of a fall."

It took me an embarrassingly long moment to realize he was frowning at me in *concern*. Slowly, as if a part of me expected it to be a trick, I reached up and clasped his hand. He pulled me to my feet, and I winced as my abused side protested.

"I'm fine," I muttered as I tugged my hand from his. I twisted side to side to test my ribs and somewhat awkwardly added, "Thanks."

Keaton tilted his head as he studied my brighter than usual eyes. "You can let go, Atticus. I've got her."

"Stupid team leader can't tell me what to do! I do what I want!"

A huffed laugh escaped my control at my griffin's outrage, and I quickly schooled my expression before Keaton could think I was laughing at him. "Um, he says thanks."

A slight smile tugged at Keaton's lips. "No, he didn't."

As we splashed out of the pit, I gave Atticus a gentle but firm shove and told him to go play. He muttered and grumbled, but by the time Keaton and I stood on solid ground, my eyes were my own again. When I would've run—or limped—to the next obstacle, Keaton grabbed my arm.

"You know what your problem is?" he asked quietly.

I bristled and ripped my arm out of his grasp. "Got a feeling you're going to tell me."

"Tavros . . . no, *Harpy*, wait."

The sound of my griffin name in that gruff tone pinned me in place far more effectively than his hand. He waited until I met his gaze, and his intense amber eyes stripped away all my armor and left me vulnerable. I hated it.

"Fine, what's my problem?" I snarled.

"You're too used to being the best," he said quietly.

Torn between outrage and chagrin, I just stared at him. My fists clenched, and my jaw tightened, but I could think of nothing to say in response. Nothing. Ironically, Instructor Bayard broke our standoff and saved me from myself.

"*Keaton! Tavros!* This isn't a gods damned staring contest. Get through that last obstacle, double time!"

Heat swept across my face, almost a welcome relief from the cold, and I turned away from Keaton and broke into a shuffling run. Everything hurt, and my ribs and right hip twinged with every step. I could've walked faster, but I didn't think pissing Bayard off further was the best plan, so double time it was.

After his unexpected and entirely unwelcome observation, I fully expected Keaton to run ahead. He didn't. He stayed by my side as we made our way through the last obstacle, and he crossed the finish line in lockstep with me ... even though he could've easily left me behind.

Bayard knew it, too. Approval flickered across his face as he glanced at Keaton before he ordered us both into the ditches.

"Since you finished together, you can run together." He raised his voice to a battlefield roar as he addressed our clutchmates. "As for the rest of you, stretch it out and do a cool-down lap around the field while you wait!"

If crawling through the ditches the first time around sucked, the second time was *so* much worse. Again, Keaton could've finished much faster. He was bigger and undeniably in better shape for this kind of torture.

"Why?" I gasped out as icy mud crawled up my neck and into my ears.

Keaton didn't bother pretending not to understand. He just looked at me, his stare less soul piercing but no less intense—even with the mud sliding down his face.

"Because none of us should suffer alone." His lips twitched, though whether in a smile or frown was impossible to tell. "And like it or not, you *are* one of us."

CHAPTER 7

Rest days at the Tennessan Bonded Training Academy were a bit of a misnomer. While there weren't any classes or training events, we still had light activities and griffin care. As our team leader, Keaton also had some input into how we spent those days, and he'd decided a group breakfast was a good way to start. After we'd seen to our griffins' breakfast, of course.

While in theory we were allowed to sleep in on rest days, hungry griffins approaching their next growth spurt had no concept of mercy for their bondmates, and we were rousted from our beds before dawn by a chorus of cranky squawks, trills, and roars. By the time they were all satisfied and sleeping off full bellies in the crèche, the sun was well over the horizon.

"Gods, I would kill for coffee," Reese muttered as we stumbled out of the hatchery in a sleepy, hungry mob. Elias, never far from his side, groaned.

"We already missed the first round at the chow hall," he said, shoulders slumping in dejection. "I bet the coffee's already gone."

"No bet," Hawthorne mumbled from behind me.

I tilted my face up to the sky as we ambled across the quad in a loose formation that would've earned us a reprimand on any day but a rest day. Between one step and the next, my eyes drifted shut and a smile kissed my lips. The sun felt good on my skin, its warmth a nice contrast from the chill morning air. At a distant roar, my eyes snapped open as a frisson of tension tightened my shoulders. That hadn't been a playful roar.

97

Only two weeks had passed since the raid. I wasn't the only one on edge, and I definitely wasn't the only person to stop in their tracks and search the skies in earnest for any incoming threats. But the sirens didn't scream their dire warnings, and the dragons sunbathing in front of their eyries didn't stir.

A few seconds later, a pair of green dragons flew over the hills, a gray dragon hanging between them from a carry net. Even with the netting distorting the dragon's body, it was obvious there was something very wrong with him. As they glided toward the landing field behind the walls of the dragon rider campus, they flashed by overhead and I got a clear view. My gut tightened when I realized who he was.

"What's that all about?"

"Which dragon was that?"

"That was Pharaoh back from the medics," I said over the murmurs of my clutchmates. All eyes swung my way, and I lifted my chin to hide my nervousness. "One of our wounded from the raid."

"He looked . . . small for a gray," Hawthorne said as his gaze followed the dragons, a faint furrow marring his brow.

"No, just young," I replied quietly. "His rider, Kyle Dockery, is a senior cadet. They're going to keep them here as ground instructors after he graduates this spring." My belly twisted uncomfortably in sympathy for poor Pharaoh. "For obvious reasons."

"Found that out from your little dragon rider friend, huh?" Langston called over his shoulder.

"Little?" Elias laughed mockingly. "My girl put you on your *ass*, Langy."

"Yeah, she did, because she's a badass," I agreed. My gaze went back to the young dragon cradled in the net, and my smirk faded at the glimpse of bandages where a wing used to be. "They got lucky."

Elias' brows shot up. "You call *that* lucky?"

"Yes. When Pharaoh fell, Dockery was ripped from the saddle. If it weren't for his wingmate—"

"Who gives a shit?" Langston muttered loudly.

"I do," Bex snapped as she shoved her way past him. Her topaz eyes seared into mine. "What happened?"

For a moment, I was taken aback by her intensity. Then I remembered—she was mountain griffin bound. With their stocky build and vicious claws, the mountain griffins were the shields and escorts to dragons. The Talons of the Dragon Corps.

And their riders often flew with one of the dragons they were assigned to guard.

Jealousy twisted through my gut. At least *she* would get to fly. Immediately, I stuffed both the errant thought and the emotion behind a mental wall. Atticus might be sleeping off breakfast, but I still didn't want to take the chance he'd pick up anything. My griffin deserved better than that.

"Well?" Bex's hands flexed and she took a step closer in her eagerness when I took too long to answer. I shook off my distracted thoughts as the dragons descended out of sight behind the dragon campus walls.

"Pharaoh's wingmate caught Dockery, but it was a close thing." I swallowed hard, only vaguely aware of the shorter girl as a memory gripped me in its claws. "I was on a training flight where the dragons practiced catching sandbags. The higher the altitude, the easier it was to make the catch."

A shudder ran down my spine. The number of burst sandbags littering the ground had haunted me for weeks. I shook off the memory and refocused on the shorter girl in front of me.

"But a lot of aerial combat happens at lower altitude," I added with a forced shrug. "Dockery used up every last bit of his luck that night."

Bex turned white as a sheet and hurried off. I stared in confusion.

"Nice work, Tavros," Reese growled before he chased after her.

My shoulders slumped as I remembered how her hands had twisted her shirt. That hadn't been eagerness. That had been *fear*. And I'd made it worse.

The rest of my clutchmates shook their heads at me with varying degrees of disgust and walked on to the chow hall, but it was Keaton's look of disappointment that really gutted me. Without waiting for him to speak, I spun on my heel and walked away. I wasn't hungry anymore.

A few hours later, the door to the barracks slammed open and heavy bootsteps rang out in a determined rhythm. Just as determined to be left alone, I stayed curled up in Atticus' empty nest and kept my nose in my book. The fact that I'd read the same page roughly twenty times and retained none of it was irrelevant.

The boots stopped in front of my bunk. *Damn it.*

Reluctantly, I glanced up at Keaton's expressionless face. His head tilted in the way of griffin riders, his amber gaze sharp on mine.

"Bex could use some help with her riding," he said gruffly. "You willing?"

I stared. How had I ever given him the impression I wouldn't help if asked?

"Five minutes." I snatched up my riding leathers and boots and hurried off to the girl's bathroom to change. As I tugged on the comfortable breeches, I reached out to Atticus. *"Hey, you feathered miscreant. Want to go see the horses today?"*

An annoyed grumble and a sleepy yawn whispered down the bond. A glimpse of tawny front legs stretching out across the sand flashed across my mental vision, all wide paws and flexing claws. Soft darkness and the rasp of warm sand on fur and feather replaced the sight as he curled up and threw a paw over his eyes.

"Felix sleepy now. Harpy have fun . . ."

Rolling my eyes at his insistence on that ridiculous name, I left him to his nap and finished getting changed. All of the griffins in Echo Clutch were bouncing between insatiable, cranky, and exhausted, but the Mavens said it was normal at this point in their development. As I braided my hair back, my fingers paused at a sudden realization. Whenever his impending growth spurt truly kicked in, I wouldn't be able to carry him anymore. No more strained arms, no more excited shouts of *"Harpy catch!"*

Pushing aside the sharp pang of sadness that lanced straight into my heart, I hurried back out and nodded at Keaton.

"Let's go."

We walked out of the barracks in tense silence. I wanted to grill Keaton for more information, but his expression was more closed off than usual. If it weren't for the smile lines around his mouth—and the fact that I'd heard him laugh at least once before—I'd think the other cadet never smiled at all.

Positioned halfway up the slope, our barracks gave us an excellent view of the academy grounds. The rhythmic *thud* of hammers and *whirr* of wood saws echoed across the valley as one Engineer Corps team worked to rebuild Bravo barracks from the ground up, while the rest worked to repair . . . everything else.

Slowly, the signs of the raid were being erased. Yesterday's icy rain had even washed the lingering smoke out of the air, though scorch marks remained here and there, and the grass in the quad would take time to regrow. My smooth stride faltered for a beat as my gaze drifted with unerring precision to one particular blackened patch of ground. The bloodstains had been washed away, but it didn't matter.

I'd always know exactly where Zathrid had breathed her last.

With a harsh breath, I caught back up to Keaton and reminded myself it could've been so much worse. As Commandant Pulaski had made *abundantly* clear, Keaton and I could've breathed our last too, along with our griffins.

As we tromped down the sloped path to the quad, we were forced to step aside as a gaggle of unbonded griffin cadets moved in the opposite direction. I nearly jumped out of my skin when Keaton *grinned* and called out to one of the unbonded cadets.

"Marcos!"

I felt the blood drain out of my face. Marcos? *That* Marcos?

"Hey, asshole!" a deep voice shouted back happily.

The cadet who maneuvered through the crowd could've been Keaton's brother. Same dark brown hair cut short to military regulations, same general build, same natural air of command. The biggest difference was in their eyes. Where Keaton's were a brilliant amber, Marcos' were an unremarkable shade of brown. Dark shadows kissed the skin below them, as if he hadn't been sleeping well.

Tension drew my shoulders tight. I knew those eyes, knew that handsome face, especially when his broad grin fell away as if it had never been. I'd passed him in the classroom halls, felt his gaze on me in the quad. I'd had no idea he was the griffin cadet I'd displaced, the team leader Keaton had supplanted . . . the intended bondmate to Atticus.

It explained the hatred in his eyes when his dark gaze landed on mine.

A shiver that had nothing to do with the weather raised goosebumps on my arms, but I lifted my chin and refused to show my unease. I wasn't quite able to force a smile, but I managed to give him a little nod.

"Hey." When Marcos just glared at me in undisguised hostility, I drew in a deep breath and stepped forward. "I'm guessing you already know who I am."

His gaze flicked down to my outstretched hand as if he were contemplating cutting it off, and I let it drop. Heat flooded my face, but I kept my chin high and my shoulders back. I should've sought him out weeks ago and apologized properly, even if it wasn't my fault.

"I just wanted to say I'm so sorry for—"

"For what?" His voice turned gravelly as he stepped into my personal space. "For stealing my griffin? For setting my career back by a year? For playing the victim these last few weeks?" He leaned down until his hot breath washed over my face. Traces of alcohol lingered, and I fought to keep my expression impassive. "All three? I've been watching you, Harper Tavros. You can keep your bullshit apologies. They're worthless. Just like you."

Despite my resolve to stand firm, I retreated a step, and it *was* a retreat. Satisfaction flared in his bloodshot eyes.

"Enough, Marcos." Keaton stepped between us with a deep frown. "None of what happened is on her."

Marcos tilted his head, but there was nothing of the griffin in the gesture. It was predatory in a way the griffins simply weren't, and his expression held no hint of mercy as he stared at me over Keaton's shoulder.

"Isn't it?"

"It *wasn't*..."

Trapped under Marcos' hateful glare, I couldn't get the rest of the words out. For the first time, I considered the uncomfortable idea that maybe I wasn't blameless. Even if I hadn't been the one to switch the eggs, hadn't I played dozens of pranks of my own on Dimitri, Zayne, and Callum? Our prank war had been epic, and I'd been a willing instigator. Guilt twisted through my belly in a sickening swoop.

"I'm sorry," I said in a hoarse whisper, but I forced myself to hold his gaze.

"I don't care." He forced a smile on his face that was somehow so much worse. "But you will. *Harpy*."

My griffin name on his tongue sounded *wrong*, every discordant note dripping with hate and malice, rotten at the core. Fear shivered down my spine, and I felt Atticus stir from his deep sleep. Lately, it had been almost impossible to wake him from his growth-induced naps, but my distress had roused him, and I shielded *hard*.

It wasn't enough to stop him from surging forward, because he was both fiercely protective and endlessly curious, even when more than half asleep. As my eyes burned and brightened, Keaton shifted further between us, his wide shoulders all but blocking the other cadet from my view. I could still see his eyes though, could still *feel* them.

"Marcos—"

"Save it, asshole." This time, there was nothing playful in the insult. His gaze bored into mine over Keaton's shoulder, that unhinged smile still on his face. "I'll see you soon."

It didn't sound like a threat. It sounded like a promise.

Marcos gave me a jaunty wave before he turned around and walked up the slope to his barracks in an unhurried stroll, whistling cheerfully. I stared after him with wide eyes until he was out of sight.

"Go to sleep, Atticus," I crooned gently, silently praying he would and *fast*, because I wasn't sure how much longer I could shield from him.

"Felix," he corrected muzzily. With one last sleepy mumble, Atticus drifted back into dreamless slumber.

Only then did I let my spine sag and my shoulders curl inward. Only then did I let out a shuddering sigh of relief. Only then did I allow myself to look at Keaton. He winced at whatever he saw on my face and awkwardly patted my shoulder.

"Sorry about Marcos. He's not normally a . . ."

"A raging psychopath?" I suggested shakily.

He got us moving toward the stables again by the simple expedient of walking off, leaving me the choice to stand awkwardly to the side of the path or follow. I followed.

"He's had a tough few weeks," he finally said.

"I can relate," I murmured, then immediately wished I could snatch the words back for fear that I sounded like I was whining or "playing the victim." But Keaton patted my shoulder again, just as awkwardly as the first time, and led us across the quad and out the main gate.

The walk to the stables was a silent one after that, but my clutchmates more than made up for it when we arrived. Reese and Elias were leaning on the split-rail wooden fence surrounding one of the smaller round pens watching Bex trot in a lopsided circle. The normally impassive girl wore the most miserable expression I'd ever seen, and the large pony she rode didn't look much happier.

Elias glanced over his shoulder as we walked up and immediately spun around to confront our team leader. His typical smirk was absent as he scowled at Keaton and crossed his arms.

"What's *she* doing here?" he demanded.

Keaton didn't give the lanky cadet the confrontation he was evidently looking for. He just walked up to the fence between Elias and Reese and rested his forearms on the top rail, his serene amber gaze focused on Bex. When Keaton didn't respond immediately, Elias heaved a sigh, his purple eyes flicking toward me as I stood awkwardly off to the side.

"Keaton, come on, man. Seriously?"

"Name a better rider"—Keaton arched a brow as Elias opened his mouth—"who isn't an instructor."

Elias snapped his mouth shut again. Reese didn't take his focus off Bex, calling out encouragement and jumbled advice that seemed to be making her more frustrated than anything else. Cautiously, I stepped up to the fence next to the dark-haired cadet.

"That's not helping," I said quietly.

"You think you can do better?" Reese growled back without taking his eyes off the struggling girl. Keaton turned to look at him and nodded.

"She can help," he said with a firm conviction in his voice I wasn't sure was deserved.

Reese's hands tightened on the top rail, his tone belligerent and sharp with doubt, "Can you?"

I glanced into the ring as Bex bounced past and winced. "I mean, I can't possibly make things worse."

Reese finally tore his gaze off her and pinned me in place with a turbulent glare. "You did this morning."

I hadn't meant to. At least, I didn't *think* so. I'd gotten lost in my memory and hadn't paid attention to the other girl's body language, but . . . it was possible I'd allowed jealousy to influence my words. Even as shame swirled low in my belly, I straightened my spine and owned it.

"You're right. I fucked up." I held his gaze for an endless moment and didn't try to hide my genuine determination to help, to get something *right*. "Let me try to fix it."

Reese's jaw clenched so tight muscles popped out in sharp relief, and I was certain he was going to tell me to go to hell. But he didn't.

He stepped aside so I could get to the gate, and even held it open for me.

Drawing in a bracing breath, I strode through the deep sands of the round pen to the center. Bex shot me a distracted look before she refocused on her riding with a hopeless sort of determination. As she rode around the pen, I turned a slow circle and watched her bounce in the saddle.

"Is she going to do anything today, or what?" Elias said loudly. Reese growled something too low for me to catch the words, but his annoyance came through loud and clear. Keaton was silent, but I could feel him watching me.

I did my best to ignore them all.

While the air was still cool, the sun beat down on the top of my head, and a lone bead of sweat rolled down my spine—though whether from the riding leathers or the pressure was impossible for me to guess. Being a good rider didn't necessarily translate to being a good *trainer*, and Reese had already proved that shouting out things like "keep your heels down" and "get your head up" weren't going to solve Bex's problem. Out of better ideas, I shifted my gaze to her mount—and paused. *Huh.*

"Hey, Bex, bring him back to a walk for me?"

The other girl didn't even question me, she just gritted her teeth, sat back in the saddle, and tugged on the reins. Her hands were soft on the bit at least. Her little gelding immediately dropped into a walk, and I fell in beside her as she walked him along the rail.

"The boys must really be desperate if they brought *you* in for help." Bex flushed a bright red and cast me a sidelong glance. "Sorry, that came out wrong."

"It's fine." I shrugged it off and eyed her chestnut pony. With the white blaze down his face and the perfect white stocking on his back left leg, he was fairly distinctive. "You rode him the last couple of lessons, right?"

"Yeah, Buster's my regular mount since I'm so short."

The longer we walked, the more she relaxed into his stride, but her spine was still too stiff, and her hands were white-knuckled on the reins. Even though she wasn't pulling on the leather, Buster would still feel the tension, but the patient little gelding just paced forward placidly. I could see why he was a lesson pony.

"Did George pick him out for you?"

She frowned. "Who?"

I sighed in exasperation. "George, old stable hand with a limp, knows more about horses than all of the instructors combined. Ringing any bells?"

"Oh, him." Bex smiled almost wistfully. "He reminds me of my grandpa. But no, it was Instructor Clements my first year, I think."

Clements had less than zero patience for new riders. There was a reason the academy had shifted him from teaching first years to second. "Okay, have you ever ridden a different horse?"

"No."

I stopped in my tracks and stared.

"What?" She glanced back as she pulled the gelding to a halt. "Ride one horse, you've ridden them all."

Wild laughter exploded from deep in my belly, and I doubled over, clutching at my ribs. Every time I looked up at Bex's confused expression, I giggled harder until I was laughing like a lunatic.

"I'm sorry," I gasped out. "It's just that's like asking what's the difference between your running style and Elias'. Boy's got legs for days, you think he runs the same way you do?"

"Thanks for noticing," Elias called out, stretching out one long leg into a ridiculous pose. He let out a startled squawk when Reese shoved him over. Bex blinked and looked down at her short legs, and then over to where Elias was picking himself off the ground.

"I guess not?" she said doubtfully.

"Definitely not," I said, finally getting my laughter under control as I walked up to stand beside the pony's neck. "Look, each horse has their own rhythm. You just need to relax and catch it. It's no different than riding different dragons."

She paled, and I gentled my voice as much as I was capable of in that moment.

"When do you start training flights?"

"Next week," she said steadily enough—but her hands clenched into fists, and dread darkened her topaz eyes. As she stared straight ahead, her voice shifted to a chilling monotone, washed of all emotion. "I'm going to die. I'm going to fall, and splat on the ground and die, and I'll take Merlin with me."

"No, you're not. I'm going to help you, and you're going to be *fine*."

At my snarl, Bex snapped her gaze to mine, desperation and hope all tangled up in her expression. The words had burst out of me without any conscious decision on my part. Now I had to live up to them, and I still wasn't sure *how* to help her.

Panic crawled up my throat. It wasn't just Bex looking at me with desperation and hope. It was all of them, and the weight of their stares threatened to crush me where I stood. And then the pony idly shifted his weight, and an idea struck.

"Dismount. I want to try something."

Bex leaped out of the saddle like it was on fire. The *thud* of her boots hitting the sand almost hid her sigh of relief. I half expected her to run away, but she held the reins while I quickly adjusted the stirrups for my longer legs.

"Stand in the center and watch," I directed as I clicked my tongue and urged the little gelding into a walk.

"How is showing off going to help Bex?" Reese demanded, but Keaton held up his hand in a silent request for him to wait.

Again, I did my best to ignore the boys as I rode past the gate. When we'd ridden a single lap around the pen, I touched my heels to his sides and clicked my tongue again—and almost immediately regretted every life choice that had led me to this moment.

Bex's pony had the *worst* trot I'd ever attempted to sit. Bone-jarring was the nicest description I could think of, and I had to grit my teeth to keep them from clacking together. As he did his best to jam my spine through my skull, I tried my damnedest to find his rhythm. It was in there somewhere, buried deep beneath his jarring strides. Really deep.

I endured a full two laps before I gave up and guided him to the center.

"What's his name again?" I could hear peals of laughter from Elias, quite possibly because my words came out in staccato bursts punctuated by escaped huffs of air. Bex planted her hands on her hips and smirked. She was enjoying this a little too much, but it was better than the despair that had marked her face a few short minutes ago.

"Buster," she called out as I slowed him to a walk and patted his neck in thanks for an . . . interesting ride.

"I bet you his full name's Ball Buster."

Bex snorted a surprised laugh. "Why?"

"Because if either of us had balls, they'd be busted by this point," I said with a wide grin. "On the plus side, I think we found your problem, Bex."

The hopeful smile on her face was just as good as the teasing smirk, and I found myself grinning down at her. Our clutchmates on the rail went very still.

"Really?" she whispered.

"Really. Sweet boy has a terrible trot. Sorry, Buster, but you really do." I gave the calm pony another pat on his neck in apology before my gaze flicked back up to Bex. "It's not your fault."

The color drained out of Bex's face and she swayed on her feet. Reese didn't bother with the gate. He planted his hands on the fence, vaulted over the top rail, and steadied her with a hand on her upper arm before I could even think about swinging out of the saddle. The shorter girl braced her hands on her knees and bent over, her harsh breaths overly loud in the silence.

Every last bit of Reese's attention was on Bex, but Elias stared at me like he'd never seen me before, and Keaton . . . an odd expression flitted over his face that *might* have been approval.

A little unnerved, I swung out of Buster's saddle and led him out of the round pen.

"I'll be right back." I gave them a hesitant smile. "I've got an idea."

A few minutes later, I came back with my second favorite horse. Reese stared at Piper and caught my arm.

"Are you sure about this, Tavros?"

"Yes. It's not enough for Bex to be told it's not her fault. She needs to *feel* it." I smiled as he eyed the tall mare with open concern. "Don't worry. This sweetheart's gaited like Renegade, but on easy mode. Even a child can handle her."

"Well, Bex is kind of child sized," Elias said with a snicker.

"I dare you to say that to her face," Reese shot back.

"No, thanks. I like living."

Keaton just held open the gate for me and ignored their bantering like he usually did. Bex had been leaning against the fence on far side of the round pen, her head tilted back as she watched a pair of dragons dogfighting in one of the nearby training airspaces, but at the *creak* of the gate, she twisted around. Her jaw dropped.

"Are you crazy?" Bex stared at the bay mare with wide eyes. "I can't ride her! She's like, a bazillion hands tall."

I snorted a laugh. "Don't be ridiculous, she's only sixteen three."

As I held the mare for her, Bex picked one foot up as high as it would go and glowered at me when she didn't come close to the stirrup. She couldn't even get a hand on the saddle to pull herself up.

"Like I said," she said with a mutinous glint in her eyes, "a bazillion hands tall."

"Boys!" I barked. When they just stared at me, I impatiently gestured to Bex. "One of you make yourselves less useless and give her a boost."

Reese belted out a laugh and easily boosted Bex up. As soon as she was settled in the saddle, we hopped back out of the round pen to give her room.

Apprehension twisted her expression, but at my urging, she nudged Piper's sides and got her walking. After a few laps to warm the mare up, I gave her the signal to trot. Bex stiffened up so much it was a miracle she didn't fall out of the saddle, but grim determination tightened her jaw. She tapped Piper's sides smartly with her heels, and the well-trained mare broke into her smooth-as-silk trot. Bex's expression remained frozen the whole first lap, as if she expected something awful would happen if she smiled, but then the biggest grin I'd ever seen stretched across her face.

"This is *amazing*!" she shouted with an enthusiastic *whoop*.

Her seat wasn't perfect, but her spine finally unlocked and she moved *with* her horse. Just like she'd need to move with a dragon in flight.

"I'm curious," I said cautiously we watched her ride. "If Bex has been having long-term problems with riding, how did she ever get assigned a mountain griffin?"

"She didn't." Reese shot me a pointed look. "When your friends messed with our eggs, the clutch got a little jumbled up."

Cold slithered through my belly. "Who was supposed to have Bex's griffin?"

Elias leaned around his friend, purple eyes dancing in mischief and malice. "Langston."

"That . . . makes sense." The muscular, aggressive cadet would've been a perfect fit for a fierce mountain griffin like Merlin. "It also explains why he hates me."

"I'm not sure Langy likes any of us, to be fair," Elias said in a musing tone before he grinned. "But yeah, that definitely didn't help. Personally, I'm not sure how that grumpy bastard has a girlfriend back home. He must save all his cheerfulness for her."

"She broke things off after he bonded," Keaton said quietly, a flicker of anger breaking through his impassive expression. "She sent a letter."

I winced. There was a reason most riders ended up with each other. Bonding changed us, made us more than we'd been before—but it also made us different. How could it not when we shared our souls with someone decidedly not human?

"It didn't matter as much that Bex sucked when she was 'just' a forest griffin–tracked cadet," Reese continued with an irritated growl. "Now that she's mountain griffin..."

"It matters," I said firmly.

A slow grin creased my face as another idea struck, and I waved Bex over.

"Come on," I said, leading her away from the pen. "You said you start training flights next week, right?"

"Yeah," she said, that tight thread of apprehension weaving through her voice once again. Her grin faded, but her shoulders remained unbowed and her spine didn't stiffen back up. Progress.

"Flying is the best fucking thing in the world, but I'll tell you a secret." I dropped back so I was walking at her stirrup and met her wide topaz gaze. "You can't fly if you're afraid to fall."

I twined my fingers in the reins and led Piper to the right, away from the stables, away from the safe, fenced-in arenas and round pens. Bex tilted her head back and back, staring at the hill towering over us . . . and the steep path that led to the top. The blood drained out of her face and she turned a terrified expression on me.

"I can't do that."

"Yes, you can."

"No, you don't understand," she said frantically. "I've *tried* to do that, and I *can't!*"

"Tavros, you better know what the hell you're doing," Reese growled as he stopped next to us. I kept my focus on Bex, but raised my voice to make it clear I was talking to all of them.

"Flying isn't some magical experience where dragons glide into the air like they're powered by pixie dust and unicorn wishes," I said with a derisive snort. "They beat the air into fucking submission, and they fight for height with every flap of their wings. Yes, there's straps to secure you to the saddle, but you have to do better than ride like a sack of potatoes." I jerked my chin toward the steep path. "You want to know what takeoff feels like? Ride the slope like a dragon rider cadet."

Bex's eyes narrowed at the blatant challenge in my voice. "Fine, if it's so easy, you do it."

"Sure—"

"Without stirrups." Judging by the smug tilt to her lips, she didn't think I could do it.

Reese arched a brow, throwing as much challenge in that small gesture as I'd managed with a whole speech. Elias smirked, crossed his arms, and leaned against a fencepost as if anticipating a good show. Keaton watched and he judged without saying a word.

They all kept accusing me of showing off, when I hadn't even *begun* to show off.

"Okay," I said casually.

Keaton's gaze sharpened, but Bex didn't notice, slipping out of the saddle and hitting the ground lightly despite the drop.

"But I won't do it without stirrups." I met her eyes when she protested—and smirked. "I'll do it without a saddle. And then you will too."

"*What?*"

Laughing under my breath as anticipation coiled low in my belly, I quickly took Piper's saddle and pad off and dumped them in Elias' arms. Keaton took a step forward to give me a boost, but I waved him off and led Piper over to a nearby rockpile some long-ago cadets had set up for this exact purpose.

"Stubborn," he muttered as I smoothly pulled myself across her wide back.

Suppressing a grin, I walked the mare in a quick circle. As soon as I'd found my seat, I tightened my legs around her barrel, pointed her nose at the slope, and dug my heels in. Piper's ears perked up, and she launched herself up the hill, pushing hard on her hindquarters. I flexed with each leaping stride, hands loose on the reins and resting gently on her neck. She didn't need guidance from me—she just needed me to not ride like a sack of potatoes.

When we reached the top, I patted her neck. "Good girl."

The path down the back of the hill was a gentle, winding switchback that the mare navigated with ease, and we quickly made our way back to the starting point. Bex still hadn't picked her jaw up off the ground.

"How did you do that?"

"It's easy." I slid off Piper's back and smirked at the smaller girl. "Just remember—chin up, tits out, and squeeze those thighs like you're riding something else entirely."

Elias' eyes bulged wide with shock and he nearly dropped the saddle in his arms. I winked at him before turning my attention back to Bex.

"Seriously, you just need to relax and *feel* what she's doing." I led Piper over to the pile of rocks and held her until Bex was secure on the mare's bare back. While the other girl was smaller than me, she was all muscle, and her legs were more than up for the task. "You can do this."

Bex repeated what I'd done, walking Piper in a few circles before pointing the mare's nose at the slope and digging her heels in. The mare promptly lunged up the hill, and Bex just as promptly tumbled off her back—and popped right back up. There was a reason dragon rider cadets used this hill. The sandy path cushioned falls nearly as well as the arenas. She tried again and ended up overbalancing and falling across the mare's neck before sliding to the ground. Another try, another fall, but she just brushed off her leathers and led Piper back to the rocks again without missing a beat.

Back to the rocks, back up the slope—fall, rise, repeat.

Every time she tried again, she made it a little higher up the slope. Every time she fell, her fear faded a little more. Every time she got back up, her determination shone a little brighter.

As she led Piper back down the slope yet again, I was about to call knock-it-off when the girl shot me a fierce look.

"One more try."

"One more try," I agreed after I checked the mare for signs of fatigue or strain.

I couldn't help it. I held my breath as she pointed Piper's nose at the slope one last time, even though it truly didn't matter. All that mattered was she wasn't afraid of falling. Not anymore. She could learn to fly now . . . even if I no longer could.

"This is why you wanted her to do this," Reese said in a low murmur as he moved up to stand next to me. "It wasn't so she'd make it to the top, it was so she'd get over her fear."

Bex dug her heels in and moved with Piper as the mare lunged up the steep path, her spine flexing with every push of the mare's hindquarters, and her balance damn near perfect. In moments, they passed the highest point they'd ever reached and kept going.

"Why not both?" I slanted him a smug glance, but he only had eyes for Bex.

Keaton had watched from the side the whole time, never speaking, never moving. When Bex made it to the top without falling, I shot him an excited, triumphant grin. He stared for a long moment before he growled a curse and stomped away.

To my shock, Reese roared a laugh.

"Finally! Somebody *finally* broke Keaton's legendary bearing. Nice work, Tavros." His gaze shifted back to Bex at the top of the hill, where she was punching her fist in the air and laughing like a lunatic, and he sobered. "Seriously, nice work."

I forced a smile, but couldn't help but watch Keaton stalk past the last of the barns and out of sight. My shoulders slumped, any sense of accomplishment draining away. Even when I did something right, it still wasn't good enough for my team leader.

I couldn't sleep. No matter how much I tossed and turned, no matter how much I burrowed beneath my blankets or cuddled close to Atticus, I couldn't sleep. Everyone else in the damn barracks was sleeping—and in many cases snoring—but not me. After the third straight hour of staring into the darkness, I gave up and did what so many cadets had done before me.

I went up to the roof.

With the way the entire hill was terraced, it was an easy matter to sneak up to the next level, tromp a short way back down the slope, and jump to the roof. Honestly, it was more a step than a jump, as the barracks were practically built into the hillside. Keeping my footsteps as silent as possible, I moved to the center of the roof where the wide brick chimney would hide me from casual view and sat down. While we weren't supposed to be out after curfew, the instructors didn't really care so long as we weren't making a nuisance of ourselves...like attempting to find the secret entrance to the Mavens' fabled underground lair.

The night was freezing cold, but I'd dressed for it, pulling on my warmest jacket before tiptoeing out of the barracks. Even so, I drew my knees to my chest and wrapped my arms around them. I told myself it was for warmth, not comfort, because it was easier to lie to myself than to my bonded.

Sadness along with an unhealthy dose of self-pity weighed down my soul. Even when I managed to do something right, something *good*, it hadn't been enough. While Bex had been grateful, she'd quickly disappeared with Reese, and judging by the looks they'd given each other, it wasn't a celebration I was interested in crashing. Elias had stuck around long enough to help with Piper but had slipped away soon after, and nobody had seen Keaton since he stomped off in a temper.

And while I had Atticus, while I'd *always* have Atticus, he was grumpy and growing and more interested in food and sleep than conversation.

I was alone, and desperately trying not to feel that way. With a low sigh, I tilted my head back to the crisp stars above and breathed in the night. Time passed, but it couldn't have been long before the gentle *thud* of boots hitting the roof told me I wasn't alone anymore. Footsteps moved toward me—quiet enough, but too heavy to be Bethany—but I didn't stop looking up at the stars. Because if it was one of the three morons who'd tracked me down, I couldn't be held responsible if I punched him in the face.

"Thought I might find you up here," a gruff voice said.

My head snapped around. It wasn't Dimitri, or Zayne, or even Callum—it was Keaton.

He sat next to me, legs all sprawled out in the way of guys everywhere, and looked up at the stars too. Without so much as a glance my way, he held out a flask. The kind cadets weren't supposed to have but kept squirreled away where the instructors couldn't find them during inspections.

I squinted at it suspiciously. "What's that?"

"A peace offering."

I snorted something that was almost a laugh. "I meant what's in it."

"I'm . . . not actually sure." He shrugged, unscrewed the cap, and took a sip. His grimace pulled a real laugh from somewhere deep inside me, so loud I startled myself. Still laughing, I accepted the flask and gave it a cautious sniff that set my nose on fire. At his challenging stare, I drank—and coughed violently at the raw burn.

"Is this a peace offering or a declaration of war?" I gasped as I passed the flask back.

"Why not both?" Keaton said with a chuckle before he bravely took another sip. He tilted the flask toward me with a questioning lift of his eyebrows. When I wrapped my fingers around the top, he didn't let go. "Thought I had you all figured out, Tavros. I was wrong."

He shook his head ruefully and let go of the flask. I watched him warily, because once again, I couldn't interpret his expression.

"What's that supposed to mean?" I asked quietly.

Rather than answer, he looked back up at the stars. In the summer, the heat was so intense even at night that they would drape across the sky in a hazy, soft glow, but tonight the lingering winter cold turned them to diamond-bright pinpricks of light. Still beautiful, just different.

Keaton was silent for so long, I gave up on him and took another sip from the flask. The questionable alcohol tasted like ass, but it provided a horrid sort of warmth that reached places my jacket couldn't. Quite possibly because it was literally burning off the lining of my esophagus and stomach.

"You weren't showing off the other day, were you?"

His quiet question shattered the peaceful night, his tone not accusing, but rather triumphant, as if he'd finally figured out a puzzle that had baffled him for far too long. I snapped my head around to see him looking at me with an intense stare.

"Huh?" Well, that was an eloquent response. I cleared my throat, and the alcohol maliciously tried to climb back up it. The resultant coughing fit ended with me desperately dragging in air while tears poured down my cheeks.

"You gonna live, Tavros?" Keaton smirked even as he awkwardly patted me on the back.

"No," I wheezed miserably. "Your peace offering killed me."

"It *was* also a declaration of war," he pointed out with exaggerated reasonableness.

"Against what? My internal organs?" I cleared my throat and tried again. "Showing off when?"

His smirk vanished between one blink and the next, and he regarded me soberly.

"When we were riding and shooting last week. You weren't showing off, you were...happy, proud." His jaw tightened. "You looked at us the same way you looked at me when Bex conquered that hill today. And we stomped all over it."

Keaton's intense amber gaze stripped away my armor and left me vulnerable again. I didn't hate it quite as much as before, but it was still uncomfortable. I dropped my gaze and twisted the flask between my hands.

"It was nice to finally be *good* at something, to not look like such a screw-up around you guys." I hesitated before I glanced back up with a slight grin and an embarrassed shrug. "And maybe I didn't want to be dead last for once."

As I tilted my head back to look up at the stars again—and to escape his scrutiny—a shadow crossed the night sky, the graceful shape of the outstretched wings identifying it as a green. Atticus remained soundly asleep, curled up in his nest below and in the back of my mind, content and warm, so I didn't bother to suppress my shiver of longing.

"I was a dragon rider cadet, Keaton," I reminded him softly. "Consistently ranked in the top five, good enough to be offered my choice of dragons. Good enough to be offered the *black* dragon egg."

His sharp inhale told me the significance wasn't lost on him, but I wasn't done yet. Maybe if I'd been honest with my team leader sooner, I could've avoided some of my issues with my clutch. I set the flask down between us and wrapped my arms around my legs again to ward off the chill, both inside and out.

"To get to where I was, you had to be competitive as fuck, and it's...it's a hard habit to shake." I finally looked at him, and the judgement I'd been expecting was absent. He was just listening. My mouth quirked into a small, lopsided smile. "You were right. I keep trying to be the best."

"The best what?"

When I just looked at him in confusion, he raised his brows expectantly.

"Are you trying to be the best cadet, or the best partner to your bonded? There's a difference, you know." He stood up and stretched before he glanced back down at me. "Don't stay up too late, Harpy."

My griffin name didn't sound wrong when he said it, and it didn't sound like he was teasing me. In his gruff voice, it sounded like a badge of honor and a sign of respect. More than anything, it sounded like acceptance.

"Hey!" I called after him as he crept across the roof. "What's your griffin call you?"

Keaton jumped onto the sloped hill and glanced back. The moon had risen enough that I could see he wasn't just smiling anymore. He was *grinning*.

"I'll never tell."

And then he was gone, and I was alone again, but not lonely. I spent the rest of the night thinking about his question, sitting on the roof until the eastern horizon lightened with the gray of predawn's light.

I wasn't happy with the answer I came up with.

CHAPTER 8

The next few days were a frantic dance between physical training, dealing with an increasingly grumpy griffin whose wings *ached* with the start of a growth spurt that might actually see him flying long before I was ready, and cramming every last bit of academic knowledge I could into my increasingly muddled brain. Not even a Savinian night raid of unprecedented scale could throw off the Tennessan Bonded Training Academy's rigid testing schedule. Midterms were next week, whether we were ready or not.

I . . . was not.

It wasn't enough for me to pass. I wanted to do well, but the coursework was wildly different from the dragon rider classes, and there was *so much* to catch up on.

Apparently, I also wasn't ready for endurance training with my clutchmates. We were only three miles into our run, and everyone was leaving me in the dust. Everyone except for Keaton, who fell back to match my incredibly slow pace. I frowned over at him, but I didn't have the breath to say anything.

"Just keep putting one foot in front of the other, Harpy," Keaton said in quiet encouragement.

Reese and Elias glanced over their shoulders, exchanged a wordless nod of agreement, and fell back to run just in front of us. Then Hawthorne, red-faced and sweating buckets but still running faster than me, dropped back as well.

A sizable gap opened up in our formation.

"I got this, boss." Hawthorne tossed a quick grin over his shoulder. "HOOAH, ECHO!"

The rest of the clutch—minus Bex and Volkow, who were out on their first training flights—snapped their heads around, saw that we were straggling, and slowed down. Everyone except Langston, who now held a considerable lead over everyone else.

"Come on, Langy," Elias bellowed, his long legs eating up the miles with ease. "Don't be a dick!"

Langston heaved a sigh I could hear all the way from the back, but he slowed until the rest of us caught up, and he didn't try to push the pace past what I could currently manage. If anything, the big bastard slowed even *more*, and I was able to somewhat catch my breath.

"You're all nuts," I panted, but I couldn't keep a grateful smile off my face. "This...is a timed...event."

Keaton just grinned, pride for his clutch shining bright in his amber eyes as he panned his gaze over everyone. "We started this together, we finish together."

"HOOAH ECHO!" Hawthorne bellowed again before breaking into an old military jody, the measured cadence more or less keeping us in step.

What we'd started was the twelve-mile ruck trail that looped around the academy. We didn't even have rucks yet. This was just an unencumbered run to get us ready for a true ruck march, but I honestly wasn't sure I could finish it. Dragon rider cadets were required to run like everyone else, but most of the endurance training leaned toward long hours in the saddle to build up the correct set of muscles for flying. Which meant I was good in a sprint, and I could ride for hours, but long-distance running was the *worst*.

"I'm going to die," I managed between heaving breaths, not sure if I was joking or serious.

"You're not going to die," Elias said with a roll of his eyes as he slowed so he was running on my other side. "But damn, we have *got* to work on your stamina."

"That's what she said," I gasped out with a smirk. Elias stared at me for a beat before he huffed a laugh.

"You're all right, Tavros." He lightly slapped me on the shoulder and grinned. "I take back half the things I've said about you."

I gave him a little side-eye. "Only half?"

"Only half." He dragged his gaze over me with a playful leer that lasted for all of half a second before he cracked up. "Kidding, Harpy, just kidding. Oh man, the look on your face."

Still laughing, he lengthened his stride to catch up to Reese and immediately picked a fight about which senior griffin clutch would win the annual relay race that afternoon. It was a good distraction until Hawthorne lost patience with the squabbling pair and forcibly separated them.

It left Keaton and me alone at the rear of the formation. Shaded by winter-barren branches and evergreens, we ran side by side through dappled sunlight and shadow, the silence only broken by the steady beat of our boots against the dirt path, the soothing chirps of birds recently returned from their migratory journey, and my less than soothing explosive exhales.

By mile four, every lungful of air I dragged in felt like fire, and the stitch burrowing into my side had long since passed painful. It felt like I was going to die, or possibly pass out. But I shoved sweaty strands of hair out of my face and did what Keaton had told me to do—I put one foot in front of the other and kept going. Even though all I wanted to do was collapse, or maybe vomit and *then* collapse, I kept going.

As we jogged past the mile-five marker, the trail cut through a grove of trees sprouting pure white flowers. Matthews immediately broke into an uncontrolled sneezing fit, and more than one of us gagged at the potent reek. The flowers were beautiful, but they smelled like rotting fish, and Langston picked up the pace to get us out of range. My thighs trembled from the strain of trying to keep up, and the gap slowly opened up again as I fell behind.

"Why are forest griffins considered more valuable than mountain griffins from a strategic standpoint?" Keaton asked, abruptly breaking his silence.

More than a little confused by the random question, I shot him a quick glance and decided I hated him a little. His breathing was slow and even, and he looked as if he could keep going at our current pace for hours. The bastard wasn't even sweating. Keaton was good at damn near everything a forest griffin rider was supposed to be good at, and it was annoying as fuck. The fact that I'd been annoyingly good at damn near everything a dragon rider was supposed to be good at before bonding to Atticus was irrelevant.

Keaton met my scowl with raised brows and a slight smile.

"You said you needed help on your midterms," he explained patiently. "I'm helping."

"Are you though?"

"Yes." Keaton's expression remained impassive, but I was beginning to learn how to look beyond his admittedly impressive bearing. His face might be a perfect, professional mask, but his eyes were full of amusement, and I fought back the urge to flip him off.

"And you couldn't have . . . picked a better . . . time . . . for this?" I demanded in exasperation as I struggled to catch up to Reese, the next cadet on the trail.

"No."

As his smug grin broke free, I gave in to the urge and held up my middle finger. When he just laughed at me, I clamped my jaw shut for a quarter mile before I broke with an audible sigh. And if that sigh sounded like it came from a dying moose, it was because we had only just reached the halfway point and we still had *six* more miserable miles to go. At least Langston had slowed the pace again once we'd left the disgusting fish flowers behind, and I was able to close the gap once more.

"I don't know," I finally admitted.

It didn't make sense to me. Mountain griffins were larger than forest griffins, stronger flyers than forest griffins, fiercer fighters than forest griffins. Dragons and griffins weren't the only ones who soared through the skies on outstretched wings, and the Savinians controlled monsters who could take out the toughest red if unopposed.

The mountain griffins had been designed to take them on and *win*.

"Yes, you do," Keaton said with a calm confidence that was infuriating. "I know the kind of marks you usually get. Use that big brain of yours and figure it out."

"My brain is currently oxygen deprived . . . and not interested in braining." I sucked in a deeper breath and dug the heel of my hand into the burning stitch in my side. "Please try again later."

"So you do have a sense of humor in there somewhere," Keaton said with a wide grin.

I jabbed a finger at his face in accusation. "Says the guy who hated me so much I wasn't even sure he knew how to smile."

"Who says I still don't hate you?" Keaton neatly dodged my elbow without breaking stride. "Come on, Harpy, you've got to be able to think under pressure. What are the forest griffins called?"

"The eyes and ears of the Tennessan military," I replied without hesitation. That response had been drilled into me by every classroom instructor I had until it became just as rote as "inside leg, outside rein."

"And the mountain griffins?" he prompted with exaggerated patience.

"The Talons of the Dragon Corps."

He stared at me in a silence only broken by the sound of boots hitting the trail and the harsh breathing of more than one cadet. At least I wasn't the only one who sounded like they were dying now. Only four more miles to go before I could collapse.

I kept putting one foot in front of the other as I thought through Keaton's original question. It still didn't make sense, because the mountain griffins were the guardians of the *dragons*—

I blinked.

"The mountain griffins support the dragons as shields," I said slowly as Keaton nodded in encouragement, "but the forest griffins support the whole military as scouts. Strategically speaking, that's more valuable."

"Exactly. We are the eyes and ears. Without us, commanders are blind and deaf. Without *us*, people die." He paused and corrected himself slightly. "The wrong people die. The mountain griffins provide a vital defense to the dragons. They shield them, and they make a difference doing it. But commanders don't stop and listen when their riders speak."

"But they do for us."

"They do for us," he repeated with a firm nod. "We are the difference between a battle lost and a battle won. Remember that." A faint grin creased his face. "For more than just your midterms."

We rounded the last bend in the trail and passed the wooden marker for mile nine. Only three more to go. I felt myself break somewhere around mile ten, and I thought I might actually die when we passed eleven. But Keaton kept quizzing me, and I kept putting one foot in front of the other until we crossed the finish line.

The only reason I didn't collapse immediately after was because Keaton wouldn't let me. He forced me to keep walking with a firm hand under my elbow and ignored my gasping curses. Langston crossed his arms, barely even winded, while my legs trembled so badly I could barely support my own weight.

"Dragon rider p—"

Hawthorne snapped his head around, his expression fierce with unspoken warning. Langston cut himself off and held up his hands.

"I was going to say *princess*, not *that*. Calm your tits, man."

Keaton and I weren't the only ones walking in slow circles, and even Langston quit posturing and started stretching. Right up until Lieutenant Osbourne, our PT instructor, called out our time. There was a collective groan. Our time wasn't just abysmal—it was an outright failure.

"Well done, Echo," Lieutenant Osbourne added with pleased smile. We all stared at the sincerity in his voice, but only Langston was ballsy—or stupid—enough to challenge him.

"Our time sucked, sir," he said with a disgusted glare in my direction. The second the instructor's back was turned, I straightened up long enough to flip Langston off. I was done taking his crap. Surprise flickered in his muddy green eyes before he flipped me off in return with what almost looked like a grin.

"Yes, it did. But it was never about the time."

"You told us it was an *individually* timed event," Keaton said, his bearing perfectly professional, but his eyes narrowed ever so slightly. Not as if he was annoyed, but as if he was trying to figure out a puzzle. "You said our time was everything."

"I did." Osbourne tilted his head like a griffin, brilliant turquoise eyes gleaming with approval. "And yet, instead of leaving your slowest teammate behind, you stuck together. You operated as a team, just like you need to do in the field."

Keaton's face lit up in understanding. "It was a test."

The lieutenant nodded. "Yes, it was."

My eyes widened. A test we would've failed without Keaton.

"And you all passed with flying colors. Make sure to stretch, and don't forget to hydrate *slowly*. Dismissed." As the rest of Echo went back to cooling down, our instructor ambled over to where I was stretching next to Keaton. "Don't sweat your time today, Tavros. You'll adjust. I did."

My head snapped up. "Excuse me, sir?"

"What, you thought you were the only cadet to ever have to switch to the griffin track?"

Young lieutenants who ended up as academy instructors for their first assignment after graduation invariably fell into one of two extremes—total hard-asses, like they hadn't just been a cadet themselves, or easygoing. It seemed Lieutenant Osbourne fell into the latter category, because he laughed at my shocked expression.

"Admittedly, your case was a little more unusual." He shrugged. "I just couldn't stop puking on my poor instructor's dragon, and my spatial D was ... bad."

I winced. Airsickness could usually be overcome fairly quickly, but if a cadet couldn't shake spatial disorientation, it was a fast track to washing out before they were bonded to a dragon they couldn't fly with. There was no shame in it, but a pang of sympathy stabbed me in the heart. He'd lost his chance to fly ... like me.

"I'm sorry, sir."

A shadow passed overhead, and a griffin landed neatly in the center of the small field. Her rich chestnut feathers lightened to nearly white at the wingtips, and her beautiful turquoise eyes were a match for the lieutenant's. As she crouched slightly, he slung himself onto her back, casually rested a hand on his bondmate's shoulder, and grinned down at me.

"I'm not."

The walk back to the academy grounds was a slow, painful one. My sweat-soaked PT gear had chilled and clung unpleasantly in all the wrong places, and my calves threatened to cramp with every halting step. As I took a slow sip of water from my canteen, I gave Keaton an irritated glance.

"You're going to miss the start of the griffin relay race if you wait for my slow ass."

"I know, but I'm afraid if I don't stay with you, we'll find you curled up in a ball on the ground tomorrow." His amber eyes glinted with amusement, and he strolled along next to me as if he hadn't just run twelve miles. "Besides, we can use the time to keep prepping you for midterms. I took all those classes last year, remember? In fact, see if you can sweet talk Elias into helping you with Navigation 202. He's already helping Langy."

"Seriously? *Elias*?"

"He might look like an idiot, but he's the best at land nav."

"Didn't he get lost on the way to the chow hall last week?"

"If by 'lost' you mean chasing after that hot dragon rider friend of yours," he said, lips twitching into a smirk.

"What Bethany does or doesn't do with Elias is none of my business." I held up a finger when Keaton snickered. "None! Do you hear me? I have zero follow-up questions, thank you."

He was silent for a beat as we passed through the academy gates. The towering stone walls encircling the grounds were still scorched in places, but the last of the repairs had been completed. Even the grass had begun to recover. It was odd seeing the grounds so empty though. Everyone must have already left for the race.

"Well, I have one for you."

I braced myself as we ambled across the silent quad toward the hatchery. Thanks to Keaton's insistence on extra stretches and a slow walk, I wasn't quite hobbling anymore, though a tiny surge of nausea caught me off guard. I dismissed it as a result of drinking too much water too fast, or maybe the thought of Bethany and *Elias*, and arched a brow at Keaton.

"What?"

"What are the known blasted zone locations, and what are the earliest signs of the mist sickness?"

I stared at him for a long moment to see if he was serious. He was.

"I think I liked it better when you hated me," I said dryly.

"I never hated you, Tavros. I just couldn't figure you out." His sly smile was more than a little evil. It said he'd definitely figured me out, and no amount of armor was going to keep him out. That was okay. I understood him now, too. "Answer the question, *Harpy*."

"Technically, that was two questions."

"You're stalling."

"Am not."

I raised my canteen to my lips to stall some more, but just as quickly lowered it at another, stronger surge of nausea. Definitely too much water too fast for my abused stomach. I stumbled to an abrupt stop and concentrated on slow breaths until the feeling passed. Keaton's smile faded and was replaced with a concerned frown.

"You okay?"

"Nope," I replied cheerfully, popping the "p" for added emphasis. "Somebody made me run all twelve miles instead of letting me fail gracefully, and now he's quizzing me on the midterms I'm probably going to fail less than gracefully, and all I want to do is curl up and sleep for the rest of the day." I stabbed a finger at the ground and smirked. "That patch of grass is looking awfully good right now."

"Who knew you were this dramatic?" He shook his head at me and gripped my arm under the elbow to tug me into motion again. Even after I'd forced tired muscles to do their job, he didn't let go of my arm, as if concerned I really would curl up on the ground if he gave me the slightest opportunity. "Blasted zones, Harpy. Where's the nearest one?"

"Um . . ." I poked at my tired brain until an answer floated to the surface. "About a week's ride to the northwest where Nash used to be?"

Keaton raised his brows. "Are you asking or telling?"

I opened my mouth to tell him where he could shove it when the warm breeze shifted, stirring the sweaty strands of hair clinging to my face and carrying a shout to my ears. My head tilted like my griffin's when they were trying to catch a distant sound. It didn't count as stalling if it sounded like someone had called your name. The shout came again, closer this time, at once borderline aggressive and a plea for my attention.

"Harper, wait up!"

My steps slowed of their own volition at the sound of that achingly familiar voice. Any amusement I'd felt dried up in a heartbeat, and I flexed my fist, my knuckles aching with the memory of the last time we'd spoken.

Reluctantly, I turned around.

Dimitri hurried out of the dragon campus, his gaze focused on mine with unwavering intensity as he ignored the paths and strode directly across the new grass. Judging by the leather jacket slung over one shoulder and the crumpled flight cap and goggles hanging from one hand, he'd just returned from a training flight. As he drew near, he dragged a hand through his sweaty hair, leaving it standing up in short spikes and showing off impressive definition in his bicep. He'd put on more muscle in the weeks since I'd seen him last, but that wasn't what captured my attention.

It was his eyes.

The soft brown had changed to a striking amber with a dramatic black ring. They were arresting, and I was caught between wanting to run away from what they meant and wanting to stare. Keaton coughed something that sounded almost like a laugh, and I tore my gaze off Dimitri to glare at his suspiciously blank face.

"I'll, uh, just leave you to catch up with your *friend*."

"Ex-friend," I shot back with a scowl. He smirked, amber eyes dancing in amusement.

"Whatever you say, Harpy," Keaton replied before fixing Dimitri with an unfriendly stare.

It was the one I'd been on the receiving end often in the beginning, and I suddenly realized I wasn't exactly sure when Keaton had stopped looking at me like I was an enemy, or a problem, or a puzzle to solve. All I knew was I was grateful to have him on my side, even if he did have the worst timing when it came to studying. His eyes softened slightly as he glanced at me.

"I'll wait for you," he said over his shoulder as he walked toward the hatchery. "Tavi will appreciate the extra nap time before we head over to the races."

My gaze snapped back to Dimitri as he closed the distance between us with confident strides. Unfortunately for him, even with our time apart I still *knew* him, and I caught the uncertainty hiding behind those pretty new eyes as he stopped in front of me. For just an instant, his gaze drifted past mine to where Keaton leaned against the hatchery wall. Something that looked very much like jealousy flickered across his face. I could've corrected his assumption, because Keaton and I were absolutely *not* like that, but a very petty part of me didn't want to.

"Hey, hotshot." Dimitri winced, another crack in his mask, and he held up his hands. "Sorry—Harper."

"Asshole," I replied coolly enough, but my stomach roiled with nerves.

He rubbed the back of his neck before he dropped his hand and met my gaze firmly. "I deserved that."

I crossed my arms and said nothing. Not too long ago, we wouldn't have been able to shut up around each other, but now we just stood in awkward silence, neither of us knowing what to say. It hurt.

His eyes caught my attention again, and I couldn't look away. Because I'd remembered where I'd seen eyes like that before—the black dragon hatchling. Because *of course* that charismatic bastard had managed to fail upward. The less petty part of me knew out of all of us he'd been the best suited—if we'd had a leader, it would've been Dimitri—but I didn't feel like being charitable right now. I wanted to be petty.

I also wanted to ask what he'd named that adorable baby tank, but that would've required speaking, and it seemed like all my words were caught behind the knot constricting my throat.

"Harper..." A deep sigh escaped Dimitri as regret darkened his expression.

No, not just regret—*pity*. Rage swept through me, so powerful my vision flashed red and my gut clenched.

"I just wanted to say I'm—"

"Finish that sentence," I snarled as my hands balled up into fists. "I dare you."

Oh, look. There were my words.

"Harper—"

"*No.*"

"Would you just let me apologize?" he shouted as his own fists clenched.

A chill washed through me, sweeping away the rage and leaving misery in its wake. My stomach cramped, and I swayed on my feet.

"Gods, you are such a stubborn..." Dimitri's anger faltered and faded into concern. "Harper?"

My stomach cramped harder. I spun away from him, doubled over, and vomited everything I'd ever eaten. Distantly, I heard Dimitri curse, heard Keaton call out in alarm, but I was too busy trying not to collapse into the nasty puddle at my feet to answer either of them. My vision blurred, and the world swam sideways on me.

Dimitri caught me before I could fall.

I sagged in his arms, leaned over, and vomited again. Tears poured down my face, but I couldn't stop heaving long enough to catch my breath. The sour tang of vomit filled my nose, and my throat burned. A broad hand rubbed my back in small, soothing circles, but urgency rode Dimitri's voice as he murmured in my ear.

"Come on, hotshot, breathe for me."

Footsteps pounded to a halt next to us as my stomach abruptly stopped trying to turn itself inside out and settled into an uneasy truce with the rest of my body. I sucked in breath after ragged breath, and if they sounded more like sobs, I was too busy appreciating air in my lungs to care.

"What did you do to her?" Keaton roared in anger, something I'd never heard before, and I whimpered as his voice seemed to spike directly into my brain. Another cold chill washed over my skin, and sweat beaded on my brow. I couldn't stop shaking, couldn't even open my eyes, and my head throbbed in time with my pulse.

"Nothing," Dimitri snarled, but his grip was gentle as he half carried me to a clean patch of grass. One hand remained on my back and steadied me, while his other brushed strands of hair out of my face. "Come on, Harper, open your eyes and tell us what's wrong."

"Don't know," I mumbled, my voice little more than a harsh croak and my eyes refusing to open. "Feel like I'm gonna die."

Keaton barked a strained laugh. "Has she always been this dramatic?"

"Harper was born dramatic," Dimitri replied easily, though I could hear the worry underlying his words. "She's just usually better at hiding it."

Dimitri's hand on my back was the only reason I hadn't curled up into a ball on the ground. My stomach clenched again, but this time I managed to ride out the surge of nausea without vomiting. Small victories.

"Just let me die," I panted. "I'll feel better then."

"You can't die." Keaton awkwardly patted my shoulder. "You'd take Atticus with you, remember . . ."

Whatever else Keaton might have said melted into nothing more than white noise. Atticus should've been in my head the instant I got sick, but he hadn't and he wasn't.

"Atticus?"

Silence.

My heartbeat thundered in my ears as I reached for him. For a terrifying moment, I couldn't find him, just like that first day in Commandant Pulaski's office. We'd been bonded long enough that he couldn't hide from me for long though, no matter how tightly he curled up in the back of my mind. Relief pulled a trembling smile to my lips.

"There you are, sleepyhead. I was worried." He didn't stir. *"Atticus?"*

Nothing. Nothing but an aching silence that felt *wrong*. His mind was silent and still, but he didn't feel like he was sleeping. He felt *muffled*, as if something had wrapped around him, a barrier to separate us and keep him asleep.

"Atticus? Atticus! Wake up!"

My hand pressed against my chest, where the hooks of the bond had sunk deep. The bond itself felt fine, but when I reached for my griffin, a wave of nausea washed over me and threatened to drown me in sickness again, forcing me back before I could touch him.

"It's not me . . ." I forced my eyes open and blinked the tears away. Black-ringed amber eyes stared at me in concern. Dimitri. He wasn't who I needed right now. My wild gaze darted past his worried face and latched onto Keaton. "It's not *me*."

Understanding flashed across his face. "Atticus."

My team leader took off for the hatchery at a dead sprint, and I scrambled to my feet to follow. Dimitri grabbed my shoulder when I staggered, but I shook off his grip and ran for my griffin. The world dipped and swayed with each step, but I knew what to do now that I knew the sickness wasn't mine.

I shielded.

What happened to one half of your soul happened to the other, but we'd been taught how to minimize the impact on our bondmates if we were hurt. Sickness like what I was feeling was much rarer. Bond candidates tended not to get sick often, even as kids. Once bonded, we rarely got sick at all. Something about the entanglement of two souls resulted in an enhanced immune system that chomped diseases for breakfast.

My vision tunneled until the gray duracrete walls of the hatchery were all I could see. Behind me, Dimitri swore and huffed as he ran after me. He could run me into the ground over a distance, but I'd always been faster in a sprint, and I had the motivation. The tired, trembling ache in my abused legs didn't matter. Only Atticus did.

I barreled through the front door of the hatchery and raced down the hall. My lungs struggled to drag in enough air, and my legs burned, but a door was suddenly in front of me. I shoved it open without slowing, took a single stride into the sticky humidity of the griffin crèche, and slammed into Keaton.

His hands wrapped around my upper arms and steadied me, kept me from bouncing off him and onto the hot sands, but I was too busy trying to get past him to be grateful.

"Atticus!"

"Harpy, wait." Keaton's hands tightened, refused to let me go. He shook me when I fought his hold and raised his voice. "He's not here!"

"What are you talking about? He has to be here!"

A dappled, tawny brown griffin pressed against Keaton's leg, a rough purr rumbling in his chest. For a split second, my heart leaped, but then he looked up at me through amber eyes, not purple. My heartbeat thundered in my ears, and I couldn't suck in enough air.

"Where is my griffin?" Frantic, I leaned around Keaton's bulk, but only found empty sands. Everyone had already picked up their griffins and headed out to the races to get a good viewing spot.

"Tavi says Atticus was gone when he woke up a few minutes ago," Keaton said grimly.

"Gone? He wouldn't just *leave*."

Understanding sucker punched me in the gut and my knees buckled. This time, Keaton was the one who didn't let me fall. I latched onto his shirt and stared up at him, panicked and pleading and a razor's edge away from shattering.

"Somebody took him." My whisper was a lost, desperate, broken thing that I barely recognized as my own. "Why would somebody take him?"

"I don't know, but we're going to find him." His gaze hardened as it flicked past mine. "Go get the griffin Maven on duty. She's not in here."

"On it," Dimitri's voice snapped out behind me before pounding footsteps raced away.

"He's gone, he's gone, and I'm alone, and I can't, I can't . . ." Panic constricted my throat, and gray sparks danced along the edges of my vision. When I swayed, Keaton's hands flexed around my arms.

"Breathe, damn it."

I tried to breathe, I really did, but Atticus was *gone*. I was never supposed to be alone again, but I couldn't hear him, couldn't *feel* him. Keaton snarled under his breath—and slapped me. I sucked in a ragged breath and jerked back in shock, but he didn't let me pull away.

"You listen to me right now, Tavros. You are *not* alone. I'm right here—" Tavi shrieked a challenge, his undersized wings mantling, golden-brown feathers puffing out. "—*we're* right here. Atticus is too.

You just need to reach for him. You know how, so suck it the fuck up and do it!"

At his roar, I stared up at him, swallowed hard, and nodded. Grim determination pushed down the panic. Keaton was right. I could do it. We were bound, soul to soul, and only death could break that bond.

"Don't let me fall," I said hoarsely, fingers digging into his shirt.

Distantly, I heard Keaton whisper, "Never," but I had already squeezed my eyes shut. As I unshielded, a wave of sickness slammed into me, and my stomach twisted uncomfortably. I didn't let it stop me from reaching for my griffin this time.

The hazy film was still wrapped around his mind, but it felt thinner, almost patchy in places. I pushed against it, calling for him, desperately trying to break through.

"Let me in, please let me in," I pleaded, but I couldn't get past whatever it was, couldn't force my way to his mind, couldn't see through his eyes. I couldn't *find* him, and despair threatened to unleash my panic once more.

And my griffin stirred.

Not awake, not yet, but he'd felt me, I was sure of it. So, I stopped trying to control my panic. I let it rage, along with my fear, my anger at whoever had taken him, my desperate need to find him. All of it, every last bit of it, driven by my love for him.

Atticus stirred, stretched, woke up, but something was definitely wrong. His bright, curious mind felt groggy and slow. Another wave of nausea slid through me, but it was a weak echo of the sickness I'd felt before. My breath caught. Not sick. Drugged. He'd been *drugged*. Confusion and fear shot through him and into me, and I sucked in a sharp breath.

"What is it?" Keaton asked sharply.

"He's scared," I whispered, most of my attention firmly with Atticus.

"Harpy?" His mental voice was slurred, and I did what I should've done the moment I realized the sickness was coming from him—I sent him a boost of my own energy. We'd only been taught how to do it a few days ago, and we'd been told to visualize pushing a warm ball down the bond. Dizziness swept over me, dragging cold in its wake, and I felt Keaton's hands tighten again when I sagged.

"That's enough, Harpy," he said quietly. "Don't give him any more."

It didn't matter. I'd given my griffin enough. His confusion sloughed away, and his mental voice came through sharp and clear. So did his fear.

"Harpy!"

"I'm here! Where are you? Please let me in!"

Without warning, my terrified griffin latched onto my mind. His mental claws sank deep, and he *tugged*. It felt like falling, like the instant before a dragon pulled out of a dive, when gravity surrendered its hold and everything felt weightless. A startled breath, an endless eternity, and then, for the first time, I tumbled into *his* mind.

Darkness shrouded his eyes, but there was nothing wrong with his sharp ears or his sense of smell.

"Hold on, Atticus, we're coming for you."

"Felix," he shot back with stubborn bravado. It immediately faltered, and I felt his fear like a knife to my heart. *"Hurry, Harpy. Scared."*

My eyes snapped open, the sweet scent of hay lingering in my nose. "I know where he is."

CHAPTER 9

"Tavi's calling for help, but nobody can hear him," Keaton snarled as we sprinted out of the academy gates. "The whole damn academy's at the races, too far away for his mental voice to reach. Everyone except for Atticus. He's trying to keep him calm."

I just nodded, already too out of breath to answer. The stables were only a mile or so beyond the academy walls, but I'd run so much today. Combined with the energy I'd sent to my griffin to help him shake off whatever he'd been drugged with, and I was spent before we even started.

Keaton could run faster than me.

Legs shaking, lungs burning, I sucked in enough air to speak. "Please go . . . save him."

"I won't leave you alone—"

"I'll stay with her," Dimitri panted as he finally caught up.

He'd been nowhere in sight when I'd figured out where Atticus had been taken, and we hadn't bothered to wait for him. His angry shout as he burst out of the hatchery and chased after us had mingled with Tavi's fierce shrieks, the young griffin no happier than the dragon rider to have been left behind.

Keaton nodded sharply and took off at a sprint. In seconds, he disappeared around a bend in the trail, and I was left with my ex–best friend. Betrayal and all the toxic hurt aside, I was glad to have him at my side again.

"Found the griffin Maven." Dimitri grimaced. "She was unconscious next to a puddle of her own vomit. Sound familiar?"

"Drugged too," I forced out.

Dimitri shot me a concerned glance when my breath rasped in my throat, but I kept my gaze fixated on the trail. I had to get to Atticus. Nothing else mattered.

The trees abruptly gave way to grassy paddocks, then riding arenas and round pens, and finally the long, low barns that housed the academy's riding horses. The fields were strangely empty, but a horse's piercing neigh echoed in my memory, and I knew there was at least one horse within the barns.

A burst of discomfort and misery flooded the bond. Whatever Atticus was wrapped in was making it difficult for him to breathe, and he was overheating.

"Harpy!" His voice sounded like a sob, and my eyes burned with unshed tears.

"I'm almost there."

My steps automatically veered toward the central barn. Not because it was where I normally went, but because the bond tugged at my soul, pulling me toward my terrified bondmate.

I staggered through the open double doors, the dim interior defying my sun-blinded vision, casting everything in various grades of shade and shadow. Dimitri grabbed my arm but promptly tripped over a pitchfork that had fallen across the aisle, and we both nearly tumbled to the hay-strewn ground. Fortunately, the loud snorts and huffs of an irritated horse covered any noise we might have made.

Atticus whimpered in my mind, and it felt as if he tried to look through my eyes but couldn't quite manage it. So, he twisted the bond instead, pushing a tiny burst of energy toward me at the same time. Everything jumped into sharp relief as if I were seeing with his vision, even though I was still looking through my own, no-longer-entirely-human eyes.

The first thing that came into focus was a large gray gelding taking up most of the aisle at the rear of the barn. His ears were pinned and he kept shifting his hindquarters as someone roughly tacked him up. Another person held the gelding's halter, his legs spread wide, planted like a tree and just as immovable. One of his legs was twisted oddly.

George, my favorite stable hand.

There was no sign of Keaton.

"I can't let you take him, son," George said as Dimitri and I crept down the aisle.

"It's just a stupid horse," another man snarled, rage and desperation riding his words. "I'll bring him back later."

"I ain't talking about the horse, son," he said in his whiskey-rough voice. "I'm talking about the griffin."

"What would you know?"

"I know that your eyes are like mine, normal, not tangled with that griffin you're trying to hide in a sack. That means he ain't yours to take."

"Last chance, old man," he replied, his voice hard with warning. "Get out of my way."

The man shifted around the nervous horse, face still in shadow as he ripped the girth tight with a brutal pull. The gelding threw his head back and bellowed his displeasure, one back hoof striking out and thudding into a stall door. The sharp *snap* of a breaking board competed with the man's snarled cursing. He danced aside, quick on his feet, and stepped into a patch of sunlight shining through the open back doors.

Recognition slammed into me as I took in the dark hair, the shadowed eyes, and the lines of hate carved into his face in a heartbeat. Marcos. Marcos had stolen my griffin. I couldn't let him leave. Before I could get closer, George's expression hardened with determination. He let go of the gelding and lunged forward on his bad leg, one hand outstretched for the squirming brown sack on the floor, dangerously close to the gelding's shifting, stomping hooves.

"He's mine!" Marcos roared, latching onto the old stable hand's outstretched wrist and twisting in a move Reese had demonstrated on me dozens of times. No matter how hard I tried to learn the countermove, Reese always sent me flying . . . but Reese also held back.

Marcos didn't.

George tumbled head over heels and slammed into the wall with a sickening *crack* audible even over the gelding's alarmed cry. The old man slumped to the ground, his neck at an angle that was all wrong, his faded blue eyes open and staring.

My lips parted, a scream climbing up my throat, but Dimitri clamped his hand over my mouth before a sound could escape. I tore my gaze off George as Dimitri shook his head sharply. His black-ringed eyes were wide, and the amber shone brightly as his baby dragon looked through them, no doubt summoned by the alarm stamped into Dimitri's expressive face. He pointed at himself, then the back doors of the barn. As soon as I nodded my understanding, he crept back outside, and I was alone.

No, not alone. Atticus was *right there*, and Keaton was here, somewhere. He wouldn't let me down, any more than Dimitri would.

Sucking in a slow breath, I ghosted down the aisle. Marcos was too busy staring at the stable hand's lifeless body to notice me—yet. Bloodshot eyes stared unblinking and his lips moved soundlessly. He repeated the words again and again, a little louder each time until I could hear him.

"I didn't mean to," he said, his voice shriller with each iteration.

Marcos skittered backward and slammed into the gelding's hindquarters. The poor horse decided he'd had enough. He popped up onto his back legs in a short rear, lashed out with a hoof that narrowly missed Atticus, and took off out the back doors and across the field with a trumpeting scream that sounded more like it came from a stallion than a gelding. A muffled roar erupted from the sack as Atticus decided he'd had enough too.

"Want out! Want out now!"

Another muffled roar escaped his bound beak, loud enough to set off the few horses remaining in the stalls at the far end of the barn. The chorus of nervous whinnies and nickers were enough to snap Marcos out of his shock, and he turned his back on George to scowl down at the wildly squirming sack.

"Calm down and quit acting like you didn't know I was going to save you. I told you, didn't I? I told you I'd see you soon. Because I keep my word, because you're mine, because *she doesn't deserve you!*"

Cold realization washed over me. That's what Marcos had meant when he'd said "See you soon" the last and only time we'd spoken to each other. He hadn't been talking to me—he'd been talking to my griffin, who had been looking through my eyes at the time.

"Wrong! You're wrong! Not yours, Harpy's. She's mine, I'm hers."

Marcos couldn't hear him, because his soul wasn't entangled with the griffin's—mine was. And while Atticus could hear Marcos perfectly fine, he had less than zero interest in what he was saying.

"Let me out let me out let me out!"

He shrieked and thrashed in a frantic rage, but he was unable to free himself, though at least it felt as if the drugs had burned themselves out of his system.

"I said *calm down!*" Snarling a curse when Atticus blatantly refused, Marcos whipped around and dropped to his knees next to the squirming sack. A knife flashed in the sunlight, and Dimitri wasn't there to stop me this time.

"*No!*"

A howl tore from my throat as I sprinted down the aisle, past empty stalls and through golden dust motes hanging in the still air. Marcos jerked his head up, but the swing of his knife didn't slow. Terror stole the breath from my lungs, but the knife didn't plunge into the sack— it sliced through the ropes holding the opening secure, and Atticus tumbled out into the aisle.

I took in each broken feather, each rumpled tuft of fur, the heavy binding wrapped around his beak, and the ropes tied around his paws. I saw his terror as his purple gaze snapped to mine. Relief touched his mind, and in that moment of stillness, Marcos snatched him up against his chest, one muscular arm banding around small wings and easily holding the struggling griffin.

"That's close enough, *Harpy.*" Marcos smiled. Raised the knife. Pointed the tip at one soft purple eye. Atticus froze, and so did I. At a scuff in the aisle behind him, he snapped his head around and put his back to one of the stalls so he could watch both of us. "You too, dragon rider asshole."

Dimitri stopped just inside the back doors, his hands up and empty. "Take it easy, man. Nobody else has to die."

Marcos' head twitched, as if he'd started to look at where George lay in the dirt and stopped himself. "It was an accident!"

"I know, I saw everything," Dimitri said soothingly, nothing but complete sincerity in his voice. He'd always been the charmer, the one who talked us out of trouble. "It wasn't your fault. He should've listened and gotten out of your way."

"Exactly," Marcos mumbled, his gaze drifting to George before darting back to me. "You should do the same." His hand tightened on the knife, the tip of the blade slipping that much closer to Atticus' eye. "You won't like what happens to him if you don't."

A shudder rippled down my spine at the pure venom in his voice.

"You're right, she should definitely listen to you," Dimitri said, smiling and relaxed as he took an easy step closer to Marcos, recapturing his attention. "Why don't you tell me what you want?"

"I want what was supposed to be *mine*!" The tendons in his neck stood out with the force of his bellow. "I want my griffin!"

"Of course you do . . ." Dimitri kept talking, but his words blurred into background noise as he closed the distance between them one step at a time. His gaze never dropped to the knife, but I knew his whole body was focused on it. He made it look effortless, but I could hear the fear behind his words, could see the sweat dampening his skin.

Dimitri was terrified. For me.

And then he took one step too many.

"Any closer and I'll kill him," Marcos crooned with an unsettling eagerness dripping from his voice, as if he wanted Dimitri to take that last step. "She'll die too."

Dimitri froze. The length of a single stall was all that separated them, but it might as well have been an entire barn for all that it mattered. Even if Dimitri lunged forward, there was no way he could grab the knife in time. Marcos' gaze slid toward mine and dread sank through my gut like a stone. There was a distinct lack of sanity in those cold brown eyes.

Hoofbeats sounded in the distance. Whether it was the proverbial cavalry riding to the rescue, or just an innocent rider returning to the stables, it was enough to destroy the delicate balance.

"Looks like we're out of time," Marcos said, his arm tightening around Atticus. "I'd just kill *you* if I could, Harpy, but it doesn't work like that, does it? No, kill the rider, kill the griffin." His head tilted in that predatory way that held nothing of the griffin in it. "But it's not always the other way around is it?"

"*He's right*," Atticus said. "*Griffins sneakier than dragons. Can save riders.*"

My griffin never looked away from me. Not once. There was so much love, so much trust, so much *terror* in his eyes. But his voice was steady.

"*Save Harpy. Sever?*"

Everything stopped.

And then I dropped every barrier between us, threw the bond wide open, and roared my denial with my entire soul.

"*NO!*" My heart thundered in my ears, and I could no longer separate my terror from my griffin's. If Atticus severed the bond, he wouldn't take me with him when he died, but I shook my head over and over. "No, no, no. Don't you dare."

"*Love Harpy.*"

But it wasn't just quiet words he whispered into my mind, it was an outpouring of wild emotion and memories. The joy he felt when he leaped into the air and I caught him, his contentment when my arms wrapped around him, his love for me from the moment his eyes first met mine. I felt it all in the space between the rapid beat of our hearts.

"Don't do this," I begged, tears pouring down my face. "Please don't do this."

"Sorry, *Harpy*," Marco said with a deranged laugh. "But if I can't have him . . ."

Marcos thought I was talking to him. I wasn't.

My gaze never left my griffin's. Not when Dimitri tensed, every muscle in his body ready to act, not when Marcos' wild eyes burned into mine, not even when he raised the knife high, blade glinting in the hazy sunlight. I kept my gaze on the other half of my soul and begged him not to go.

"*Don't sever, Atticus. Don't leave me alone.*"

"*Atticus stupid name,*" he whispered, winking one purple eye at me as steely resolve flared bright. My heart shattered.

Marcos smiled. "No one can."

The knife started to move.

My griffin dug mental claws into the bond.

And Keaton rushed out of the shadows with a roar.

All three of them went down in a tangle of limbs. My griffin let out a muffled squawk and scrambled away, little wings beating against the ground, strands of hay and puffs of dust kicking into the air with each frantic beat. Keaton and Marcos struggled for control of the knife, rolling down the aisle, first one on top then the other.

I was frozen, unable to move while my griffin held our bond so tightly, a claw's breadth from severing it forever . . . but Dimitri wasn't bound, and he exploded into motion, lunging forward to help. Before he reached them, a strangled scream split the air, and they stopped struggling. Fear stabbed into what was left of my heart. Neither man moved.

Dimitri grabbed Marcos by the back of his shirt and hauled him off Keaton. Dark red stained Keaton's PT shirt, but the knife had been driven into Marcos' chest. Marcos weakly clutched at the hilt, but his fingers fell slack before he pulled more than an inch of bloody blade free. His head lolled, eyes searching, desperate and lost and afraid.

"Mine . . ." His breath rattled in his chest and he stilled, his gaze open and staring at my griffin.

Carefully, oh so carefully, those mental claws slid out of our bond, leaving it intact, whole if slightly torn. It would heal. And so would we. I dropped to my knees next to my griffin with no memory of taking the steps between. Dimitri was there in the next instant, a small pocket knife at the ready. His hands were steady where mine were shaking too badly to be any use. He cut my griffin free and then I had an armful of fur and feathers, trembling just as badly as I was.

"HarpyHarpyHarpyHarpy!"

I cradled him against my chest and buried my face in his feathers, breathing in his sun-warmed cinnamon scent and fighting for control.

"You're right." My mental voice wavered. *"Atticus is a stupid name."*

Dimitri sat next to me, rested a comforting hand against my back, and I lost it. My whole body shook with the force of my sobs, and my griffin keened and purred and did everything he could to burrow deeper into my arms. I wrapped myself around him and let my tears soak into his feathers.

"You're okay, you're both okay," Dimitri murmured as he stroked my back.

"You're still an asshole," I mumbled without raising my head, but I blindly reached out with one hand and he gripped it tight. Just like he used to when I was homesick and scared.

"I know, hotshot. I know."

He wasn't forgiven. I might *never* forgive him, but I could forget, if only for a few moments. Eventually, I lifted my head and wiped away the tears, searching for Keaton, who hadn't made a sound this entire time. I found him sitting next to the body of his friend, his shoulders bowed with grief. His amber gaze flicked up to mine.

"Thank you," I whispered.

He nodded once, and we both pretended I couldn't see the tears running down his face.

✢ ✢ ✢

There were questions. So many questions.

The relay races had ended not long after our deadly confrontation with Marcos. Instructors, students, and bonded alike had flooded back to the academy, escorting the triumphant Bravo Clutch to their victory feast. The discovery of two dead bodies in the stables had put a damper on things, and Commandants Pulaski and Iverson had been quick to separate all of us for questioning.

That order didn't include separating me from my traumatized griffin. Neither of us would've allowed it, and nobody was stupid enough to try. I talked myself hoarse during those long hours, my griffin huddled in my lap the entire time. I had no idea where the guys had been taken, but I was escorted to the hatchery, where a Maven—not the one who'd been drugged—could look over my griffin.

Commandant Pulaski herself had handled my interrogation, that iron-willed woman sitting in the warm sands next to me without a moment's hesitation. While her expression had remained impassive, a sort of horrified sympathy had lurked in the back of her green eyes, which had brightened halfway through as her griffin took an interest in the discussion. Even though I had her sympathy, she didn't let it affect her bearing, and her questions were brutally direct and probing and uncomfortable.

On, and on, the questions went, round and round until my head spun and my eyes drooped with weariness.

It helped when the griffin Maven had woken up and confirmed Marcos had drugged her—with her favorite cookies, no less.

It helped more when Dimitri's dragon, Riven, woke up from his nap and "spoke" with Commandant Iverson's dragon. His testimony counted more than anyone else's, even my griffin, because griffins would lie for their riders in a heartbeat, out of mischief as much as loyalty.

Dragons didn't even understand the concept of lying.

The black hatchling had witnessed everything that happened in the stables through Dimitri's eyes, and while he was too young for words, Tiberius was able to glean enough from his mind to confirm our stories. And our innocence.

We were finally released, long after darkness had fallen.

I stepped out of the hatchery, tilted my head back to the sky, and took a moment to just breathe.

Marcos had timed his kidnapping attempt well.

The griffin relay race was a "mandatory fun" event. The academy had emptied out rapidly, with very few left behind, and almost nobody to interfere.

If it hadn't been for George delaying Marcos, he would've gotten away with my griffin. If it hadn't been for Dimitri distracting Marcos, Keaton wouldn't have been able to sneak into the stable unseen. And if it hadn't been for Keaton tackling Marcos... my griffin would've died.

My arms tightened around my griffin, and he sleepily nuzzled my chest.

"*Still here, still alive, still with you.*" His purr was constant, steady, threading between and around his murmured reassurance.

George wasn't. Sorrow ricocheted through the bond. My sorrow, my griffin's sorrow. Not magnified, but shared. I sent up a silent prayer laced with gratitude to the old stable hand, and sighed.

"Let's go home."

Arms burning with effort, I carried my griffin across the empty quad with only a few tentative *chirrups* from early crickets as company and the moon to light my way. I didn't hesitate when I hit the path leading up to the barracks. If I paused for even a second, Keaton really would find me curled up in a ball on the ground tomorrow.

While it was after curfew, muffled shouts and laughter rang out from the various dormitories and barracks, and the newly rebuilt Bravo barracks was still lit as they celebrated their victory in the races. My whole body was shaking with fatigue by the time I made it up to Echo, and I pushed open the door with one hip. Or at least, I tried. I couldn't quite manage to get the door open, not without letting go of my griffin, and that wasn't going to happen any time soon. Maybe not ever.

Before I could do something ridiculous like cry, or scream my frustration, Elias ripped open the door. His eyes widened an instant before a relieved grin creased his face.

"Harpy! Thank fuck." He yanked the door wider and bellowed over his shoulder. "Hey guys, Harpy and Atticus are back!"

Out of all the imagined reactions of my clutchmates, somehow, outright concern and relief had never crossed my mind. There were happy shouts, and grins, and everyone was talking at once. Even Langston gave me a nod and what almost looked like a smile.

It was overwhelming... and amazing.

Griffins slunk between their riders, eager to see their clutchmate, but none was more enthusiastic or relieved than Tavi. He stretched up on his back paws and nuzzled my griffin as I carried him toward our bunk.

"Nest," my griffin said in a tired mumble. I guess I was letting him go sooner than I wanted, but if he wanted his nest, he was getting his nest. The instant I set him down, Tavi hopped in and curled up around him, one wing spread over his clutchmate like a blanket. Within seconds, both griffins were soundly asleep.

Everyone crowded around my bunk, eager to hear what had happened, but Matthews of all people bulled her way to the front.

"Save it, assholes," she said firmly. When there were protests, she glared at our clutchmates. "Look at her! She ran the ruck trail with us, then dealt with all that crap. The girl needs a shower and fresh clothes. Then you can grill her for all the details Keaton left out."

"But..." My gaze shot to my griffin, and Hawthorne stepped forward and positioned himself like a guard in front of the nest.

"Nobody will touch him," he said in a quiet rumble. "You have my word."

"And mine," Reese said gruffly.

"Mine too," Elias chimed in. As the rest of my clutchmates murmured agreement, the lanky cadet sprawled on the floor next to the nest and gave me a wink. "We'll watch him, Harpy. Go get clean. For our sake if nothing else."

I rolled my eyes when he wrinkled his nose, but he wasn't wrong. After the day I'd had, I could barely stand my own stink. The sour tang of sweat and fear and just a little horse manure hit my nose, and abruptly I wanted to claw my skin off. Before I could so much as twitch, Bex was digging through my locker for a clean set of PT gear, and Matthews was gathering up my shower supplies. Both girls escorted me to the bathroom and set everything up before leaving me to get clean.

Showering was heaven, and fresh clothes were the best thing ever.

The second I collapsed onto my bunk, everyone gathered around again expectantly. I hesitated, but judging by the shadows in their eyes, they already knew about Marcos. Keaton must have told them, though he was nowhere in sight. I told them everything, sipping steadily at the water Bex had given me, and munching on the snacks Elias and Reese had snitched from the chow hall for me.

Somber silence fell when I was done, and my gaze went back to my griffin. I watched the steady rise and fall of his chest, needing the reassurance that he was still here, still breathing, even though I could feel him curled up in the back of my mind, warm and content. Finally, I let out a low, exhausted sigh and looked at my clutchmates.

"Where's—"

The door burst open and slammed against the wall with a *bang*. I whirled around, expecting to see Keaton's grumpy face, but it was Bethany. She charged across the barracks and barreled into me, wrapping me up in the tightest hug I'd ever experienced in my life.

"Can't. Breathe."

"Deal with it, bitch." Bethany's arms didn't loosen an inch. "Never do that again!"

I could've protested that I hadn't done anything, but I was too busy hugging her back just as tight, if not tighter. Then I had to recount the whole experience *again*. Her fiery orange eyes were by turns bright with fear and shock and rage, and I pretended not to see her lean against Elias halfway through the story. I glossed over a few details this time around, not interested in reliving everything.

Eventually, she had to sneak back to her dorm, and the rest of my clutchmates drifted off to bed. Before he ambled down the aisle to his bunk, Hawthorne gave me a slight smile.

"He's on the roof."

I took one last, reassuring look at my griffin before I slipped out of the barracks. Before I could take more than a single, weary step, Reese stepped outside and held out a flask.

"Thought you might need this," he explained with a wry, fleeting smile.

"Thanks." Alcohol probably wasn't the answer tonight, but I appreciated the gesture. Reese accurately interpreted my less than enthusiastic expression and huffed a sad laugh.

"It's not for you."

Oh.

It only took a few minutes to reach the roof, and I found Keaton sitting exactly where we'd sat last time, his head bowed. I settled next to him, held out the flask, and waited. After a few minutes, Keaton lifted red-rimmed eyes.

"Is that a peace offering or a declaration of war?" he asked, his voice a ragged, rough sound that tore at my heart.

"Neither."

I waited for him to take it, to drink. Watched as he kept drinking, far more than he should. The flask was much lighter when he passed it back, one brow quirked in silent challenge. I held his gaze, raised the flask to my lips, and tipped it up. Fiery alcohol burned a path straight to my belly, but I managed not to choke this time.

"It's an apology."

"Why are *you* sorry?" Keaton growled, snatching the flask out of my hand. It looked as if he couldn't decide between hurling it off the roof and draining it dry. In the end, he just strangled it in his hands and turned bloodshot amber eyes on me, teeth bared in a parody of a smile. "My best friend tried to kill your griffin, tried to kill you! So what the hell do you have to be sorry for, Harpy?"

There was so much anger and grief in his eyes that my own burned, as if the fire in my belly had jumped to my eyes. I swallowed hard.

"I'm sorry you had to be the one to stop him. I'm sorry you had to be the one to kill him." I held his gaze and ignored the wetness tracking down my cheeks. "And I'm sorry because you're hurting, and you lost a friend."

Slowly, the anger drained out of his gaze, leaving only heart-wrenching sadness behind.

"Fair enough," he finally said.

We sat in silence for long minutes, Keaton staring across the academy grounds while I tilted my head back and gazed at the stars. They were beautiful tonight, but my mind wouldn't stop replaying scenes from the barn. They were disjointed, out of order, but razor sharp, leaving me bleeding with each cut. I let out a shuddering breath as Marcos' hate-filled eyes flashed in my memory.

"Why did he do it?" I asked quietly. Keaton sighed.

"I talked to him a few times after you accidentally bonded Atticus. He wasn't just upset, he was obsessed." His laugh was a hollow, strained thing that held nothing of amusement. "He'd spent months forming a bond with his intended bondmate, only to have it ripped away at the last moment. It messed him up in the head."

"You buy into that magical bullshit pre-bond theory?" I glanced up at him from the corner of my eye to see if he was serious. He was. My scoff echoed in the chill air. "Bonding only happens when we look into their eyes and trigger the entanglement. Anything before that is just . . . wishful thinking. There's no magic left in this world, Keaton."

He stared. "We're literally bound soul to soul with *griffins*. We can talk mind to mind, feel what they feel, see what they see. That's magic, Harpy. There's a reason the Mavens have us handle and care for our eggs so much, there's a reason you knew something was wrong the instant you picked up Atticus' egg before he hatched . . ." He shook his head sadly. "There's a reason Marcos couldn't let him go."

I paused. There was a lot of truth to what he said beyond the obvious. I remembered my horrible reaction to finding out Zayne had bonded the green who was meant to be mine, remembered my unreasonable, completely illogical attachment to her.

Maybe there was something to the theory after all.

"But what about Bex and Langston?" My brow furrowed. "Those idiot friends of mine mixed up their eggs, but they seem fine. I mean, Langy's a dick, but I'm pretty sure he was born that way."

"I think they were okay because they had each other's griffins to fill the void. But Marcos? He had nothing." Keaton's eyes shone suspiciously bright, and it wasn't because Tavi was looking through them. "I watched my best friend spiral, and I couldn't do anything to help him." Misery stamped his features, and he sounded so damn lost. "I wasn't trying to kill him. I was just trying to save your griffin."

I was silent for a beat before the question I'd done my best to suppress burst out of me.

"But *why*?"

"Why what?"

A tendril of anger stirred, driven by an echo of fear more than anything else. The moment where I wasn't sure if Keaton was alive or dead or somewhere in between, the terror I'd felt for him and for his griffin . . . it was seared into my memory as deeply as the moment my griffin had bravely offered to sever our bond.

"Why did you risk yourself like that?" Guilt twisted through my belly much like the nausea from earlier that day, leaving me feeling just as sick. Marcos might have set events in motion, but *I* was the one who'd begged Keaton to save my griffin. I was the one who'd put him in the position of choosing between my griffin's life and his best friend's. I shook my head slowly, my eyes burning again. "I know I asked you to save him, but . . . you didn't even *like* me until recently.

You could've been killed in that fight, *Tavi* could've been killed. So *why?*"

"Because of Tavi."

My head tilted as I stared at him.

"Tavi and Atticus aren't just clutchmates—they're twins."

"What?" The two griffins *did* look nearly identical. It also explained why they were usually near each other, and Tavi's extreme reaction when we'd gotten back to the barracks.

"Same breeding pair. Atticus might be a little bigger, but Tavi's a few minutes older. He wanted to save his little brother." Keaton's gaze slid toward mine. "And I wanted to save you. You're a pain in my ass, Tavros, but you're one of mine, and I look out for my people. Just like you look out for Atticus."

Warmth bloomed in my belly and banished the guilt.

"Felix," I told him firmly. "My griffin's name is Felix."

A slow smile spread across his face. It didn't banish his grief, but it lightened it, if only for a moment.

"It's about time you called him that." He nodded in approval as the corner of his mouth kicked up in something adjacent to a smile. "Felix told the other griffins he offered to sever, and you refused. Loudly."

"Is *that* why everyone was being so . . . nice?"

"I guess they finally know where you stand." A shadow crossed his face, and his voice dropped low. "I can still hear you screaming, you know."

"So can I," I whispered hoarsely.

Keaton awkwardly patted my shoulder, drew in a breath, and hesitated, as if he wasn't sure how to say something, or if he even should. Finally, he shrugged.

"If he'd severed . . . you could've bonded a dragon, Harpy. You could've been free."

"No." Another shudder wracked my frame as the ghost of mental claws dug into the bond. "I would've followed him."

That was the thing with a severed bond. We weren't forced to follow our griffins into the dark, but that didn't mean we *couldn't*. When the sever was fresh, a raw and bleeding wound, a griffin rider could just . . . let go. After that, well. There were other ways to follow. More than half the griffin riders who survived a severed bond didn't last a year. But our griffins loved us enough to try to save us anyway.

Keaton nodded in quiet acceptance and went back to staring out into the night, his eyes seeing things, *memories*, that I couldn't.

"You don't have to sit here with me," he muttered after a few minutes.

"Yes, I do."

"Go be with your griffin, Harpy."

"Tavi has him covered." I laughed softly as I remembered what he'd done with his wing. "Literally."

"Would you quit being so damn stubborn—"

"You said I wasn't alone." I leaned my shoulder against his. "Neither are you."

After a moment, he relaxed and pressed his shoulder against mine.

"I did say that, didn't I?" He looked at the flask cradled in his hands and held it up. Amber eyes met mine. "Here's to never being alone."

He drank and passed it to me. I curled my fingers around the flask and held his gaze. He hadn't said the words like they were a toast. He'd said them like a promise. I gave him a crooked smile.

"Never alone."

CHAPTER 10

The months flew past. That impending growth spurt hit our griffins and hit hard. Felix had quickly grown too big for me to carry, but he wasn't quite big enough to carry me yet. Even though he was the size of a young horse, just like that young horse, his joints weren't ready to bear weight. He also wasn't even close to done growing, and his shoulders were already even with mine.

The Mavens had no doubt Felix would end up being the largest forest griffin of our entire year group, with Tavi only a feather's width smaller.

To my everlasting relief, the novelty of a dragon rider cadet turned accidental griffin rider faded. My clutchmates had not so subtly spread the word about my refusal to let Felix sever, and they'd made it damned clear that Marcos had brought about his own death.

It also helped that the collective attention span of the cadet population was short. People were always eager to grab onto the newest scandal, whether it was horny cadets getting caught with their pants down, another group of cadets getting caught trying and failing to find the secret entrance to an underground lair that might or might not exist, or the latest prank. Anything to distract from the grim reality of our war with Savinia.

As bonded cadets, in addition to the random lectures from shanghaied active duty riders, we were required to attend a weekly briefing where we were read into declassified battle reports. After the initial invasion push where we'd lost a wide swath of territory and people, we'd managed to hold the new border steady, but in recent months things were changing for the worse. More deep air raids like the one that had hit the academy, more massed attacks. The Savinians kept constant pressure on the front lines, eating away at our country one bite at a time. The last briefing reported the loss of territory that included Aubrewiss Lake. Strangely, they'd dug in around the lakeshore and had made no moves elsewhere along the border.

Breathing room, for now at least, but the war grew ever hungrier.

I tried not to think about graduation.

Thanks to Keaton and Elias' relentless tutoring, my marks were back up where they should be. Thanks to spending extra time in the saddle with Bex, my riding was better than ever. And thanks to Reese spending extra time throwing me around on the mat, my hand-to-hand combat was improving... slowly. But Commandant Pulaski had held firm on not allowing me to drive myself into the ground, and I could only get so far ahead in my classes.

I'd spent my first two years at the academy unbonded, bonded Felix in my third, but I wouldn't graduate in my fourth. No matter what I did, I'd be stuck here while everyone I knew and cared about went out to defend our country. Even Callum, who'd bonded last of all, would graduate next spring.

The first time I'd let my frustration get the better of me, Keaton had dragged me out to the archery range for extra practice. The repetition of putting arrows into targets helped. When I'd calmed, he'd taught me how to do better. Keaton was so good at concealing his true feelings that it wasn't until the third time he'd dragged me out that I realized it was as much for him as for me. Shooting quickly became an outlet for us both, a way for him to escape the pressures of leadership, and a way for me to do something constructive with my frustration. Our griffins would lounge under the shade of an oak, and offer snarky, entirely unhelpful commentary.

By the time the summer heat hit, our griffins were old enough to train with us. We started doing short patrols together, both on foot and horseback, and began learning the basics of scouting. Our griffins also got to experience the joys of the obstacle course and the ruck run, though the instructors were careful to work them up to the distance gradually—unlike me—so as not to strain their developing joints.

They were also old enough to fly, and the quad quickly became hazardous as young griffins tumbled through the air and across the thick grass. They were just as quickly rounded up by instructor griffins for proper lessons while their bondmates were stuck in the classroom.

One early summer morning, I was struggling to stay awake in history class. Only Adderley could make the Prisoner of War treaty between Tennessan and Savinia—a treaty that might very well keep us alive if we were ever captured—so utterly boring. The hypnotic drone of his voice was effectively putting most of us to sleep when a trilling cry of triumph echoed in my mind and startled me wide awake.

"Harpy! You've got to feel this!"

With no further warning than that, Felix gave an excited tug and pulled me into his mind. The bottom dropped out of my stomach as my mind spent a second, an eternity, in free fall. Despite practicing, I still hadn't quite mastered doing that on my own, but my precocious griffin was more than happy to make up the difference in our skill level. In fact, he took delight in doing it at the most ridiculous times.

"Felix, I'm in class—"

My breath caught. My bondmate wasn't playing a prank. He was flying. And thanks to him pulling me into his mind, so was I. Or as close as I could get.

The wind rushed over his feathers. I could *feel* it.

It had been so long...

For just an instant, my longing to fly surged beyond what I could shield from him. It was almost impossible to keep anything from him anyway, especially when we were entangled like this, but I tried. I never wanted him to feel a moment's doubt or guilt that I'd bonded him instead of a dragon.

Rather than sadness, he let out another happy trill with the slightest edge of mockery.

"I know you want to fly, silly. It's why I'll bring you with me whenever you need, Harpy!"

Felix's mental growth and his corresponding improved vocabulary over just a few short months were nothing short of amazing. *He* was amazing. I sent him a burst of love and affection and settled in to enjoy the ride as he dipped and soared. A flash of tawny brown feathers flashed in the corner of our eyes—Tavi, swooping dangerously close to his brother before darting away, enticing him to play tag.

Another griffin joined in the game, and another, until the sky became a chaotic swirl of fur and feathers, and excited trills and roars filled my ears. I could feel my lips pulling into a grin, and I held back a laugh by the thinnest margin when Felix successfully tweaked Bailey's tail.

The *thud* of a heavy textbook dropping onto my desk startled me back into my own head. I blinked my vision clear and winced as Adderley glared down at me.

"Cadet Tavros, since it seems you feel like you already know the course material and no longer need to pay attention to my lecture, allow me to assign you bonus material. I expect you to analyze this treatise on water management techniques and provide a full report along with how you think it affects our current war with our neighbors by next week." Adderley looked down his hooked nose and arched a brow. "You can present your findings to the class."

"Yes, sir," I muttered, barely holding back my dismay at the size of the text. *There goes my rest day.*

"*Sorry, Harpy,*" Felix whispered, remorse dampening his exuberance.

"*Don't be.*" I let him feel my joy at feeling the wind on my face again. "*It was worth the cost.*"

A full morning of classes and a quick lunch later, I met the rest of Echo out on the dreaded obstacle course. Lieutenant Osbourne was our instructor in utilizing our bonds, and he'd directed us to the wooden obstacles near the lowland ditch run for today's session. Once again, we were going to work on seeing through our griffin's eyes. I wasn't the only one struggling to pick up the skill. It was easy when emotions were heightened, but it needed to become as easy as breathing and about as much effort.

Lieutenant Osbourne had apparently also decided to switch tactics as well as location. He passed out blindfolds with a smile that was more than a little evil. Langston pinched his between two fingers and held it away from his body with a curled lip.

"What are these for?"

"Your face," the lieutenant replied dryly, but his brilliant turquoise eyes danced in amusement. "We need to reduce the external stimuli to make it easier for you to follow the bond."

"Huh?"

"Making sure you can't see through your own eyes will make it easier for you to find your griffin's, Langy," Elias said with exaggerated patience.

"Oh." Langston scowled. "Why didn't he just say that?"

Lieutenant Osbourne chose to ignore Langston's grumpiness and quickly passed around the rest of the blindfolds before directing us to take a seat next to our griffins. I sank down onto the sun-warmed grass, Felix sitting on one side and Keaton on my other, with Tavi on his far side.

It was still a little disconcerting to look *up* at my griffin, considering the fact that just a few short months ago he'd been small enough to curl up in my lap. Felix caught the flow of my thoughts and clacked his beak softly in amusement.

Drawing in a deep breath laced with the sweet scent of wildflowers, I tied the thick cloth around my eyes, tuned out the chatter from my clutchmates and the *buzz* of industrious insects, and searched for Felix's mind. I found him curled up in the back of mine, where he always was, but I couldn't figure out how to bridge the gap between us. It was like hitting a barrier I couldn't breach, no matter how I used the bond that entangled our souls together.

"Having trouble?" Felix asked after a few minutes, muffled laughter underlying his voice.

Behind the blindfold, my eyes flew open and narrowed. I knew that teasing tone. It meant I was missing something obvious, but I screwed my eyes shut again in a stubborn refusal to give up. When I let out a frustrated huff, Keaton leaned close and bumped my shoulder with his.

"Did you try *asking* to see through his eyes?"

"How is that different from letting him pull me in?" I growled, bumping his shoulder slightly harder than he'd bumped mine.

"Just try it, you stubborn bitch," he muttered with a smile in his voice.

"Fine." I dropped back into my mind and brushed up against Felix. *"Can I see through your eyes?"*

"Always," he purred in satisfaction.

I gasped as the barrier dropped, and I slid into his mind. Unlike the other times where he'd pulled me in, it wasn't a wild tumble, though there was still a breathless moment of free fall. My stomach swooped at the dizzying sensation before the world steadied around me.

All of my senses sharpened in an instant. The sweet scent of wildflowers gained deeper notes my nose couldn't pick up, and the quiet rustle of the breeze through the grass was razor sharp in his ears.

And then he opened his eyes.

Just as it always did, my brain struggled to adjust to the increased visual input. Griffins could see shades of color we couldn't, could see a level of detail we couldn't, could see across distances we couldn't. And this time, I didn't have the joy of flying to distract me from the sensation.

"That wasn't so hard, was it?" he said teasingly. He tilted his head so I could see myself sitting quietly next to him. My shoulders went tense as understanding hit.

"You were messing with me, weren't you, you fancy chicken!"

"Maybe," he said with a snicker before his tone sobered. *"You forgot you weren't trying to force the bond—you were trying to force* me. *The first time you tumbled into my mind, when I was lost and afraid, what did you do?"*

A shiver of remembered terror crawled across my skin, but I forced myself to shift through the memories until I found the right one. *"I asked you to let me in."*

"That's all you ever need to do, Harpy. Just ask."

I felt myself smile, watched it stretch across my face though his eyes . . . because that wasn't weird *at all*.

A sharp *clap* rang out across the field as Lieutenant Osbourne smacked his hands together. "And now for something completely different. There will be times where you need to move but your griffin needs to see for you."

"Like when?" Reese called out, a frown in his voice.

"Oh, I don't know," Lieutenant Osbourne said dryly. "Maybe when it's too dark for you to see, but you still need to do your *job* and scout an enemy encampment. Or maybe when it's too dark for you to see, but to remain in place means capture or death. Or maybe when your instructor blindfolds you, because he's bored." He paused as a round of chuckles rang out before his tone sobered. "You need to learn to move your body while your perspective is skewed."

My brow furrowed as I remembered how Felix had helped me see in the dim barn when my eyes were too blinded by the sun to make anything out.

"Can't our griffins sharpen our vision instead?"

The lieutenant stilled. His head tilted as he studied my blindfolded face.

"Some griffins can do that, yes. But that's a more advanced class. For now, how about I teach you to crawl before you try to sprint." That evil smile returned to his face. "Literally. I want everyone to get through the wooden obstacles as a warm up ... and then you're going to low crawl through the ditches while your griffins fly overhead. Good luck."

I was pretty sure our griffins weren't the only ones laughing at us as we clumsily made our way through the obstacles, because I heard the lieutenant's slightly maniacal chuckle more than once. I'd also heard he was being sent out to one of the border forts soon, so I supposed he was entitled to a little fun with us before he left.

By the time I'd gotten through the last obstacle, my knuckles were bleeding, my knees were bruised, and a decent headache was building at the base of my skull. At least this time I hadn't fallen from the apex of the wall, though I'd once again abused my ribcage on one of the log jumps when Felix blinked at the wrong moment.

It wasn't until we began our ditch run that I understood the purpose of the training exercise beyond providing Lieutenant Osbourne some entertainment. It was one thing for our griffins to slink along behind or beside us on the ground through the wooden obstacles. Quite another for them to soar overhead, to fight the wind and their wings to keep the perfect position to allow us to see where to go, what to do. The exercise was as much for them as for us, and I felt Felix's amusement fade into determination as he guided me through.

"I've got you, Harpy. I won't let you down."

"You couldn't let me down if you tried, Felix." My muscles burned as I low crawled along the twisting ditch at a steady pace, but I sent him a warm burst of pride and encouragement. *"You're doing great."*

He preened and turned his head toward his brother. Instead of seeing myself, now all I could see was Tavi, hovering over Keaton further within the maze of ditches.

"Did you hear that, you smug peacock? I'm doing great!*"*

In the next instant, the mud beneath my forearms abruptly vanished as the water deepened into a pool, and my head went under.

"Uh, oops?" Felix mumbled as chagrin burned through the bond.

"*Medium. You're doing medium.*" I spat out a mouthful of muddy water, adjusted the soggy blindfold so it was securely around my eyes again, and kept crawling to the sound of my griffin's trilling laughter.

"Remind me again why you're reading that dusty old book instead of helping us with Jasper's itchy hide?" Bethany grumbled as she rubbed oily hands along her red's wide back. Bex worked on the other side, the tips of her choppy brown hair barely visible over Jasper's spine.

Jasper was sprawled on the warm stone outside his assigned eyrie in the sun, his tail tip dangling off the ledge and his wings hanging loose on either side of his back. The academy stretched out below us, but the irritable dragon was oblivious to the view, his eyes closed and a faint snore drifting from his open maw.

Dragons didn't get short growth spurts like griffins. They grew fast and constant, and their thick hide needed daily oiling in order to keep it from splitting. Jasper, like all reds, also had narrow bands of scales running along his hide, additional armor to protect vulnerable areas, though they wouldn't harden until he reached his full growth. Already half the size of Tiberius and growing larger every day, there was a lot of hide for Bethany to oil, and I'd promised to help before I'd been slapped with an extra assignment.

"Because my griffin doesn't think the rules apply to him," I grumbled though a smile tugged at my face at the memory of flight.

"*I do what I want,*" he said in amused agreement, even as misery pulsed along the bond.

Felix sat next to Jasper's head, beak buried in one wing as he preened old feathers. Merlin sat on his other side working on his own wings. Like every griffin in Echo, they were going through their first molt and were nearly as itchy as Jasper. In fact, I was fairly certain they'd all bonded over their shared misery, despite their inability to communicate, because the fierce red wouldn't let anyone else that close to his face.

"Also, my history instructor is a jerk," I added as I glowered at the thick book in my lap.

"You've got Adderley, right?" Bex rolled her eyes as she drizzled more oil over Jasper's hide. "That man has a stick so far up his ass I'm amazed he isn't spitting out splinters when he talks."

I snorted a laugh and went back to reading. I could only manage a paragraph or two at a time before I lost focus. Whoever had written the treatise was also a jerk. I paused, checked the first page, and snorted a laugh. Adderley had written it himself, because of *course* he had, which meant I couldn't bullshit my way through my report. Determination thrummed through me as I flipped back to the last page I'd read. I couldn't allow my marks to slip, not now that I'd finally crawled out of the hole. Adderley would *not* delay my graduation any further than it already was.

After a few minutes of working in companionable silence, Bethany cleared her throat. My shoulders tensed at the pointed sound, because she only did that when she was about to stick her nose where it didn't belong.

"What?" I asked warily.

"Not that it's any of my business—"

"It's not," I said flatly.

"—but I heard that you shut Dimitri out again. I thought . . ." She waited until I looked up at her, and her fiery orange eyes softened in concern. "I thought you guys patched things up after he helped rescue Felix from that psychopath."

My fingers clenched around the edges of the book, and I dropped my gaze.

"More like it was a temporary truce."

"He won't say it, because he's an idiot, but he misses you." She snorted softly. "It's painfully obvious. Why not put him out of his misery?"

"Because I haven't forgiven him." I stared down at the open page, unable to read a single word. "I don't know if I can."

"Girl, it would help if you let him apologize," she said in exasperation.

"It's not the apology that's the problem." I flexed my hand. "The last time he tried, there was so much pity in his eyes that I wanted to break my fist against his stupid face. Every time I've seen him since, it's still there. I can't . . . I can't deal with it."

"It's not pity—"

I shot her a look and she had the grace to wince.

"Okay, fine. It's pity, and regret, and a metric fuckton of guilt." Bethany wiped her hands on a cloth, slid off Jasper's back, and walked over to rest a hand on my shoulder. "But Harper . . . it's been months, and you know he didn't mean for any of this to happen. None of those morons did."

"I know," I said hoarsely, painfully aware of how still Felix had fallen. I turned to him, and laughter burst out of me, banishing the toxic sorrow. My griffin had frozen with one wing awkwardly outstretched, an old feather sticking out of his beak. "You look ridiculous."

Felix spat out the feather. *"Do not."*

He turned his back on me, tail lashing the ground, and went back to teasing out the old, itchy feathers. Bethany grinned, but my laughter faded.

"It's not Dimitri I need to see right now. It's Zayne."

"That's not a bad idea, but . . ." She crouched down next to me, orange eyes searching mine. "You know you're not like Marcos, right?"

"I know." But I didn't know, not really. And until I'd spoken with Zayne and faced up to the fact that he'd bonded the green dragon, *my* green dragon, I couldn't be sure that I wouldn't break like Marcos had. At the doubt I was unable to hide, Bethany narrowed her eyes.

"Harper Tavros, you listen to me right now—you're *nothing* like that psychopath. Go see Zayne if you need to, forgive him if you can, but I know you. You wouldn't hurt him anymore than you would hurt your griffin." She squeezed my shoulder gently. "You don't have to do it today."

"If I don't do it now, I might chicken out." I cleared my throat. "Again. Besides, it's either today or after we get back from our first scouting patrol."

Bethany sighed wistfully.

"I can't believe you guys will be gone all week. I'll miss you both."

"You mean you'll miss Elias," Bex called out with a teasing laugh.

"Maybe." Her smirk was positively wicked. "The things that boy can do with his—"

I slapped a hand over her mouth. "Finish that sentence and I will *vomit* on you."

As much as I teased Bethany, she handled her relationship exactly as required by the regulations. It helped that from day one at the academy, the instructors had made their conduct expectations clear— while on duty, we were sisters among brothers.

So while they were on duty, Bethany and Elias were utterly professional.

Off duty was another matter. Hence, vomiting.

Jasper grumbled low in his chest, the deep sound vibrating through my bones. One orange eye cracked open, and he gave his bondmate a glare as he pointedly stuck out a back leg. Bethany rolled her eyes, grabbed the pot, and dumped a ridiculous amount of oil on his red hide. It was highly entertaining watching her expressions change as she mentally conversed with her rapidly growing dragon. A snicker escaped me as I wondered if *I* looked that ridiculous when I talked with Felix.

"You do."

"Thanks, featherhead."

Jasper let out a pleased grunt when Bethany worked her fingers under the swath of scales running along the leg, and he shut his eyes again. She gazed at her bondmate, her normally fierce expression almost painfully tender, before she glanced back at me.

"Zayne should be on the dragon rider campus this afternoon. You know him, always studying."

"I remember." I sighed. "But first, I need to finish reading this incredibly light and entertaining treatise on..." I flipped back to the cover and squinted at the handwritten title. "*Conflict drivers: Water management techniques during periods of low rainfall and the impact on socioeconomics and population count.* And then put together a verbal report for class tomorrow."

"Yikes." Bethany winced. "That sounds about as delightful as the paper Callum had to do on the differences between Tennessan's elected civilian government and Savinia's hereditary lordship system after he mouthed off to the poli sci instructor."

"I'd help you if I could, but I'm terrible at public speaking. My words get all tangled up." Bex moved around Jasper's bulk to Merlin and scratched his neck feathers with a rueful grin. "Maybe it's a good thing I ended up a mountain griffin rider. No verbal reporting required."

"Gee." Bethany arched a pointed brow. "If only we knew someone who *is* good with that sort of thing."

"I'm more likely to punch Zayne in the face than ask for his help," I said wryly. Mischief danced in her gaze as she grinned down at me.

"Aim for the nose. It makes such a lovely sound when it breaks."

Later that afternoon, I stood just outside the dragon rider campus, my feet firmly rooted to the path. Behind me, the quad was full of cadets enjoying a lazy rest day, but their raucous shouts and laughter washed over me without touching me. I couldn't seem to convince my feet to move. There were no rules against griffin riders being on the dragon rider campus or vice versa, but a part of me wasn't ready to face my old stomping grounds—or my old classmates. I didn't want to see the satisfaction, didn't want to deal with the pity. It was why I couldn't stand to be around Dimitri, even though I missed his stupid ass . . . even though he'd helped save Felix's life. Saved my life.

"Are you sure you don't want me to come with you?" Felix murmured in my mind as a phantom sensation of fur and feathers brushed against me in comfort.

"I'm sure. Go tweak Tavi's tail. He's getting too serious for his own good."

Drawing in a deep breath, I walked through the dragon gates for the first time since I'd bonded Felix. There were a few wolf whistles, and one loudly grumbled, "Harper Tavros is back?" but most didn't give a shit, and I was perfectly happy that way.

The campus was only lightly populated today, and I strode down the deserted path toward the library. If Zayne was still studying, he'd be in one of the private rooms in the back. My steps slowed of their own volition as I neared the ancient building. The griffin rider campus had their own library, of course, but it was nothing like this one. Ours might be newer, but this one had a sense of permanence to it that ours lacked.

There were rumors that the library was older than the academy, that the academy had been built *around* the library—and the hatchery. Lending credence to the rumor, both buildings were made of the same material, a harder-than-stone duracrete we could no longer replicate. And just like the hatchery, the library had the same small square panels at the doors. While their magic was long since lost, the library endured.

I had a feeling it would survive the destruction of the academy, if it came to that.

Hauling open the reinforced steel door, I strode inside. The slightly musty scent of old books slapped me in the face, and a smile danced on my lips. I'd always loved that smell, boring old treatises on water management aside. Sunlight streamed through the high windows, highlighting the dust motes hanging in the still air, and cadets sat at tables and wandered through the stacks under the watchful gaze of the Librarian.

Nobody knew her actual name, everybody feared her wrath. And rightly so, because many of the books contained in this library were completely unique and utterly irreplaceable.

Her dark gaze briefly landed on mine. With a single glance, she managed to convey that she remembered me, had no issues with a griffin rider in her library, and expected me to follow the rules. Or else. I dipped my head in a respectful nod, and headed for the back, trying not to look as if I were moving too quickly... even though a part of me very much wanted to run away from her eagle-eyed gaze.

I checked all the private study rooms, but while they were occupied, none of them had the tall, broad-shouldered, gold-shot green-eyed cadet I was looking for. My fingers tapped against my leg as I wracked my brain. A slow smile crossed my face. If Zayne hadn't been able to get one of the study rooms, there was only one other place he would be. Unless things had changed more than I thought possible...

Suppressing a nervous flutter in my belly, I walked back out of the library at a sedate pace, giving the Librarian ample time to note that I wasn't trying to sneak out any of her precious books under my shirt. That same rule had never seemed to apply to Zayne. We'd always teased him that his special privileges were because he was a general's son, but the truth was the Librarian had a sweet spot for quiet, studious young men who preferred books to fighting.

The late afternoon sun beat down on my head as I walked around to the back of the library, where a small weeping willow was kept meticulously trimmed. The drooping branches provided ample shade for the wide ring of wooden benches encircling the trunk. Sure enough, Zayne lounged on one, his back propped up against the smooth bark of the willow and his nose buried in a thick book like the one I'd just finished slogging through.

For a moment, I stood in the shadow of the library, studying his face. He *had* changed, the rounded lines of his face a little sharper, muscles a little bigger... but even though the color of his eyes had also changed when he'd bonded, the quiet pleasure in them when he was reading hadn't.

A curl of mischief stirred in my soul, and I felt Felix ease forward in response. A single glance out of my eyes, and he retreated, snickering his approval. Zayne was so lost in his book that I managed to ghost across the courtyard and sit on the bench without disturbing him.

My head tilted, and I leaned in close enough to whisper in his ear. "Boo."

"*Fuck!*" He startled, dropping the book onto the ground with a muffled *thud* before he pinned me with a wide-eyed stare. "Holy shit, Harper. When the hell did you get so sneaky?"

"When I bonded a griffin," I said dryly as I leaned down and picked the book up. Carefully, I dusted it off and handed it back, one brow arched high. "Don't let the Librarian see you mistreating her children like that."

"She'd skin me alive." Zayne shuddered before he set it aside and stared at me. He seemed at a loss.

I searched his green-and-gold eyes, the eyes that he'd gained when he'd bonded the green who'd been meant for *me*. But no matter how I poked and prodded at my brain, there was no murderous rage, no sudden urge to kidnap a dragon who was bigger than a horse by this point.

As I stared at him, the furrow in his brow deepened. "Harper, what—"

"This is going to sound dumb, but I needed . . . I needed to see if I would break." I swallowed hard and admitted, "I almost did when I saw *her*."

Zayne stiffened before remorse stamped his features. He sighed.

"For what it's worth, I'm not sure you know how to break."

"For what it's worth, I'm glad it was you who bonded her."

Awkward silence settled over us, broken only by the chirps of the birds nesting in the tree and the playful roar of a dragon soaring overhead. The green branches of the willow swayed around us, providing not just shade from the hot sun, but a shield from the rest of the academy. I could see why Zayne had always liked to read out here. It was almost magical, like we were a step removed from the world. A safe place. One where I was brave enough to finally say the words that had eaten at me for long months and a short eternity.

"Whose idea was it to switch the eggs?"

The question landed between us like an unexploded firebomb. The answer could be a complete dud, or it could burn what was left of our friendship to the ground. Zayne twisted slightly on the bench, his shoulder brushing mine before he settled again, facing me dead on and unafraid. The peacemaker of our group, the one who'd always mended the broken bonds between us. I just wasn't sure he could manage it this time. I wasn't sure if I even wanted him to try.

"I'll tell you whatever you want to know, but you have to promise me one thing."

My eyes narrowed. "What?"

"You have to listen to all of it." He waited for my nod of agreement before he continued. "It was Callum's idea." He let out a slight huff of laughter. "You really pissed him off with the itching powder in his best flying leathers."

"He deserved it for switching out *my* flying leathers with progressively smaller sets so I'd think I was gaining weight," I said tartly, but Zayne smirked.

"He was really proud of himself for that one. If Bethany hadn't caught him in your room you might not have figured it out as quick." He rolled his eyes and pointedly jabbed me in the ribs. "I can't believe you fell for it in the first place. As if any of us could get fat with the crap they feed us. Remember those awful casseroles a few months ago?"

"So much sadness," I agreed with a shudder. "Not to mention all the exercise. Still, he had me going for a while there. Any tighter and the seams of my leather pants would've popped."

"I'm pretty sure Dimitri didn't mind the view." Zayne roared a laugh as heat swept across my face. I shoved him, and for just a moment, it was as if nothing had changed and no time had passed. But his laughter faded quickly and was replaced by shame. "It might have been Callum's idea . . . but I figured out how to do it."

"You always were the smart one." I hesitated, wasn't sure I wanted to know, but the words tumbled out on their own. "Who switched them?"

Zayne briefly shut his eyes. Drew in a deep breath. And said exactly what I'd thought he would.

"Dimitri."

My hands curled into fists. Of course it was him. Of *course* it was. That charismatic bastard was the one who'd made so many of Callum's ideas and Zayne's plans work. Rage and betrayal stirred, the wounds still raw and barely scabbed over, and I squeezed my eyes shut to fight back the burn of tears. Maybe this had been a bad idea.

Felix brushed against my soul. *"Be brave."*

"Harper."

Reluctantly, I opened my eyes again and found Zayne staring at me with a familiar mulish expression. The one that meant he was determined to get me to listen, even when I didn't want to. I sighed.

"What?"

"He doesn't feel guilty for switching the eggs so much as for not standing his ground."

My brow furrowed. "Okay, more words please."

"He said no, Harper. When Callum first came up with the idea, he said *no*. Too risky, too dangerous, too likely to backfire. And it did, fuck did it ever." Zayne shook his head slowly as his look of shame intensified into something bone deep, soul deep. "But then I figured out how to do it because . . ."

"Because you're like a dog with a bone." I gave him a fleeting smile. "Never found a puzzle you didn't want to solve, and Callum dangled it like bait in front of your nose. Didn't he?"

"Maybe." He sighed. "So there we were, with an idea, and a plan, but Dimitri still said no . . . and then you and Dimitri had a fight."

Cold spiraled through me. I remembered that fight. It had been a stupid, nothing little argument. The kind we always had when one of us got a little too arrogant, a little too competitive. I couldn't even remember what had started it, but I remembered I'd won, something that only rarely happened, because that boy could charm a snake when he put his mind to it. I remembered how he'd smiled, how mischief had gleamed in his eyes before he sauntered away. I remembered what he'd called back over his shoulder.

Just you wait, hotshot. I'll win the next round.

I shot to my feet and stared down at Zayne as my heartbeat thundered in my ears.

"You're telling me you guys screwed with my egg, with my *future*, because Dimitri actually lost an argument with me *for once*?" My laugh echoed off the willow branches, full of bitter disbelief and pain. It took effort to cut it off, and my voice came out slightly higher pitched and far more vulnerable than I wanted. "Okay, well this has been fun, but I think I need to get going. Lots of studying to do, you know how it is."

Zayne's hand snapped out and wrapped around my wrist before I could walk away. "You promised to listen to all of it."

I wrenched my arm free. "Yeah, well, you guys promised you'd always have my back, and look how that turned out."

Zayne's face hardened, and then his eyes brightened as his dragon peered out through them. I couldn't look away. Slowly, I let my breath out, blinked back another surge of tears because I'd be damned before I let either of them see me break, and turned on my heel. I ducked out from beneath the willow branches and made it halfway across the courtyard before Zayne called after me.

"Don't you want to know what I named her?"

"*No,*" I replied without slowing.

"Cassia."

The name hung in the air, something entirely breakable, entirely precious. I froze in my tracks, wrapped my arms around my belly. He'd kept it. He'd kept the name I'd picked out for her. A tremor shook my whole body, and Felix surged forward. Slowly, I turned back around.

Griffin eyes met dragon eyes.

"Why?" Instead of aggressive like I wanted, the word came out plaintive, almost begging. I desperately wanted, no, *needed* to understand. At the same time, I wanted to run fast and far, until his voice was nothing more than a distant memory.

Zayne stepped closer cautiously, as if well aware I was poised to run. "We discussed it, but Cal was stuck with grays. And then Dimitri was offered the black. I was the only one who had a chance."

"What chance?" Felix purred within my mind, steadying me, giving me the strength to stand there and listen to all of it. Like I'd promised.

"The chance to change my specialization." Another step closer. "The chance to make things up to you, to protect what should've been yours, to fix our mistake. Dimitri and Cal are too good at fighting, they weren't going to let them go to greens, but me?"

Zayne's laugh rang across the courtyard, sharp with self-deprecation. While it was true he'd never been the best fighter in our group, he'd always been the best rider. Even better than me.

"You wanted to save people." Another step, and he stood in front of me, eyes burning bright with his dragon, with *Cassia,* and with something else—determination. "I figured that was a hell of a thing to live up to, but I could try. I had to try."

I scowled. "For me?"

He shook his head. "No, for me."

Silence again. It wasn't awkward this time or fragile, but it was heavy, and I wanted to move, if only to shed its weight. But I'd given my word to listen, even if I'd almost broken it out of self-preservation, and my feet wouldn't move until I'd made sure I'd kept my promise.

"Can I go now?" I swallowed hard but managed to hold his gaze. "Is that everything?"

"Just one more thing." Zayne forced a smile. "I won't speak for the other two, because whether they fix things with you or not is up to them. But for what it's worth, I'm sorry, Harper." His voice was raw, honest, *shredded*. "Forgive me?"

Zayne held out his hand and waited. I pretended I couldn't see how his fingers shook, and he pretended he couldn't see the tears running down my cheeks.

I took his hand.

His fingers wrapped around mine and a smile broke out across his face, bright as the sun.

"Now that we're friends again—"

"We are?"

"—did you want help with Adderley's assignment?" His smile widened at my confused expression. "Bethany relayed through our dragons a few hours ago. I already read his water management book."

"Of course you have," I murmured, the beginnings of my own smile banishing the tears. He dragged me back to the willow bench as he rattled off a list of key talking points.

"...don't forget the change in weather patterns and the ten-year drought after the Sea Burn War, the death of the oceans, the quakes that destroyed or destabilized a lot of the dams and shifted riverbeds out of Savinia, and their crop failures as a result."

Zayne picked up a notebook and scanned his chaotic notes before he tossed it back on the bench and kept talking. Shaking my head at his enthusiasm, I shifted aside the heavy book he'd been reading when I'd first walked up so I could sit next to him. Absently, I turned it over to look at the title—and froze. *Conflict Drivers: Water management techniques during periods of low rainfall, and the impact on socioeconomics and population count.* He'd checked out the second copy and read it *today*, without knowing if I'd forgive him or accept his help.

"Tennessan, of course, has the biggest river on the continent flowing through it, not to mention our mountain lakes and rivers—"

I tackled Zayne in a hug.

CHAPTER 11

Public speaking was the absolute worst.

I'd rather clean out stalls for a week. I'd even take cleaning out latrines over public speaking. Not with my own toothbrush, of course. There were limits.

Thanks to Zayne's help, I muddled through my presentation, mostly keeping the dry facts and figures straight, and nailing his key talking points. My classmates' eyes had fully glazed over, and one skinny guy in the back was snoring, by the time I wrapped up.

"There were other factors at play, but it can be argued that the drought and the loss of old water-management techniques paved the way for our current conflict with Savinia."

I swallowed hard as flashes of the night air raid filled my mental vision. Flickering flames raged, tattered wings flared wide. The acidic burn of smoke tickled my throat, a defiant roar filled my ears. My jaw tightened, and I shook off the memory of blood-smeared gray scales and brilliant sunset eyes and retook my seat.

Adderley gave me a slight nod of approval.

"Acceptable, Cadet Tavros. To avoid a repeat of this painful exercise, I suggest that in the future, you don't let your griffin steal your attention from where it belongs."

A sharp *clang* rang throughout the building, signaling the end of the current period. The skinny guy startled awake, and everyone stirred in anticipation of being dismissed. Our history professor was lost to dark thoughts though and didn't seem to hear it.

"War destroyed the old world," he said in a low voice, more as if he were talking to himself than his class. "If we're not careful, it'll destroy this one too."

My feet itched to move, to run. I'd known I'd be late to meet Echo at the stables thanks to my class schedule being slightly skewed from theirs, and I'd planned for it. My gear had been packed this morning before dawn's light kissed the horizon, and Keaton had promised to bring it with his own gear. That didn't mean I had time to loiter in the classroom after the bell rang. As it was, I'd have to run all the way to the stables.

I gently cleared my throat, and Adderley's gaze snapped back into focus.

"Dismissed."

The humid summer air slapped me in the face like a wet cloth as I sprinted outside, and my lungs spasmed in protest before they adjusted. By the time I burst out of the griffin gates and into the expansive quad at the center of the academy, sweat rolled down my face and trickled down my spine—but my breath was steady, and I ran easily.

Lieutenant Osbourne had been right. I'd adjusted.

I wove my way between a gaggle of untracked first-year cadets, and cut around a tight formation of dragon rider cadets marching toward the chow hall. Their faces flashed by, some familiar, some not.

One of the girls shouted after me with a laugh. "Where's the fire, Harper?"

"Stupid late," I shouted back without slowing. "Can't stop to chat! Enjoy the casserole!"

A chorus of groans chased after me, and a grin stretched across my face even as I stretched my legs out into a full sprint. I actually had no idea what was on the lunch menu for the day, but it was fun messing with them. Felix snickered in approval.

"Harpy should run faster, or the next joke will be on you."

My grin died. I had no idea what that meant, but the muffled laughter underlying his words spelled nothing but trouble—for me.

My legs ate up the mile to the stables in seven minutes flat. I ran past the fields, and the paddocks, and the arenas. All empty. My steps didn't slow until I hit the barns. The *quiet* barns. The only time they were that quiet...was when most of the horses had already been checked out.

Apprehension twisted low in my belly. Echo wasn't the only clutch going out on their first long scouting run this week. We were just the last. And thanks to my tardiness, I was the last of all. *Damn it.*

My clutchmates were already out in the stable yard, horses tacked up and gear neatly rolled up behind each saddle. Their griffins sat off to the side, or slunk through the yard, or tussled with each other. The academy's horses were well used to the antics of griffins and stood placidly, tails swishing to keep the buzzing flies at bay. Rumor had it the Mavens had a hand in their breeding, while the stable hands maintained it was just a matter acclimating them to the predators in their midst while they were young. Whether it was one or the other, or maybe a little of both, the academy horses never seemed to have a problem with even the dragons, who would absolutely eat one if given half the chance.

As I dashed up, sweaty but not out of breath, Keaton grinned and tossed over my gear.

"Took you long enough."

"Shut up," I muttered, slinging my bag over one shoulder. "Adderley was in one of his moods again."

As I glanced around the yard, Elias passed his reins over to Reese and strode over to me with an unhappy expression. My apprehension deepened into alarm. I'd asked Elias to get a decent horse for me, but all of the horses already had a rider.

"Elias, which one is mine?"

"Um, about that . . ."

Elias rubbed the back of his neck and looked vaguely guilty. Felix though? That featherhead laughed his tail off as a weathered old stable hand led a chestnut pony out of the barn. A very familiar chestnut pony with a white face blaze and a perfect white stocking on his back left leg.

"No. *Hells* no." I crossed my arms and shook my head firmly. "I am *not* riding Buster."

An hour later, Reese glanced over his shoulder with a wide grin. "How you hanging in there, Harpy?"

My teeth hurt from gritting them so tightly together, my spine ached, my thighs burned from posting every time we picked up the pace to a trot, and my ass was no longer on speaking terms with the rest of me.

"I'm doing *great*," I said sarcastically.

Reese roared a laugh at my miserable expression, but Elias glanced back from his spot next in line with a wince. He'd felt so bad about me getting stuck with Buster that he'd offered to trade mounts, but the lanky cadet had more than six inches of height on me. There was no way he could comfortably ride a pony Buster's size, even if his weight wasn't a factor.

At the head of the line of horses and griffins, Keaton picked up a trot again, and I bit back a groan as the others followed suit.

"Poor Harpy," Reese said as he easily sat his bay mare's smooth trot. "Sucks there weren't any other horses left."

"You could've taken him," I growled as I forced my legs to post, because there was no sitting Buster's trot. "You're barely taller than me."

That earned me a dry look. "Do I look dumb to you?"

"Do you want me to answer that?" Elias called back with a laugh.

"No."

Despite the little chestnut gelding doing his earnest best to drive my spine into my skull, riding was still my happy place, and something deep in my soul relaxed as we rode down the quiet trail.

The day was perfect—warm sun overhead, a decent breeze to keep the bugs to a minimum, and shade from the surrounding trees. This close to the academy, the trail was well-maintained, with room for two riders abreast . . . or a rider and a griffin. Once again, I was at the back of the formation, but this time it wasn't because I was the slowest. It was because I was the most experienced rider, and Keaton had asked me to bring up the rear so I could keep an eye on everyone.

Our orders were to ride out to the Alpha Training Grounds, specifically Base Camp Two, where we'd meet with Lieutenant Osbourne for further instructions. If we were lucky, Charlie and Delta Clutch would still be there. If we were really lucky, the other cadets would have everything set up by the time we finished the three-hour ride.

I'd just finished my unappetizing ration bar, which still beat a casserole of sadness any day, when the brush rustled deeper in the forest. My head snapped around, and my eyes widened when I caught sight of something large moving through the trees. Large, brown, and *fast*.

"Contact right," I called out in the low but carrying voice we'd been trained to use.

My words swiftly traveled up the line and Keaton pulled his gray gelding to a halt, sharp amber eyes scanning the forest on both sides.

Keaton was smart. While we rode in pairs with our griffins beside us, he'd staggered horse and griffin so there were five griffins on each side of the trail. Which meant while Felix didn't have a good visual, Reese's griffin did . . . or he would have if he hadn't been digging at his itchy wing and missed whatever it had been.

"Gage says he can't see anything moving out there now," Reese reported after a long moment of strained silence where the only sound was impatiently stomping hooves and swishing tails.

One by one, the others reported the same. No movement, nothing to see.

"Probably just a deer," Langston said from his position at the center of the column. While dismissive, his tone wasn't as belligerent as it might have been a few months ago, and his muddy green eyes were still scanning the trees.

Keaton twisted in his saddle and raised his brows at me in silent question. Hesitating, I took one last look at the brush before I shrugged.

"Yeah, probably a deer."

My gut churned with unease though, and I was on edge for the rest of the ride, jumping at random noises and irritating Felix with my constant demands for him to keep his eyes open. The hair on the back of my neck refused to lie down, and I kept catching glimpses of movement out of the corner of my eye, as if something stalked us through the trees.

By the time we hit the wooden sign marking the turnoff point, I wasn't the only one jumping at shadows, and I wasn't the only one to sigh in relief when Keaton guided his horse off the trail and down the narrow path toward our campsite for the night. My shoulders refused to relax until the camp was in sight, and even then, a thread of tension remained.

Base Camp Two was about as barebones as a camp could get. There was fresh water from a small pump for humans and a fast-running creek for horses and griffins, a sturdy shed full of rations, and a lean-to with firewood and stone rings to contain the flames. That was it.

It was far from empty though. Two dozen cadets, griffins, and horses were already there. There was no sign of Lieutenant Osbourne or his griffin yet.

"About time!"

"Took y'all long enough!"

"Hey, Delta!" Lorna Wallace, their team leader, shouted. "Think they took their time so we'd do the work for them?"

Keaton grinned as a wave of laughter rolled through the camp and strode over to clasp hands with the curvy brunette. Her gaze lingered just a fraction too long, and I suppressed a grin. Objectively speaking, Keaton was hot. Subjectively, I'd rather kiss my actual brother—if I had one—than him. Keaton didn't miss her interest, and his voice gained a husky edge.

"I mean, it worked didn't it?"

She snorted and punched him in the arm. Griffin rider flirting at its finest.

Working quickly, we got our horses settled on the picket line with the others, then we took care of our griffins. Always them before ourselves, even when we were tired. And since the other cadets really had gotten everything set up, including starting a couple of roaring campfires, Keaton decided we should gather replacement firewood per base-camp protocols.

"Stay close," he ordered with a frown at the creaking, rustling trees. The gentle breeze had picked up with the approach of sunset, and the shadows beneath the tangled branches had grown deeper.

"Why?" Wallace sauntered up with a smirk. "Scared of a little work?"

"No, Harpy spotted something on our way in. Probably just a deer, but the griffins got jumpy."

The other team leader shot me a considering look, and then surprised the hell out of me by giving me a serious nod. She turned back to her clutchmates as if about to say something, but Charlie's team leader glanced over at us from where he was lounging against his griffin by one of the fires.

"You're telling me she got scared by *one* little deer?" Tobias "Lobo" Lorenzo's mocking laugh was echoed by more than one cadet, with even a few trills of griffin laughter. "We saw at least four on our way out here. Maybe Harpy should rethink the scouting gig if she's going to let a single deer spook her."

Reese scowled and looked seconds away from throwing himself at the other cadet. Even Langston glared, but Hawthorne clamped a big hand on their shoulders. They weren't going anywhere, which was probably a good thing. Nobody needed a punishment detail for fighting.

Lobo got to his feet with lazy grace and looked at me. "No offense meant, sweetheart."

"I'm not your sweetheart," I snapped. Felix stalked over to stand at my shoulder, his wings rustling in irritation.

"I mean, you could be." Lobo dragged his gaze over me with an appreciative smirk. "I wouldn't say no."

More laughter, this time with some wolf whistles added to the mix. Heat flashed across my face even as my fists curled. Hawthorne wasn't holding *me* back, after all, and if there weren't any instructors around then nobody could assign me a punishment detail for beating Lobo's smug ass. I'd only taken a single step forward when a new voice called out from behind me.

"Well, now, I'm glad you knuckleheads are having a great time!"

I whirled around as Lieutenant Osbourne stalked into base camp, his gorgeous chestnut griffin slinking along at his heels. Neither of them looked pleased.

"I mean, that's what you're all out here for, right? A fun little camping trip, maybe drinking by the fire, maybe a little dancing under the trees." His pointed look made it clear it wasn't *dancing* he was talking about. He swept a withering gaze over us before he barked, "Fall in."

There was a bare second's hesitation, because we'd never seen the young officer quite so angry, and then the camp was full of scrambling cadets and griffins as we fell into formation.

"Team leaders, report."

One by one, Lobo, Wallace, and Keaton gave a concise report of the trip out and what they'd done to set up camp since arrival. The lieutenant's eyes narrowed.

"Anything else you'd like to report? Details from the trail ride in, perhaps?"

Silence for a beat before Keaton cleared his throat.

"Cadet Tavros spotted what we determined to be a deer. Charlie Clutch also reported seeing several deer on their ride in." Keaton hesitated. "Our griffins got a little jumpy, but it might have been nothing."

"Or," Lieutenant Osbourne said as shadows moved beneath the trees behind him, "it could've been the team of rangers I had shadowing you along the way."

Eight men dressed in the tan-and-gray leathers of rangers stepped out of the forest. One of the rangers, a young man barely older than me with light brown hair and a roguish air caught my eye. He gave me a slow wink and a slower smile as he leaned back against a tree and crossed his arms. My "deer," I assumed.

Lobo stiffened. "Our orders said the scouting run wouldn't begin until we reached base camp. We weren't expecting—"

"No, you weren't, because you forgot anything can be a test. Everything we do at the academy is designed to help prepare you for active duty." There was no sign of a smile on his face, only grim determination. "Scouts need to keep their eyes open and ears up at all times, even on the 'safe' trails near the forts. The *moment* you step beyond those gates, you have to behave as if you're moving through enemy territory, because you never know when the enemy might be moving through ours!"

From the way our griffins were all tucking their wings and tails in tight, it was clear they were also getting a lecture from the lieutenant's griffin. Keira's turquoise gaze was hard, and she snapped her beak in emphasis as the rangers made themselves comfortable in our camp.

"Your griffins are more human because your soul is entangled with theirs, but you have to remember the opposite is also true." He shook his head, disappointment joining the determination. "You're all griffin enough to have their instincts, and if you see something that triggers those instincts I expect you to *pay attention!*"

I wasn't the only one to flinch at the mild-mannered lieutenant's sudden roar. My shoulders tightened in shame, but I managed to keep them from curving inward and remained at attention.

"Understood?"

"Yes, sir!" we all chorused. He let the silence stretch out before he sighed.

"Everything is a test," he repeated quietly. "And I won't be here much longer to help you. So pay attention to what I'm trying to teach you and start acting less like cadets and more like griffin riders. It won't be long before they throw you into the real world too, and I've lost enough people already."

On that grim note, he dismissed us, and we settled in for a quiet night. Keaton and the other team leaders didn't need the lieutenant's direction to set up sentries, and I stood my one-hour shift with a Charlie and Delta cadet in watchful silence.

The next morning, we were up before dawn, tending to griffins and horses before gathering around the lieutenant for our assignments. There were six patrol routes, six scouting targets, and only three clutches. From the pre-brief the week prior, I'd expected Echo would be split into two five-man squads.

I hadn't expected Keaton to put me in charge of squad Echo-two.

"Me?" I dragged him off to the side and dropped my voice low. "Why not Hawthorne?"

"Hawthorne led on our first day trip, it's your turn to lead. You can do this, Harpy. You *need* to do this. Ever since..." Keaton drew in a deep breath as shadows darkened his eyes. "Ever since the kidnapping, you've been so happy to fit in, you've forgotten how to stand out." He smiled, more with his eyes than his mouth. "Time to show me that hotshot dragon rider cadet again. Just remember to be a griffin rider this time around."

Hold on to that fire.

Drawing in a deep breath, I nodded. "I've got this."

"I know you do." He clapped me on the shoulder, awkward as ever with his affection. "We'll see you at Base Camp Three tonight."

I always felt the wind first.

After the endless fall, smoother and more controlled each time, it was the wind that anchored me to Felix's mind more than anything else when I looked through his eyes. I retained enough awareness of my own body that I could feel the leather saddle beneath me, could smell the sweet, slightly pungent mix of horse and sweat, but all I could see were blue skies and trees so very far below.

Felix tucked his legs in tighter and tilted on one wing as he circled over our scouting target—a small clearing set a hundred meters back from the trail we were patrolling. He was so high up, if anyone had been in that rough campsite, they would've mistaken him for a hawk. His vision was incredible though, and we easily picked out details.

A circle of stones to contain a campfire, a stack of rotting firewood, and oddly even rows of . . . sticks?

"*Felix?*"

My griffin did something with his eyes, something humans weren't capable of, and everything leapt into even greater clarity, as if we were only a dozen feet away instead of hundreds of feet in the air. The strange sticks resolved into wooden markers like the one we'd passed on the main trail yesterday.

Troop markers that we were supposed to pretend were real, as if each one represented an enemy soldier or spy.

As Felix circled again, we both counted the markers and verified our count with each other. There was a strong possibility there were more troop markers beneath a decrepit lean-to. We couldn't quite see under it, no matter how Felix angled his wings, but that was fine. We worked in teams for a reason, and I'd ordered Reese and Matthews to have their griffins scout from the ground. Meanwhile, Langston and Elias watched over our bodies, and their griffins guarded all of us.

As Felix banked away from the rough campsite, his sharp eyes caught the faint signs of Nell—Matthews' griffin—and Gage slinking through the woods below, but only because he knew where to look. With more practice, we wouldn't be able to spot them at all. But that was why we were out here, to practice before we had to do this for real, risk our lives for real . . . risk our griffins' lives for real.

A blink, two, and I tumbled back into my own headspace. For a heartbeat, everything seemed miserably dull in comparison to my griffin's eyes, and then everything snapped back into place. Elias arched a brow and I gave him a thumbs-up. We hadn't actually spoken out loud since we'd left base camp that morning. All communication was either relayed through our griffins, or via simple hand signals.

A few seconds later, Matthews and Reese blinked back to awareness and gave me a thumbs-up.

"*They counted six additional troop markers,*" Felix relayed as Nell and Gage stalked out of the trees. "*That's twenty-five total.*"

I nodded and filed the information away to report to the lieutenant. A few seconds later, Felix trotted into the tiny clearing. He'd had to land farther away where there was a decent break in the canopy. Langston glowered at me, which seemed to be his method of letting me know he was passing along a message between our griffins. Honestly, it was probably preferable to him *smiling* at me.

Felix stretched his wings out before tucking them tight to his sides. *"Bailey and Astra didn't find any threats."*

Lieutenant Osbourne had looked particularly evil when he'd told us to expect opposition. That was *all* he told us, but the rangers had disappeared sometime during the night, and it didn't take a genius to figure out they were around here somewhere.

According to the map we'd been provided, our target had been near the beginning of our patrol, and the closest to Base Camp Two. Either the rangers had decided it was too obvious an ambush point, or they were off messing with another squad.

I shrugged, circled a finger in the air and pointed back to the trail. Time to move. Elias nudged his gelding into a walk and smirked at me, obviously waiting for Felix to relay his words.

"Well, that was rather anticlimactic."

"Don't jinx us." I leaned sideways in the saddle and punched him in the arm—hard. *"We've still got the rest of our patrol to go."*

CHAPTER 12

For being a smartass, I set Elias to riding point on the narrow trail, with me directly behind him, then Reese, Matthews, and Langston bringing up the rear. We moved as silently as unshod horses could travel. This time, our griffins didn't walk the trail with us—they ghosted through the forest in a wide net around us with their eyes open and ears up, as if we really were moving through enemy territory.

Our assigned patrol route swung further south than the others. The further south we traveled, the thicker the forest grew, until we rode through a tangled mess of green, with the trail a bare suggestion beneath the horses' hooves and the sky a faint memory. Sunlight seeped through the thick canopy in a golden haze, with the occasional thin spear of light angling down to the forest floor.

If there was a breeze, it didn't reach us beneath the trees.

Before long, our riding leathers stuck to sweaty skin, and the high heat and humidity sapped our energy. I kept a close eye on everyone, but especially the horses, as they were the only ones who couldn't demand a drink when they got too thirsty. George's whiskey-rough voice murmured in my memory.

No more than four hours on the trail without water, girl. Three if it's hot. A good horse will run his heart out for you, so you best make sure that you're a good rider for him.

I nodded agreement with the old stable hand's wisdom and quietly patted Buster on his damp neck. None of the horses were showing any signs of distress or overheating, but I'd rather be cautious.

"Elias, how much further until the next creek?"

Saying "tell" or "ask" wasted too much time, so we'd started to just state the name first, then what we needed to say or ask, and our griffins handled the rest. It cut down on relay time.

A few beats of silence, then, *"Another twenty minutes if our map is accurate."*

"Stop us before we're in sight."

Felix relayed Elias' agreement, and I refocused on our surroundings. The forest might be a wild tangle, but it was full of life. Rabbits and squirrels were everywhere, and birds flitted between the boughs, their bright songs doing as much to mask the noise of our slow passage as anything we were doing. Rustles in the brush proved there was far more wildlife out here than what we could see, and more than once we caught the white flash of raised tails as deer bounded away. Once, a great stag paced into view, his wide antlers a regal crown above his head.

I thought he looked majestic. Felix thought he looked like lunch.

Roughly twenty minutes later, we neared a bend in the faint trail. Elias raised a closed fist, held it a beat, then waved forward once. We all obeyed his silent command to halt, and then I urged Buster forward until we sat side by side, so close our legs brushed against each other. Elias scanned the trees before he turned to look at me. His expression was serious, for him, but his lips twitched a few times as if holding back another smirk while he waited for our griffins to relay his words.

"The creek should be around the bend and maybe a quarter mile down the trail."

"Nice work. According to the map, it's a good ambush point."

I was about to hand him my reins so I could scout it with Felix when I remembered Keaton's advice. A dragon rider was trained to be self-sufficient, but griffin riders were trained to work together . . . and Elias needed practice scouting through his griffin's eyes too. A slow smile curled my lips, and I tilted my head at Elias like a griffin.

"Want to scout it with Astra?"

Elias' expression didn't change for a few seconds, then a wide smile broke through his semiserious expression.

"Felix, stay close while Astra checks out the creek."

My griffin grumbled in annoyance at staying back. *"Why can't we scout it while she stays close?"*

"Because we did it last time. Besides, Astra is further out than you. I can see your tail feathers."

Outrage flared along the bond, and a feathered tail tip flicked out of view.

"No, you can't."

I held back a laugh and looked at Elias. He nodded his readiness, and I wrapped my fingers around his reins. If anything spooked his stolid trail horse while he was in Astra's mind, it would be my job to hold him steady.

In the next instant, his purple eyes glazed over as he joined his griffin and looked through her eyes. While Elias was occupied ensuring the creek was safe for us to stop at, I kept my gaze moving and my head on a swivel.

"Langy, send Bailey to check our backtrail again."

When Felix didn't relay an immediate response, I twisted around in the saddle to check on Langston. His muddy eyes narrowed before he nodded sharply.

"Bailey is thirsty, but she'll range out a mile before heading back. Make sure she gets the time she needs at the creek, Harpy."

I dipped my head in acknowledgement before straightening in the saddle. A few minutes later, Elias reported back.

"Clear! No sign of rangers or any kind of ambush. Deer and mountain lion tracks in the mud, but the scents are old. No bridge, but the creek isn't running high and the ford is in good shape. Easy crossing, even for that pony of yours." Laughter edged Felix's tone, and it was equally likely that he was relaying Elias' laughter, or laughing on his own. Possibly both. *"Water is running clear and fast enough that it should be safe to drink."*

A moment later, Elias' gaze sharpened once more, and he grinned at me as he took his reins back. I gave him an approving smile before issuing orders. Being in charge still felt . . . weird. I was getting a taste of what Keaton dealt with on a daily basis, and I was grateful once again that he was Echo's team leader.

"Langy, tell Bailey we're moving. Everyone, let the griffins and horses drink one at a time in trail order. If your mount isn't drinking, stay alert. Let's get it done and move on quickly. We've got another few hours to go, and I want to get to Base Camp Three before sunset."

Elias touched his heels to his gelding's flanks and headed around the bend in the trail. When his horse was roughly two lengths ahead, I urged Buster to follow. Not that it took much urging. His nostrils flared wide as he caught the scent of running water, and it was more of an effort to hold him to proper spacing than to get him moving.

Soon enough, I heard the burbling splash of running water, and Buster sped up into a fast walk nearly as bone-jarring as his trot. I gritted my teeth but didn't fight him. Up ahead, sunlight sparkled and danced on the water, shining down through a rare break in the canopy. Elias guided his horse into the creek downstream of the ford, while Astra was already drinking from upstream, where the water was cleanest.

As soon as Elias' gelding finished drinking, he walked his horse out of the water, and Buster and Felix got their turns. Reese surprised me when he passed his reins to Matthews and slid out of the saddle. He held up their canteens and shook them pointedly before he moved further upstream and refilled them. As soon as he had them filled, he splashed over to me and Elias and grabbed our canteens.

My fingers started tapping a nervous beat. Ten minutes had already flown past, and Langston's massive gelding and Bailey still needed to drink. As if sensing my urgency—or feeling his own—Reese moved faster, tossing us our canteens before splashing across the creek toward Langston.

His boots had just cleared the water when he stumbled to a halt on the bank with a hoarse cry. My gaze traveled over him, but I couldn't see any injuries. Felix tensed, paws flexing and claws digging into the dirt.

"Bad snake."

Only then did I pick out the tan-patterned loops of smooth scales scant inches from the tips of Reese's boots. A wide, triangular head rose up and the mouth opened wide, exposing white flesh and needle-sharp fangs.

Fuck the exercise.

"Don't move, Reese!" I called out sharply.

"Does it look like I'm moving?" he growled, panic riding the edge of his words. Gage mantled his wings and looked seconds away from charging in, but he was behind Reese and liable to scare the snake into biting.

"Back away, *slowly*." My pulse thundered in my ears, and tension wound through my frame, but I kept the fear out of my voice. Calm. We needed calm. "No sudden movements."

As Reese edged backward, the snake's head rose higher, the jaws stretched wider—and Bailey burst out of the brush and snatched it in her beak. With a sharp snap of her head, she flung the snake into the trees, where it disappeared with barely a rustle of foliage.

With an explosive breath, Reese dropped to one knee. In the next instant, his distressed griffin charged out of the creek and curled around his bonded, a rough purr tumbling from his open beak. Reese pressed his forehead against his griffin's and they both fell still as they silently reassured each other.

Matthews blew out a sharp sigh of relief and slumped in her saddle. I could probably tap dance on Buster's back and he wouldn't care, but Matthews' bay mare was more high-strung. At her rider's unexpected movement, the mare snorted in alarm and skittered sideways through the creek, hooves flashing and flinging water everywhere. Fortunately, Matthews' riding had improved, and she stuck to her mare's back like a bur.

"Nice work, Bailey," Langston said pointedly as he scratched behind her tufted ears. Reese lifted his head and gifted the griffin with a rare smile.

"Thanks for the save." With a sharp breath, he untangled himself from Gage and filled Langston's canteen while the other cadet saw to his horse.

I'd expected to feel relief that Reese was unharmed, but if anything, my tension grew worse, digging sharp claws of apprehension into my gut. My gaze swept over the creek, searching for threats and finding none. But the ever-present birdsong had grown . . . subdued.

Picking up on my tension, Felix's feathers slowly puffed out and his wings mantled. It was entirely possible it was an overreaction to Reese's near miss. Or it could be a ranger team closing in on our vulnerable position. Elias nudged his horse into a sidestep until his leg brushed mine again, his purple eyes sharp as he scanned the trees.

He felt it too.

"*Something's out there,*" he said through our griffins.

Bailey stopped drinking abruptly and snapped her head up, her tufted ears flicking back and forth. As she slunk closer to Langston, she clacked her beak gently, droplets of water dripping from the hooked tip.

"Agreed."

"Need to leave."

"Something smells wrong."

"Go, need to go."

The hair on the back of my neck rose, and my hands tightened on the reins. The griffins murmured each other's words, and while Felix was the only voice I could hear, he mimicked the others' tone, intentionally or not. It was eerie. Heads bobbed, beaks clacked, and wings flared in increasing agitation. Their instincts were speaking, and their riders were definitely listening. Reese capped the half-full canteen and sprinted for his horse.

As soon as he'd flung himself into the saddle, I jerked my head at Elias.

"Let's go!"

Thoroughly spooked, we moved faster down the trail than was prudent for exercise purposes but entirely appropriate for getting clear of whatever the hell was near the creek. I didn't even care when Buster's trot rattled my bones. All that mattered was putting enough distance between us and the threat.

Our griffins moved with us in a tight formation, weaving between the trees and brush on either side of the trail, unwilling to range further afield. It was fine. I didn't want Felix out of my sight right now either.

First one mile, then two passed beneath our horses' hooves. Feathers began to settle, beaks stopped clacking . . . and the hair on the back of my neck finally settled. Another mile, and the tension left my shoulders.

"Anything?" I asked Felix. His tufted ears rotated, sharp eyes scanning the tangled forest, before he snapped his beak decisively.

"No."

Sighing in relief, I pulled ahead of Elias and gently pulled Buster back to a walk. The other horses followed his lead, and I glanced at Felix.

"Any idea what the hell that was?"

"No." An annoyed growl rumbled in his chest, loud enough to be audible over the rhythmic *clop* of hooves hitting the trail.

Another mile went by, and slowly, we all relaxed. We were past any reasonable ambush point by the creek, everyone had gotten water,

Reese hadn't been bitten by a venomous snake, and the scary whatever-the-hell-it-was hadn't chased us. I was willing to call it a success.

That, of course, was when the rangers ambushed us.

Padded arrows flew out of the surrounding trees, striking not at our griffins, but at us.

Kill the rider, kill the griffin.

The Savinians knew griffins could sever if death wasn't instantaneous, so they always targeted the riders. We trained appropriately.

I grunted as an arrow thudded into my shoulder. Padded didn't mean it wasn't painful, and I'd have one hell of a bruise to show off tomorrow. Judging the "wound" to be nonfatal, I kicked Buster into a run, only to be hit from the side.

Not by another arrow, but by a ranger. He literally tackled me out of the saddle, though he was nice enough to twist and take the brunt of the impact. Not so nice that he didn't flip us over and "slice" my throat with a knife hand to simulate a blade.

A familiar young man winked down at me with a roguish grin. "You're dead, griffin girl."

I let my head fall back onto the forest floor with a groan. *Damn it.*

An older, grizzled ranger leaned over us and roared a laugh. "So are you, Maddox."

Confusion twisted the young man's face until a very large, very furry paw pointedly tapped him on the shoulder. As furious as Felix was, it was a remarkably restrained, polite tap. He'd even left his claws sheathed. His beak, on the other hand, was perfectly positioned to rip out the ranger's spine.

Maddox shook his head and scowled. "No, I killed the rider. The griffin can't do that."

"Think again, boyo," the older ranger said sternly. "A dragon will fall dead the instant you kill the rider, but a griffin? A griffin might just hold on long enough to take his rider's killer with him. Remember that." Amusement creased his leathery face as he shifted his gaze to me. "Speaking of the rider, you planning on letting her up any time soon?"

To his credit, Maddox had the grace to wince. "Sorry, griffin girl."

"Oh, no, it's fine," I said sarcastically, though in entirely different circumstances, I might not have minded. "I'm perfectly comfortable down here, *deer.*"

"I didn't think we were at the pet-name stage." Maddox winked a perfectly normal green eye at me. "Yet."

He tried to shift his weight off me but froze as his back bumped against a deadly sharp beak. Felix had decided to be himself and hadn't moved an inch.

"Deer as in d-e-e-r," I explained with a slightly vindictive grin. "You know, like you pretended to be on our way into camp."

"Okay, fair. Can I get up now?" Maddox chuckled, but Felix wasn't amused, and he snapped his beak—the one still uncomfortably close to the ranger's back. A trace of nervousness flashed across his face. "Your griffin knows I'm not *actually* a deer . . . right?"

Felix chuffed a laugh before he *very* reluctantly slid to the side. I smirked.

"He says close enough."

As soon as Maddox gracefully rolled to his feet, I sat up and examined my shoulder. My sleeve was stained an obnoxious blue from the padding, a deliberate marker for training exercises to show any hits. Kept us honest, and gave the shooters feedback on their aim.

I didn't need to check Maddox's quiver to know his markers were blue.

Experimentally, I flexed my arm and winced at the dull throb. Definitely bruised, but Reese had given me worse on the practice mats. So had Callum. Dismissing it as unimportant, I ignored the hand Maddox held out in favor of checking on my clutchmates first.

Langston stood next to his griffin, scowling so hard it was a wonder his face didn't break. There were no less than four impact markers on his chest. The color was probably originally red. A very light red.

My lips twitched as I fought back a grin. I was pretty sure he was more pissed about the exercise death, but it was entirely possible having his riding leathers stained pink wasn't helping.

Reese looked irritated, but that was normal. Whoever had shot him was good. Very good. There was just a single white marker, dead center over his heart. Elias also sported a single white marker, but he seemed amused, trading good-natured banter with the ranger who had taken them out, while Matthews was absolutely flirting with hers. Roughly the same age as us, the guy was not only stupid hot, he was flirting back. He gave her a charming smile and helped her back onto her skittish mare, holding the reins for her like she was a lady instead of a cadet who could hold her own.

The rest of the horses didn't seem to care that we'd just been ambushed. In fact, they were taking full advantage of our distraction to munch on the surrounding vegetation. My nose wrinkled. Cleaning those bits tonight was going to be a bitch.

"You comfortable down there?" Maddox asked with a slow grin, still holding his hand out. He gave the impression he'd continue to do so until I took it or got to my feet on my own. Before I could decide one way or another, Felix shoved between us, not so subtly herding the ranger away from me.

I snorted a laugh and hooked my hand around the leg my griffin extended. His tufted ears were flattened as he glared at Maddox.

"Felix, be nice," I said out loud for the benefit of the ranger as he pulled me to my feet.

"Don't wanna."

Great. One little exercise death, and my griffin had reverted to the maturity of a cub. Suppressing my grin, I looked around the ambush point, but unless the others were still hiding in the woods, we'd been taken out by only four rangers. They must have split into two teams, much like we had. Even though rangers never wore rank in the field, three of them seemed to be about as experienced as us, while the older ranger carried the unmistakable air of someone who'd been at this game longer than I'd been alive.

"Now what, sir?" I asked him quietly.

"Sergeant, not sir," the older man corrected me with a grin. "Now we all head over to Base Camp Three, where you can explain to your lieutenant how easily we took you all out. Gotta say, lass, you weren't the first squad we took out today, but you were surely the easiest. Walking down the trail all clustered up like a bunch of kids out for a walk in the park." He shook his head with more than a hint of disapproval. "I know you lot have been trained better than that, even if you are newly bonded."

I grimaced. "Yeah, whatever you guys did back at the creek had our griffins spooked."

"Us too," Elias called out, all traces of laughter fading from his expression. Reese shifted to stand at his friend's shoulder and nodded agreement. Even Matthews took a break from flirting to scowl at her new "friend" as Nell edged as close as the bay mare would allow.

"Yeah, scaring our griffins wasn't cool."

The sergeant stilled, his sharp gaze shifting to the tangled forest pressing close to either side of the faint trail. Even the griffins couldn't see far through the thick mess of green.

"We weren't at the creek, Cadet," he said in a deadly calm tone. The kind of tone I'd used when Reese had almost been bitten. "What'd you see? Describe it."

"We didn't *see* anything," I said uneasily, my hand dropping to brush against the hilt of my dagger, as if I needed the assurance it was still there. "The birds went quiet though, and one of the griffins said she smelled something *wrong*. Whatever it was, we all felt it and we got the hell out of there."

"Think it's the mountain lion we crossed paths with earlier, Franks?" Maddox asked quietly, unslinging his bow and nocking an unpadded arrow with practiced skill, though he didn't draw it yet. "She was in heat, could be what set the griffs off."

"Not a chance," Sergeant Franks murmured before he tilted his head up the trail. "Time to go, kids."

Silence dropped over the forest like a bomb. Nell's head snapped up, beak dropping open in an alarmed shriek just as *something* reared up from the tangled foliage behind her.

My eyes struggled to make sense of what I was seeing even as I stumbled backward and ripped my dagger from its sheath. My first thought was diseased bear, but it was too fast, too . . . *wrong*. Not enough fur, too many teeth, and limbs that were oddly proportioned with claws that put even a dragon's to shame.

"Broken beast!" Franks shouted, warning thick in his voice.

Horror twisted through my soul, amplified by Felix, crouched protectively in front of me with his tail lashing and every last feather standing on end. Broken beasts were malformed creatures, warped by the same war that had ended the old world. Or worse, a deliberate attempt by someone to re-create the magic that had given us our griffins and dragons. The Savinians weren't the only ones who liked to create monsters. They were just the best at it.

The bear that wasn't a bear struck out with a lightning fast paw and caught Nell on the side of her head. The power behind that blow must have been tremendous, because the griffin's head snapped around, her eyes glazing even as she flew across the trail in a tumble of limbs and wings. She fetched up against a tree and went limp.

My gaze shot to Matthews in horror, but she was still alive, so Nell must just be unconscious, not dead.

"Nell!" Matthews' howl of terror and fury rose above roars of the other griffins. Her delicate face twisted into a snarl as she held the reins with one hand and yanked out her dagger with the other. Her bay mare reared up, screaming defiance and lashing out with her hooves. The rest of the horses screamed in alarm and bolted back toward the creek.

The broken beast blurred forward and struck Langston's massive gelding, the slowest of the horses, with its claws, carving a bloody path through its flank. Blood sprayed, and the horse went down with a shrill scream of agony, hooves flashing and eyes wide with terror. Another slash of oversized claws, and the horse fell silent, his throat torn out. The coppery stench of blood hit my nose and I staggered back a step.

The broken beast snapped its head up and looked at me. I froze.

It had no eyes.

It wasn't even as if it had lost them to some other predator, but as if they'd never existed at all. Instead, deep pits full of strange bumps stretched across the face where eyes should be.

Franks yanked an arrow out of his quiver and snapped off a shot. The razor-edged broadhead barely sank into the beast's strange, pale hide. Maddox stood calmly off to my side and fired two arrows. One nicked the thing's throat, the other ricocheted off its arm, careening dangerously close to Matthews before it disappeared into the undergrowth.

"Get away from it!" I shouted, clutching my useless dagger and feeling utterly helpless.

"I'm trying," Matthews shrieked as her horse trumpeted in fear and reared up again, so high this time that I thought the mare would topple over backward. Still rearing, the mare spun on her back legs and took off like a shot back down the trail, carrying Matthews with her despite everything the other cadet did to stop her.

That was one of my clutchmates out of immediate danger at least.

As the broken beast made an aborted lunge for the fleeing horse, the rangers spread out and riddled it with arrows. All except for the one who had taken out Reese and Elias with a single shot. The dark-haired young ranger held an arrow nocked but only partially drawn, his narrowed gaze intent on the monster, his expression a mask of calm.

"Any time you want to join in, Pearson!" Maddox snarled. The corner of the other ranger's mouth ticked up, but his sharp eyes remained focused on the beast. In the next instant, his gaze hardened, and he fully drew and fired in one smooth motion.

Thwack!

Pearson's arrow sunk halfway to the fletching into one of the pits where eyes would be on a normal beast.

Keening a high-pitched wailing cry, the broken beast blurred forward, its movements jerky but *fast*. With a frightening display of intelligence, it ignored everyone else and focused on the one person who'd managed to truly hurt it.

The broken beast was so determined to strike at Pearson, it never saw Astra and Gage. Griffin claws sliced ribbons down the monster's side and back. Dark red, nearly black blood trailed down the pale hide. It spun, fast, so damn fast, but the griffins flowed out of the way, and Bailey glided in, slashing wicked claws into the back of its leg, seeking tendons to cut. It whirled again, and my heart stopped as Felix darted in and leaped on its back. Back paws dug into dense slabs of muscle, front claws slashed along the spine, and his beak snapped at the thick neck.

Keening in frustration and pain, it flung Felix off and retreated to the forest, disappearing within the tangled mess within seconds. Too fast, even for that thing. My eyes widened.

"Please tell me it can't camouflage like a green," I hissed as Felix rolled to his feet.

"Okay, we won't tell you," Maddox muttered without taking his gaze off the trees.

Tension rose as we all waited for it to reappear. The rangers didn't lower their bows, and the griffins didn't sheath their claws. Hands tightened on knife hilts, and hard eyes scanned the trees. Nothing. We saw nothing.

One by one, birds started chirping again, single calls, as if asking each other if it was safe. A few seconds later, birdsong resumed full force, and the griffins shook their fur and feathers out, slowly calming.

I ran for Felix, who bumped against my side in reassurance.

"I'm fine, Harpy." He held up his paw for my inspection. *"I don't think I'd want to eat that thing though."*

I shuddered at the nearly black blood coating his claws and silently agreed. *"Definitely not for eating."*

"We've got to go after it. Can't let it rampage through our damn training grounds." Franks stalked up to me and gripped my arm, his fingers like iron bands around my bruises. "Take care of your wounded griffin, get your runaway girl, and get your asses to Base Camp Three." When I just stared at him, wide-eyed and more than a little shaken, he gave my arm a sharp shake. "Understood, Cadet?"

"Yes, Sergeant."

The rangers disappeared into the tangled forest as silently as they'd arrived, leaving us alone with an injured griffin and a missing cadet . . . and no horses to help with any of it.

"Son of a *bitch*," Reese snarled.

"Yeah, that about sums it up," Elias muttered, one hand resting on Astra's shoulder. "How's Nell looking?"

Langston glanced up from where he knelt next to the brown-and-white griffin, big hands carefully checking her for injuries while Bailey tried to wake her. Sighing, he shook his head as Bailey curled around Nell protectively, a soothing purr rumbling in her chest.

"All I can tell is she's out cold and not waking up. If she's got additional injuries, I can't see them." He stood up, his big hands curled into fists. "The broken beast might double back. We can't stay here."

"What do we do about Nell?" Elias demanded. He glanced at Langston's butchered horse and shuddered. "It's not like we can carry her."

"And what about Matthews?" Reese reminded us grimly. "If she'd been able to get control of Marylou, she'd have doubled back by now. She might be lost or hurt, and the only one who could tell us is unconscious."

They all fell silent and looked at me. It slowly dawned on me that they were looking at me because Keaton had put me in charge. While we were well and truly past the bounds of the exercise, I was still the squad leader, still responsible for everyone's safety. *Fuck my life.*

"Okay," I said after a brief moment where I completely panicked and my brain was full of nothing but white noise. I huffed out a sharp breath, ignored the sweat trickling down my spine, and nodded. "Okay, here's what we'll do. Langy's right, we can't stay here, and we can't carry Nell—but one of the griffins could drag her."

Elias' gaze shifted to the surrounding trees. "You thinking a sled?"

"And a harness." I strode over to the nearest tree and tugged free one of the many vines slowly suffocating the trees in the area. "Vines will do the trick if we double up enough."

Reese scowled. "What about—"

"I'm not done," I said sharply before I turned to Felix. "Can you climb up above the canopy and take off safely?"

My griffin directed a considering gaze toward the tangled canopy blocking out most of the sky before he shifted his attention to the trees. His head tilted, and he glanced at Gage. The other griffin shifted his wings in a shrug, but Astra slapped her paw against one of the bigger oak trees. Felix tilted his head back, gaze following the myriad branches, mapping a path. He snapped his beak decisively.

"I can do it."

"Okay, buddy, I need you to look for the rest of the horses. If we're lucky, they stopped at the creek. If we're really lucky, Matthews already regained control of her crazy-ass horse and is delayed because she's rounding them up."

"Got it," he said, tail lashing behind him, the fan of feathers at the end snapping open and closed with equal parts eagerness and excitement. I held up a hand when he would've just leaped at the tree.

"Be careful," I murmured, my worry seeping through despite doing what I could to shield it from him. He was still so very young, and so very new to flying, with so many things that could go wrong if he messed up his takeoff . . . a broken wing being the least of them. Felix bounded over and dropped his forehead to mine. A wave of love and confidence washed through me.

"I've got this, Harpy."

"I believe you." I lifted my chin. "Go."

Felix bounded across the trail and launched himself at the hapless oak, all of his claws sinking deep into the bark. Then he climbed up as easily as any cat and disappeared into the canopy. My hands slowly curled into fists, tension shivering through my frame as I waited. A few seconds later, a burst of joy hit me.

"I'm airborne. Heading for the creek now."

I turned back to the guys and found them already busy building a sled for Nell, lashing together branches with the ever-present vines, while Astra and Gage stood guard. Nodding in approval, I got to work on the harness. A few minutes later, Felix tugged on my attention.

"I found three of the horses near the creek, but Matti isn't there."

I tucked Matthews' griffin name away for later and asked to see through his eyes. *"Show me?"*

At his ready agreement, I told the others what I was doing and dropped the endless drop into Felix's mind. The wind anchored me, and I sternly told my stomach to behave as it swooped and dipped queasily along with my griffin as he turned in a wide circle over the creek where the trail intersected. Buster was lazily drinking, while Elias and Reese's horses were sampling the lush plants along the far bank.

There was no sign of Matthews or her bay mare.

"Check our backtrail. With as freaked out as that mare was, she could've carried Matti all the way back to Base Camp Two."

Felix dropped one wing low and cut his circle tighter to turn west, a wild shriek of joy escaping his beak as he caught a friendly thermal. As the heated column of air cushioned his wings and carried him in an ever-higher spiral above the creek, his feathers made millions of tiny adjustments that made my shoulders twitch in reaction.

Finally, with a snap of his wings, he leveled out and glided high above the ground, the trail a barely visible thread weaving through the tangled forest. Felix followed it until he flashed over Base Camp Two, but it was empty, with no sign of anyone, let alone Matthews.

Hissing out a breath in frustration, I wracked my brain. There was no way the mare had made it any farther than that, and even the base camp had been a wild stretch. But the forest was far too dense here for a horse to navigate, even a panicked horse. My eyes widened in realization.

"The creek! Check along the creek. It's the only other place the mare could've gone."

As Felix wheeled back around, I fell back into my own mind. Fatigue unexpectedly slapped me in the face, and I swayed as the world slid sideways on me. A hand landed on my shoulder and steadied me. When the dizziness passed, I blinked my eyes open, expecting to see Elias, or even Reese.

"You okay, princess?" Langston grumbled.

A sarcastic retort hovered on the tip of my tongue, but I held it back. Though his blunt features were impassive, even annoyed, concern lurked within his muddy green eyes. I nodded.

"Just dizzy. I'm good now."

He dug out a ration bar from a pouch on his belt and handed it over without comment. Between bites, I relayed what we'd found. And what we didn't find.

"Let's get Nell on the sled if it's ready," I said after I'd checked in with Felix. Still no sign of Matthews or her stupid horse.

Elias wiped sweat off his face, reached for Nell—and hesitated. "What if her neck's broken?"

"Gods, I hope not," Reese muttered, and even Langston paled slightly.

"Gently then, but we can't wait around for her to wake up." I swallowed hard. "I'll brace her neck, Langston and Elias lift, Reese you get the sled under her."

Working together, we managed it, though Elias wasn't the only one sweating by the time we were done. I held up my makeshift harness and looked at Langston and Reese.

"We need to divide and conquer—"

A keening wail rose up in the distance, startling the birds into momentary silence and others into panicked flight. We all froze—and then another wail answered it. Further away than the first, but a second broken beast anywhere within hearing distance was far too close for comfort.

Langston snatched the harness out of my hands as a hard, determined expression settled on his face.

"Bailey and I don't need any help. We can get Nell to camp on our own." With gentle hands utterly at odds with his harsh words, he slipped my shoddy vine harness over Bailey's head and adjusted it until it was as snug as it was going to get. "We'll let the LT know what's going on."

Elias roughly clapped him on the shoulder. "Be careful, brother."

"Those wails didn't come from the direction *I* need to travel." Langston hesitated, jaw flexing. "Go get our girl back."

CHAPTER 13

Getting the horses turned out to be the easy part. Even finding where the mare had abandoned the creek for the woods was easy once Astra took to the air and helped Felix search north and south along the creek.

North would've been great. North led back toward the academy and the heart of the training area. And while I wasn't sure how safe that was right now with at least two broken beasts roaming the forest, it was known territory at least. South was dangerous, if only because our map only went so far . . . and it took us farther away from help.

So of course the panicked mare went south.

Astra quickly found where she'd abandoned the creek in favor of charging through the forest like a ninny, leaving a trail of broken branches and trampled greenery behind her. We pulled our horses to a halt in the middle of the creek, eyeing the trail with trepidation and no little exasperation while we waited for Felix.

Grumbling, he landed on the bank and glared at the fresh trail. *"Why can't I stay on overwatch?"*

"Because Astra hasn't been flying this whole time and I can feel your wings aching."

"Can not." Felix carefully stretched his wings against the gentle throb of overexertion pulsing through them. When I arched a brow, his ears pinned flat in irritation and he stalked over to stand guard with Gage, flexing his shoulders and grumbling as he went.

Once again, I put Elias in the lead—but while he could out-navigate the rest of us blindfolded, even he needed reference points. Reference points that were quickly lost once we rode under the thick canopy. The trees were a little thinner on the ground here, but vines stretched from branch to branch in a thick, impenetrable web of green.

Even a griffin's sharp eyes couldn't see through it, and it stretched as far as Astra could see.

Still, if it weren't for Elias, we would've lost Matthews' trail within a quarter mile. About a half mile in, he pulled his horse to a stop and pointed at a wooden marker. I squinted at it, and realized it wasn't a marker. It was a rotting fencepost. A glance left and right showed a few more in the distance, equally as rotten, with no sign of the fence they'd once supported.

"Southern border of the training area," Elias said grimly. "We're officially off the map once we go past it."

Behind me, Reese snorted. "We didn't come this far to turn around now. Move it, Eli."

Elias ignored him and twisted around in the saddle, his purple gaze firmly on mine, searching for approval ... and conveying without words that the decision to leave the training area was my call. Lieutenant Osbourne had ordered us to remain within the boundaries, but that was for the exercise.

"Let's go," I said firmly.

A shiver rolled down my spine as we rode between the old fence posts, but I ignored it and nudged Buster into his bone-breaking trot. The sooner we found Matthews, the sooner we could get back.

Beyond that suggestion of a border, the ground sloped downward for nearly a mile before it leveled out again. The ground grew soft, almost marshy, beneath horse hooves and griffin paws. The vines thickened until they completely enshrouded this section of the forest, hanging and creeping and twining around *everything*, as if they wanted nothing more than to strangle the trees until there was nothing left but the vines. Some were thick, massive things bigger round than my arm, others as diaphanous as a spider's web, with everything in between.

With sunset fast approaching, the diffuse light shifted and darkened, leaving the marshy woods gray or sickly green at best. In the distance, mist rose off small ponds, but the air wasn't just humid. It felt heavy and dead, a suffocating shroud that held only silence, as if nothing living lay within.

Horses and griffins stopped, ears swiveling, muscles twitching. Apprehension tightened my shoulders, and goosebumps rose on my exposed skin.

"Harpy...I don't like this place," Felix said in a bare whisper, as if afraid the forest would hear him. He sidled over to me, his tufted ears constantly moving, feathers ruffled and wings mantled. A faint *shick* drew my gaze down, and I saw his claws flexing in and out of soft paws. Flecks of dried blood still clung to them. *"It feels...wrong."*

Alarm raced through me.

"Wrong like the broken beast?"

"No, just...wrong."

"Elias—" I broke off abruptly, uneasy with how the sound seemed to bounce and echo, and relayed through Felix. *"You're sure Matti went this way?"*

He silently pointed at the ground in three places. Hoof marks. Judging from the depth and distance between them, the mare had still been running, if not at full speed, then still at a gallop. I nodded at Elias, and he urged his gelding into a reluctant walk. As we followed I glanced back at Reese.

"Reese, what did you say the mare's name was?"

"Marylou."

Unexpected pain stabbed at me. No wonder the name had felt vaguely familiar earlier. The mare had belonged to George. He'd once called her half endurance, half racehorse, and all heart. He'd also said she was as high-strung as a mouse in a griffin crèche. I'd had no idea she'd been added to the cadet herd, but it made sense with him gone.

"Explains how she was able to get this far," was all I relayed.

We'd gone maybe a hundred meters before both Felix and Gage snapped their heads up.

"Astra found her!"

"Show me," Elias whispered, thrusting his reins into my outstretched hand. His eyes glazed over. With Astra guiding him, he led us through the creepy forest to an irregular clearing—and to Matthews.

Her sharp cry rang out the instant we broke through the trees, so much relief in her voice and on her face that it was painful to witness. There was surprise there too, as if she hadn't really believed we'd come after her, and pain. She sat on the ground with her back propped up against a vine-covered tree, left leg stretched out in front of her and her right arm held awkwardly against her side.

A brilliant smile stretched across her face. "Thank fuck you guys found me." Her eyes darted past us and her smile dimmed. "Langy?"

"Dragging Nell back to camp. Is she awake yet?"

Her smile dropped away completely. "No. What happened with the broken beast?"

"Griffins drove it off, rangers went after it," Reese said shortly as he slid out of the saddle and knelt to inspect her leg. "Twisted knee?"

"And a broken arm." She tossed a glare across the clearing, where her idiot mare gazed calmly enough next to a steep-sided hill. "She got the bit in her teeth. I couldn't stop her, and she was going too fast to safely ditch."

"You did fine . . ." I smirked. "Matti."

"Damn it," she mumbled, then sucked in a sharp breath through her teeth as Reese gently prodded at her arm.

"Definitely broken," he said brusquely.

"Get her ready to move." I took a closer look at Marylou. Her sides heaved a little too fast, and even from here I could see the fine shivers that ran through her sweat-darkened flanks. She was dangerously exhausted. "Matti can ride double with you, and we'll lead the mare."

"I'll see if I can find something to splint her arm." He tilted his head at Gage, eyes going vague for a brief second. "Gage will try to herd Marylou over here without spooking her."

"She's used to griffins, and she's worn out—he can probably just pick up the reins in his beak and walk her over," I said with an amused snort before I headed over to Elias. The lanky cadet was staring up at the darkening sky where Astra was circling, an uncharacteristic frown on his face. "What's wrong?"

Wordlessly, he held out his compass for my inspection. The needle swung in wide arcs, never settling or even slowing.

"Astra's disoriented, she's not sure which way to go."

He flexed his shoulders and shifted his frown over to the creepy forest. A shudder wracked my frame. The clearing seemed normal enough, and I was *not* looking forward to heading back under the vines.

"I'm not sure if I can lead us back without a proper bearing," Elias said grimly. "It's almost dark under there and it'll be easy to lose our hoofprints and get stupid lost."

"Shit," I muttered.

Felix, on the other hand, seemed delighted. *"I'll go help Astra!"*

He didn't wait for approval, he just bounded across the clearing and beat his wings, smoothly lifting into the sky despite the fatigue I could feel burning through his muscles. With an exasperated sigh, I sent him a tiny burst of energy. He sent back gratitude as his wingbeats smoothed out.

"I'm going up the hill." Elias handed me his reins. "It's above a lot of the canopy, and I might be able to get a good bearing from up there. Worse comes to worse, the stars will be out soon and I can use them."

Nodding, I ground tied the horses and followed Elias to the hill. From across the clearing, it hadn't seemed that tall, but standing at the base it looked like it was easily a forty-foot climb, all of it nearly straight up.

"Be careful."

Elias grunted dismissively and started up the hill. It was so steep he had to use his hands and feet, climbing more than walking. He was roughly halfway up when Reese shouted. At the sharp alarm in his voice, my head snapped around, searching for whatever had spooked him. Reese jogged through the tall grass, a rusted piece of metal clutched tight in one hand.

"Found it looking for a splint. Looked like it was a railing of some kind." He frowned up at Elias and raised his voice. "Careful, brother, I think this is a pre-War ruin!"

Unease tightened my gut. "Elias, maybe you should come back down! Gage hasn't flown yet, we can send him up to lead us back."

Elias didn't stop climbing.

"Would you quit worrying? I'm almost there—ha! That's what she said." He pulled himself to the top and grinned down at us. "See? Nothing to it."

My unease spiked into alarm, but it wasn't mine. It was Felix's. And he was circling over the hill, his head tilted as he studied it.

"Something's not right. It's too . . . straight."

"Elias, come back down!"

"Geeze, Harpy, would you calm down?" He strolled along the flat hilltop, head tilted back and compass raised to the sky. "Keaton puts you in charge of one little thing and—"

Between one step and the next, he vanished from sight. A short, startled shout rang out before it cut off with an awful finality.

And then Astra screamed.

I could live a hundred years and never forget the heartrending agony in that cry. Like half her soul had just been ripped away— because it had been. The *thud* of her body hitting the ground hit me like a blow, and I wasted precious seconds staring into those open, purple eyes. Eyes just a shade or two more blue than my own. Eyes that had usually been filled with laughter, with mischief. Dull and with lingering traces of agony now.

Even knowing it was too late, even knowing that if Astra was dead so was Elias, I screamed for Felix. He pulled me in before I could ask, and I looked through his eyes as he hovered over the hill that wasn't a hill at all. It was some kind of building, so thickly enshrouded by vegetation that none of us had recognized it for what it was until it was far too late.

The vast expanse of green was broken by a jagged hole where Elias had fallen through. Only plants had stretched across that section of the roof, and they hadn't been strong enough to hold his weight. I'd always envied Felix his sharp vision. Better than most griffins, better by far than the best dragon. I didn't envy it now. His sharp eyes easily pierced the shadows, and I saw everything.

Elias lay on a cracked stone floor, dark liquid pooling around his body that I knew would be red if the sun had been higher. His eyes were open, but there wasn't even a hint of agony on his face. Just surprise, as if death had claimed him before he'd even registered the pain. Only his griffin had suffered, and not for long.

Felix keened a mournful cry, and I slid back into my own body, my own eyes. I pressed a hand against my mouth and slumped to the ground next to a dead griffin. *Oh gods...*

With Gage flying above the trees, Reese guided us out of the creepy forest. By that time, twilight blanketed the trails, but it was just enough light to guide our way. We stumbled into Base Camp Three before full dark, exhausted and hurt and grieving. But we weren't the only squad who had run into broken beasts, and we weren't the only clutch who had lost someone. Delta hadn't had the benefit of a team of rangers with them when not one but two broken beasts had crashed into one of their squads on the trail.

All six cadets and their griffins were gone—including their team leader, Lorna Wallace.

The rangers had taken losses of their own. While we'd been out tracking down Matthews, our rangers had tracked down the wounded broken beast. It had led them straight to a nest in the center of our training grounds. A nest that hadn't been there the week prior.

They'd lost two rangers taking it out. Only Franks and Maddox had returned.

Lieutenant Osbourne, along with solid backup from Keaton and Lobo, had rallied Charlie and the other half of Echo and fought off the two broken beasts who had attacked the camp. They came away from the fight with only minor injuries. Keaton had taken a claw to the face saving Lobo, of all dumbasses, and would probably have a wicked scar to show for it. He was lucky he hadn't lost an eye with his heroics, and I'd scolded him soundly before he'd told me to shut up and pulled me into a rough hug.

"Twenty minutes," he said in a gruff voice that did nothing to hide his relief. "That's how long you had before I was going out after you."

His arms tightened, and my fingers dug into the thick leather of his riding vest. It wasn't until that moment that I realized how badly I was shaking, or how badly he was.

"Thank fuck you guys made it back."

"Not . . . not all of us," I choked out.

Keaton stiffened and pulled away. His gaze skipped from a red-eyed Reese, to a pale Matthews, and landed on Astra. We'd built another sled for her, and used Elias' gelding to drag her back. Keaton stared at that empty saddle, his expression impassive but his eyes anguished.

"Oh, hells," he mumbled as Lieutenant Osbourne strode up.

"Cadet Tavros, report." Despite the brisk order, his tone was gentle and his eyes were kind. When I stiffened to attention, he waved me back to at ease as exhaustion creased his face. "Just . . . just tell us what happened, Tavros."

So, I did, with as much detail as I could remember. While we'd brought poor Astra back with us, we hadn't been able to recover Elias' body. The hole was too narrow for a griffin, too dangerous for a rider.

That last nearly broke me, but none of us could afford the luxury of breaking down—we had to assume there were more broken beasts roaming the training grounds.

Lieutenant Osbourne had sent Keira, his griffin, back to the academy. Help was on the way, we just had to hold on until it arrived.

The remainder of the night passed in tense silence, the pall hanging over the camp broken only by the occasional sob or groan of pain. Some cadets had wanted to retreat to the academy even though it was a moonless night, but the lieutenant held firm on his decision. The horses wouldn't be able to see well enough on the trails, and it was too dangerous.

We stood guard in shifts, and waited for first light.

Help arrived in the form of green wings flashing across the dawn sky. A flight of green dragons to take our wounded back to the academy. Keaton refused to go, even though the bandage on his face was bloodstained, but three riders from Charlie weren't given a choice, their injuries too severe to make riding back wise. With her broken arm and twisted knee, Matthews also wasn't given a choice. Not that she protested, because her griffin was also being airlifted out.

Nell still hadn't woken up.

My nails dug into my palms as I watched the greens take off with our wounded, but for once, it wasn't because I desperately wanted to fly, or even because this kind of medevac was *exactly* what I'd wanted to do. It was because I was desperately afraid for Nell, and for Matthews. If her griffin never woke up...

On our slow, painful trip back, several teams of griffins flashed by overhead, with a flight of dragons backing them up, no doubt to do an aerial recon for any more broken beasts or nests. We even passed a grim-faced ranger unit, twenty-five strong, who would sweep through the training grounds on foot.

By the time we'd turned over our horses to the stable hands and trudged the mile to the academy proper, the sun was setting in a glorious display of reds and oranges that none of us gave a shit about. All we wanted was to take care of our griffins, scrub the dirt and blood from our skin, and collapse. Later...later we would grieve for everyone we'd lost.

But the instant we stepped through the academy gates, a swarm of medics descended on us, along with a bevy of Mavens, and the inevitable crowd of morbidly curious cadets. Somehow, I'd come through physically unscathed, with nothing more than bruises and strained muscles. A brusque medic had checked me over with brutal efficiency and cleared me within minutes, and I was allowed through the gauntlet of medical personnel.

Meanwhile, the Mavens had rounded up those griffins who didn't need medical care and were leading them off to get them fed. While they'd outgrown the crèche months ago, the Mavens had left the hatchery to help, and I was grateful.

Felix hesitated, his ears tilted back and his tail lashing with uncertainty. He didn't want to leave me, but I could feel his gut cramping with hunger pains, and his thoughts were edged with that red haze that meant he needed to eat sooner rather than later.

"Go," I whispered to him, too tired to make the effort to speak out loud. *"I'll be okay."*

Too exhausted even for mindspeech, Felix sent a burst of love through the bond and joined Tavi, who had waited for him. Together, the brothers walked off shoulder to shoulder, wings drooping with exhaustion. I looked for Keaton, but he'd been beset by that same brusque medic, a formidable woman who rather reminded me of Commandant Pulaski, all iron will and grim determination as she cleaned the jagged claw mark that had split his skin from temple to jaw.

He wasn't going anywhere anytime soon, which meant neither was I.

I just wished there was somewhere other than the ground to sit. Not that I minded the ground, I just didn't think I'd be able to get back up again. Sighing, I braced my back against the sun-warmed stone of the academy wall and settled in to wait for him.

My mind drifted. Overlapping voices washed over me in a wave, nothing more than white noise—until a familiar voice broke through my exhausted haze. Hands gripped my shoulders and shook me slightly until I lifted my eyes high enough to meet Bethany's concerned orange gaze.

"Harper!"

I had the distinct impression it wasn't the first time she'd said my name, and I did my best to focus. A quick glance showed Keaton was still getting treated, pain creasing his face as the medic placed tiny, neat stitches to pull the wound closed. Maybe it wouldn't scar . . .

"Harper!" Bethany gave my shoulders another shake, reminding me she was there. Her fingers rested directly over the bruises from the padded arrow, and the dull throb of pain did more to focus my mind than her voice.

"Sorry," I said, my voice little more than a harsh rasp in my throat.

"What *happened*?" Bethany darted her gaze around the chaotic crowd, searching for someone who wasn't there, who would never be there again, before she looked back at me. "Are you okay?"

"No." Slowly, I shook my head as my eyes burned. "No, I'm not."

Steeling myself, I told her about the broken beasts. I told her how half of Delta was just *gone*. I told her about Nell, and how she wouldn't wake up, and how Matthews was half out of her mind with terror. I told her how Matthews had gotten lost, and how we'd found her, injured but alive. My voice broke then, but the tears still wouldn't fall. I stared at my friend through blurred vision, the words caught in my throat. If I forced them past the tight ball of grief, if I said them out loud, it would make it real.

I didn't want it to be real. I didn't want my friend to be gone.

But he was, and whether I said it or not, it wouldn't change anything. It wouldn't make him any less dead, and it wouldn't bring his griffin back.

As I struggled, fear tightened Bethany's expression, and her fingers dug in harder. I didn't mind, the pain grounded me.

"There's more, isn't there?" she said, her voice hard as she ruthlessly suppressed her fear.

I nodded. Swallowed hard as the tears built higher. Her eyes widened.

"Keaton?"

"No," I whispered.

My voice broke again. I tightened my jaw to keep it from trembling . . . and I saw the exact moment when she knew.

"No." She shook her head, slowly at first but faster and faster. "Not him. Not Elias."

My tears spilled over, tracks of guilt and sorrow burning down my cheeks. As if they'd unlocked my voice, I finally managed to get the words out.

"I'm so sorry."

❖ ❖ ❖

Elias and Astra's deaths weren't my fault.

The academy review board said so. Keaton and the rest of my clutchmates said so. Even Bethany said so.

And if I repeated it enough times, maybe one day I'd believe it.

My head understood there was literally nothing I could've done differently, not knowing what I did then. The only other choice I could've made was to order everyone back to Base Camp Three and abandon Matthews to an uncertain fate—which wasn't a choice at all. We didn't leave our own. Even when I'd been at my lowest, when my entire clutch had hated me, they wouldn't have left me out there alone.

Elias and Astra's deaths weren't my fault, but while my head understood, my heart didn't believe. Deep down, I was convinced if I'd done just a little better, *been* just a little better, they'd still be alive and teasing everyone incessantly. But I hadn't, and they weren't.

Echo was a more somber clutch without them.

Even Nell waking up, confused and weak after being out for a solid three days, wasn't enough to break us out of our grief. The relief was there though. If Nell hadn't woken up, she'd eventually have taken Matthews with her. An unconscious griffin couldn't sever, after all.

Before departing for his active-duty assignment, Lieutenant Osbourne gave us a bit of intel as a parting gift. Word hadn't worked its way down to the cadets yet, but he told us the nest of broken beasts had been planted. The rangers had found evidence of a carry basket in the heart of the nest before they burned the whole thing to the ground. Even though the academy had tightened the patrols after the air raid, the Savinians still found a way through. Running into those broken beasts hadn't been a mistake or misfortune—it had been enemy action.

Some of my guilt abated, but not all. While Felix vehemently disagreed with my stubborn insistence on shouldering the blame, he agreed we needed to be better. We threw ourselves into training, much like Bethany had with Jasper to bury her grief, and it was only because of Keaton and Tavi that we didn't burn ourselves out.

They never tried to stop us from training. They joined us. No matter how hard I tried to push Keaton away, he never left me to suffer alone, and I wasn't so lost to my guilt and my grief that I failed to notice he was suffering too. We spent a lot of free time on the archery range and a lot of nights on the barracks roof that summer.

One gloomy fall day, when Felix and I would've gone out to get in extra training on the obstacle course, Tavi decided he'd finally had enough of our overzealous bullshit and sat on me. Literally. Like his brother, the griffin was the size of a horse and still growing, and there had been no escaping.

"Enough, sister," Felix had relayed in the slightly deeper tones of his twin. Amber eyes stared into mine before Tavi gently nuzzled the side of my face. *"You've punished yourself enough."*

Tavi had refused to let me up until I'd agreed to spend my rest day . . . resting.

With the skies overcast and drizzling, it was a perfect day to curl up with Felix and read. So that's what we did, with Tavi and Keaton curled up next to us and the rest of Echo hanging out in the barracks. That day saved us, saved all of us. It was the first day that felt like a good day since we'd lost Elias and Astra.

Things got better after that. Slowly, but they did get better.

While Alpha Training Grounds remained closed, there were others we could utilize, and we did. We learned how to scout in large groups, how to scout with just our griffin as our partner, and how to work in pairs. We learned how to fight alongside our griffins, who were now as large as full-grown horses, only leaner and far more agile—and deadly.

Just as importantly as the how, we learned the why.

My class schedule was adjusted so I could take the Strategy and Tactics course with my clutchmates. The instructor led us through different tabletop scenarios, covering the standard tactics and ideal scout-team size for each. But even with that addition to my schedule, I was still nearly a year behind on classwork. On the plus side, I got a glimpse of the senior classes my clutchmates were taking, and I learned quickly who would give me helpful tips for when I took the classes and who wanted me to suffer like they were suffering. Keaton, for all his impassiveness, took the most delight in withholding anything that would make passing the tests easier, though he was always quick to offer help with my current classes—help I no longer needed.

I might not be graduating on time, but at least I was no longer struggling.

With a shock, I realized a year had passed since I'd accidentally bonded Felix. He and the other griffins in Echo marked their hatching day with the start of their final growth spurt. At the end of it, they were ridable.

Riding horses had been my joy, my happy place. It was nothing compared to riding Felix. When he ran, we moved as one. It was almost as good as flying. Almost. By the time the first hints of spring warmed the air, we exclusively rode our griffins on scouting missions and patrols.

Eventually, we returned to the old training grounds. Our instructors weren't heartless. They'd given us time to recover, time for the memories to fade, but the real world wouldn't give us the same courtesy. So, we set out on our griffins one cold spring morning and rode into Alpha Training Grounds, stayed the night at Base Camp Two, and split up to hit all the scouting targets and patrol routes.

Keaton hadn't given me a choice. I'd led one squad, and he'd led the other. I'd felt sick the entire time, and had a really bad moment when we hit the creek, but the tension slowly leaked out of my spine when I couldn't pinpoint the exact spot where first the rangers, then the broken beast, had ambushed us, and the rest of the patrol route went well. The team of rangers lying in wait just before Base Camp Three never stood a chance against us, and the ambushers became the ambushed.

When we rode into camp just before sunset, triumphant and maybe a little smug, the first thing I saw was Keaton's proud smile. The second was the new stone marker at the center of camp.

I slid out of Felix's lightweight scout saddle, my gaze locked on the carved block of granite. The rays of the dying sun caught on the polished face, picking up subtle glints in the gray stone. It was a memorial dedicated to everyone who'd lost their lives to the broken beasts, carved in stone so their names would never fade.

My knees hit the dirt, and I reached out a trembling hand to trace two names in particular. Felix pressed against my side, a mournful trill spilling out of his beak. In the next instant, Tavi was there, pressing against *his* side and draping a wing over his brother's back, purring reassurance. And then Keaton knelt next to me and gripped my shoulder tight. My brother, in every way that mattered.

"I miss them." My voice was steady at least, even though my eyes burned with unshed tears. Keaton rested his free hand on top of mine, on top of those names.

Elias and Astra.

"We won't forget them, Harpy," Keaton said with quiet determination.

"Damn right, we won't."

I held onto their memory . . . and let the guilt go.

CHAPTER 14

Graduation for my clutchmates was fast approaching, and with it the annual griffin rider relay races. Classes for the semester had been completed, final exams had been taken, and one last mass briefing by the academy instructors had been endured. We'd even gone through a grueling two-week-long scouting exercise, our last practical exam, and passed with flying colors.

The relay race was our reward, a way to have fun together as Echo Clutch one last time before we were scattered to the four winds.

Ruthlessly, I suppressed the surge of resentment-tinged anger that I'd be left behind to finish the senior year classes I hadn't been able to take with my clutchmates, alone but for Felix. He brushed against my mind, a mental caress and a warning that I hadn't shielded quite as well as I'd thought, before he retreated with a trilling laugh. A reluctant smile pulled at my lips as I returned my attention to the race strategy session.

Everyone in Echo was huddled up around our barrack's work table, where we studied or repaired our riding leathers. Everyone except for Bex and Volakis. As mountain griffin riders, they were exempt from the race. While Merlin and Prue were perfectly capable of walking and even running, mountain griffin feet were more talon than paw, and they would never be the runners forest griffins were. Instead, they'd be participating in the annual war games and mock aerial battles with the dragon rider cadets, which was where their training had been focused.

Silence fell over the group. When Keaton stared at me expectantly, I realized I'd missed something directed at me.

"I'm sorry, what did you say?" I asked him sheepishly.

"I want you to go high." He grinned and gestured to the course map. "Look, this last section of the relay cuts right through the lowland valley. This time of year, it's all mud, and with all the griffins running through it'll only get worse. *But*, if you go high, you bypass all of it."

Keaton pointed out a particular area near the obstacle course, one I was well familiar with. A series of hills ran alongside it like stepping-stones, and they were technically within the bounds of the relay race. Legal by every official rule. Also incredibly useless, since running up and down the grassy hills would take longer than slogging through the mud.

My lips parted as understanding slammed into me.

"You want us to glide." I stared at him and wondered if he'd lost his mind. "Are you insane?"

"Hear me out. Felix is the biggest griffin," Keaton explained, that crazy grin still on his face. "Outside of Bex, you're the smallest rider. He might not be able to fly with you, but I bet you he can glide if he's got enough height. And you've got the training."

At his pointed look, my belly tightened with an odd mix of apprehension and anticipation. He meant dragon rider training. I tugged at Felix, who was outside playing with, or possibly tormenting, his brother.

"Is he right? Can we do it?"

Felix went very still. Barely suppressed longing strained to break free from the shield I'd placed around it, and I held my breath. Exhilaration shivered through the bond, and my shoulders flexed in unconscious mimicry as he snapped out his wings.

"I think so—"

In the next instant, a muffled squawk reverberated in my skull as Tavi tackled his brother while he was distracted. Felix managed to come out on top in the scuffle, triumph and smugness rolling through his next words.

"Tavi thinks so, too."

Snickering, I refocused on the planning session again.

"Charlie Clutch is the one to beat." A shadow crossed Keaton's face, darkening his bright amber eyes. "Delta isn't a contender. Even with them weighing the times to account for uneven teams, none of them are fast. They're workhorses, while Charlie has some real sprinters. The only way we can take them is if we stack the deck." He glanced around the table. "I'll lead off and get us a good start, but Harpy's still our strongest rider so she'll ride tail."

There were murmurs of agreement, with none of the resentment there would've been last year. Warmth bloomed in my belly, both at the casual acceptance of my hard-won skill and the praise, and I smiled as Keaton continued to strategize. Echo had nine riders participating, which meant we'd have to do three laps of the obstacle course. After breaking us into three-man teams, Keaton took suggestions on riding order and which section of the course everyone thought they were best suited to handle. He was a disgustingly good leader.

If I didn't love him like a brother, I'd be tempted to prank him like I used to prank the three morons. He caught my smirk and arched a brow in return.

"Harpy, you're the one who'll have to make up any lost time. Taking the high route through that section will definitely do the trick." For the first time he hesitated. "That is, if you think you can handle it?"

"Of course Harpy can handle it." Bex shoved her way into our huddle and bumped her shoulder against mine. She smirked, topaz eyes dancing with mischief. "You're not afraid to fall, are you?"

"No." A slow grin crossed my face as I nudged her back. "Let's do it."

The day of the races was unseasonably warm, but that was to our benefit. Hot air meant thermals, which meant Felix could glide longer distances. We hadn't been able to practice nearly as much as I would've preferred, and not on the course at all. We didn't want Charlie to know what we were up to, because they had at least one griffin rider who could duplicate the feat. If he thought of it.

Felix fidgeted beneath me as we waited impatiently for our turn to run. Since Delta only had to do two laps, they'd already finished, leaving just me and a Charlie griffin rider waiting to take up the relay and finish the course. A mocking laugh spilled out of the other griffin's beak, and my thighs flexed automatically as Felix sidestepped and snapped at him. His beak came within inches of the other griffin, but his rider smirked at the near miss. Probably because there were instructor griffins monitoring from the skies who'd disqualify us in a heartbeat if we put so much as a scratch on our competition.

"Don't give them the satisfaction," I said firmly, pressing my right leg gently against his side to encourage him to move away. He didn't budge.

"But Titus said you weren't a real griffin rider!" Felix eyed the other griffin as if deciding the best place to bite. *"I should rip his flight feathers out. They'll grow back. Eventually."*

I snorted a laugh at his viciousness and patted his shoulder soothingly. "Just ignore them."

"You might as well give up now, sweetheart." Lobo smirked. "You know we're faster than you."

"Are you?" I gave Lobo a slow grin that was more teeth than smile. "I guess we'll find out."

The thud of paws striking ground reached our ears, and both griffins tensed, ready to run. I glanced over at Lobo and arched a brow.

"Also, I'm not sure you want to brag about how *fast* you are."

A lazy smile stretched across his face, and he winked. "Anytime you want to find out, you just let me know."

I didn't bother to respond. I just relaxed into the saddle, deepening my seat as much as possible and adjusting my legs so I gripped Felix's sides tightly. Nerves fluttered in my belly. Unlike a dragon's saddle, there were no straps to hold me in, nothing to keep me from falling but my own grip and the griffin beneath me.

"I won't let you fall, Harpy," Felix said earnestly, so much love in his voice that I had to blink tears away.

"I know you won't, Felix."

The thuds grew louder, and I glanced over my shoulder in time to see one of Charlie's riders race around the bend in the trail, her griffin bounding closer with every leaping stride. Lobo's griffin trotted forward, then accelerated into a smooth run, while Lobo held one hand out. His clutchmate flashed past him, flawlessly passing over their messenger tube before her griffin slowed to a panting walk.

"See you at the finish line," Lobo called out over his shoulder as they dashed down the trail. "Sweetheart!"

"I'm going to murder that ass one of these days," I said conversationally to the other girl as she slid out of the saddle and paced next to her panting griffin.

She rolled her eyes. "We've got a betting pool going on how long he's got before he finally pisses off the wrong woman. You want in?"

"Yes," I said with a laugh, even as I strained my ears for signs of my clutchmate.

Felix's tufted ears flicked back, and he tensed. Moments later, Langston rounded the bend, sweat dripping down his face and a messenger tube held in one hand. Bailey's beak gaped as she sucked in air, and sweat darkened her flanks, but she stretched out her legs and *sprinted.*

"Ready?" Felix asked, tail lashing in eagerness. I felt his muscles bunch in anticipation and leaned forward slightly.

"Ready!"

Felix took off like a shot, almost too fast for Bailey to catch. She put on one last burst of speed, Langston slapped the messenger tube into my outstretched hand, and we were off. Felix's paws beat a steady rhythm on the packed dirt of the trail, and my spine flexed with every stride. There was no bridle, no need to control him like a horse. My hands rested lightly on either side of his neck, the messenger tube securely hooked to my belt.

Green blurred past on either side, trees and underbrush. No vines, thank fuck. Up ahead, I could barely make out Lobo and his griffin. They had a considerable lead on us, and Felix pushed himself to close the gap. A growl rumbled through his chest, something I felt through my legs more than heard, and I stroked his neck.

"Remember the plan."

"I'm going to make them eat the plan," he growled, but he slowed, running just fast enough to keep them in sight.

Sweat trickled down my spine beneath my riding leathers, but my breathing was steady, and so was Felix's. The worst part of the course was coming up—the lowlands. All muddy ditches and marshy ground guaranteed to slow the fastest runner down. Unless they went high.

I was just hoping that Lobo hadn't thought of the same plan, because if anyone from Charlie could handle those stepping-stone hills, it was him. But his griffin raced out of the trees and directly into the lowland valley. At my relieved *whoop*, Lobo cast a sharp look over his shoulder. I lifted my hand just long enough to give him a little finger wave. His eyes narrowed, and then widened in shock when Felix veered off the trail and sprinted for the first of the hills lining the western edge of the valley.

The first hill was both the tallest and steepest, and Felix had to dig his claws in as he launched himself up the slope. I flexed with each leaping stride, hands gently resting on his neck. He didn't need anything from me—he just needed me to not ride like a sack of potatoes.

My legs were already wrapped tightly around his dappled sides as he raced across the top of the hill, but I squeezed tighter, my heartbeat pounding a frantic rhythm in my chest. His wings brushed my thighs as he unfurled them. Nerves tightened my belly, but I kept my eyes up as he counted down his strides, just like we'd practiced.

"Three . . . two . . . one . . . and go!"

Felix gave a mighty leap with his back legs and launched us into open air, front paws outstretched and reaching as if he meant to jump to the next hilltop. For just an instant, we hung in midair, defying gravity as momentum carried us. The only sound was the rush of the wind and my sharp gasp—and then I screamed in pure joy as his wings snapped out and we fucking soared.

It only lasted seconds, but I felt the wind on my face again, and my cheeks hurt from grinning so hard. The next hill rushed up with frightening speed, but I had faith in my bondmate. A faith that was well rewarded when he flared his wings and smoothly hit the ground running. Shrieking in triumph, he raced across the hilltop and launched himself again. This flight lasted just a little longer, and I rejoiced in every second of it.

Felix hit the next hilltop a little harder, but my grip didn't falter, and I urged him on.

"Go, go, go!"

Laughing wildly, he launched us off the last hill, his wings stretched out as wide as he could. Feathers twitched and flight muscles made a thousand tiny adjustments. Grunting with effort, Felix beat his wings hard, fighting for every last bit of speed he could get. We flashed past Lobo and his griffin from a hundred feet in the air, the ground nothing more than a blur beneath us.

I'd treasure the dumbfounded shock on Lobo's stupidly handsome face for the rest of my life.

"Hold on!" Felix called out as he angled his wings just enough to catch a friendly thermal.

Buoyed up by the column of warm air, we rose higher before Felix angled his wings again and traded in that extra altitude for speed.

Exhilaration flooded my heart, tangled up with my griffin's, and rebounded until we were both screaming our triumph. There was no way Lobo could catch us now. We'd *won*.

"Harpy, look up! They came to watch us!"

At his happy cry, I risked a glance up but saw nothing but the achingly blue sky. Felix tugged on my mind, nudged my eyes to where they needed to look. That's when I saw the dragons—and their riders.

Black, gray, and green wings stretched wide, all three dragons keeping pace high above as we soared across the finish line.

No matter how I wished for time to slow, it didn't oblige. If anything, the remaining days flew by, faster and faster until graduation day arrived. Sleep had eluded me the night before, and Keaton and I watched the sun rise for the last time from the roof of Echo barracks.

It was a beautiful sunrise. I hated it.

A flight of gray dragons flew across the academy, the first rays of sunlight turning their hides silver as they spiraled down to land on the dragon campus. Keaton stirred and nudged my side, but his amber gaze didn't leave the sky.

"You're going to their graduation, right?" he asked quietly, his gruff voice unusually soft.

"Yeah." My lips twitched into a smile. "Bethany made me promise not to punch the morons in the face. Their guts, on the other hand, are fair game."

Keaton barked a laugh. "Just don't break your hand. You've got our graduation this afternoon."

"Wouldn't miss it." I forced my smile to stay in place, but Keaton knew me too well. He threw his arm around my shoulders and pulled me into his side. Still a little awkward, but I'd grown used to the rough affection.

"It'll be fine, Harpy." His amber gaze slid toward mine. "Never alone, remember?"

A faint trill of laughter echoed in my mind, and I gave my griffin a friendly mental smack. Keaton was right though. I was never alone, not as long as I had Felix.

"Yeah, I remember." Sighing, I slid out from under Keaton's arm and stood, stretching my spine until the vertebrae snapped into place with a satisfying *crackle*. "I'd better go get my dress uniform on."

"Have Bex or Matti double-check you," he said as he settled back on his elbows, gaze drifting back to the sky. "Don't want to ruffle any dragon rider feathers."

Snorting a laugh, I flipped him off before I jumped from the roof to the sloped hillside behind the barracks. As if I needed the help. The dragon side of the academy was far stricter than the griffin side, and I'd helped the others more than once with uniform standards on the rare occasion Commandant Pulaski required us to wear formal dress.

Felix lifted his head from his nest when I slipped inside, purple eyes squinting against the sharp ray of sunlight I'd inadvertently allowed in with me. Snores and muffled groans drifted through the cavernous room, and I quickly closed the door. As soft darkness enveloped the barracks once again, I ghosted down the aisle, as silently as if I were on a scouting mission through enemy territory. The clean, spicy scent of griffins hung heavy in the still air, nearly obscuring the less pleasant odors of a dozen cadets living in close proximity.

Most of Echo was still sleeping. Our griffins had long ago progressed to being able to feed themselves, so the last year we'd had days where we could actually sleep past dawn. Today, all Echo had to do was get up before noon and show up to their graduation in their dress uniforms. I bit my lip to keep my laughter contained at the sight of Reese and Bex's empty bunks. Either they'd also had a sleepless night of a much different flavor than mine and Keaton's, or they'd slipped out to start the day early.

I hoped they got posted together.

Active-duty assignments would be announced during graduation. Cadets were allowed to submit their preferences, but at the end of the day, the needs of our country came first. Bex would be assigned wherever mountain griffin support was needed most. The Mavens had been having difficulty producing them in the past few years, and the war had a nasty habit of chewing through their numbers at a terrifying rate. Forest griffins were typically sent to the border forts, but there were a number of assignments that had both types of griffins, so their situation wasn't hopeless.

Before I'd retreated to the roof last night, I'd spent the time prepping my uniform. All I had to do was shower, braid my hair so it was within regs, and get dressed. As I buttoned the last button and tugged the stiff jacket straight, my stomach grumbled with hunger but it was so twisted with anxiety I didn't think I'd be able to eat much. Besides, the chow hall had actually brought those godawful casseroles back, and today would be hard enough without adding that kind of sadness to the mix.

Fortunately, I kept a healthy stash of ration bars in my locker. At this point, I was practically living off the damn things. Felix clacked his beak quietly in disgust.

"So gross."

"Says the griffin who prefers his breakfast still kicking," I retorted, shoving another bite in my mouth and chewing obnoxiously at him. He trilled a sleepy laugh and tucked his head under one wing.

"No getting into trouble without me," he mumbled as he drifted back to sleep.

I rolled my eyes at him and slipped out of the barracks. If there was any trouble, I wouldn't be the one to start it.

Squinting against the brilliant sunlight, I strode down the slope, across the open quad, and toward the only place large enough to hold everyone attending graduation—the amphitheater. I wasn't the only one headed in that direction, and I fell in behind a group of dragon rider cadets I vaguely recognized from the class behind mine. One of the guys glanced back and gave me a little nod of recognition, and I took a seat in the stands next to them.

Not that there wasn't plenty of room.

Family members used to be allowed, but not after the Savinians had snuck in operatives a few years ago. Several cadets and their dragons had been killed in the bombing, and so had a lot of innocent civilians. The academy was closed to outsiders now, though members of the Tennessan military often attended the graduations. I spotted a fair number of high-ranking officers in the reserved section of the stands, including a general who bore a shocking resemblance to Zayne. I smiled, happy his father had managed to break away from his duties to attend. The last time we'd talked, Zayne hadn't been sure he'd make it.

Commandant Iverson made an incredibly brief opening remark, and then got down to business, calling out each new lieutenant's name and assigned duty station. After a few minutes, the names blurred together, and I passed the time watching the dragons perched high on the amphitheater's curving stone walls, or peering down at us from their eyries. My attention snapped back to the stage when the commandant got to a familiar name.

"Lieutenant Bethany Sturman," he bellowed, his voice carrying across the amphitheater like the roar of his red dragon, Tiberius. "Fort Oakburn."

Pride and excitement shone in my friend's fiery orange gaze, and she stood tall as he pinned on her gold bars. I was so damn proud of her, and so was Jasper. His roar of approval boomed across the academy as he watched his bondmate from his eyrie high above. As she strode off the stage, Iverson called the next name.

"Lieutenant Callum Blackwood, Fort Ashfall."

My jaw tightened as Callum stalked onto the stage. I hadn't seen him in almost a year. His slight frame had grown wiry and tough, and while he'd always been confident, there was a dangerous air to the way he moved now.

"Lieutenant Zayne Serrano, Fort Ashfall."

A slight smile graced my lips when the commandant pinned on Zayne's gold bars, and General Serrano's proud grin could be seen all the way across the amphitheater.

"Lieutenant Dimitri Thompson, Fort Ashfall."

Dimitri strode across the stage, seemingly as confident as ever, but his gaze searched the stands—and found mine. My heart stuttered at the flash of relief that crossed his face. I'd told Zayne I was coming, but Dimitri apparently hadn't been sure.

I'd been avoiding him and his damnable pity for so long, but this was my last chance to settle things with him before he left. He'd been my best friend once, had been there for me and Felix when it had mattered most. For that reason alone, I'd try to forgive him.

If only for today.

The rest of the graduation ceremony passed in a blur, and soon enough, it was over. Zayne found me first, and he snatched me up in a hug before I could ward him off.

"Put me *down*," I snapped, squirming free of his overexuberant embrace and straightening out my dress uniform with sharp, irritated tugs. "Yours isn't the only ceremony I need to attend today, you know."

"Sorry," he said with a grin that said he wasn't sorry in the least. "I'm glad you came. *Somebody* didn't believe me."

I snorted as I caught a glimpse of that somebody making his way through the crowd of cadets, instructors, and visiting officers. "He better not try to apologize today."

"Don't worry, I talked to him," Zayne said with a confidence I wasn't sure was deserved. Dimitri's dramatic black-ringed amber eyes were fixated on me, and he had that familiar, stubborn angle to his jaw. Zayne glanced over his shoulder and winced. "Please don't cause any trouble today."

"Why does everyone think I'm going to cause trouble?" I demanded in exasperation.

"I wasn't talking to you," he muttered before he slid aside to make room for our friend. Dimitri dragged a hand through his dark hair, one of his few nervous tics, and gave me a crooked smile.

"Hey, Harper."

I arched a brow. "Hey, asshole."

His lips twitched into a smirk before it fell away, replaced by determination. *Here we go . . .*

"I'm glad you made it," he said carefully, so carefully I couldn't decide between laughter, tears, or violence.

His amber gaze slid sideways toward Zayne, and his jaw flexed. For a second, I thought he'd be able to hold back the words, until one of the dragons perched on the stone wall let out a happy roar. My hands curled into fists as guilt flooded his eyes. I gave him credit for trying to hide the pity, at least.

"Harper, I'm so sor—"

"Nope."

Violence it was.

"Gods damn it," Zayne mumbled.

My fist snapped out, and I twisted my hips to put a little more power behind the strike. I'd tried subtle. I'd tried avoidance. Maybe if I pissed him off enough, he'd finally get it. My knuckles cracked against his face, and he doubled over with a low growl. I grinned and shook my fist out.

Bethany had been right. Noses really did make such a lovely sound when they broke.

Dimitri glared at me through his hands as he tried to stem the flow of bright red blood and keep his dress uniform clean. I'd definitely pissed him off. There wasn't a trace of guilt or pity in those striking eyes now, just a metric fuckton of anger.

My grin widened. Good. Dimitri and I had always been at our best when we were fighting. This guilt-trip pity fest had to stop, or what was left of our friendship wouldn't survive.

"Damn it, Harper," he roared. "Would you stop doing that!"

"Stop trying to apologize, and I'll stop breaking your nose," I shot back tauntingly. When his hands curled into fists, I beckoned with one hand. "Bring it, bitch."

"And we're done," Zayne snapped, one big hand clamping down on Dimitri's shoulder. "Let's go get you cleaned up." As he forcibly marched Dimitri across the stands and away from the crowd, his voice drifted back just loud enough for me to hear. "You're such a dumbass, man. I *told* you to leave it alone, but you just couldn't stop yourself, could you?"

"We ruined her life, the least we could do is apologize for it . . ."

My grin faded. Any sense of accomplishment I'd felt at riling him up drained away. It wasn't the apology that was the problem, but he *still* didn't get it. Felix stirred, my distress rousing him from his late morning nap.

"You okay, Harpy?" Felix prodded at the ache in my knuckles, and his concern was replaced with amusement. *"I told you no trouble without me."*

"Yeah, yeah, featherhead." I shook out my hand in a futile attempt to banish the discomfort. *"I'll be back soon, why don't you get yourself some breakfast? I can feel your stomach cramping."*

"Five more minutes," he mumbled before a fierce itch distracted him. His flight feathers were molting again, and he turned his attention to plucking out the old feathers.

Sighing, I turned to look for Bethany, and found Callum instead. I jerked backward, because the sneaky bastard was standing a bare foot away and I hadn't heard a thing. Even distracted by Dimitri and Felix and throbbing knuckles, I should have.

Sadness replaced my surprise as I studied his silvery-gray eyes. We'd been close once, but it was like a stranger stood before me, one I hardly recognized. We hadn't spoken since that day in the quad, when he'd accused me of betraying them to Commandant Iverson, and I had no idea what to say to him.

Callum solved that problem with typical aggression.

"Did you know General Serrano paid us a visit after you bonded Felix?"

My lips parted in shock. Not because Zayne's father had visited the academy, but because Callum knew my griffin's name. Slowly, I shook my head, and a humorless smile twisted his lips.

"He chewed us out worse than Iverson did, tore a literal strip off our hides. You know what he told us when he was done?" Callum didn't wait for me to answer, he just plowed on, throwing words at me, sharp as my knife and just as likely to draw blood. "He said you spoke for us. We stole your fucking wings, and you spoke *for* us. Why the *hell* would you do that?"

My head tilted at the boiling anger in his eyes, and I studied him for a long moment before understanding hit. Callum hated to be in debt to anyone, and he'd been nursing resentment because he thought he owed me his career this whole time . . . when in reality it had nothing to do with him at all.

"I thought about it you know. Revenge." I swallowed hard as I thought back to that conversation in Commandant Iverson's office and the temptation he'd dangled in front of me. "But I didn't want to be that person."

"I would've been *exactly* that person," Callum said in a low, seething tone. "I would've thrown you to the rampaging dragon in a heartbeat."

I smiled and leaned closer, because this wasn't a stranger after all. He was still *Cal*, the guy who ran his mouth and pretended he didn't need anyone at all. The same guy who was unfailingly loyal once you'd gotten past his spiky exterior.

"No, you wouldn't have."

"Don't be too sure of that," he growled before he drew in a deep breath and slowly let it out. "The general said you were a big part of the reason we weren't expelled or reduced to griffin riders like—"

"Like me?" I asked with a wry smile. He had the grace to wince.

"Yeah, like you." His jaw flexed and his eyes darted to a lithe gray dragon perched on the wall. He kept his gaze fixed on her as he hoarsely whispered, "If it weren't for you, not even General Serrano could've saved us. So . . . thanks, Harper."

When he glanced back at me, it was with a mischievous grin I hadn't seen in over a year. The one he wore whenever we'd pulled off an exceptionally good prank.

"He also told us you were the reason we spent two weeks cleaning latrines with toothbrushes."

I arched a brow. "Did you have to use your personal ones?"

"No."

"Damn." I crossed my arms and fought back a grin. "You're still a dick."

"And you're still a brat." Callum gave me a serrated smile. "So, you gonna forgive me?"

I snorted. "You gonna apologize?"

He smirked and turned on his heel. Over his shoulder he called back, "Maybe next time, Harper."

After spending a few hours hanging out with Bethany and Jasper, it was time for the griffin rider graduation ceremony. Bethany went to save us seats, while I snuck into the back to wish my clutchmates luck before they crossed the stage and officially became officers in the Tennessan Griffin Corps.

The area behind the stage was cramped, with more than a few curious griffins making it even more congested. Charlie Clutch was lined up at the front, and I met Lobo's annoyed glare with a wide smile and a little finger wave. He was still holding a grudge over the race, and I was still having far too much fun riling him up over it. *New game.*

Weaving around the rest of Charlie and what was left of Delta, I finally made it back to Echo. As I strolled up to Keaton, I casually tucked my hands behind my back. He wasn't fooled for an instant.

"Did you break your hand?" he asked gruffly.

"Of course not." I held up my reddened knuckles for his inspection and smirked. "Reese taught me better than that."

"Damn right I did," the dark-haired grumpy cadet muttered from where he stood next to Hawthorne. Bex leaned out from behind him and grinned at me, her topaz eyes sparkling with mischief.

"Who and where?"

"Dimitri." I flexed my throbbing hand and smirked. "Broke his nose. Again."

She punched her fist in the air and cheered before she spun around to Matthews. "Pay up, Matti."

My jaw dropped. "You guys were *betting* on it?"

"Duh." Bex winked at me. "And you won me the whole pot."

Matthews shrugged and shifted her weight with a pained grimace. Her knee had never healed completely. Unsurprisingly, Nell was one of the griffins who'd decided to stick close, and the sleek griffin pressed against her bondmate's side, encouraging her to lean her weight against her.

"Honestly," she said, "I figured Cal would win if only because he's *such* a dick."

I paused. "And you know this how?"

"What?" Matthews gave me a slow grin. "Cal's hot and we had a fling a few months back."

My nose wrinkled. "Oh, ew. Please never use the words 'hot' and 'fling' in relation to Cal again." I held up a hand, my grimace nearly as pained as hers had been. "No judgment, Matti, but that's as gross as calling Keaton hot."

"Thanks?" Keaton asked with a bewildered glare. "Harpy, get out of here before you get into trouble." He paused, and his gaze dropped to my bruised knuckles. "More trouble."

Hurt stabbed unexpectedly deep, but he caught my arm when I would've stalked past him without a word. He dropped his voice low like we were out on a scouting mission.

"They're about to start, and Pulaski is glaring at you like she's about to have *you* scrubbing latrines."

My head snapped around, and sure enough, there was our commandant, staring directly at me. Lobo stood nearby, looking entirely too smug. He gave me a little finger wave and a wink. If it weren't for Pulaski, I'd have returned it with a one-fingered salute.

Sighing, I waved at my clutchmates and slunk back to the stands. My spirits lifted when I found not just Bethany waiting for me, but Felix. He'd draped himself along the top of the stands like an overgrown cat, with Jasper perched on the stone wall directly above. I leaned on their support as I watched my clutchmates—once hostile, resentful strangers, and now as close as family—graduate without me.

It hurt, but I kept a smile on my face. It helped that I really was proud of them all, and I cheered like a lunatic when Reese and Bex ended up stationed together at Fort Arcadia. Keaton went last of all, and I braced myself when his gold bars were pinned on, waiting to hear where he'd be going next.

"Lieutenant Tyler Keaton, first assignment instructor, Tennessan Bonded Training Academy." Commandant Pulaski gave him a sharp grin. "Welcome to the dark side, Lieutenant Keaton."

I froze, hardly breathing, hardly daring to hope. And then Keaton's gaze found mine, and he smiled. Felix relayed his words for me.

"*Never alone, Harpy.*"

I grinned down at him, deliriously happy that my brother had stayed behind for me.

Keaton snorted as we stood at attention outside of Commandant Pulaski's office. "Don't flatter yourself, Harpy," he muttered out of the side of his mouth. "Tavi just didn't want to leave Felix."

I kept my gaze locked forward but couldn't help my snicker. "Whatever you need to tell yourself, Keaton."

"Keaton, Tavros, get your butts in here!" Pulaski called out.

My shoulders relaxed slightly at the edge of amusement in the older woman's voice, but I still marched inside and saluted.

"Cadet Tavros, reporting."

"Ca—" A dull red flush traveled across Keaton's face as he cleared his throat. "Lieutenant Keaton, reporting."

"At ease, both of you." Pulaski grinned at Keaton. "Still feels weird, doesn't it?"

"Yes, ma'am."

"Don't worry, you'll adjust." She shifted her formidable gaze to me. "Speaking of adjusting, I'm reworking your class schedule again."

Hope flared up higher than when I found out Keaton was staying.

"So I can graduate earlier, ma'am?"

She held my gaze for a long moment. And then she smiled.

"Yes. Professor Adderley has volunteered to personally tutor you in several subject areas. With his assistance, you'll graduate at the end of the fall semester." Before I could do something embarrassing—like squeal—she held up a hand. "There's a catch."

Of course there is.

"I have a problem you're in a position to solve for me. One of my instructors has orders to report to Fort Mayberry at the end of the semester, so I'll be short. Since you're now graduating early, you'll take over his slot as a first assignment instructor." She tilted her head toward Keaton. "And at the end of the year, you'll both be assigned to an active-duty fort."

A slow smile spread across my face.

"I'm not done yet," she cautioned, the beginnings of sharp amusement in her eyes. "You and your griffin have already passed all the physical requirements, but we can't let those new skills languish. While you finish up your classwork, you'll also assist our newest instructors."

My smile grew. "No offense, ma'am, but I'm not seeing the catch."

"While you're still a cadet, I'm pairing you with Lieutenant Lorenzo." When my shoulders slumped, she grinned. "You'll survive, Tavros."

Of all people, Lobo just had to decide to apply for one of the other first assignment instructor positions. He was the *last* person I wanted to spend time with, but despite that minor setback, my smile didn't dim. I was going to graduate early *and* I'd be able to stay with Keaton. Working with Lobo was a small price to pay—even if that ass would probably make me call him Lieutenant Lorenzo. I rolled my shoulders back.

"Yes, ma'am."

"In addition to your classroom and instructor duties, the pair of you will be added to the duty roster and assigned a patrol route." Her grin turned sharp as she arched a brow at Keaton. "If you thought you were getting off lightly as an instructor, you were sadly mistaken."

"Never crossed my mind, ma'am."

"Good. You'll both need to be out of Echo barracks by sunset so it can be prepped for the next clutch. Since you spent the past year and a half living together, I assumed assigning you a shared room in the instructor dorm wouldn't be an issue." Her iron-gray brow arched. "Will it?"

We both shook our heads. If nothing else, our griffins would appreciate nesting together, and I was more or less used to how loudly Keaton snored. She nodded and waved a hand to dismiss us before she paused.

"One more thing, Tavros." She tossed a new set of cadet rank pins on her scuffed desk. They weren't a lieutenant's bars, but they were gold, unlike my current silver chevrons. "Your exact situation might be unique, but you aren't the first cadet who's had to stay longer. The new rank marks you as above a normal cadet and exempts you from most of the bullshit we put you through the first four years."

"Thank you, ma'am," I said with quiet sincerity. As my fingers wrapped around the new chevrons, her gaze hardened.

"*Don't* abuse it."

"I won't, ma'am."

"Good. I expect those back in the same condition. I wore them once too, a very long time ago."

When I blinked in surprise, the corner of her mouth kicked up in a slight smile. Her attention fixed on my bruised knuckles as I swapped out my rank, and amusement twinkled in her brilliant green eyes.

"And Tavros? Stay out of trouble."

"Yes, ma'am." As we closed her door behind us, I scowled at Keaton. "Why does everyone keep saying that?"

"Because you *are* trouble," a deep voice muttered.

My gaze snapped around. Lobo stood in the hall with his arms crossed. *Fuck my life.*

"Commandant Pulaski said you'd be helping us out, Harpy." Unexpectedly, he grinned without a trace of his earlier irritation. "I asked her if I could have you for the obstacle course. You have *got* to teach me and Titus how to glide like that. You guys helped Echo break the course record, you know."

I blinked. That was *respect* in his voice. His grin faded.

"Besides, gliding like that could save a scout's life out in the field. You guys heard about Bradford, right?"

I frowned. Fort Bradford was in the eastern hill country, one of the border forts that had been built at the apex of one of the tallest, rockiest hills in the area. That hill was practically a baby mountain and wouldn't have been out of place in the Smoke Mountains. The fort itself was small but tough, and acted as an anchor point for one of our main patrol routes in that region.

"No." I exchanged a quick glance with Keaton, but he seemed as clueless as me. "What happened?"

"It's gone," Lobo said grimly. "Along with every griffin rider stationed there. I heard the dragon riders made it out. No clue if the arrogant bastards bothered to evac anyone before they flew off."

The bottom dropped out of my stomach.

Lieutenant Osbourne had been stationed at Bradford.

"Remember to request Fort Oakburn," Bethany said before she gave me a hard hug. "I'm going to miss you, girl."

My throat tightened, but I threw my arms around her and hugged her back. "I'll miss you too."

The sun hadn't even crested the horizon yet, but the landing field was packed with newly commissioned dragon rider officers and their dragons preparing to depart. Bethany and Jasper would travel to their duty station with the other riders who'd been assigned there, led by a rider from Oakburn.

She reluctantly pulled away when the rider's heavily scarred dragon, his hide so dark a gray he nearly seemed black, let out an impatient roar. She forced a smile.

"Don't worry. The year will fly by before you know it."

Then she was gone.

I watched the sky until I couldn't spot the flash of red wings anymore and turned to go. My breath caught. Dimitri, Callum, and Zayne stood across the field next to their dragons, looking damned impressive in their new flying leathers. My chin lifted and I held their gazes for a moment that stretched into eternity.

My brothers, my rivals, my betrayers.

All three brought their fist to their chest in a dragon rider's salute. The one they only gave to their own. My body moved automatically, returning the salute without any conscious direction on my part.

And then they were gone, too. But I wasn't alone. I never would be as long as I had Felix . . . and Keaton and Tavi.

CHAPTER 15

Bethany was right. The year flew by.

Keaton and I fell into a natural rhythm, juggling instructor duties with patrolling around the academy and my classes. Professor Adderley's private tutoring sessions were less than fun, but when he wasn't randomly assigning me extra work, or falling into one of his strange moods, he really did have valuable insight into the war with Savinia. I absorbed everything I could—when Felix wasn't being a brat and trying to distract me because he was bored.

Out of all of my duties, I'd dreaded working with Lobo the most. To my shock, he'd turned out to be a good guy under the arrogant exterior and a great instructor. That didn't mean he didn't make another pass at me, but he not only understood the word "no," he also proved a good student. He'd been serious about learning to glide, and we spent long hours training on the obstacle course after dismissing the cadets.

While he was far too big for Titus to glide any great distance with, he had an excellent seat and good balance, which were key. After a few weeks of practice, they managed to nail the stepping-stone hills perfectly, gliding long past the finish line.

The wide grin he'd given me had been pure happiness and excitement, without a shred of arrogance or artifice. I'd stared at that grin, stunned into silence.

Oh...do that again.

That was the day no turned into yes.

As summer heat began its slow slide into winter cold, I finished up the last of my classes. My days as a cadet were finally over. While my overall scores weren't as good as they might have been if I hadn't had a compressed schedule, I'd passed. Not being the best was a small price to pay to graduate early.

When Commandant Pulaski pinned on my gold bars, she dropped her voice low, her words meant only for my ears. And my griffin's.

"Proud of you, Tavros. The Griffin Corps is damned lucky to have a rider like you."

I blinked back tears. "Thank you, ma'am."

"As if my bonded would be anything less than amazing," Felix purred deep in my mind, pride and love washing over me. I grinned.

"Love you, too, featherhead."

When I tried to hand Commandant Pulaski back her old cadet rank, she shook her head. "Keep 'em. And remember to hold on to that fire. You'll need it."

Before long, spring rolled around again and the last semester, where I was a full instructor, flew by until there was only one day remaining before Keaton and I left for our active-duty assignment. Commandant Pulaski had pulled a few strings and ensured we were assigned to Fort Ashfall together.

I owed her...so much.

Keaton and I lounged on the grassy slope overlooking the quad, relaxing in the warm afternoon sun while we could before we had to finish packing. It would take about three weeks of overland travel to get to Fort Ashfall, even riding our griffins, and we weren't exactly in a hurry to begin the grueling trip. Fortunately, the griffin rider tasked with escorting us was running late, so we weren't leaving until the next day.

A smirk stretched my lips as I watched Keaton's eyes track a senior dragon rider cadet as she walked past with her friends. Her gaze briefly slid his direction before she laughed a little louder, swayed her hips a little harder. I elbowed him pointedly.

"She thinks you're hot."

Objectively, he really was, especially with the amount of muscle he'd put on in the past year. Combined with his brilliant amber eyes and dark hair, and Keaton wasn't lacking for willing partners. It also meant he didn't always come back to our room, and any night I could escape his snoring was a bonus.

"How do you know?" Keaton demanded, but he stared at the dragon rider with undisguised interest.

"I'm a girl, I know these things," I said smugly.

"It doesn't matter." He tore his gaze off her and scowled at me. "I'm an officer. It wouldn't be appropriate."

"You're an officer in the *Griffin* Corps. She's a dragon rider cadet. Entirely different chain of command." I waved a dismissive hand. "You're fine. Besides, we're leaving tomorrow. Who cares? Go have fun."

"Harpy . . ." He trailed off as the curvy brunette glanced over her shoulder, a sultry smile on her lips, and my brother was a goner. "Never mind."

I smothered a laugh as he rolled to his feet. He definitely had a type.

"I am the best wingwoman ever," I muttered as Keaton sauntered over to her with confidence in every stride.

"Does this mean you'll have your room to yourself tonight?" Lobo dropped down into the grass next to me with lazy grace and a lazier smile on his face. "You know I'm always happy to keep you company, sweetheart. Wouldn't want you to be lonely."

"Beast." I grinned and poked at his side. "You're lucky you're hot."

He caught my hand and brushed his lips over my knuckles with a wink. "Yes, I am."

"Don't forget arrogant."

"You say that like it's a bad thing," he said in a low voice. When I tugged him close and kissed his sly grin off his lips, he waggled his brows. "Is that a yes, Trouble?"

"Try my door tonight, Lo." I pushed him away with a snicker. "If it's unlocked, you'll have your answer."

"You've never locked me out before, why should our last night together be any different?" He flopped back on the sun-warmed grass and crossed muscular arms behind his head. His crystalline green eyes slid toward mine. "What time do you and Keaton leave for Fort Ashfall tomorrow? And why do you look like you just bit into a sour apple?"

"Because we leave before dawn, and Ashfall is where the three morons were stationed," I grumbled, still annoyed that our request for Oakburn had been denied.

"One, that's stupid early. Two, Ashfall's a major fort. Plenty of room to avoid them." He hesitated. "At least you and Keaton were assigned together."

My head tilted, and I studied him for a moment. We'd never pretended to be anything more than what we were—friends with benefits. My gaze drifted over his muscled body and anticipation coiled low in my belly. Friends with very *good* benefits, but never anything more, so I was surprised at the genuine sadness in his eyes.

"Are you . . . okay, Lo?"

"Don't worry your pretty head about it, sweetheart." He sat up abruptly, any trace of emotion disappearing beneath his usual arrogance. "I'll be just fine."

Well, I knew one way to make sure of that. I rolled to my feet and stretched. Lobo's gaze grew heated, but I just turned on my heel and sauntered up the slope toward the dorms.

"Fine, just leave me here, all lonely and shit," he grumbled good-naturedly.

"I'm going to go pack." I glanced back and smirked. "In my empty room."

Understanding dawned on his face, and he scrambled to his feet with an amusing lack of grace. I took off up the slope, giggling like a fiend. His husky laughter rang out, and he gave chase, just like I knew he would. As I ran, I cast a teasing grin over my shoulder, silently daring him to catch me, before I stretched my legs into a sprint. Just because I wanted to be caught didn't mean I'd make it easy on him.

He caught me long before we reached my room.

I didn't mind in the least.

Judging by Keaton's rumpled hair and bloodshot eyes the next morning, he got about as much sleep as I did. Our griffins were highly amused by our questionable life choices. As Felix snickered and flicked his tail against my leg, I gave him a smug grin.

"You can tease all you want, you fancy chicken. I regret nothing."

"Me neither, but please, no details," Keaton mumbled as he leaned against the academy gates. "There's some things I don't need to know about you."

"Agreed," I said with a shudder. Our griffins exchanged identical grins, and I swiped a hand over my face with a groan. "One of these days, we'll learn not to give them extra ammunition."

I switched to mindspeech and glared at Felix. *"I swear, if you tell me anything about what Keaton got up to with that girl, I will pluck all your tail feathers while you sleep."*

Felix whipped his tail out of reach. *"You wouldn't dare."*

"Try me, featherhead."

When he snapped his beak in irritation, one of the geldings shifted his weight and let out a nervous nicker. Our escort had brought a trio of Fort Ashfall's packhorses with him to transport our gear and travel supplies, but while they were used to griffins and dragons, they weren't as stoic as our academy-bred horses. Crooning gentle reassurance, I stroked the gelding's neck until he settled again.

"Remind me why we had to get up this early again?" Keaton grumbled without bothering to open his eyes.

Morning mist lingered in the trees beyond the academy gates, and the sun hadn't yet crested the horizon. As warm as it was already, it was going to be an unseasonably hot day, and I was grateful for my lightweight summer riding leathers. We'd have to keep an eye on the packhorses today.

Assuming we ever left.

Our escort, Lieutenant Nikos, had been closeted in a meeting with Commandants Iverson and Pulaski and their senior staff since he'd arrived in the predawn darkness, bearing messages from the border forts. The whipcord lean man hadn't bothered to tell us anything other than to load our gear on the packhorses and wait for him. That was over an hour ago.

Finally, long after the sun had risen, Nikos strode out of the griffin campus. He paused and tilted his head back toward the morning sky, faded copper gaze searching. With a flash of reddish-brown feathers, his griffin, Erra, flew over from the livestock pens where she'd helped herself to the first breakfast she hadn't had to hunt in weeks.

As she prowled across the grass toward us, Nikos matched her pace and swung himself up in her saddle. They didn't stop or even slow as they approached, they just walked through the main academy gates at that smooth pace that would eat up the miles.

"Let's go, newbies," Nikos said over his shoulder.

My gut tightened, and I turned back to look at the academy one final time. This place had been my home for five years, and while it hadn't always been easy, it had been constant, unchanging, *safe*. My gaze caught on the now well-recovered patch of grass near the hatchery where Zathrid and her rider had perished, and Elias and Astra flashed in my memory. For just a second, I saw his teasing smirk, heard her mischievous laughter.

I bowed my head in remembrance. *Okay, maybe not safe, but safer than the frontlines anyway.*

Keaton swung onto Tavi's back, the lead line for the packhorse string already secured to his saddle. His eyes were alert now, his smile understanding. "Come on, Harpy. Time to go."

I nodded as Felix sidled up next to me, and reached for the saddle.

"Harpy!"

I whipped back around in time to see Titus gliding down into the quad from the top of the barracks slope, Lobo perfectly balanced despite the lack of saddle. Titus nailed the landing and smoothly trotted across the grass to us.

"Was afraid I'd miss you," Lobo said as he slid off his griffin's back and grinned down at me. He didn't leave until tomorrow and had been soundly asleep when I'd crawled out of bed that morning. We'd thoroughly said our goodbyes already, and I hadn't seen the point of waking him. I was oddly touched that he'd come to see me off.

My lips twitched into a teasing smile as I arched a brow. "Are you? Going to miss me?"

His gaze traveled over me as his lips stretched into a first-class leer. "Well, I'll miss certain things about you."

He roared a laugh at my mock glare and pulled me into a brief embrace and a longer kiss. Long enough that Keaton grumbled something about being sick. He trotted through the gate on Tavi, the packhorses following in an obedient line. Lobo snickered as he stepped back and rested a hand on his griffin's muscled shoulder.

"Be safe out there, Trouble."

Felix snapped his beak at Titus, his tufted ears flattened as he deliberately turned his back on the other griffin. He still hadn't forgiven him for what he'd said about me not being a real griffin rider, even though Titus had only said it to get under Felix's feathers. Smothering a laugh at my irritated griffin, I pulled myself into the saddle and smiled.

"I'll see you around, Lo."

Almost before the words were out of my mouth, Felix spun around and dashed out of the academy gates for the last time. He only took a few leaping strides under a brilliant blue sky before we raced beneath the green canopy of the forest surrounding the academy. As we ran down the familiar trail to catch up to the others, I glanced over my shoulder. Lobo stood next to his griffin, watching us go. He lifted a hand in farewell, and then the trail curved and they were gone.

An unexpected pang of sadness shot through me, but I didn't think it was because I loved him. Not really. That didn't mean I wouldn't miss him. Felix purred as he ran, a soothing rumble I felt as much as heard, and I patted his shoulder.

It didn't take Felix long to catch up to his brother. Soon enough, I shook off my melancholy and just enjoyed the ride through the sun-dappled woods. The trail was wide enough our griffins could trot next to each other, but we fell into patrol habits—eyes and ears open, mouths shut.

Lieutenant Nikos glanced back a time or two, and I thought I caught a flash of approval in his copper eyes.

After a quick stop at a fast-running stream to care for the packhorses and eat a quick lunch, we kept going until the sun began its descent to the western horizon. We'd relayed through our griffins all day, so it was almost a shock when Nikos broke the silence.

"All right, newbies. We've got two choices for the night. There's a good spot to camp just a mile further up the trail, or we can push on to the next village and sleep at the waystation." His head tilted slightly in the way of griffin riders as he watched us. "Your call."

My eyes narrowed slightly as I thought through the choices.

Every village and town was required to maintain a waystation for riders as part of their civic duty to support the Tennessan military. However, stopping at one meant the village would have to replace any supplies we used up, and spring was the lean time of year for the smaller villages.

"How big is the village?" I asked.

"Not very."

I blinked in surprise when he offered no more detail than that. Nikos was an experienced scout. Withholding information from us could only be a deliberate choice on his part.

He was testing us.

My fingers tapped a steady beat against the saddle as I tilted my head back and scanned the sky through the overlapping branches. Camping would come with its own set of challenges, but the sky was clear, and it was warm enough to sleep under the stars. We also had plenty of trail rations to tide us over until we passed through a larger village. Water was the biggest concern, both for drinking and bathing. We'd all sweated through our leathers, and at a minimum we'd need a quick wash and change of underclothes and socks tonight. Otherwise, we were at risk of developing sores. Proper camp and personal hygiene had been drilled into us from year one at the academy.

Keaton hummed thoughtfully under his breath, his quick mind following the same trail as mine. "Is there running water at the camping spot?"

"Yes."

Keaton and I exchanged a quick glance and nodded.

"Camp," we said in unison.

That earned us our first smile. "Good choice."

Less than ten minutes later, we turned off the main trail and rode single file down a faint track through the trees. The brush was thick here, and I was grateful for my leathers when more than one thorny branch *thwacked* against my leg. As the burbling song of running water reached our ears, the packhorses whickered, nostrils flaring in eagerness for a drink, and we soon broke out into a narrow clearing flush up against a creek so tiny it probably dried up during the hottest months.

Apparently, Erra had been testing our griffins much like her rider had tested us. Felix and Tavi declined their field rations and followed her into the woods to hunt, while we took care of the packhorses and set up camp. Nikos didn't sit back and watch, he pitched in, and between the three of us we soon had the horses settled, our supplies secured, and a small fire going. Our griffins returned with the onset of night, bellies full and beaks bloody. They cleaned up in the creek, and we bedded down for the night.

It wasn't the first night I'd camped beneath the stars by a long shot, but sleep refused to come, and I tossed and turned. As the moon rose over the trees, bright enough to wash out the weaker stars, Felix padded over with silent grace and curled around me.

"Thoughts too loud," he mumbled in a sleepy complaint. *"Go to sleep or I'll smother you with my wings."*

I rolled my eyes even as I pillowed my head on his sleek furry side. *"If you smother me, you won't have anyone to scratch behind your ears."*

"I'm adorable, I'll find somebody. Sleep, Harpy."

I tried and failed miserably—until a faint snore hit my ears. Keaton must have been awake too, otherwise I would've heard him hours ago. Something tight in my chest relaxed at the annoying sound, and I finally drifted off to the familiar rattle of his snores in one ear, and the beat of Felix's heart in the other.

Midmorning the next day, we passed through the village Nikos had mentioned. While there was a definite sense of relief that we weren't stopping, every last person had a smile or a friendly greeting for us, and more than one thanked us for our service. That last felt more than a little uncomfortable. Yes, we'd volunteered to serve, but we hadn't actually *done* anything yet. From the impassive expression on Keaton's face, he was just as uncomfortable, but Nikos would just smile and thank them.

As we hit the far side of the village, an old farmer with dirt permanently ingrained into his hands stopped us long enough to press bags of fresh snap peas on us, sweet enough to eat straight out of the bag. He refused payment, but Nikos dug out a pair of Erra's old flight feathers from his travel pack, in perfect condition and shining in the bright sunlight. He tilted his head toward the pair of boys hiding behind a split-rail fence, adorable young faces near-identical to the farmer.

"For your grandkids."

The old farmer grinned as the boys darted out with squeals of excitement, and they hugged those pretty burgundy feathers to their chests like they were the greatest gift they'd ever been given. And then we moved on and kept moving until it was time to stop.

That night, we camped out again. Setup went smoother, hunting went well enough that our griffins brought back a pair of rabbits to supplement our rations, and sleep came easier.

The rest of the first week passed in much the same way. We were on one of the major east-west roads, and we passed through plenty of small villages. More often than not, the villagers were friendly. They would give us smiles and thanks, fresh vegetables, last-season fruits, and sometimes even dried meat for the griffins.

Things changed the closer we got to the Mistmurk River.

The forests gave way to vast farm fields, and the small villages to proper towns, and the townsfolk weren't as friendly as the villagers. There were no more random gifts of food and very few thanks, and even though they were still polite, more than one person regarded our griffins with unease instead of wonder. The bigger the towns grew, the more unease I saw.

And fear.

That bothered me more than the people who had thanked us . . . but not as much as it bothered Felix.

The day we crossed the Mistmurk River, there wasn't a cloud in the sky, and the sun threatened to sweat every last drop of water from our bodies. I walked next to Felix as we crossed the first bridge. The river was so wide, I could barely make out the far side, and we couldn't build a bridge long enough to span it. Instead, a narrow island in the middle anchored a pair of bridges.

I wiped sweat from my brow before it could trickle into my eyes, and stared down at the murky waters. Despite their placid appearance, the current was fast, and a tangled mess of branches flashed past before I could blink.

"I wouldn't want to swim in that," I muttered to Felix, wrinkling my nose at the heavy scent of old fish and fresh mud.

"Me neither."

Nikos huffed a quiet laugh. *"Dragons* don't swim in that river."

Keaton's brow furrowed. "Why not?"

Beckoning us to follow, Nikos pulled a rabbit Erra had caught that morning out of the small game bag hanging off one of the packhorses and led us over to the chest-high rail. With quick, efficient slices of his knife, he gutted the rabbit, tossed the good parts to our griffins, and chucked the offal into the water.

"Watch," he said quietly as he wiped his hands clean.

Within seconds, the water churned as the local denizens honed in on the bait. Fins sliced through the surface, sharks lured in by the blood scent, but they scattered as something else rose up from beneath. Something much bigger. I caught a glimpse of dull scales and a mouth large enough to swallow a griffin before it too vanished into the murky depths.

"Bull sharks, gators, and fish large enough to eat a dragon are why not. Not to mention the current. You're like as not to get swept down to the ocean as make it across Old Muddy." Nikos caught our confusion and smiled. "Local name for the river. It's older than our country, and it's had a lot of names. That's one of the oldest."

My brow furrowed as a faint memory of dry history lectures surfaced. "I think Adderley called it that once."

Nikos barked a laugh. "Is he still convinced water rights started the war?" When we nodded, he stabbed a finger at the river. "Lifeblood of our country or not, that is the most dangerous natural hazard within our borders next to the Smoke Mountains and the things that live there."

"What about the blasted zones?" Keaton asked.

Any amusement faded from the other rider's face. "There's nothing natural about those." He stalked back to Erra. "Come on, newbies. We're wasting daylight."

As we crossed the second bridge, Felix tugged at my mind.

"Look."

I squinted against the harsh glare of sunlight on water and could just make out the remnants of a great bridge in the distance. Support pillars marched across the river in a straight line. Several sections of the bridge still stretched between the pillars, but there were massive chunks missing, as if something very large had taken bites out of it, and gaps where there was no bridge at all.

Proof that not even duracrete lasted forever.

We'd just reached the far bank when a pair of dragons flew downriver, gray wings stretched wide as they utilized the thermals to glide. One swung closer and gave us a friendly wing waggle, and I grinned and tossed him a griffin rider salute.

Nikos stiffened though, and his copper eyes glazed over as his griffin tracked their flight. A moment later, he blinked and relaxed.

"Sir?" I asked quietly. He waved an irritable hand.

"This isn't the academy, Nikos is fine." His gaze followed the dragons' flight path for another few seconds before he gave us a hard look. "If you see riderless dragons, say something. Odds are they're not friendly."

Keaton's jaw tightened in understanding, but it took me a second longer for Nikos' meaning to sink in—and then Zathrid's sunset eyes flashed in my mind and I understood. "Tennessan dragons, but Savinian controlled."

Griffin wings rustled with unease as fear ricocheted through our bonds, growing stronger with each rebound. The fear of being captured and tortured until we broke and allowed ourselves to be used against our country... against our brothers- and sisters-in-arms. Terror shivered down my spine as I remembered the scars on Zathrid's limbs, the hopelessness in her eyes.

And the desperation.

Felix pressed against my side, and I wrapped my arm around his neck, both of us trying to reassure the other. As Keaton pulled himself onto Tavi's back, I caught his amber gaze and saw the same fear reflected in his eyes.

"Savinia honors the Prisoner of War treaty in name only," Nikos said, his expression hard, almost as impassive as Keaton's, but beneath lurked the horror of someone who'd seen things he desperately wished he hadn't. "At the last POW exchange, they sent back a dozen men bearing the marks of long-term starvation and torture, nothing more than broken shells. No women, no riders. And I don't think they'll release any more captured riders, not after the last time we found one of their POW camps and broke them out."

Nikos slung himself back into the saddle and calmly attached the packhorse lead line, but his hands were white-knuckled, and a muscle in his jaw ticked. Something in the way he'd said "we" made me think he'd been personally involved in that rescue. A low growl tumbled out of Erra's open beak, and her claws flexed, digging into the muddy ground.

"Whatever fucking hole they're keeping them in now, not even the rangers have been able to find them." Nikos glanced back at us as Erra prowled down the road, her tail lashing in agitation with each step. "So here's a bit of advice for you both—don't get caught."

Keaton and I exchanged a long glance. Sleep didn't come so easy that night.

CHAPTER 16

Our route to Fort Ashfall took us toward Stonehaven. I'd never been to the capital city of Tennessan, but Keaton had grown up in one of the surrounding towns on the southside. It still amazed me that a city could be so large that it collected smaller cities, like an honor guard, or a mother with a flock of unruly children. The towns grew larger, and the packed dirt road turned to paved stone, like the paths at the academy. Felix and Tavi flicked theirs ears in distaste before they very reluctantly walked on the smooth surface, and only after Erra trilled a mocking laugh.

The closer we got to Stonehaven, the quieter Keaton grew. He buried whatever was going on beneath his normal impassive mask, but I caught the growing anxiety he tried to hide. It was in every jerky movement, in the tense set of his shoulders, in the stiff way he sat in the saddle. Keaton was many things, but a terrible rider wasn't one of them. Tavi stuck close to his bonded, and I heard his rough purr on more than one night. Finally, one morning, I couldn't take it anymore. I caught his arm before he could mount up on Tavi.

"What is going on with you?"

"Nothing," Keaton growled. He yanked his arm out of my grasp, but paused when I wasn't quite able to hide the flash of hurt. He flexed his shoulders and let out a slow breath. "This is where I grew up, remember?"

"Yes," I said impatiently.

"Yeah, well..." His gaze went distant, seeing things I couldn't. "It's where Marcos grew up too."

Oh. Guilt twisted my belly.

"I'm sorry," I whispered.

"Me too." He gave me a strained smile and didn't relax again until we swung north of Stonehaven, bypassing the city in favor of one of the northside towns for resupply.

"Let's go, newbies," Nikos called out as he led the string of packhorses toward the central market. "Time to teach you how to bargain in the big city."

I tried to pay attention to what Nikos did, I truly did, but everything was so loud and crowded, so chaotic and *messy*, that I had a hard time focusing. Something was always catching my eye, or grabbing my attention, and if Keaton didn't stop silently laughing at my wide-eyed awe, I was going to punch him in the face.

My latest distraction was ridiculously adorable.

I'd been attempting to dutifully listen to Nikos as he bargained for more grain for the packhorses, when I felt a tentative tug on my leather vest. My eyes snapped down, expecting to see a pickpocket or worse, and found a tiny child with big blue eyes and neat blonde pigtails staring up at me. I blinked, because she was almost too cute to be real, but then she piped up in a high, sweet voice.

"Wow, look at your eyes," she gasped. "They're so pretty!"

Unless pickpockets wore expensive dresses and smelled of lavender, this was the child of a well-off family. I pinned her age at six, maybe seven years old. Far too young to be in the crowded market alone.

"Thanks," I said with a bright smile. "Are you lost—"

Another, bigger gasp as Felix crowded close, tucking his wings tight as someone jostled him to get to a vegetable stand. "Oh, wow, her eyes match yours!"

An amused giggle escaped me at Felix's grumble. "Yes, sweetie, *his* eyes match mine. How else are we supposed to look through each other's eyes if they don't match?"

She squealed and bounced, her little hands clasped in front of her chest and her eyes shining in excitement. "I want matching eyes with a griffin! I want a griffin!"

Slightly mollified, Felix flicked his ears forward. *"Well, who wouldn't want a griffin. Especially a griffin as awesome as me?"*

I rolled my eyes at my bondmate's arrogance and crouched next to the girl. "Well, before you can be a griffin rider, you have to test bond capable."

"I don't like tests." Her little button nose wrinkling up adorably. "My teacher gives us a lot of them."

"Ah." I shook my head with a smile. "It's not that kind of test. The Mavens will test your blood when you're sixteen and see if you have the right kind."

For just an instant, I flashed back to when I was sixteen, standing before a Maven and breathlessly waiting to see if my blood tested positive.

"Will it hurt?" the little girl asked, recalling me to the present.

"No more than pricking your finger on a thorn."

"That *hurts*." She snatched her hands behind her back. "But . . . then I could have a griffin?"

Felix's eyes narrowed and his tufted ears angled back. "Have *a griffin? We're not* pets!"

"*Hush.*" I patted his side. "*She's just a baby. She doesn't understand.*"

Erra sat with her back to her rider, observing the crowd and not so incidentally keeping anyone from getting too close to our packhorses. She trilled a soft laugh at Felix's outrage. The little girl was captivated, her gaze bouncing between the griffins as if trying to decide which was prettier. I took the opportunity to scan the crowded street. Surely *somebody* was missing this sweet baby.

When the little girl tugged at my vest again, I returned my attention to her.

"If I have the right blood then I get a pretty griffin and pretty eyes, right?"

"No, then you'd have to finish school." I chuckled at her crestfallen expression. "After that, if you still want to be a griffin rider, you'd have to enroll at the Tennessan Bonded Training Academy when you turn eighteen. It's like a college for griffin and dragon riders. That's where we just graduated from."

I gestured to Keaton, standing with one hand on Tavi's shoulder, and her eyes seemed to take up half her face as she looked between the nearly identical griffin twins.

"Wow, he's so handsome!" She tore her gaze off Tavi and gave Felix the sweetest smile I'd ever seen. "But she's prettier. What's her name?"

Felix huffed in disgust and turned his back, tail lashing in annoyance. I smothered a laugh, but Tavi didn't bother. He dropped his beak in a full griffin grin and trilled with laughter. Keaton bit back a smirk as he turned back to the stall to watch Nikos bargain.

"*His* name is—"

"Get away from my baby!"

A young woman who couldn't be more than a few years older than me shoved her way out of the milling shoppers and snatched the girl up as if she thought I was about to feed her to my griffin. Slowly, I stood up, making sure that my hands were relaxed and open to show her I was unarmed.

"I'm sorry, ma'am. I was just trying to answer her questions. She looked lost, but she was so excited by the griffins she wouldn't focus on anything else." I faltered when her hostility seemed to get worse, rather than better. "I was just trying to help."

"Trying to help yourself to my child, you mean!" The woman held her daughter close and glared, jabbing a finger at me in accusation. "Freaks of nature like you should stay where you belong!"

My jaw dropped, and Keaton snapped his head around, his eyes narrowed dangerously. Nikos stilled for a heartbeat before he turned away from the vendor he'd spent so much time bargaining with.

"And where's that, ma'am?" Nikos asked smoothly, like velvet over steel. "Risking our lives and our bonded's lives out on the border, protecting ungrateful civilians like you?"

"Exactly," she snapped as a slightly older man bulled his way through the gathering watchers. "That's the entire reason for your existence, so get out there and do it! And stay away from our children!"

My stomach sank when I noticed her hands were shaking. She wasn't just afraid of us, she was *terrified*. The man pushed his way between us and roughly shoved me away, even though I hadn't threatened the woman or even talked back to her. A low growl rumbled in Felix's chest, but Keaton reacted first.

"Back off." There was nothing impassive in Keaton's expression as he faced off against the larger man. "Now."

The man snarled and punched Keaton in the face, hard enough his head snapped sideways. Tavi roared and Felix's dappled wings flared wide, eliciting mingled gasps and muttered curses from the crowd as our griffins moved up to flank us. The man stumbled backward before he spun around and herded his family away from us, darting wide-eyed glances over his shoulder every few steps. Within seconds, the crowd swallowed them up, and the gathered watchers, deprived of further entertainment, drifted back to their shopping.

Breath shaking from anger more than fear, I stroked a comforting hand down Felix's neck before I turned to Keaton.

"You okay?"

"Yeah, guy could throw a fast punch," he muttered. Rage boiled in his amber eyes as he wiped a thin trickle of blood off his chin and spat more blood onto the paved road.

A tremor born of equal parts anger, frustration, and bewilderment rocked through me. "How did we go from people thanking us to *that*?"

"Later," Nikos said in a low growl. He dropped a handful of coins on the vendor's worn counter, snatched the bags of grain, and secured them on the packhorses. "Time to go."

We rode our griffins out of the market, through the town, and down the road in strained silence. It wasn't until the pavement turned to dirt beneath our griffins' paws that Tavi stopped stalking along like he was looking for something to kill, and it wasn't until the sounds of civilization had been replaced by birdsong that Felix's stiff-legged strides smoothed out.

As the trail cut through a tame little woodland, I glanced back at Keaton. My jaw clenched at the traces of dried blood on his split lip, and my frustration boiled over.

"Why did that mother act like that? I don't understand. I don't understand any of them! Why would they act hostile toward us? Why were they *afraid*?"

Erra whirled around on the trail, and Felix and Tavi stopped shoulder to shoulder, facing her. And her rider. Nikos' expression was calm, but his shoulders were stiff with tension.

"Because this deep in the country, the war hasn't touched them. Not really. Dragons and griffins and riders are bedtime stories they tell their children, not flesh and blood people they run into at the market." Nikos let out a slow breath and squinted at me. "Where'd you grow up?"

Taken aback at the randomness of the question, I shrugged. "Royal Oak."

His brow furrowed as if trying to place it, then he nodded. "Southern border town. Explains the accent."

"I don't have an accent!"

"Yeah, you do." Keaton snorted a laugh at my murderous glare. "You've got a little drawl, especially when you're tired."

Nikos waved us to silence before I could argue.

"Okay, it's like this, newbies. Border folk understand the war with Savinia is a real and present danger to their lives and livelihoods. Because of that, they tend to make up almost half the military, and more than half the bonded ranks." He shook his head in disgust. "Central folks like back there? The only real impact the war has on their soft lives is when they have to stock the waystations, or when they grudgingly allow the Mavens to test their teenagers."

"But the villagers near the academy didn't act like that, and they're even farther from the border," I said in protest.

"They exist in large part to support the academy," he said. "They're also closer to the western wastes, and they know that wastelanders and broken beasts aren't just scary stories."

"He's right," Keaton said quietly. "We were taught about all those things, about the border clash and the broken beasts and the bonded, but the first time I saw a griffin was when a pair of riders escorted the Mavens through Stonehaven for blood testing. That was the first time it felt real to me." He shrugged at my shocked stare. "Seeing is believing, Harpy."

"Meanwhile, we fight and we bleed and we *die* protecting these people, but let me tell you a secret, newbies." Nikos leaned forward in the saddle, his intense gaze full of rage and the dark shadows of old grief. "We don't do it for them. We do it for each other."

His words hung in the air between us for a long moment.

"Any more questions?" When we remained silent, Nikos tilted his head toward the southwest, where towering gray clouds were building. "Great, I have one for you. What do we do about that incoming storm?"

Always a test with him.

I shook my head and gave Nikos a small grin tempered by sadness. "You remind me of Lieutenant Osbourne."

He smirked. "Who do you think trained him?"

As we'd traveled, the land had gradually changed from wide fields and woodlands to rolling hills. A faint haze grew on the eastern horizon, the first indication of the Smoke Mountains. Deceptively soft and green, they were ancient, red in tooth and claw, and full of monsters we had no name for. Broken beasts and worse haunted those mountains, and they were a far more effective guard for that border than we'd ever be.

Midday rolled around, and the only thing that kept the sun from scorching us in our leathers was the steady breeze blowing from the north. We'd already halted for lunch an hour prior, so I was surprised when Nikos stopped at the crest of one of the low hills. His somber expression as he dismounted caught me off guard even more.

"Unsaddle them," he said with a sharp gesture to our griffins. "It'll be easier for them to fly without them."

Keaton and I exchanged a puzzled glance before we did as ordered. Our griffins shook their fur out and stretched their wings eagerly. They hadn't gotten nearly as much flying in as they'd prefer with all the riding we'd been doing, and I felt Felix's eagerness as he jostled Tavi playfully. Erra snapped at them, and they settled down somewhat, but their tails lashed with barely restrained excitement. Trees dotted the wide hill, but it was mostly grass and wildflowers, with plenty of room for agile griffins to take off.

As Nikos directed his somber gaze south, his hands curled and uncurled, and he shifted his weight. Not once, but several times, as if unable to hold still.

"You newbies need to see the blasted zone, but this is as close as I'm willing to take us. You might think you know what they are, but you don't. Stories and lectures and pictures in school textbooks aren't enough. You need to see it with your own eyes to understand." He let out a faint snort. "Failing that—because while I'm many things, stupid isn't one of them—seeing it through your bonded's eyes will have to do."

Both Keaton and I looked south, but it was just more rolling green hills, more green trees, with maybe the faintest smudge of gray in the distance, like a low-hanging cloud or morning mist...in the afternoon. A distressed purr rumbled in Erra's chest, and she pressed against her rider, one wing curling around him, though whether she needed the reassurance or he did was unclear. What *was* clear was Nikos—unflappable, irritable, experienced Nikos—was *uneasy*. And that, more than anything, drove fear into my heart.

I locked my gaze onto Felix as he wiggled his hindquarters in anticipation. *"Be careful, featherhead."*

"Always am," he claimed with a trilled laugh.

"No, you're not," I muttered as Nikos gestured sharply at our griffins.

"Daylight's burning, you overgrown chickens. Get up there!"

With eager roars, Felix and Tavi bounded across the grassy hilltop side by side. They snapped their wings out in unison and leaped into the air, wings pounding a rapid beat as they reached for the sky. They quickly caught a thermal and spiraled up around each other, shrieks of joy spilling from their beaks as they soared ever higher.

I wanted to fly with them so badly that my longing reached Felix.

"Come with me, Harpy!" He laughed brightly and tugged at my mind. *"You know I'll always take you flying with me."*

With his eager permission, I slid into his mind. There was a breathless moment of free fall where I felt his joy and his happiness as if they were my own, and then my stomach swooped at the sudden drop into his mind, the dizzying moment where I saw through his eyes. As my mind struggled to accept the visual input, I felt a frisson of guilt slice through Felix, sharp as any knife.

Guilt that he couldn't carry me with him in true flight. Guilt that he could only bring me along in his mind, and not on his back. Guilt that I couldn't feel the wind on my own face, only his.

I slammed my shields into place so hard a bolt of agony shot through my skull, locking the longing away where it couldn't hurt him. Gasping in shock and pain, I scrambled to think of the right words to say to reassure him, but I couldn't find them. So I let him feel my love for him, my joy at feeling the wind on his feathers once again, and his guilt melted away.

"Love you, Felix," I whispered into his mind. *"And I love flying with you."*

He roared in delight and tilted on one wing, his desire to indulge in aerobatics—for *me*—temporarily distracting him from the very reason he'd been sent up in the first place. Tavi snapped at him, his dappled wings stretched wide as he rode the thermal, and Felix heaved a sigh and tilted in the other direction so he faced south. Dismay ricocheted through the bond as Felix reared back midair, wings beating hard as he fought to hold his position, to look, to see. I really wished he hadn't.

Shock held me rigid as dread sank through my gut like a stone.

The rolling hills gave way abruptly to a flat plain where nothing grew. The land was barren for miles in every direction, and the ground didn't look right. It looked . . . dull. Grayish brown and lifeless, as if nothing had ever grown there or ever would.

In the center of the blasted zone was a massive crater, so massive Felix couldn't see the far side. The crater itself was curved, but it wasn't a smooth curve. It was wavy, as if it was composed of overlapping circles.

Understanding hit.

It wasn't one impact crater—it was several.

Sunlight caught and sparkled off the sloped sides as if off glass, the reflected colors strange, almost irritating to Felix's sensitive eyes. He looked at his brother, and they both spiraled higher, nothing of joy in their flight now. They were going for more height to try to show us the bottom of the crater, but it was impossible. A strange, churning mist filled the crater, just like our textbooks and stories claimed.

Those same stories told of the odd, twisted things that sometimes crawled out. They never lived long, but they did terrible things while they still drew breath.

Most who tried to explore the craters, to see what was at the bottom, never returned. Those who did make it out alive emerged from the mists feverish and sick, covered in bleeding sores and so disoriented their words made little sense. They never lived long either.

And any griffins or dragons who flew overhead invariably sickened. Some recovered. Most wasted away within a year and took their riders with them.

Fear shuddered through my soul as I stared at that horrible landscape. The blasted zones were as unnatural as the broken beasts, but so much worse. Distantly, I felt wetness on my cheeks and realized with a faint shock I was crying.

Nikos had been right. We had to see it to understand.

Steady, vicious snarls reached my ears—Keaton, cursing and urging Tavi to return. Out of the corner of Felix's eye, I saw the other griffin drop one wing low and swoop back around to where we waited on a green hilltop so very far below. Felix hesitated, head tilting as he studied the blasted zone.

Revulsion twisted through him, but so did curiosity. A bolt of terror shot through me.

"No!" I shrieked before he could so much as twitch in that awful direction. *"Come back. Come back now!"*

"I was only going to go a little closer!" he protested even as he swung around and spiraled toward the ground. I didn't pull back from his mind until I was dead certain that he was going to land. As soon as he did, I sprinted forward and threw my arms around his neck and buried my face in his feathers.

"That was the opposite of careful!" I scolded him. I couldn't stop shaking, not even when his sun-warmed cinnamon scent filled my nose and his soothing purr rumbled in my ears.

"Sorry, Harpy," he whispered contritely as he dropped his head and pressed his feathered cheek to mine. *"I didn't mean to scare you."*

When I finally pulled back from him, I found a grim-faced Nikos waiting. Tension held him rigid, and his fists flexed a few times before he spoke. Not to me, but to Felix.

"When I was a baby lieutenant, fresh out of the academy and traveling to my first post with a group of other newbies, my escort did the same thing for us. So we could see, so we could understand. Only he brought us much closer. My friend's griffin decided he was *curious*, and he didn't just fly over the blasted zone. He flew over the crater." Something flashed in his copper eyes, something very like horror and old grief. "By the time we reached Ashfall, we had to drag Merrick on a sled. He was sick, clearly dying, but he was too far gone to sever. It took him *weeks* to die, and when he went he took my friend with him."

My nails bit into my palms as Nikos turned that intense stare on me. I couldn't look away, though I was aware of Tavi pressing close to his brother, felt Keaton press his shoulder against mine as he slid past the griffins to stand at my side. Nikos ignored them all and leaned closer to me.

"Rafferty gave everything he had to his griffin to keep him alive that long." A shudder ran through him, and suddenly he looked... young. With a shock, I realized Nikos wasn't that much older than us, he just carried himself with so much confidence that he *seemed* so much older. But if he'd been a first-assignment instructor for Osbourne, he couldn't be more than three years our senior. His voice dropped to a hoarse whisper. "It would've been more merciful to kill them, but Merrick rallied and for a few days we hoped..."

Nikos gave himself a sharp shake and turned his back on us.

"Saddle up." He took his time remounting Erra and waited for us to tack up our griffins again. Tremors ran through Felix when I tightened the flexible girth, and remorse swamped his mind. When we were ready to go, Nikos took lead once more and glanced back, his expression impassive, as if nothing had happened. "Three more days to go, newbies. Let's get it done."

I wasn't sure what I'd expected from the largest eastern border fort, but the tiny guard outpost manned by a pair of conventional Tennessan soldiers was a bit of a letdown. Situated between two towering hills, almost mountains in their own right, the outpost stretched across the gap. A heavy-duty metal gate blocked the very center, with twin blocky buildings on either side—presumably combination living quarters and armory.

Even though the guards on duty clearly recognized Nikos, they went through the full sign and countersign exchange with the griffin rider before they snapped out salutes and began the process of opening the gate. The very boring gate.

Felix felt my disappointment and he nudged me to take a closer look at the smooth gray buildings. He'd been nearly silent the last few days, and I regretted every time I'd wished he'd stop talking. I let him feel that regret, and my loneliness.

"Sorry, Harpy."

His mental voice was hoarse, as affected by disuse as a human's would be if they went days without speaking out loud. A full-body shiver ruffled his fur just before he shook himself violently, as if he was trying to physically shake off his melancholy—and shook me right out of the saddle.

My high-pitched yelp cut off as I hit the ground *hard*. Startlement tinged with merriment flashed through Felix, and he craned his neck back to stare down at me, his purple eyes wide.

"Um, oops?"

"Oops?" I demanded as I sat up, so outraged I didn't even bother with mindspeech. "*Oops!*"

Keaton and Tavi burst out laughing, and even Nikos broke out into a wide grin. Both the guards leaned on the gate, doing their best to maintain a professional bearing but mostly failing as I stood up and dusted off my leathers. Rather than remounting, I stalked past Felix and walked through the open gate on foot, valiantly ignoring the amusement on the guards' faces.

Felix took a bounding leap and caught up with me, trilling laughter spilling from his beak. *"The look on your face! New game!"*

My outrage faded, replaced by relief to have my mischievous griffin back. *"Oh, heck no. Not new game! I will pluck your tail feathers if you do that on purpose, you smug peacock!"*

He whipped his tail out of sight with a snicker before he tilted his head toward the smooth gray walls anchoring the gate, and I finally took a closer look. My eyes widened at the first clue that the little outpost was far more than it appeared—and far older.

"Duracrete," I said in surprise.

The guards closed the gate behind us, not a whisper of sound until the locks engaged with heavy *thunks* that spoke of solid, well-maintained mechanisms. Nikos allowed me to keep the lead as we left the outpost behind. It wasn't as if I could get lost. There was only one way we could go—forward. The small mountains towered overhead, the sides sheer in places, rocky in others, and the path between them so narrow we had to go single file.

Admiration replaced disappointment. Even if those heavy gates were breached by an enemy, a small force could hold this pass until reinforcements arrived.

Again, Felix tugged on my mind, and I briefly looked through his eyes. There were smaller observation posts on top of the mountains. A flash of feathers and fur on one side and a glimpse of a lashing tail on the other told us they were manned by griffins.

It took us fifteen minutes to get through the pass. The trail ended at an identical guard outpost and heavy-duty gate. Again, they clearly recognized Nikos, but still required a sign and countersign exchange, different from the first one. Only when they were satisfied did they open the gate and wave us through.

Sunlight blinded me for the first few steps, and I stumbled forward far enough to clear the gate and allow the others through before stopping next to Felix. I brought a hand up to shade my eyes and felt my jaw drop.

Ashfall wasn't a simple fort—it was a self-sustaining fortress.

Backed up against sheer-sided rocky cliffs and encircled by a series of hills connected by stone walls, the fort encompassed an entire mountain valley. I felt my jaw hanging open as I dragged my stunned gaze over the expansive grounds.

It was larger than the academy by far, with livestock pastures, agriculture fields, archery ranges, armories, smithies, supply warehouses, stables and pastures dotted with horses, and barracks and training grounds for conventional troops. There was not one but two dragon eyries built into a pair of towering manmade hills, big enough to support two full wings of dragons, forty at a minimum. There was even a small lake, one of the clear, underground spring-fed lakes the area was known for, and probably the reason the fort had been built here however many years ago.

"Whoa," Keaton mumbled from next to me. His expression was just as stunned as mine as he tilted his face to the sky.

Dragons flew overhead, wings flashing in every color, and the smaller shapes of griffins darted around and between them. People moved through the fort, some with the brisk efficiency of soldiers on duty, while others were more relaxed.

At the rear of the valley, a massive fortress was built against the rocky cliffs, quite possibly *into* the cliffs. Just like the protective walls, it had the distinctive smooth gray construction of duracrete, more than I'd ever seen in one place before. All that duracrete meant this fort was as old as the hatchery and library at the academy, if not older.

Tavi nudged Felix, his tufted ears standing straight up and his beak dropped in a griffin grin. I followed his gaze. There was another manmade hill on the opposite side of the valley from the dragon eyries. Not quite as tall, but with wide ledges for sunbathing, trees for shade, and a cluster of buildings with the distinctive construction of griffin rider dorms.

A proper griffin eyrie.

Nikos grinned at our expressions. "Welcome to Fort Ashfall."

PART II
RISE FROM RUIN

CHAPTER 17

Our tour of Fort Ashfall went by in a whirlwind of blurred impressions, new people, and far too many places. By the time we'd handed over our packhorses to a stable hand—who bore no physical resemblance to my old friend George but who treated his charges with the same care and respect—and got our griffins cleaned of travel dust and fed, the sun had set.

As twilight stretched across the sky, all dusky purples and soft stars, we stumbled up to the griffin eyrie, travel packs slung over aching shoulders and exhausted beyond measure. Nikos had us drop our packs inside one of the dorms and herded us over to a small building tucked away behind the dorms.

"Never go to the main chow hall if you value your taste buds," he said in cheerful warning as he pushed open the door.

A quiet wave of voices washed over us before silence fell across the small dining hall. Over a dozen griffin riders stared at us with varying levels of interest, their eyes every shade from amber to purple to red. One older man had brilliant green eyes like Commandant Pulaski.

"Ah, there's our fresh meat," the older man said with a wicked grin. "Good trip, Nik?"

"Good enough," Nikos replied as he shoved us over to the table. "Sit, eat, then sleep. Think you newbies can handle that?"

I retained exactly zero names that night, but by the time Nikos led Keaton and me back to the dorms, we had full bellies at least. Felix and Tavi had elected to sleep with their new clutchmates that first night, though our rooms also had nests for our griffins. Rooms, plural, because while the dorm was a lot like our barracks back at the academy, it was sectioned off into individual rooms instead of an open bay.

Nikos barked a laugh at our confused expressions. "This isn't the academy. Officers in the Griffin Corps rate their own rooms. You're welcome, now kindly both of you fuck off, and I'll see you in the morning. *Late* morning."

With that, he left us standing in the wide hallway. Keaton shifted his weight, yawned, and shrugged.

"See you in the morning, Harpy."

Sighing, I hauled my travel packs into my new room. Unlike the academy and its old built-in lights, there was only a lantern on a side table. Fortunately, there was more than enough moonlight pouring in the open shutters of the lone window, and it took mere moments to light the oiled wick. A soft yellow glow spread over the room, illuminating the narrow bunk along one wall, the wider nest taking up the back corner of the room, a wardrobe for gear, hooks in a neat line along the wall, and a set of shelves built into the headboard of the bunk.

That was it, but it was *mine*.

For the first time since I'd left home as a teenager, I had my own room again. I was too tired to decide how I felt about it. I dug through my travel packs, pulled out one of my last relatively clean sets of clothes, and dragged myself to the communal baths at the far end of the building just as Keaton was stumbling back, his hair wet and eyes glazed.

Scrubbing off weeks of travel dust felt amazing, but I almost fell asleep in the shower. Forcing myself to keep moving, I made it back to my room, quickly made the bed with the bedding that had been left at the foot of the mattress, collapsed—and stared up at my new ceiling.

I couldn't sleep.

Grumbling under my breath, I slid out of bed and dug through the nearest travel pack until my hand brushed against a well-wrapped bundle at the very bottom. Slowly, I unwrapped the ratty PT shirts I'd used to cushion my oldest possession. Relief gusted through me when I found the little carved dragon had survived the trip intact, and I stroked a finger down the smooth wood before I placed it on the shelf built into the headboard.

A faint frown marred my brow as I crawled back into bed and

resumed staring at the ceiling. A quick mental check found Felix curled up in the back of my mind, warm, content, and soundly asleep. But something was still missing...

Keaton's obnoxious snores drifted through the thin wall separating our rooms. A slow smile tugged at my lips. *Now it's home.*

I curled up under the blanket and was out like a light.

Nikos let us sleep all the way to noon before he pounded a rough fist on our doors. "Rise and shine, newbies. Time to get chow and handle your inprocessing."

After a quick check in with our griffins and a quicker lunch, Nikos led us outside. As we walked across the wide, grassy hill, a red dragon flashed by overhead, so close the wind of his passage stirred my hair and kicked up dirt into my eyes. Unlike the gray dragon who'd buzzed me back at the academy's obstacle course, there was nothing friendly about the low pass.

Nikos' eyes narrowed to slits as he followed the dragon's flight back to the larger of the two dragon eyries.

"Here's some more advice—steer clear of Captain Westbrook," he said, his voice full of distaste and warning. "He was a massive asshole to griffin riders *before* he got passed over for promotion. The kind of dragon rider who couldn't let old academy rivalries and prejudices go, if you catch my drift. But when Major Zeddemore was transferred here to take command of the Dragon Corps detachment and *our* commander supported him, we became a convenient scapegoat for everything wrong in his miserable life."

A grimace of distaste twisted my face. I remembered Captain Westbrook. Remembered his amused arrogance after my last flight, his pitiless candor when he'd briefed the mountain griffin riders.

"We've met," I said dryly. "The academy shanghaied him into briefing us about active duty. Commandant Pulaski was less than impressed."

Nikos arched a brow. "The academy ropes a *lot* of riders into those godawful briefings. You actually remember him?"

"He left an impression," Keaton said with a wry smile.

"Yeah, he tends to do that."

With a final glare across the fort valley, Nikos brought us to a small command post with a green GRIFFIN CORPS sign above the front door.

Unlike the older duracrete buildings, this one was simple stone, but sturdy enough, with narrow windows cleverly placed to maximize airflow throughout. Nikos knocked briskly on an office door just inside the main hall, opened it, and gestured for us to go in. He didn't follow.

The older rider with the brilliant green eyes turned out to be Major Levi "Dash" Anderson, our detachment commander. He very much reminded me of Commandant Pulaski as he delivered a lightning fast overview of our typical scouting duties, including patrol schedules and message relays, as well as our duties when at the fort. He finished with what he expected from his griffin riders.

"Forget whatever silly rivalries you had with the dragon riders at the academy. There's no place for it at Fort Ashfall. We are the heart and soul of the eastern border defense, and I expect my riders to keep that in mind at all times." A grin creased his face as a spark of mischief lit up his eyes. "That being said, I also expect my riders to stand up for themselves. Understood?"

"Yes, sir," we chorused just as there was a sharp knock on the door.

"Ah, right on time," Anderson said as a slim, handsome woman sauntered inside. She was maybe ten years my senior with purple eyes much like my own. Her riding leathers were scuffed and her boots well-worn, but her blonde hair was immaculately braided and her bearing was intimidating as hell. "This is Major Tori 'Mayhem' Mayhew, executive officer and my second-in-command."

"I prefer to think of myself as the director of chaos," she corrected blandly before her professional mask broke into a broad grin. "Because commanding griffins—and their riders—is rather like herding cats."

Anderson arched a brow at his XO. "Well, what'd your griffin think?"

"Havok assessed their griffins. He approves of his new clutchmates, and so does your Loki." Mayhew gave us an appraising once-over and nodded. "You'll do. I've assigned trainers to each of you. For the next six months, they'll show you the ropes and get you acclimated. Fort Ashfall isn't technically in a combat zone, but that's always changing, and with dragon air raids, no fort or outpost is safe." She paused, and her head tilted in the way of griffin riders everywhere. "But then, you were both at the academy when it was hit, weren't you? So you'd know better than most."

"Yes, ma'am," we chorused grimly.

"Sometime in the next few weeks, I'll take each of you out on a short solo run. In the meantime, pay attention to your trainers." She winked. "Maybe you'll live long enough to get wrinkles."

A small smile tugged at my lips at the old joke. When we weren't killed in combat, bonded tended to live longer than the average, and we didn't show our years until we were quite old. That same quirk of entanglement that made us disease resistant coming into play again.

"I'd also like to meet your griffins," Anderson said as he stood up from behind his desk. "Human or griffin, you're all under my command."

We tromped back outside as a large male griffin with light brown feathers and a deep scar marring one cheek padded over, Felix and Tavi in tow.

"Twins?" he asked in surprise, looking from Felix to Tavi as if comparing the brothers.

Keaton nodded. "Same breeding."

"Rare for a griffin female to produce two eggs at once—"

"Are those my new scouts?" a harsh voice bellowed.

"Oh, hey, look at the time, Dash," Mayhew muttered. "Got to go do that . . . thing."

"Traitor," he muttered back.

"The perks of *not* being in command," she said as she strode off, laughing quietly under her breath.

"Major Anderson!" the harsh voice bellowed again.

Anderson's left eye twitched slightly before he spun on one heel. A gray-haired older soldier in the conventional military's mottled green uniform with the rank pins of a full-bird colonel marched up the hill, two younger aides scrambling to keep up with their leader's swift strides.

Keaton and I both stiffened to attention and saluted sharply, while Anderson's salute was a touch slower. His spine was stiff with tension, or possibly annoyance. The colonel returned our salutes with harried distraction.

"Yes, Colonel Harborne, these are our new scouts." Our detachment commander pointed to us in turn. "Lieutenants Tyler Keaton and Harper Tavros, and their griffins Tavi and—"

"That's it?" The colonel glanced around the hilltop, squinting against the bright sunlight, or maybe hoping if he squinted just right more griffin riders would materialize. "Just the two of them?"

"Technically sir, there's *four—*"

"Bah." Colonel Harborne waved a dismissive hand. "Yes, I know your griffins are scouts in their own right, but they come as a matched pair, so that's how we have to count them." He gave Felix and Tavi a dismissive glance. "No mountain griffins?"

"No, sir."

"Blast, we only have the two. I'll have to send *another* message to the academy. We need a full wing of mountain griffins here, damn it." He heaved a disappointed sigh before he gave us a narrow-eyed inspection. "Dear gods . . . they're sending me babies."

Shaking his head, he turned around just as his aides—a red-faced captain of middling years and fitness, and a balding first sergeant who looked as if he could bench press my griffin—caught up.

"Carry on, Major," he called back over one shoulder. "Were we ever that young, Sergeant Morrison?"

"Probably not, sir . . ."

All three of us relaxed slightly, with Major Anderson muttering under his breath and Loki snapping his beak in irritation.

"Don't mind Colonel Harborne," a deep voice rumbled as the biggest man I'd ever seen ambled up. Slightly younger than Anderson, the man-mountain wore dragon rider flight leathers and an open smile. The laugh lines carved into his skin said he smiled often, and the way our commander relaxed said this was an ally or even a friend. "He's just mad Fort Mayberry down south got half a clutch of forest griffins *and* three mountain griffins. Our fort commander's always competing with his brother-in-law."

Major Anderson clasped forearms with the other rider with a broad grin. "Was wondering when you'd stop by today, Zeddie." He glanced at us. "This is Major Zeddemore, dragon rider detachment commander and my counterpart."

We snapped off sharp salutes, and he returned them with solemn respect before he waved us to at ease with a friendly grin.

"Everybody always wants a look at the new riders, dragon or griffin," Zeddemore explained after Anderson introduced us. His warm yellow eyes were cheerful and stood out sharply against his dark skin. "I'm no exception. Neither is Maximus."

My lips parted as the largest dragon I'd ever seen touched down on the landing field at the front of the griffin eyrie. I'd never seen a full-grown black dragon before, and his great wings stretched across the sky. This was what Dimitri's dragon would one day become, but blacks were slow growing, and it would be years yet before Riven reached that size.

Despite Maximus' immense bulk, he seemed . . . gentle. Though I'd wager anyone who'd faced one of those unstoppable tanks on the battlefield would think otherwise.

"That's the biggest dragon I've ever seen," Felix said, mirroring my thoughts. He tilted his head, purple eyes locked onto the dragon's flicking tail tip with predatory intensity. *"Bigger than Jasper . . ."*

"How about you not attack the tail of a dragon large enough to squish you with one foot?" I asked dryly.

"But I want it . . ."

Tavi smacked his wing into Felix's face, and my griffin trilled a laugh before he pounced on his brother. Rather than discipline them, Loki loosed a ringing cry and joined in the fun. Major Zeddemore's grin widened as he watched them play.

"And this is why I love griffins," he said with a booming laugh.

Later that afternoon, Nikos made a reappearance. His brow twitched as he looked at Keaton. "It's your lucky day, newbie. You've been assigned as my trainee for the next six months. Get your gear squared away. We head out on our first patrol tomorrow."

My shoulders slumped a little at being left behind, but Nikos belted out a laugh.

"Don't look so sad, newbie. Your trainer is out on a short scouting run, but he should be back tomorrow. I've got a feeling you're going to like him."

He was right.

"Oh my god, I thought you were dead!" I blurted as a familiar griffin rider walked into the dining hall at breakfast the next morning. Keaton and Nikos had just left, and I'd been picking at my food, trying not to feel alone. Lieutenant Osbourne grinned broadly as he dropped onto the bench next to me.

"The rumors of my demise were greatly exaggerated." His grin faded as he dragged a hand over close-cropped wavy brown hair. "The dragon riders carried out everyone they could before Bradford fell.

Not everyone made it, but if it weren't for them, none of us would have. Hells, some of those dragon riders bought it saving us. Brave bastards."

A shiver worked its way down my spine, and I wondered if I knew any of them. Felix brushed against my mind with a phantom caress of fur and feathers, and I blew out a short breath to release the tension.

"So . . ." I raised my brows hopefully. "Does this mean you're my trainer, Lieutenant Osbourne?"

"For my sins, yes. And it's just Oz." He let out an amused snort as he pointedly flicked a finger against my own rank. "No rank between lieutenants, Harpy."

"The last time I saw you, I was a cadet," I reminded him and took a bite of warm, buttered bread to hide my embarrassment.

"Some habits are harder to break than others," Oz said agreeably. He snagged a hardboiled egg from the bowl in the middle of the table and peeled it with brisk efficiency. "We'll head out on our first patrol in two days. After I make sure you've got all the right gear for a long haul."

"I thought you just got back," I said in surprise, but he just shrugged.

"It was a short run. Keira prefers being out on the trails, and so do I. Besides, somebody has to take the Bristol run. Might as well be us." He tilted his head and paused with his egg halfway to his mouth. "So long as Felix is up for it after your trip out here?"

A quick check with Felix confirmed his eagerness to finally get out there and do what we'd been trained to do. I nodded firmly and snagged the last piece of bacon with a grin.

"We're ready."

Two days later, we left the fort while the moon was still high in the sky and dawn only a faint suggestion on the rim of the mountain valley. We traveled on foot, with lightweight travel packs on our backs, daggers strapped to our hips, and unstrung bows slung over our shoulders. Instead of saddles, our griffins only wore light bareback pads. Just enough material to cushion their spine and leave them relatively unrestrained so they could range through the thick woods without a saddle catching on everything.

We logged our departure with both sets of gate guards, and then traveled due east into the rising sun. After two days of sitting around the fort, it felt good to stretch my legs again, and Felix prowled through the trees with happy thoughts rumbling through his mind. I soon broke out into a light sweat, but a gentle morning breeze kept the rising heat manageable, and Oz and I settled into a loose long-legged stride that would eat up the miles.

By midmorning, we hit the first trail marker and turned north. Oz had shown me the great map in our headquarters when we were planning our run, and he'd traced out our route from Fort Ashfall up through Bristol. We'd take this trail all the way north, shadowing our eastern border and checking in with a dozen smaller outposts and waystations along the way.

Sunset was closing in when we reached the first waystation and our stop for the night. When I would've just walked down the well-worn path through the brush, he gripped my shoulder and relayed through our griffins.

"Never assume they're safe. Always scout them out, even when you're dog tired. We're too close to the border, and it wouldn't be the first time the Savinians have ambushed tired scouts. Send Felix forward and look through his eyes."

Abashed, I nodded quickly. Scouting with Felix took only a few extra minutes, and he quickly confirmed it was clear.

The waystation was similar to the base camps we'd trained on back at the academy: a stone bunker stocked with supplies, a lean-to shelter for sleeping, dry firewood and a stone ring for safe burning, and a water pump. Barebones, but more than enough, especially in the summer. Winter would be a different story, but between the shelter, our winter gear, and our griffins, we'd survive the cold.

The griffins went to hunt while we refilled canteens and washed up before changing out the sweat-soaked underclothes we wore under our riding leathers.

"We'll be able to get proper showers and wash our gear when we hit Fort Bramble next week," Oz said as he got a fire started. He sprawled out in the grass and nodded to the cheerfully crackling flames. "This is the closest waystation to Ashfall, and this area is so heavily patrolled we can risk a good fire. Further north, we'll have to be more careful."

My eyes narrowed. "So making Felix and me scout the waystation—"

"Was good practice." A slight grin creased his face. "Remember, everything's a test ... until it isn't."

I scooted a little closer to the fire and hugged my knees. "I remember."

Felix and Keira soon returned with full bellies and bloody beaks. After they washed up in the trough we'd filled for them, they curled up behind us. With a sigh, I leaned back against Felix's furry side and stared into the flames.

"I miss my brother," Felix said abruptly. His tail twitched, the wide fan of feathers snapping open and closed as it often did when he was upset.

"I miss mine too," I admitted with a sigh. *"But we'll see them in a few weeks. And we have each other."*

"Always," he purred in agreement. His tail stilled, and the subtle tension stiffening his lean frame eased.

Oz placed another log on the fire, and a half-burned chunk of wood collapsed, sending a shower of sparks spiraling up into the night sky. I tilted my head back and followed their flight until they blended with the wide river of stars overhead. As much as I longed to fly with them . . . this wasn't a bad life either.

I somewhat regretted that thought when my merciless training officer had us up before dawn and back on the trail the next day. That set the pattern for the following week, and we quickly fell into an easy routine as we traveled north, watching for anything unusual during the day and stopping at waystations or small outposts every night.

One evening, a gray dragon had just taken off from the waystation as we arrived. Silver wings flashed overhead as he circled beneath sunset-kissed clouds. I caught a glimpse of the rider leaning over his dragon's side, one hand lifted in question. Oz raised one arm and waved forward with a slow, exaggerated movement. Disorientation washed over me as a distinct memory of learning signal recognition from the air hit hard, but I shook it off as the dragon rider waved an acknowledgment and continued on his patrol.

Dragon riders, usually young lieutenants or those with dragons recovering from battle injuries, stopped in the waystations on a regular basis, and Oz had made me memorize the schedule. They provided a link back to the main forts, and a way to pass messages faster than a griffin scout could run . . . or fly, because sometimes the only way a rider could get a message through was to send their griffin without them.

The midpoint of our run was Fort Bramble, and we spent a solid day resting and exchanging stories with the soldiers stationed there. They had no riders, no bonded, and more than one stared at our unusual eyes, though it was usually the younger soldiers. The older sergeants and their captain had been around long enough that they didn't care, though even they watched our griffins with an uneasy mix of respect and wariness.

By the time we left, tension had knotted up my shoulders, and half the day was gone before I'd fully relaxed again. While we were on the trail, Oz and I relayed through our griffins and moved in relative silence, but that didn't mean we didn't talk.

"Is it always like that?" I asked, unable to keep the slightly plaintive note from my voice. Felix purred in my mind before he passed the message along to Keira.

A moment later, Oz glanced at me with a neutral expression before he turned his attention back to the thick scrub lining either side of the trail. We were down in one of the narrow valleys, towering forested hills dominating the skyline above us, and patchy third-growth forest all around us. He slapped at a bloodthirsty mosquito and finally shrugged.

"Sometimes it's worse. The Griffin Corps is only a small part of the Tennessan military, specialists with similar numbers to the rangers, but different. *We're all a little griffin, not entirely human. Dragon riders have it a little easier, I think. They're different too, but they're also separate from the regulars. We're down here in the dirt with them, and they see us up close."* His turquoise eyes slid my way. *"They see us fight, and bleed, and die with them, and they respect us for it. But their instincts tell them we're not quite like them, and that makes a lot of people . . . uneasy."*

While I mulled over his words, I returned my attention to my side of the trail. This particular valley was so narrow that our griffins had already swept through and cleared it. Oz had sent Keira back to check our backtrail, while Felix forged ahead toward the next pass. We were just following behind him and doing our best to see anything through the tangled mess. As it was, I was more looking for motion than anything else and wondering how Felix had managed to navigate the thick scrub without snagging his feathers.

Disquiet spiraled through me as we ghosted down the trail. I didn't feel *different*, but then again, it was hard to remember what I was like before bonding with Felix. It had been almost three years—

A flash of brown where there was only green.

"*Contact right!*" I called out sharply, even as I kept my pace and expression unchanged. If it was just a deer, that could be dinner for the griffins. If it wasn't ... well. No need to alert whoever it was to the fact they'd been spotted.

"*Going high,*" Felix said after he'd relayed my words. I felt his muscles bunch and stretch, felt claws digging deep into bark as he scaled one of the taller oaks. "*Keira's circling east.*"

Oz's body language changed subtly, more relaxed, almost sloppy. Between one stride and the next, the competent scout had vanished beneath the guise of a young, inexperienced soldier out on his first patrol.

"*Savinian raiders,*" Felix whispered, wariness threading through his mental tone along with a faint red tinge. He was ready to fight. "*Three on either side of the trail, with four more moving in from the east.*"

An easy smile spread across Oz's face. He hummed a few notes of a popular drinking song under his breath before he slung his arm over my shoulders.

"Not too much longer until we hit the waystation for the night, love," he said in a suggestive tone that startled the hell out of me. He'd been so utterly professional this entire patrol, treating me as nothing more than another rider, that the abrupt shift in character caught me off guard—until I caught the hard glint in his eyes. "I don't know about you, but I'm looking forward to *relaxing.*"

Oz added an awkward wink, almost as an afterthought, and despite the deadly seriousness of our situation, I had to smother a laugh. The man was a *terrible* flirt, but if it distracted the Savinians long enough for our griffins to get in a position to ambush our ambushers, I'd play along.

I slid my compact recurve bow off my shoulder and nestled under his arm, letting the bow dangle from my right hand as if I'd forgotten all about it. Pitching my voice to carry, I purred into his ear, "Relaxing, huh? That's not what you called it last night."

To my shock, his face turned bright red, and my laugh rang out, unrestrained and full of mischief.

"*New game,*" I sang out to Felix before I sobered. "*Assuming we live through this.*"

A fierce growl rumbled through his mind as he eeled his way through the tangled canopy. The scrub forest was dense, but the individual trees were thin, and I felt his muscles burn with effort. He wanted the height advantage though, and I wasn't about to tell him how to hunt.

"I'll kill them all before I let them hurt you," he said fiercely. His tone abruptly shifted to the subtle burr that meant he was relaying for Oz. *"Try to loosen your stride a bit more. If we convince them we're harmless, they might let us pass. Then we can drop a message at the next waystation and circle back and track them."*

"Odds of them letting us through?" I asked, allowing my hips to sway just a touch more than necessary.

"Fifty-fifty," he admitted as his arm tightened across my shoulders for a beat before he relaxed again. *"Depends on if they want to stay hidden—"*

An arrow sank into the ground a bare meter from our boots.

"Or not," he muttered as we both froze. Slowly, he raised his hands, and shot me a sharp glance when I hesitated. "We're scouts, not skirmishers, Harpy."

As men in dark brown hunting leathers rose up from concealment on either side of the trail, I dropped my bow and held up empty hands.

"Keep your eyes low," Oz breathed, his voice more the memory of sound than anything else as he dropped his gaze to the dirt.

Understanding punched me in the gut. If they didn't see our distinctive eyes, they might not realize we were bonded riders. Our griffins had been ranging far enough that it was possible they didn't know about them, and Tennessan *did* utilize women as messengers. As the Savinians slid out of the brush and onto the trail, my shoulders hunched forward, and I lowered my head as if terrified.

I wished I was still playing along.

A pair of boots stopped in my field of vision, their owner close enough to touch—or knee in the balls. My fingers twitched toward my dagger, but I forced myself to hold still.

A low, appreciative whistle rang out as a lean hand reached up and brushed against the side of my face. I could feel Felix's rage, could feel his control faltering and fraying with every frightened beat of our hearts.

"Man, I'll never understand why the Tennessans allow their women into the field, but I can't say I'm sad about it," a young man said as he gripped my jaw in a hard hand, angling my face up to the dappled sunlight. It took everything I had to keep my gaze downcast and my unusual eyes hidden.

"*Wait for the right moment*," I urged Felix desperately as my breath shook.

Reluctant agreement shivered through the bond. In the next instant, he shielded his own fear and helped me control mine, as he'd done once before so very long ago. My panic receded, and my hands steadied as determination took hold. A slight creak drew my gaze to the side. Oz, one hand curling into a fist, just as determined, just as ready to act.

Another man barked a rude laugh. "Maybe she's meant to be entertainment for one of their northern forts."

There was a whisper of boots on loose dirt as someone ghosted closer, and then the man standing before me was brutally shoved away. A whimper of pain escaped me as his hand wrenched my head sideways, and I stumbled before a new hand snapped out and steadied me.

"Tennessan or not, that is *not* how we treat women," the owner of that steadying hand said in fierce growl. "Or captives."

"Yes, Sergeant," both men muttered with barely hidden resentment as they moved a few steps further away.

"I don't need to see your eyes to know what you are," the sergeant murmured.

Unable to stop myself, my gaze snapped up. The Savinian sergeant wasn't much older than us, with rugged features set in a grim expression, though there was the briefest flash of sympathy in his eyes. No, *pity*.

He glanced at Oz. "You might have fooled those boys with that tactic, but I spent too much time around my sister and her griff to fall for that one."

All traces of pity vanished as another raider strode down the trail. It wasn't until he was close that I caught the rank of a Savinian officer, the singular bar a subdued color that blended in with his leathers. The sergeant released my shoulder and turned to face his superior.

"Sir. Two captives."

The barest hint of hesitation.

"They're griffin riders."

Several raiders cursed and whirled to face the trees, bows gripped in white-knuckled hands, but the officer just nodded and sharply gestured to one of his men. A whipcord lean raider kicked out the back of Oz's knees, sending him crashing to the ground with a pained grunt. The bastard gripped Oz's hair and jerked his head back, exposing his throat as he laid the edge of his knife along it. I didn't have to fake a damn thing as my terror broke through Felix's shielding.

"Call your griffins," the officer said in a cold voice that sent shivers down my spine.

Tiny beads of blood welled up on his skin, but Oz just silently glared at our captors. A hard hand grasped my chin and wrenched my head around so I had no choice but to face the Savinian officer. A low chuckle hit my ears, and a hand trailed down my side to my belt. My heart stuttered as a different sort of fear took hold, but then there was a sharp jerk and the metallic *rasp* of my dagger sliding from its sheath.

A breath later, cool metal kissed my cheek.

"Call your griffin, girl. It would be a shame for anything to happen to that pretty face."

I drew in a shaking breath to tell him to go to hell—and Felix surged forward. I welcomed the burn as my eyes adjusted to the weight of his soul. The officer's lips curled into a smug little smile, but the sergeant sidestepped toward his commander, his hard eyes never leaving the surrounding trees.

"Careful, sir. Griffs can last just long enough to kill whatever killed their riders."

"I'm well aware, *Sergeant*," he said as his smile vanished behind an icy glare. "That's why we won't *kill* them." He tapped my cheek with the flat of my blade and smiled again. "Call your griffins in, and you might live to see tomorrow."

"But sir," a rough-voiced raider said. "We have a standing kill order for—"

His sharp protest dissolved into a horrible gurgle as an arrow pierced his throat. The officer spun away from me with a low curse, cold eyes scanning the trees, while his sergeant reached for the heavy war bow slung on his back. A second bowstring sang out, and another arrow shot out of the tangled undergrowth and sank to the fletching in the eye of the raider holding Oz at knifepoint.

Without hesitating, Oz jerked his hand up and wrenched the knife out of the dying man's hand, twisting around and cutting the man's throat in one smooth motion. Turquoise eyes flared bright, and he looked feral as he stood over the body, bloody knife clenched tight in one hand, his dagger in the other.

More arrows flew out of the trees. The sergeant went down with an arrow to the leg, while the remaining three raiders fired into the thick undergrowth ... and there I was, in the middle of the damn trail without a weapon or cover. Felix retreated from my mind as my frantic gaze landed on my discarded bow. Despite my rough treatment, the string hadn't snapped, and the quiver strapped to my hip was still full of our deadly little arrows. Against armored soldiers, they wouldn't do much, but against leather at this range? More than good enough.

I dove for my bow and came up on one knee. All those long hours of practice and drills on the archery range with Keaton came to my aid, and I had an arrow nocked and drawn without conscious thought. The Savinian officer was the closest target, and I shifted my aim as I exhaled half a breath. Fletching tickled my cheek as I held the rest of my breath—and released.

But I'd never shot anyone before. He wasn't some silhouette on the range, some lifeless target. In the instant before I fired, our eyes met ... and my hand twitched.

I missed center mass, but my arrow still sliced through leather and muscle to lodge just beneath his collarbone. Blood welled up and he bellowed in pain, even as he lurched toward me with my own dagger raised high. I fumbled for another arrow, but my hands were shaking and there was *no time* to get off a second shot. There wasn't even time to get out of his way. I whipped my bow up like a shield in a desperate attempt to block the blade as it descended toward my face.

A furious shriek split the air. Felix dropped out of the trees, wings flared as wide as the narrow trail would permit, and knocked the Savinian officer away from me. Before the man tumbled to a stop, Felix sprang forward, deadly silent now. His massive paws pinned the thrashing, screaming man to the dirt, and his sharp beak snapped closed around the back of his neck. The man's struggles ceased abruptly, body going limp as a puppet with cut strings.

My griffin snapped his head up, blood dripping from his beak, and roared. His sharp gaze panned over the trail, searching for his next target, but the only Savinian left alive was the sergeant. The man calmly knelt at the edge of the scrub forest with his back to Oz, hands on top of his head, fingers interlaced. Blood poured from a deep slice down the side of his face, and an arrow was lodged in his upper thigh. Not one of the small arrows we used either. It was a heavy arrow from a war bow, like the ones conventional archers used.

Or the rangers.

CHAPTER 18

"Can you call your griffin off?" a gruff, vaguely familiar voice called out from the trees. "I think we proved we're friendlies."

"Not yet, you haven't." Oz lowered his bow slightly, but he didn't ease the tension off the bowstring, the arrow still nocked and ready to fire. "Harvester of sorrow."

Without hesitation, the gruff voice called back, "Red cold river."

The correct countersign given, the tension left Oz all at once and his whole body slumped. Keira prowled out of the tangled undergrowth a heartbeat later and padded over to her rider, where he stood behind the captured sergeant. Carefully, Oz placed the arrow back in his quiver as four rangers walked out of the scrub without making a sound.

To my surprise, I knew two of them. Sergeant Franks was perhaps a little more weatherworn since I'd seen him at the griffin training grounds, but he moved just as well as his younger rangers. The second wore that same roguish grin, though his face had matured somewhat.

Maddox slung his bow over his shoulder and winked. "Hey there, griffin girl."

"Hey, deer," I said with a tiny smile as I belatedly lowered my own bow.

It took me three tries to properly sling it over my back. My hand brushed against the empty sheath on my hip, and I automatically looked toward the dead Savinian officer for my stolen dagger. Franks was crouched next to him. He glanced back at me as he pulled the hilt out from under the body.

Just the hilt.

The blade had snapped clean off sometime between Felix tackling him and slamming him to the ground.

Franks walked over and handed it to me. "Best requisition a new one when you get back to the fort."

"Thanks," I said on a quiet groan.

"Uh, oops," Felix said, his ears flicking back and forth uncertainly.

I stared at the broken hilt for a long moment before I let it slip from my trembling fingers. Exhaustion slammed into me, and I patted Felix on the shoulder with a harsh laugh.

"Who gives a shit about a stupid dagger? You saved us. You're amazing."

My griffin preened, his feathers fluffing out and his tufted ears standing straight up.

I laughed again, a slightly more genuine sound this time. *"You're also ridiculous."*

"Nope, I'm amazing," he replied smugly as he sauntered over to the brush and wiped his beak clean. *"No take backs."*

"Here," Franks said, holding out the officer's dagger. "This'll do until you can get one better suited to your size."

With a grateful nod, I forced my shaking hands to cooperate and grasped the leather hilt. It was heavier than mine and would drag uncomfortably on my belt, but it was better than nothing.

"What are you doing out here, Franks?" Oz asked as the ranger strode over to him. "I thought you had a cushy instructor assignment at the ranger school."

"Cushy, yes. Well paying, no." The older ranger snorted and clasped hands with my trainer. "Had to take an active-duty assignment, or I'd never be able to retire."

"Well, your timing remains incredible," Oz said wearily as one of the rangers I didn't know secured the Savinian sergeant's hands behind his back. "We're lucky you showed up when you did."

"Luck had nothing to do with it. We've been playing cat and mouse with these bastards all damn week." Franks glared at the dead raiders and spat on the dirt. "They came over the hill and cut through the scrub, trying to lay a trap for us. Just your bad luck they caught you instead."

"Bad timing, too." Oz grimaced. "They must have come through after our griffins cleared the valley."

"We were here yesterday, but we managed to shake them and double back," Maddox explained with a broad grin at the Savinian sergeant, who just gazed back with an impassive expression. "We were following them when they thought they were getting ahead of us."

"Six Savinians, and four rangers." Felix flattened his ears as chagrin washed through him. *"I thought they were more Savinian raiders."*

"Well, they are dressed similarly," I said faintly as my gaze skipped around the bodies, not lingering on the death wounds. A faint buzz grew louder as more insects found their way to the feast. I tried to tune it out. Bad enough I could smell the blood. The heavy tang of copper and iron coated the back of my tongue, and I swallowed hard as saliva pooled in my mouth.

"Thanks for slowing them down long enough for us to catch up," the last ranger called out with a teasing grin. He looked barely out of his teens, but he moved from body to body, recovering arrows with a pragmatic, unbothered air. I couldn't look away as he knelt next to the Savinian officer. There was a wet *squelch* as he tugged my arrow free and studied it with a critical eye—and then he held it out toward me, thick blood and gore coating the razor-sharp tip. "This one's yours, right?"

My stomach twisted, and acid rose in the back of my throat. With a strangled whimper, I staggered over to the edge of the scrub, dropped to my hands and knees, and vomited. Cold chills wracked my frame, and I heaved until there was nothing left.

The young ranger snickered in amusement. A hot flush traveled across my face as I tried to pull myself together, but a second later there was a dull smack, as if someone had hit him. His laughter abruptly cut off. A hand gripped my shoulder, and I let out a slow breath before I dragged the back of my hand across my mouth and pushed myself up. Maddox was crouched next to me.

"First time shooting someone?" he asked quietly.

I nodded.

"I threw up my first time. There's no shame in it." A ghost of a smile danced on his lips, and he titled his head toward the younger ranger as he stood up. "That moron over there did, too."

"Not to mention the fact that he threw up *on* himself," the third ranger said with a snort as he looted the bodies of anything useful. "Refresh my memory, Riley. Did you ever get the smell out of those leathers?"

"Shut up, Buchanan," Riley mumbled, but there was a touch of remorse in his eyes as he handed me my arrow. It was clean.

"Thanks," I murmured as Felix forced his way past the rangers and planted himself at my back. Keira had also plastered herself to her rider's side, her tail lashing in pent up agitation.

Oz met my gaze over his griffin's shoulder and gave me a nod. "Good job, Harpy."

"You too . . . *love*."

My lips twitched into something close to a smile when his face turned bright red again, but it fell away when my eyes drifted to the thin cut in Oz's throat and the tiny trails of blood staining the skin beneath. That had been close, so damn close. Shaking violently, I leaned against my griffin's warm side and sucked in deep breaths, his clean, spicy scent overpowering the stench of death.

Time did something weird, skipped or stuttered as white noise washed over me. I blinked, and Maddox stood over me.

"Come on." He held out his hand with a mocking grin, but his eyes held a wealth of understanding. "On your feet, griffin girl."

A short distance away, Franks and Buchanan were getting their prisoner ready to march.

"Might want to brace yourself, lad," Franks warned gruffly. He waited for the sergeant's grim nod before he reached for the arrow lodged in the man's thigh and snapped off the shaft. A strangled grunt of pain escaped his clenched jaw, but it wasn't until Franks dug out the arrowhead that the color drained from the sergeant's rugged face. With brisk efficiency, Franks bound up the wound and hauled him to his feet. "Are you capable of walking?"

The sergeant shuffled a few steps before he dipped his head in a cautious nod. "So long as it's not too far, I can make it," he said, his previously smooth baritone rough with pain.

Oz hadn't been lying when he'd said we were almost to the waystation. Another hour on the trail got us close enough to scout it. The rangers waited patiently with their white-faced prisoner as Oz sent Keira ahead, his eyes glazing over as he looked through hers. As soon as he called it clear, we wearily marched into the waystation.

Oz went straight for the supply bunker and emerged with a signal flag, red for urgency.

"Now what?" I asked after he'd clipped it to the signal pole.

"Now, we wait." Oz slumped down next to Keira and gingerly touched his throat. "One of the patrol dragons should swing through by midmorning."

"Are you sure you're all right?"

"It's minor," he said, waving off my concern.

While the rangers secured the sergeant to one of the trees next to the lean-to shelter, I forced myself to keep moving. There was no way the griffins would be convinced to leave us to hunt tonight, so they would have to deal with dried meat from the supply bunker. I pulled enough to feed them, plus extra to feed the rest of us, along with enough dried fruit and nuts to round out the simple meal. A white box caught my eye as I slipped out of the bunker, and I snagged that too.

Oz tilted his head back obediently and allowed me to clean and treat his cut, but he was right. It was minor. My gaze drifted to our prisoner, whose wounds were definitely *not* minor, and my lip curled at the thought of wasting precious supplies on someone like him... then I remembered how he'd defended me from two of his men, and I pushed myself to my feet with a sigh.

Maddox caught my arm. "What are you doing?"

"Treating him the way I'd want to be treated," I muttered.

He let go, and I crouched in front of the Savinian sergeant. He watched me through wary eyes, but his impassive expression was nowhere near as good as Keaton's, and it was obvious he was in pain.

"Will you let me help you?" I asked quietly.

"Why?" he asked bluntly, a faint drawl in his voice that reminded me of home.

"Because you helped me."

His eyes shifted away from mine, something very like shame darkening his face. "It was nothing."

I held up the med kit. "So is this."

At last, he dipped his head in that same short nod he'd given Franks. "Thank you."

"Don't thank me yet," I said as my gaze dropped to the bloodstained bandage wrapped around his thigh. "This is going to suck."

When it was over, I got a much fainter "thanks" as he rested his head against the tree trunk. The sun had set while I'd worked. There would be no fire that night, but twilight and a rising moon gave me more than enough light to see his wan expression.

"You're welcome, Sergeant..." I trailed off as I wiped my hands as clean as I could.

"Aral." He slit open eyes hazy with pain, and dipped his head in a deeper nod, almost a bow that reeked of old-world courtesy. "Sergeant Benjamin Aral."

"You are the strangest Savinian raider I've ever met," I muttered.

"Heard you earlier." The corner of his mouth tipped up as his eyes drifted closed. "Pretty sure I'm the only one you've ever met."

Disquiet twisted through my gut, and I packed up what was left of the supplies and left the sergeant tied to his tree. Shaking with exhaustion, I replaced the med kit in the bunker, marked the supplies used on the clipboard hanging next to the door, and stumbled over to Felix. He'd stretched out next to Keira, and Oz was curled up against her side, out cold.

Franks glanced up from where he leaned against a tree, his eyes gleaming in the moonlight. "Sleep, griffin rider. We'll keep watch tonight."

With a nod of gratitude, I collapsed against Felix's side. He curled around me and spread one wing over me like a feathery blanket. I was trembling so hard it took me a moment to realize he was shaking too. I brushed against a mind filled with confusion and regret, and the faint remnants of bloodlust and rage.

"Felix? Are you okay?" I knew he wasn't all right, but I needed him to talk to me. He was silent for so long it became a struggle to stay awake, but I forced my burning eyes to stay open. I'd wait all night if I had to.

"I never killed anyone before," he whispered at last, his voice so very small.

I burrowed deeper into his side and let him feel my love for him, and my own regret and confusion and guilt. Back at the academy, all I'd ever wanted was to *save* people, not kill them. But I couldn't deny the relief that tangled through everything else. Relief that we'd survived, even if it meant others hadn't.

"And I never shot anyone before," I whispered back and carded my fingers through his fur. *"It wasn't like practice, was it?"*

"No. Not like hunting deer either." A fierce wave of love washed over me. *"I'd do it again to save you."*

There was no hint or thought of self-preservation in his mind. It didn't matter to him that if I died so would he. It only mattered that if I died, he wouldn't want to be here anyway. My heart squeezed painfully tight. Whoever had created our griffins had given them hearts twice as big as a dragon's.

"Love you, Felix."

"Love you too, Harpy."

Gradually, our trembling eased, and I drifted off to his rough purr, my fingers still buried in his fur. The next morning, Oz officially took custody of Sergeant Aral and released the rangers to return to their duty.

"If you're sure," Franks said, but his doubt faded when Keira planted herself next to the Savinian, her deadly beak hovering close to his neck. "Yeah, I guess you're sure. Until next time, Osbourne, Tavros. Stay safe out there."

Riley and Buchanan ghosted into the trees after their commander without a backward glance, but Maddox hesitated.

"See you later, griffin girl." He gave me a crooked grin. I liked it better than his typical roguish one. It was more honest, somehow. "Try to stay out of trouble."

He winked and vanished into the thick undergrowth.

"Should I give you a minute?" Oz asked with a teasing grin. "I'm sure you could catch up to him if you ran." Heat swept across my face, and he pointed with a triumphant laugh. "Ha! How do you like it?"

I snorted and planted my hands on my hips. "Do you really want to challenge me to this game, Oz? Because I'll win, *love*, I promise you that."

I'd forgotten all about our prisoner until Sergeant Aral huffed a quiet laugh. "I'd forgotten what griff riders were like."

The humor drained out of Oz's expression, and Keira snapped her beak lightly next to the sergeant's face, her tufted ears angled back. Again, disquiet twisted my belly as I stared at the Savinian raider who was *nothing* like I'd expected, but I tore my gaze off his at the harsh roar-scream of a gray dragon.

Warily, the dragon circled over the landing field and waited for Oz's all-clear signal before descending. The morning had dawned without a cloud in sight, and silvery-gray wings flared wide and beat against an achingly blue sky. High in the saddle, her rider gripped tight with his legs and moved with his dragon, perfectly in sync with his bonded.

Taloned feet hit the ground, joints flexed, and then the front legs touched down softly. Those great wings only partially furled though, and the dragon arched her neck, scanning for threats. She only relaxed after Oz shouted back the countersign to the rider, but I tensed.

That voice...

With a gentle pat on her neck, the wiry man slid out of the saddle and dropped to the ground. He stalked across the landing field, wildflowers and weeds trying and failing to gain purchase on his leather-clad legs, and my belly tightened with every step he took. I knew that confident walk, but the slightly dangerous air had intensified over time.

The dragon rider drew to a halt in front of me and pulled off his flying cap and goggles with an impatient tug. Silvery-gray eyes a perfect match for his dragon's wings caught on my face as if I was the only person at that waystation. My eyes narrowed slightly, but it took more effort than I'd thought it would to hold back my smile.

"Cal."

It had been more than a year since I'd seen him last, and he hadn't changed much. The lines of his face were maybe a little sharper, his eyes a little harder. The scar was new. Not quite silvery, still a little pink around the edges that curled around his jaw. An icy shock traveled through me, and my nails dug into my palms—someone had tried to cut his throat and very nearly succeeded. His gaze flicked past me to the sergeant still tied to his tree, and the realization of why we'd raised the signal flag flashed across his face.

Callum might not have been book smart like Zayne, but he was quick.

"Harper." His lips twitched, and I knew he was going to be an ass. "I always thought you were an overachiever, but don't you think capturing a Savinian raider is a bit much, even for you?"

"Point of order," Oz interjected easily as he crossed his arms and leaned against the supply bunker. "Technically, the rangers captured him. We're just the delivery guys."

Callum ignored him and stared a challenge at me.

"You never wanted to be a fighter, Harper." There was a flash of worry, there and gone so quickly I'd have missed it if I'd blinked. One brow slowly arched, and his lips twitched again. "Did bonding a griffin make you reckless as well as slow?"

Casually, I moved my right leg back and shifted my weight as if I was just making myself comfortable. Not so incidentally, it placed me at the perfect distance from my old friend.

"No," I said with a slow smile. "Bonding a griffin made me sneaky."

Pivoting on my left foot, I spun around and extended my right leg, briefly touching my fingertips to the ground and sweeping my right leg out and *through* Callum's legs in a textbook-perfect sweep kick. He hit the ground flat on his back with a startled *oof* as I pushed off my fingertips and sprang back to the guard stance I'd so casually shifted to at the beginning of the move. Felix let out a sharp trill of amusement, Oz huffed a quiet laugh, and Callum's dragon dropped her jaw in an unmistakable grin.

"See?" My head tilted as a smirk pulled at my lips. I stared down at Callum as he fought to regain his lost breath. "Sneaky."

For just an instant, something dark flashed in his eyes, a reflex quickly suppressed maybe, because in the next instant he roared a laugh.

"Suppose I deserved that," he said as he sat up. "At least you didn't break my nose like Dimitri."

"Trust me, you were at the top of my 'to be punched' list for a while there." Snickering, I held out my hand, my legs braced just in case he tried to pull me down with him. But he just clasped my callused hand with his own and allowed me to pull him back to his feet. Shaking his head slightly, he gave me that old mischievous grin, like he had when we were a little younger and a lot more innocent.

"Well played, brat." Callum's grin faded, and once again his gaze slid toward Sergeant Aral. "Raiders travel in groups of six. Where's the rest of them?"

"Dead."

Despite my best effort, my voice wavered, and his hand tightened on mine in a brief squeeze that managed to convey understanding before he let go. I stepped back without looking and leaned against Felix, who had prowled up behind me, and cleared my throat.

"Sergeant Franks said the prisoner . . ." I hesitated. I didn't like how that sounded, as if by reducing someone to the status of prisoner dehumanized them. I didn't like it at all. "He said Sergeant Benjamin Aral needs to be transferred to Fort Ashfall for questioning."

"I don't have a double saddle—not that I'd trust a Savinian at my back anyway—but I've got a carry harness," Callum said briskly. "Artemis can haul him back in her talons." He leaned past me and fixed a hard gaze on Sergeant Aral. "Hope you don't get air sick."

The raider just gazed back, his expression as impassive as last night. Callum grunted and strode back to his dragon to grab the harness. The moment his back was turned, Sergeant Aral's jaw flexed a few times, and he swallowed hard as he stared at the lithe gray dragon waiting in the landing field, only the twitch of her tail giving away her impatience. Felix tensed at my back, fixated on that tail tip.

"Not the time, featherhead," I said in exasperation.

Keira stood guard over the sergeant while her bondmate cut him loose from the tree. He cautiously stood and rubbed his wrists, his gaze still focused on the dragon, who had dropped her head to her rider. My internal debate only lasted a moment.

"The carry harness isn't so bad. Just keep your arms and legs crossed, and close your eyes." I shrugged, remembering my own training experiences as a second-year cadet in the carry harness. "Or don't. I never did."

"You forgot the most important part, Harper," Callum growled as he stalked back and whipped the harness at the Savinian. "Try anything and we'll drop you so fast you'll still be wondering what the hell happened when you hit the ground."

As Oz helped Sergeant Aral into the harness, I caught Callum's arm in a tight grip. I knew that vindictive look in his eyes, and I didn't like it one bit in this situation.

"Under the Accords, Sergeant Aral has clear protections and rights as a Prisoner of War," I said in an undertone. *"Don't* mistreat him."

"Why not?" He ripped his arm free. "They would. They *have*."

"Because we're supposed to be better than that."

"What would you know?" His eyes hardened. "You just got to the fort."

Huh. So he'd been paying attention. I'd looked for the three morons the few days I'd been at Ashfall before heading out, but I hadn't caught so much of a glimpse of any of them, or their dragons.

"You have no idea what they're like." Callum flung an arm at Sergeant Aral, as if he were solely representative of all of Savinia. "They're animals."

"I know more than you think," I said evenly enough, but Callum must have seen something in my face, because he clenched his jaw and glared hatred at the sergeant. The darkness that had so briefly flashed across his gaze returned, deeper and uglier than before.

"What did they do to you, Harper?" he crooned in a dangerous whisper.

"Nothing," I snapped.

"Because they didn't have time," Oz said grimly, nothing casual in his stance now.

A shiver traveled down my spine, and I felt the ghost of a hard grip on my jaw. I shook it off and tilted my head toward Sergeant Aral. "And because he stepped in."

"Only to a certain extent," Oz shot back, his expression tight. "He did nothing to stop his commander when he threatened to murder us in cold blood."

Sergeant Aral finished tightening his harness, and I was probably the only one who noticed the slight tremble in his fingers. Oz clamped a hand on his shoulder and urged him toward the landing field and the gray dragon whose tail was twitching a little more impatiently. As they drew even with me, Sergeant Aral stopped, lifted his chin, and looked me dead in the eye.

"Killing you in combat is acceptable," he said in a hard tone. "Executing you per our standing orders is acceptable."

Cold shot down my spine, and Felix growled. My hand automatically dropped to my hip, but the unfamiliar Savinian dagger offered little comfort or protection. Not that Sergeant Aral so much as twitched in my direction. Instead, his voice dropped into that fierce growl I'd heard once before.

"Allowing my men to take liberties between either of those things is and always will be unacceptable."

Once again, Sergeant Aral dipped his head in that courteous bow, and then Oz escorted him to the field.

"I'll give you two a minute," Felix said, that slight burr in his voice telling me he was relaying for Oz. *"And then we need to hit the trail again. This bit of fun has set us back, and we're going to have our work cut out for us if we're going to get back on schedule."*

Sighing, I turned back to Callum. Darkness lingered in his eyes as he glared after the limping Savinian sergeant. I hated it. He'd always been so prickly, so quick to fight, to mouth off, but he'd never been vicious. My gaze dropped to the scar on his jaw, and I wondered just what the hell he'd been through in the past year. And if he'd even tell me if I asked.

"Cal—" I broke off when his gaze snapped back to mine.

"I'd tell you to be careful out here, but I think I'd just be wasting my breath," he said with considerable exasperation. "Only you could go out on a simple patrol and run into a full raider team—and somehow come away without a scratch *and* a prisoner."

I huffed a soft laugh. "You know me, always with the overachieving."

Callum shook his head, gaze catching on my empty sheath.

"Seriously, Harper, how do you not have a proper knife?" he burst out, lip curling in disgust at the heavy Savinian dagger hanging opposite the empty sheath. I smirked as Felix loomed over my shoulder. I could've told him mine had broken in the fight, but it was more fun to tease him. A whisper of amusement caressed my mind as Felix caught the direction of my thoughts.

"I mean, technically I have ten of them."

Felix casually held up one paw and extended his claws. What had once been tiny baby claws had long-since developed into fearsome weapons that rivaled my lost dagger for length and sharpness.

"I suppose you do," he said with a sharp laugh, some of that darkness fading away. Not gone though, just buried a little deeper. He fell silent, his silvery-gray eyes searching for something. "You gonna forgive me yet?" he finally grunted.

"You gonna apologize?" I shot back. He smirked, and I knew what he was going to say.

"Maybe next time."

Callum turned on his heel and stalked halfway across the landing field before he stopped. His shoulder flexed, as if he'd taken a deep breath, before he whirled back around, muttering under his breath with each stomping step. I tilted my head back and met his irritated stare with an arched brow.

"Here." He unclipped his knife from his belt and thrust the blade out sideways. "You should be properly armed if you're going to run around playing tag with Savinian raiders."

Almost hesitantly, I curled my fingers around the hilt. The weight of the knife was comforting. Not quite as long as my dagger, but long enough to do the job, and with the heft of good steel—and unlike the Savinian dagger, it wasn't too heavy for me to effectively wield. I tugged a quarter inch of the blade free from the sheath to inspect it, and my breath caught at the maker's mark etched near the hilt.

"Cal..." I shook my head slowly and tried to hand the knife back. "I can't take this."

"Yes, you can." He backed out of reach as that mischievous grin made a reappearance. The one that said he thought he'd gotten one over on me. "If it makes you feel better, consider it a loan. You can give it back when you find a better one."

He jogged across the field. Artemis extended one forearm, and without breaking stride, Callum leaped from her elbow up to the saddle. He always was a bit of a showoff, though if it had ever been a contest, Dimitri would've won hands down. Or possibly me.

Felix snorted. *"I've seen enough of those morons of yours. You were definitely the showoff of that group."*

"Hey!"

Oz and Keira backed away as Artemis rocked onto her hind legs and threaded her foreclaws through the thick loops of Sergeant Aral's carry harness. With a trumpeting roar, she leaped into the air in a thunder of wingbeats, kicking up a breeze that stirred the strands of hair that had escaped my braid and whipping dust into my eyes. Belatedly, I shielded my face, but I didn't stop watching until Callum was out of sight.

My lips parted on a shaking breath, and I glanced down at the knife in my white-knuckled grip. There *was* no better blade than this...and it was probably the closest thing to an apology he would ever give me.

Maybe next time I'd tell him it was enough. Maybe.

CHAPTER 19

Three weeks to the day after we left, we tromped back through the gates of Fort Ashfall.

We were only supposed to be gone for two weeks. Our run-in with the raiders had cost us half a day at most, but an unusually severe thunderstorm near Bristol had washed away part of the trail, leaving us a week overdue. Thanks to Callum, the guards knew part of the reason for our delay, and only gave us a little trouble on the way in. Felix's tail was lashing by the time we made it through the second set of gates, and Oz barked a tired laugh.

"It's their job to be suspicious." He clapped me on the shoulder companionably. "Good job out there."

"Thanks, you too." My lips quirked up in a small grin, and I panned my gaze over the massive valley, still bustling with soldiers and riders and dragons and griffins despite the setting sun. Red and orange splashed the puffy gray clouds, tiny remnants of that brutal storm. A shiver ran down my spine. If we'd been just a little slower, we might have been washed away along with that section of trail. But we hadn't, just like we hadn't fallen to the Savinian raiders. Felix caught my pride and arched his neck in response.

"*Well, featherhead,*" I said as we slowly walked across the valley toward the griffin eyrie. "*We survived our first patrol.*"

"*Together,*" he purred in agreement.

Keira tilted her head at Felix and squawked in irritation.

"*With a little help,*" he amended hastily.

291

Weary but happy, we trudged up the slope behind Oz and his bondmate. He crested the top of the wide hill and glanced back with a smile that was more in his eyes than anywhere else.

"Welcome home, Harpy."

I'd barely been here long enough for it to feel like home before we'd left, but his words struck a chord. *Home.*

In the next instant, Felix's tufted ears stood up straight and he let out a piercing shriek.

"TAVI!"

His wings snapped wide, accidentally smacking me in the face, and he bounded forward as energetically as if we hadn't been on the trail for three weeks. An answering shriek echoed off the hills, and Tavi rose up onto his back legs and flung himself at his brother. I spat out a stray feather but couldn't help my grin as the two griffins tumbled across the grass in a tangle of limbs, wings, and tails.

Oz lifted one hand in a tired wave and trudged off with his arm slung around Keira's neck, and I absently waved back. We'd see plenty of each other over the next five or so months of training. Right now, I was looking for someone else. Because if Tavi was here, so was—

"Keaton!"

He strolled across the hill, adroitly avoiding our wrestling griffins with the ease of long practice, his brows raised without a hint of a smile on his face.

"You're late," he said gruffly.

"Ran into a few . . . delays," I said with an evasive shrug. I went to hug the grumpy bastard, and he stepped back with his nose wrinkled.

"Holy shit, Harpy, you reek."

"I was on the trail for three weeks, what did you expect?" I demanded.

"You to shower before you tried to hug me," he said dryly.

His expression was impassive, but he couldn't hide the amusement and happiness in his eyes. Not from me anyway. I dropped my travel pack and bow, and spread my arms wide with a slightly loopy cackle.

"Come here and let me rub my armpits on you."

He stared at me for a heartbeat before he roared a laugh. "Damn, I missed you."

"Missed you too, brother," I said with a happy smile. "Anything interesting happen on your run?"

Instantly, I wished I could take the question back, even though I genuinely wanted to know. Regardless of what had happened on his patrol, it would prompt him to ask about mine, and I was too damn tired to go into detail. The walls I'd built in my mind trembled, and I desperately shored them up. *Tired. Right . . .*

"Not too different from our patrols back at the academy." He picked up my travel pack and bow and slung them over his shoulder. "Kind of boring, if I'm being honest, but Nikos is a good trainer, and I picked up some good techniques. How was yours? You know, outside of a week longer than it was supposed to be."

My shoulders stiffened slightly, but while there was curiosity in his voice, there was no real concern. Callum might have informed the gate guards to expect us back late, but word must not have reached the griffin eyrie. *Small mercies.*

Somehow, I managed a casual shrug as we strolled toward our dorm.

"I'll tell you about it after I shower." My stomach gurgled a complaint, and he laughed.

"How about over dinner?" he asked with a grin.

"Deal."

Our griffins fell silent with an abruptness that was louder than all their squawking, roaring, and trilling combined. My shoulders tensed even more in that ominous silence. Keaton snapped his head around to his griffin and went rigid.

"You were *what*?" Slowly, he turned back to stare at me, his amber eyes blazing. "You were captured by *raiders*?"

I winced and held my index finger and thumb slightly apart. "Only a little captured."

"Fucking hell, how were you just a *little* captured?" Keaton snarled and dropped my travel pack and bow without regard for the weapon. There was nothing impassive in his enraged expression, or awkward in the way he lunged forward and pulled me into a rough hug.

He felt familiar and *safe*—and all my careful compartmentalization crumbled in one terrible instant. Everything crashed down on me and replayed in my memory. A harsh grip on my jaw, a gore-drenched arrow held out like a present, the *buzz* of hungry flies, the sour tang of copper and terror. I shuddered, seconds away from shattering, but Keaton tightened his arms around me and held all my jagged pieces together.

"Breathe, Harpy. Just breathe."

With a gasp that was part sob, I buried my face in his chest, my eyes burning as I struggled to take deep breaths.

"What the hell happened out there?" he demanded, anger doing a poor job of masking his fear. I pushed away, dragging the back of my hand across my face and shaking my head. Keaton gripped my upper arms and didn't let me go. "Come on, you stubborn bitch, talk to me."

Another tremor shook my frame, but I kept my chin up and forced a tremulous smile. "Do I have to?"

"Yes." The determined look on his face said I wasn't getting out of talking with him tonight. A small smile tugged at his lips. "Or I'll have Tavi sit on you again."

That startled a laugh out of me, and I glanced at Felix's brother. The tawny brown griffin narrowed his amber eyes and nodded emphatic agreement. He nudged Felix, and my griffin relayed for him.

"You know I'll do it." Tavi padded over and gently nuzzled my face. *"Talk to my bonded, sister."*

"I think you need to," Felix added in his own voice, and I gave in with a sigh.

"Okay, just let me get cleaned up first," I said hoarsely. Keaton picked up my gear again and nodded.

"I'll save you some dinner."

Full darkness had fallen by the time I'd showered, changed, and eaten. Keaton had spent a little more time at the fort than me, and he'd bullied me out to his favorite place to get away from everyone.

"Of course it's a roof," I teased with a grin as we climbed up the steep hillside near the back of the valley. There were a handful of stone storage bunkers built into that hill, and it was easy to hop onto the roof of one. As our griffins curled up together nearby, we sat, the stone still slightly sun-warmed, and leaned against the grassy slope.

We had an impressive view of the valley reminiscent of our old view of the academy. Far enough away from the busier areas of the fort and back where the carefully managed trees dotted the massive hills that cradled the fort. We sat in silence for a time, just listening to the night. Summer heat made the stars overhead hazy, what few we could see through the clouds, and the crickets sang a lazy song.

At a flash of light beneath a tree, I tensed, but my apprehension vanished in a delighted gasp when another light flashed. Keaton chuckled, his laughter a quiet rumble I felt more than heard.

"Lightning bugs."

I smiled wistfully at the dancing, flickering lights.

"We called them fireflies back home." When he held up a flask, my smile widened. "Peace offering or declaration of war?"

"Only one way to find out," he said with a challenging grin.

Cautiously, I took a sip. My eyes widened at the smooth, slightly sweet burn.

"That's *good*." I took another, longer sip, and sighed happily at the pooling warmth in my belly.

"Should be, I snitched it from Oz's stash."

"You did *not*," I said with a giggle that was part stress, part exhaustion, and possibly part alcohol.

"What?" Keaton shot me an innocent look that would fool exactly nobody. "He always had the best booze back at the academy."

I took another sip, slower this time, more appreciative. "He definitely stepped up his acquisition game here. I'll have to thank him for the donation."

We passed the flask back and forth for a few minutes before he pinned me with a determined stare. But he didn't demand. He asked.

"Talk to me, Harpy?"

So I did. I somehow managed to get the whole story out without pausing for anything more than a few bracing sips of whatever the hell Oz had scrounged up from somewhere. Everything got a little fuzzy somewhere along the way, comforting without stealing my clarity.

When I was done, Keaton tilted his face up to the sky. Clouds had completely obscured the stars, but he stared up as if those clouds held all the answers.

"Damn it, Harpy," he finally said with a harsh laugh. "I leave you alone for five minutes."

"No, you didn't." I leaned against his side and sighed when he put his arm around my shoulders. *Safe*, my hazy mind whispered as the last of my tension and fear slid away. "You never have."

"Never will," he said gruffly and pulled me closer.

The next time Oz and I were sent out, it wasn't on a patrol, or even a scouting run. It was a messenger relay. Proof that none of our training at the academy was ever wasted, not even the "fun" things. And for griffin riders, messenger relays were far from fun.

While horseback messengers were used in the more open areas, and dragon riders were used in the safer areas, griffin riders were used in the most dangerous. We were sent to the smaller forts in the mountains where the paths were too treacherous for horses to run, and the forward operating bases where the skies were too dangerous for dragons to fly. Conventional soldiers held the line at the border, and Savinians on the opposite side were well equipped to shoot down any dragons who dared draw near. Worse, they had a distressing tendency to move their dragon lance and flechette artillery at unpredictable intervals, so what were once safe skies became a death trap for fragile dragon wings.

But griffins? Griffins were sneaky and fast, and they rarely caught us unaware.

The fact that Oz and I had been successfully ambushed by the raider team was considered highly unusual. Anderson and Mayhew had exchanged a grim glance after we'd reported in the morning after we'd returned from our patrol, a dark knowledge in their eyes that had sent chills down my spine. But all Anderson had said was the timing of the rangers had been incredibly good luck for us, even as the timing of the raiders to cut through that valley at the exact right moment to avoid our griffins and intercept us was incredibly *bad* luck.

Our commander had then ordered us to spend a few days recovering before he retreated behind closed doors with Mayhew. When Keaton found me sitting on the edge of my bunk a few hours later, my unstrung bow in one hand and a mineral oil–soaked rag in the other, just staring and not actually doing a damned thing to care for it, he dragged me to the archery range. He made me run through drills and basic target shooting until my hands no longer shook and I was no longer seeing the Savinian officer's eyes every time I released an arrow.

Nikos stalked out to the range halfway through, watched for a short time, and then taught us new drills. When we mastered those to his satisfaction, he roped our griffins into the impromptu practice and had us running drills from griffin-back. By the end of the day, I was hitting the bull's-eye again.

Three days later, Nikos and Keaton departed for the western fringe of the Smoke Mountains to see if there was any truth to the reports of broken beasts ranging out of their traditional territory and into the path of our conventional soldiers. Their griffins wore lightweight scout saddles in case they had to *move*, and they carried extra quivers.

Oz didn't give me time to worry. He told me about our messenger relay tasking, dragged me to the highly detailed map that dominated the entire back wall of the Ops Center in the main fortress, and told me to plan a route to Outpost West Pike, where we'd rendezvous with the griffin rider coming in from Forward Operating Base, or FOB, Decatur.

"Good," he said when I was done. "Now give me two alternates, and an 'oh shit' route."

The moment Oz was satisfied, an Ops Center staff officer issued us the sealed cylindrical message tube, and we headed out. This time, we rode our griffins, though Oz decided against the lightweight scout saddles and went with the bareback pads again.

"Just in case they need to fly," he said quietly as we passed through the outer gate. A wry grin creased his face. "Or we need to use your 'oh shit' route, because there's no getting through those particular woods with stirrups."

Keira snorted agreement, clamped her wings tight to her side to anchor her rider's legs, and took off at a run. Felix copied her, his wings a warm weight against my lower legs, and his spine flexing beneath me with every bounding stride. I flexed with him, reveling in his speed. It was almost like flying and, despite the risk, my soul sang with joy as we raced beneath the trees. As we hit the first of many rolling hills, our griffins dropped into the steady lope they could keep up for hours, even carrying our weight.

Six hours later, Oz had us stop at a waystation, but only for dinner and a short rest. The moon would be full tonight, and our griffins could see just fine in the dark. We took naps in shifts, though it seemed like I'd just rolled myself in my bedding when Oz shook my shoulder. I walked the perimeter while he napped, and then woke him when it was time to move out again.

We reached Outpost West Pike late morning the next day. Little more than a sturdy stockade surrounding a handful of wooden buildings, the hotly contested Wattspar River was barely visible as a faint sparkle of sunlight on flowing water off to the east. We found the next griffin rider in the relay pacing in front of the stockade, impatiently waiting for us. Surprise shot through me and startled a grin onto my face.

"Langston, Bailey!"

"Took you long enough, princess," Langston grumbled. He glanced at Oz and nodded respectfully. "Osbourne."

"Good to see you too, *Langy*." I rolled my eyes at the old insult and remembered why I'd never particularly liked my irritable clutchmate. His bulky frame had leaned out somewhat in the past year, but his muddy green eyes were as full of disdain as ever.

With a disgruntled sigh, I passed over the messenger tube while Felix and Bailey nuzzled each other in a fond greeting. At least our griffins got along now, something I hadn't thought possible when they were young.

"Got anything for us to take back?" Oz asked.

"No," Langston said shortly as he swung himself into Bailey's saddle. Her tail lashed, and she mimicked her rider's grumble with hilarious and incredibly mocking accuracy. His shoulders flexed and he glowered first at his griffin, then at me. "Reese and Gage should be next on the relay."

I waited for a moment, but apparently that was all he intended to say.

"Tell them we said hi," I ventured slowly before I brightened. "Oh! And tell him to say hi to Bex for me. I miss her."

He grunted and turned away, but Bailey planted her feet and refused to move. A trilling laugh spilled out of her beak, and Felix and Keira echoed it. Langston heaved an exasperated sigh.

"Reese said he's proud of you for that sweep kick," he said through gritted teeth.

I blinked in astonishment. There hadn't been many witnesses when I got Callum with my sneak attack. "How does he *know* about that?"

"Griffins gossip like old women." Unexpectedly, Langston grinned. "Of *course* that story of you putting a dragon rider on his ass spread like wildfire."

On our return to Ashfall, I found out Callum and Artemis had vanished on a patrol sweep. A few days later, the Savinians were kind enough to return his mutilated body to our front door. I spent a long time curled up with Felix that night. Tears blurring my vision as I held Callum's knife, the closest I'd ever get to an apology from him, wishing . . . wishing I hadn't been stupid enough to think we had all the time in the world to play our stupid game.

Three weeks passed where Oz took me on shorter patrol routes through the hills surrounding Fort Ashfall before we were sent out on a low-risk scouting sortie at the border. Low risk, because that area of the border wasn't hot. No forts, no pitched battles, just a stretch of second-growth forest and rolling hills north of Fort Bramble. A sharp-eyed conventional soldier had noticed unusual activity at a Savinian supply depot and reported it up the chain. A high-altitude pass by Banshee, Ashfall's lone blue dragon, hadn't revealed anything unusual, but I was learning Colonel Harborne was the thorough—or paranoid—type of commander.

He sent griffin riders in to verify.

We headed for the western bank of the Wattspar River and settled in to wait for nightfall with the rushing sound of the river in our ears. We kept our eyes open while we waited, but the supply depot wasn't visible from our current position. The available intel painted it a bare-bones facility though, little more than rough shelters for supplies designed to look like natural treefalls that blended in well with the terrain.

At last, night fell, and it was time to move. The river was narrow and fast running this far north with only the remnants of a bridge in sight, long since destroyed by one side or the other. But as a former dragon rider cadet turned griffin rider, Oz was just as good at gliding as I was, and our griffins easily got us across.

"You take the south, we'll scout around the northern edge of the depot. Banshee reported the trees thin out too much for even a griffin to get near. Use your judgement, but don't take stupid chances. Understood?" Felix's tone had shifted to the soft burr he used when relaying for Oz, and I nodded at my training officer.

Oz held my gaze for a brief moment before slipping into the thick brush, Keira prowling silently after him. Had that been doubt in his eyes? My jaw tightened with determination. I could do this. Felix nudged my shoulder, and I smiled. *We* could do this.

Silently, almost as silently as Oz, I crept through the night-dark forest with Felix at my heels. I knew the supply depot was roughly five hundred meters ahead, but if there were soldiers manning it, they hadn't elected to light fires—another change that sharp-eyed conventional soldier had noted. Somebody didn't want to call attention to this depot, which meant we absolutely wanted to pay attention to it.

Banshee had provided an accurate report of the terrain though. After two hundred meters, the trees thinned out, leaving tangled brush and the occasional scrub pine behind. A quick glance, a caress of fur under my fingers, and I left Felix behind.

"Be careful," he whispered, sharp eyes scanning the path ahead of me for threats as I slowly eeled through the brush. I sent him a quick burst of reassurance and focused, dropping down to low-crawl through a patch of ferns.

Up ahead, past a clump of scrub pines, I caught a glimpse of the rough timbers of the supply depot. And tarps. A lot of tarps. I paused beneath the wide fronds of a fern, but no matter how I shifted, I couldn't get a clear view. I had to get closer. In order to get closer, I'd need to break cover. There was a narrow stretch where there was nothing bigger than knee-high weeds, maybe three little paces across and no way around it.

Sweat born from more than the summer heat trickled down my spine and gathered under my riding leathers as I considered my options. Doubt flickered... but then I remembered the doubt in Oz's eyes, and I buried mine.

Drawing in a deep breath, I plotted out the quickest route to get to the next decent cover and slid out of concealment. My steps were soundless, my movements graceful and quick, and within a heartbeat I'd disappeared into the shadow of a pine tree.

A hard glance around showed no sentries, and no alarm was raised. Even better, I had a clear view of the supply depot. My lips kicked up into a serrated smile as triumph rushed through me—and then the familiar *creak* of a drawn bowstring cut through the still air.

I froze for an instant before my head snapped up. Directly above me, a Savinian soldier knelt on a tiny wooden platform built around the trunk and cleverly hidden within the boughs. Felix felt my panic and surged forward. My eyes burned, but I didn't so much as blink. I was too busy staring at the razor-sharp arrow aimed for my heart.

The arrow that would kill us both.

Felix's panic rebounded through the bond, ricocheting and

building in intensity until I could barely think. He was too far away, and I was too slow, too stupid, too fucking overconfident to do anything to save us.

The sharp *twang* of a bowstring sang out.

A bolt of terror shot through me and I flinched, waiting for the pain. And kept waiting—because the arrow didn't move. Not until the bow slipped from the sentry's hands.

My stunned gaze tracked that razor-sharp arrow as it tumbled to the ground, and then jerked back up as the sentry toppled out of his perch. He landed with a muffled *thud* in the bed of dead pine needles at the base of the trunk. Shaking with adrenaline and fear, I stared at the body lying at my feet . . . and at the deadly little arrow in his eye.

Oz ghosted out of the brush, bow in one hand and rare anger blazing bright in his turquoise eyes. Anger not for the dead Savinian, but for me. Felix's mental voice was shaking as he relayed.

"Never *forget to look up.*"

Dimitri's voice drifted through my memory. *How many times do I have to tell you to look up, hotshot?*

Shame rolled through me as panic faded. That was a lesson I should've carried over from dragon rider training. Another tremor shook my frame before I shoved everything behind a mental wall. Felix helped, shielding his own fading terror and doing what he could to steady me.

"*I'm so sorry, Felix. I should've been more careful.*" He curled around my mind in silent forgiveness. My hands still shook, but I nodded at Oz and relayed through our griffins. "*I won't forget again.*"

"*Good.*" Oz tilted his head toward the supply depot. "*Now, tell me what you see, newbie.*"

The echo of Nikos helped me pull myself together a little more, and I peered out from between drooping pine branches. At first, all I saw were tarps and the shadows of men moving equipment under the cover of darkness. And then a soldier flipped up the edge of the closest tarp to inspect the goods hidden beneath, and my breath caught.

"*Dragon lances. Ballistae.*" Alarm raced through me. Now that I knew what I was looking at, the shapes beneath the tarps snapped into focus. Dozens of anti-air weapons disassembled for transport. They must have just moved them to this location. I did a rapid count. "*It's a full artillery unit.*"

"*What* don't *you see?*"

I scanned the supply depot and surrounding area. This time I remembered to look up.

"*No anti-air ballistae set up for defense, no signs of dragons or wyverns in the sky.*"

Oz raised his brows. "*And what do we do when we find an unprotected artillery unit within reach of our dragons?*"

My head tilted. "*We call in an airstrike?*"

He bared his teeth in a savage smile. "*We call in an airstrike.*"

We high-tailed it back to Fort Bramble and did exactly that. When we were sent back in to verify the hit, we watched with vicious satisfaction as the entire depot went up in flames.

On our return to Ashfall, exhausted paws and feet dragging, and the cloying scent of smoke clinging to us, we were met with an enthusiastic reception from the dragon riders. Not just the handful who'd participated in the airstrike—all of them currently on post. Word had spread, and the riders were eager to celebrate the destruction of so many of the weapons that threatened their bonded.

Felix and Keira were presented with choice cows from the dragon herds, a rare treat for a griffin, and they promptly gorged themselves into happy food comas while the entire Griffin Corps detachment was swept up in the invitation to the dragon eyrie. Food and drinks were broken out, someone with no small talent pulled out a battered guitar and took requests from the increasingly inebriated riders, and bonfires were built in the space between the dorms.

The party lasted into the small hours of the morning. I spent much of the night reconnecting with Zayne, but Dimitri was out on a mission.

"Just as well," Zayne said with a teasing grin when he caught me looking for him for the dozenth time. "You'd just end up breaking Dimitri's nose again, and it looks like your knuckles have already suffered enough abuse for tonight."

I gave my scraped, scabbed knuckles a rueful glance. I'd been so twitchy after my near miss that I'd spent the first half of our trip back to Ashfall jumping at shadows.

"Yeah, that tree I hit totally had it coming."

Panic slammed into me. Once again, I saw the shadowed gaze of the sentry as he drew back on the bowstring, saw the arrow that had nearly cost Felix and me everything. I breathed through the memory, but something must have shown in my expression.

"Bad mission?" Zayne asked quietly, the ghosts of his own failures and past mistakes swimming in his green and gold gaze.

"I fucked up," I confessed hoarsely. "Nearly got myself and Felix killed because I was being a cocky little shit. If it wasn't for Oz . . ."

"You? Cocky?" He snorted a quiet laugh and gripped my shoulder. "Harper—you can do everything right and still lose. You can fuck up and still get lucky. The important thing is not to let that panic I just saw in your eyes win. Ever. You panic, you die." He tightened his grip. "Don't let it win."

"I won't." I shook off the last of my fear and managed a lopsided smile. "I mean, I'll definitely panic again, let's not kid ourselves . . . but I won't let it win."

"Good."

Laughter rang out as Zayne let go of my shoulder. He glanced across the dancing flames of the nearest bonfire to where Keaton had his arm wrapped around the waist of a brunette dragon rider. Their heads were bent close together and they were smiling as they whispered words meant only for each other.

"Your boy has some serious game," he said with only the faintest tinge of envy. "I've been trying to get Corella's attention for *months*, and he manages it in a single night."

"And I didn't even have to play wingwoman this time." I mimed wiping a tear from the corner of my eye. "I'm so proud."

Zayne chuckled and grabbed my hand. "Come on, brat. I've got some booze that'll knock you on your griffin rider ass."

My eyes narrowed at his deliberate phrasing. "In a good way, or in a revenge for Cal way?"

"Why not both?" he asked with a smirk, but his gaze darkened with loss. "Besides, I'm pretty sure he would've loved to see us drunk and falling on our asses in his honor."

Grief ricocheted through my heart, but I smiled through the sharp pain. "I mean, is there any other way to honor that dickhead?"

"Falling down drunk it is!" Zayne declared with a wicked grin.

Laughing, I let him tug me through the mingling crowd of dragon and griffin riders, the raucous melody of an old drinking song weaving through the cheerful cacophony of dozens of conversations. Sparks from the bonfires rose up and merged with the stars, while dragons watched with bright-eyed interest from their eyries and griffins played and sprawled out on the grass.

We passed by Oz, who was flirting with one of the dragon riders, a tiny slip of a woman with laughing green eyes, without a hint of awkwardness. Apparently, he was only a terrible flirt when we were under threat from Savinian raiders.

"Or maybe he was just terrible at flirting with you," Felix said with a muzzy, meat-drunk giggle.

"Shut up." I rolled my eyes even as a grin pulled at my lips. Griffins couldn't process alcohol, but they could get pretty loopy when they overindulged in meat, and Felix hadn't stopped giggling yet. I sent him a wave of exasperated affection. *"Go sleep it off, featherhead."*

Zayne bulled his way into a group of dragon riders crowded around a smaller fire. "Make a hole, you bunch of degenerates. This is Harper Tavros—"

"Harpy?" An intimidatingly large man with an impressive scar running down the side of his face, only one eye, and enough muscles to pick Felix up with one hand, scowled at me. "One of the scouts who found the weapons depot?"

I lifted my chin, mostly because he was so much taller than me if I *didn't* there was no way to meet his smoky gray eye. "Yeah."

He tossed me a flask. "Cheers."

I was still hungover when someone pounded on my door the next morning. Groaning, I turned over and accidentally rolled right out of my bunk and onto the floor. The *thud* reverberated through my skull and drew out another, louder groan. I pressed my fingertips to my temples as Felix filled my aching head with mocking laughter.

"Stop laughing so loud, you fancy chicken," I whimpered. There was a muffled snort of laughter from the other side of my door.

"You okay in there, Tavros?" a woman's throaty voice called out.

"No," I said on another groan as I struggled to sit up. "Please go away and come back when the world stops spinning."

There was another laugh, and something about the voice prodded at my memory. My eyes widened as I placed it, and I scrambled to my feet as quickly as my aching head and queasy gut would allow. Damn Zayne and his stupidly strong, incredibly tasty booze.

I yanked open my door and tried not to look as if I were hanging onto it for dear life. The fact that I *was* hanging on for dear life was irrelevant. I cleared my throat.

"Morning, ma'am."

"Good morning, Tavros." Major Tori Mayhew stood in the hall with her hip cocked and her arms crossed, wearing riding leathers and a shit-eating grin. "Have fun last night?"

"Yes?" I winced. "Uh . . . sorry, ma'am."

"Never apologize for celebrating your victories," she said as her grin softened. "Live dangerously and play hard is the unofficial rider motto for a reason. But the war doesn't wait for hangovers to fade, so get your ass in gear. You're riding with me today."

"Yes, ma'am," I said as crisply as I could manage when I was still seeing double. A sharp shake of my head that threatened to rattle what was left of my brains snapped my vision back into focus. "I'll be ready in fifteen."

"Make it thirty," she said with a chuckle as she strolled down the hall. Over her shoulder she called back, "And take a damn shower, Tavros. You smell like campfires and fun life choices."

"No regrets, ma'am." A grin pulled at my aching face, and I felt Felix brush against my mind with a fond laugh. A warm burst of energy followed, and the world stopped spinning. I gripped the door tighter at the abrupt change, but then the throbbing in my head quieted, and even my stomach settled.

"Thank you," I breathed out with heartfelt gratitude. As I gathered up my shower supplies, I sent a questioning tendril of thought to my griffin. *"Are you up for another run so soon?"*

"It's either run off that cow from last night, or sleep for a week," he shot back with a merry laugh. *"And I don't think they'll let me sleep that long, so running it is!"*

We met Major Mayhew and her griffin, Havok, at the inner gate exactly thirty-two minutes after she left me in the dorms. The second-in-command of the griffin detachment made a show of checking the time and arched a brow.

"Only two minutes late. Not bad."

Without another word, she swung up into the saddle, and we followed her out of the fort. Once we were on the trail, she beckoned me to ride beside her.

"A couple things. On post, absolutely use rank, especially around the conventionals. They expect it, and it makes them uneasy when we don't adhere to their expectations. But out in the field, last names or griffin names only, no 'sir,' no 'ma'am,' and sure as hell no rank. We don't wear it on our riding leathers for a reason. One, it's damn stupid to paint a target on yourself for the Savinians. Two, when we're scouting or patrolling or even messenger relaying, we're a team." Her broad gesture included both humans and griffins. "Yes, the higher-ranking officer has command, but you better not just blindly follow. We're the bloody eyes and ears, and it's your duty, your entire purpose, to use that mouth of yours and *speak up*. Understood?"

"Yes, m—" I cut myself off and nodded. "Got it."

Mayhem grinned, her eyes full of sharp amusement. "I think you're starting to. Now, try and keep up."

Outrage surged through Felix as Havok accelerated into a flat-out run. The other male wasn't quite as tall as Felix, but he was all lean muscle, and he was *fast*. Puffs of dust rose into the air with each strike of his paws, and his wings were clamped tight to his rider's legs, streamlining himself as much as possible. We were using the lightweight scout saddles today, which was a damn good thing for me. Without the security of leather and stirrups, Felix might have left me sitting in the trail as he took off in a dead sprint.

Wild joy filled my soul, sweeping the remnants of my hangover away, and I bent over Felix's neck and urged him on with a mental *whoop*. We weren't able to overtake the more experienced pair, but we kept up, and it was enough.

The summer heat rose with the sun as it climbed higher in the cloudless sky. Sweat soon rolled down my spine and gathered under Felix's girth, dampened the skin beneath the feathers on his neck where I rested my hands. Havok never slowed though, and Felix remained game to keep up, running easily despite the heat.

Many of the paths out of Fort Ashfall went east, but most split to the north or south. Not this one. We continued running east, and the longer we went without changing direction, the more my belly twisted with anxiety. Felix's ears flattened, and I could feel him fighting to keep his claws sheathed as his own anxiety spiraled higher.

Without warning, Mayhem leaned in the saddle, perfectly counterbalancing Havok as he sharply turned off the main trail and onto a narrow one I hadn't even glimpsed before that moment.

"Keep up, Harpy," Felix relayed in Mayhem's throaty tones as her low laugh drifted back to my ears.

"Mayhem is the perfect griffin name for that woman," I grumbled to Felix as we duplicated their feat. I flexed in the saddle, tightening my abdominals and thighs as he whipped around the turn. *"Menace would've fit too."*

"I like her, and Havok. Don't you?"

"Are you kidding?" I snorted a laugh as the trail cut a narrow path through towering trees, the land rising and falling beneath the steady beat of Felix's paws. *"I want to be her when I grow up."*

The trail had so many twists and turns there were times where we could only catch a glimpse of Havok's tail. It was the most challenging ride we'd been on in a long time, and my thighs were burning long before the trail turned into a steep switchback straight up a small mountain. Felix's sides were heaving, and I was completely out of breath by the time we crested the top.

Dropping into a slow walk, we copied the more experienced pair and paced in slow circles around the bare rock of the summit until we were breathing easily and our sweat had cooled. A broad smile creased my face, and Felix's beak gaped in a griffin grin as he came to a stop next to Havok.

"That was fun."

There were no trees to shade us from the hot sun, but a brisk wind kept the heat manageable. It whipped strands of Mayhem's blonde and my copper hair into our faces, and ruffled the griffins' dappled brown and tawny gold feathers. Mayhem impatiently swiped a hand across her face and jerked her chin to the east.

"What do you see?" she asked quietly.

Felix cautiously paced toward the edge of the summit, where the gray stone dropped away into a sheer cliff. I wasn't afraid of heights—no dragon rider cadet could be afraid to fall and learn to fly, after all—but even I was impressed at the drop. I hadn't realized we'd climbed that high on our crazy ride. We gazed out over the impressive view and relayed what we saw to Mayhem.

A sparkling ribbon in the distance highlighted the winding path of the Wattspar River. Fortifications along the river, glimpses of stockades and distant troop movement, a cavalry patrol riding along one of the old roads. And trees, rolling hills, the towering Smoke Mountains, green, so much green growing things and life. Deer and rabbits and birds who didn't care that we fought over this strip of land, who lived blissfully unaware that fire could rain from the sky at any moment, that soldiers could pour through their little glens and meadows.

"Can you tell me where Tennessan ends and Savinia begins?" Mayhem asked as Havok moved up next to us.

The river wasn't the border. It was beyond that, further east, maybe not even in sight, maybe . . . Felix tensed.

"Harpy, look."

He tugged, and I dropped the endless drop into his mind. A blink to shed the disorientation, a breath to settle my stomach, and I looked through his incredible eyes.

And found the telltale gleam of metal marking anti-air emplacements.

Based on location, they were Tennessan, and I urged Felix to look beyond them. A shudder rippled through our entangled souls when we found the Savinian emplacements. They had more than we did. A lot more. My mouth dried out, but my hand rose and I pointed at the jagged line tearing the countryside into two very separate lands.

"That's where the border is now," she said in grim agreement. "A few years ago, you couldn't see it from here. Those bastards are eating away at us one hungry bite at a time."

She let out a slow, heavy breath.

"I bring newbies out here to the border because I need you to understand how precarious our situation is. Our duty is to protect our country, but they're whittling away at our numbers, and the Mavens can't produce more griffins fast enough." She let out a bitter laugh. "Everyone always thinks the dragons are important, and they are. They're so damn important. But so are we. Savinia might have their monsters, their wyverns, one last gasp of the old power used to create our bondmates twisted into creating those evil, mindless things, but Tennessan has an advantage the Savinians squandered—griffin riders."

Cold chills pulled me back to my own mind. I blinked, breathed, and turned to the older woman. "What happened to their griffin riders?"

Mayhem shook her head, her expression tight. "Wish we knew. Nobody's seen one in years."

CHAPTER 20

Our ride back to Fort Ashfall was a slow one. Both to allow our griffins to recover from the wild ride out and because Major Mayhew apparently used these one-on-one missions to conduct counseling sessions with her newbie riders. She was also well aware of my unique academy history, and wanted to ensure I was fitting in with the rest of the griffin riders. I'd barked a laugh and told her that question implied Oz had allowed me any time to socialize between patrols and scouting sorties.

"You socialized plenty last night," she pointed out with a reappearance of that shit-eating grin as we approached the gates. I grinned right back.

"So did you, *Mayhem*. Pretty sure I saw you drinking a certain pair of detachment commanders under the table last night."

"And yet *I* wasn't hungover this morning," she said smugly. "You've still got a lot to learn, Harpy."

"Please, teach me your ways, wise one," I shot back, only partly joking. She really had out-drunk Zeddemore and Anderson, and she was half their size. By rights, she should've been passed out on the ground instead of sauntering off with steady strides and an evil laugh.

She waited until we were through the first gate and walking along the narrow pass between before she patted her griffin affectionately.

"Havok really is the best bondmate a girl could have," she said almost idly. Almost. I caught the wicked gleam in her eyes and gasped in understanding.

"He fed you energy and burned off the alcohol while you were drinking." I shook my head in admiration of the trick. "You *cheated*."

"No more than you did this morning when Felix helped you." Her evil grin broadened. "And either of those dummies of mine could've done the same."

By the time we'd passed through the second set of gates, taken care of our griffins, and showered and changed, we'd missed dinner at our own dining hall. I stood in the doorway, staring at the dimly lit interior mournfully. While there were always snacks available, the others had already eaten all the hot food, and the kitchen staff was off for the night.

Sighing, I trudged down the hill toward the main chow hall. After that ride, I needed a real meal. Mayhem intercepted me before I could go inside.

"Didn't anyone warn you?" she demanded in exasperation. "*Never* eat at the main chow hall."

My mouth twisted to the side as my stomach gurgled a hungry complaint. "Can't be worse than the academy."

"Trust me, it's worse," she said dryly as she tugged me around toward the dragon eyrie. "Come on, newbie, we've got a standing invite to the dragon rider's dining hall. Theirs is open all hours."

We strode up the slope of the nearest dragon eyrie, where we'd spent the night partying. The air was heavy with humidity, but it lacked the overwhelming heat of the day, and the dragon riders' dining hall had the windows and doors open to catch the evening breeze. Light poured out onto the grassy lawn, along with cheerful banter. It sounded like a flight had just returned from a patrol, so we wouldn't be dining alone.

As I followed Mayhem inside, a group of dragon riders glanced up from one of the scarred wooden tables. I froze as a pair of black-ringed amber eyes landed on me.

Dimitri.

Slowly, he pushed his way up from the table, his gaze locked to mine. Mayhem glanced between the two of us, bit back a smirk, and got out of the way. Conversation in the dining hall resumed as Dimitri drifted to an uncertain stop, so close and so very far away.

I couldn't breathe. Unlike Callum, there were no scars, no hidden darkness in Dimitri's dramatic eyes. In the year since we'd last seen each other, he'd gained more muscle, more definition in his face, and maybe another inch of height. I'd wager he was as tall as Zayne now, and I had to tilt my face back to look him in the eye.

"Hey, hotshot," he murmured before he sighed. "Harper."

I licked dry lips and managed to force a single word out.

"Hey."

"Oh, very good, Harpy," Felix purred. *"Maybe you could manage to string two words together next? Oooh! Or maybe talk about the weather?"*

I gave Felix a mental shove and ignored his mocking laughter. It was harder to ignore the hot flush that swept across my face, and I mentally cursed myself for always turning into an idiot around Dimitri. As I drank in the sight of my oldest friend almost hungrily, I noticed the tiniest bump in the bridge of his nose that hadn't been there before I'd broken it. *Oops.*

Dimitri dragged a hand through his short, dark hair and gave me a hesitant smile. "Can we talk outside?"

In answer, I turned on my heel and walked back into the embrace of the warm twilight.

"I see we've regressed to nonverbal status," Felix teased as I paced over to the remains of one of last night's bonfires.

"Shut up, *Felix,"* I hissed and clenched my fists, ignoring the way the scabs pulled on my abused knuckles. Anxiety swirled low in my gut and mixed with the annoyance.

I'd wasted my chance with Callum . . . I had to get this right.

Felix retreated with a mental caress that managed to convey apology and amusement all at once as I turned to face Dimitri. He eyed my fists with raised brows, some of his hesitancy falling away beneath his old arrogance.

"I let you have that last hit because I thought I deserved it," he said in a low, warning tone, "but I won't be your punching bag, Harper."

"I never said you couldn't fight back," I said with a challenging grin, but he shook his head, stepping back. That flash of guilt and pity made a reappearance and I let out a bitter laugh. So much for getting it right. "Have you figured it out yet?"

He gave me a cautious look. "Figured out what?"

"Why I keep hitting you. Why I won't let you apologize." Despite my best efforts, my voice rose. "Why you're such a moron!"

His lips twisted into a wry smile. "You forgot 'asshole.'"

"I've forgotten *nothing*," I snapped, but he let out a frustrated snarl and stomped closer.

"Neither have I! I've never forgotten what a stubborn brat you are, or how infuriating you are, or how much you drive me *insane*." His shoulders heaved as he drew in a deep breath, staring down at me with blazing eyes. "And I've never forgotten what we did to you."

I stilled, caught in the strength of his glare, but he spun away with another snarl. He paced around the firepit, a muscle in his jaw flexing as he fought to control his temper. As he stalked back to me, his gaze landed on Callum's knife on my hip. Grief twisted his expression, and I realized I'd been wrong. So very wrong. There was darkness there, too, he just hid it better than Callum had.

"How could you forgive Cal?" he demanded. "Gods, how the hell could you forgive *Zayne*?"

His voice had dropped into an angry growl, but I heard the unspoken, plaintive words beneath. How could I forgive *them*, but not him?

"We stole your wings, and you won't even let me apologize for it..." The anger in his gaze faded, replaced by that awful pity that made me want to scratch his stupidly pretty eyes out. I took a stomping step forward and glared up at him, pain and rage and my own grief for our lost friend swirling in a toxic mess in my stupid heart.

"Gods damn it!" I snarled. "You want to know how I could forgive them but not you? Because they didn't look at me like I'm something to be pitied!"

He faltered. "Is that what you think?"

My jaw dropped at the genuine surprise on his face—and an ear-piercing wail shattered the night.

The air-raid siren.

"Son of a *bitch*," Dimitri snarled.

As well trained as we'd been at the academy, it was nothing compared to the response of an active-duty fort. Within seconds, the previously quiet grounds boiled with personnel. Conventional soldiers spilled out of their barracks and raced for their duty stations. The guards already manning the anti-air emplacements along the hills and duracrete walls went from a ready status to actively searching for targets in the purple twilight sky. Griffins spilled out of their eyrie, wings flared and piercing shrieks rivaling the warble of the siren. Loudest of all were the dragons, quite possibly because I was standing in the middle of one of their eyries.

A deep roar vibrated my bones, and I spun around as Major Zeddemore's great black dragon Maximus crested the taller dragon eyrie, neck arched and jaws spread wide as his roar rolled on like thunder. I'd been right—there was nothing gentle about him now. His call was answered by the harsh roar-screams of grays, the booming roars of the reds, and the echoing cries of our small wing of greens.

Black wings flared wide, blocking out a wide swath of bright evening stars, and Maximus roared again. Major Zeddemore sprinted into view and took a running leap onto his outstretched elbow. The arm flexed, and the rider sprang up into the saddle. They must have been getting ready to fly a patrol, because other dragon riders were already taking to the skies, while more frantically worked to saddle their dragons.

A pair of mountain griffin riders sprinted into sight and launched themselves into the saddle behind Zeddemore. They would guard the detachment commander's back even as their mountain griffins would guard the less agile black dragon. Maximus crouched before leaping into the sky, great wings beating the air into submission, two mottled gray and white mountain griffins flanking him.

"I've got to go," Dimitri said hurriedly.

He was gone before I could yell at him to stay safe.

A moment later, Mayhem latched onto my arm with hard fingers and dragged me into a run. As we sprinted down the hill, griffin riders raced out of the gates and into the night, while a pair of unsaddled griffins raced for us. More dragons launched with bellowing roars, gray and red wings flashing, but no green. Their turn would come after the battle, when rescue and recovery was needed.

"Retaliation for our airstrike on the artillery, you think?" I gasped out as we ran.

"Maybe. No way to be sure." But the look in her eyes said she thought I was right. "Send Felix up. We need eyes overhead until Banshee can launch and give us top cover."

"Yes, ma'am." I nudged Felix, but he'd already spread his wings and followed Havok into the air.

"We'll need to relay for our griffins to Ops," she added, voice steady despite our sprint for the rear of the valley, where the fortress blazed with light and personnel. Her gaze drifted upward, but the sky overhead was clear of enemies, despite the incessant wailing of the air raid siren.

An eerie cry rang out as we reached the guarded entrance to the fortress. I glanced back at the secondary dragon eyrie as narrow, *long* blue wings spread wide, and a sinuous dragon shot into the air. Banshee wore no saddle. The heights a blue could achieve were death for a rider, but those strange, multifaceted eyes could see so much.

In seconds, Mayhem got us past the guards and we darted around conventionals crowding the halls and into the hectic Ops Center. The detailed map on the back wall was ignored in favor of a smaller map of Fort Ashfall and its immediate surrounding area spread out on the massive oak table in the center of the room. Normally a vast, echoing space, the room was now packed with staff officers, most huddled around the table and focused on the base commander.

The slightly querulous old-man routine Colonel Harborne had pulled at the griffin eyrie was gone in favor of an experienced, battle-hardened soldier well used to command. He snapped out orders, no hesitation in that gravelly voice and a determined gleam in his utterly normal brown eyes. More than that, he *listened* to his staff officers and scouts.

Should've known the commander of the largest fort on the eastern border couldn't be useless.

Major Anderson broke away from the huddle of officers and waved us to a pair of open seats next to a gaunt man in riding leathers. Even the bones of his hands and wrists stood out, as if he hadn't so much as a spare ounce of fat on his attenuated frame. His eyes opened as we dropped into our chairs, and I was arrested by their crystalline beauty, as if a prism was reflecting back moonlight.

The blue dragon rider.

"Banshee's up," Lieutenant Qualls said in a voice as colorless as his eyes were colorful. "Your griffins are no longer needed."

Colonel Harborne snapped his head around. "Disregard that, Anderson. Keep those griffs up in the air. I want a standard search pattern above Ashfall."

"Yes, sir," Anderson said crisply.

The blue rider's beautiful eyes narrowed into an annoyed glare before he closed them.

"I've got our scouts out," Anderson said in a low voice meant just for us. "And a pair in the observation posts above the gates. If Felix doesn't know the pattern yet, Havok can teach him."

"Keep a sharp watch on Felix," Mayhem said. "We ran our griffins hard today, but just like the war doesn't wait for hangovers, it doesn't wait for us to be rested either. We can always switch with the observation pair if they get too wing-sore."

She closed her eyes, and I followed suit.

"Felix?" I asked, waiting for his permission.

"Come fly, Harpy!" he said eagerly.

Tension and anxiety swirled in his mind, but it was balanced by a rising bloodlust. I let out a slow breath and fell into his mind. The stars leapt into brilliant clarity, edged in colors human eyes could never see, blues and purples and greens and pinks. They wheeled and blurred as Felix turned on one wing, flying just outside the perimeter of the hills and duracrete walls. His sharp gaze slid northeast and a gasp escaped my lips.

Dragons fought a short distance away. Grays, reds, coppers, and one massive black dragon dueled for air supremacy, the Tennessan dragons doing everything they could to keep the Savinian dragons away from Ashfall. Roars of anger and screams of pain echoed across the hills, and several bombs tumbled prematurely out of enemy claws. Fire splashed across the forest below and guttered out, the trees too wet for the flames to spread far.

Felix shuddered as a gray dragon plummeted toward the ground, wings limp, either unconscious or already dead. No way to tell from this distance if he was ally or enemy. And then Felix wheeled again, the battle passing out of his sight as he dropped his piercing gaze to the land just beyond our walls. Again, he wheeled, and again I saw the battle.

True night hadn't fallen yet, but the long summer twilight was steadily fading, and it wouldn't be long before our dragons fought in darkness. Spurred on by the loss of light, slowly, painfully, our dragons gained the upper hand. Between one turn of Felix's wings and the next, the Savinian dragons broke, turning en masse and fleeing back toward the border. Cheers rang out across the room as Mayhem relayed the news.

"*No!*" Lieutenant Qualls bellowed, alarm pulsing through his flat voice. "Pull them back, pull them back now!"

Enraged by their losses, our dragons were racing after the fleeing Savinians. Felix beat his wings hard to gain altitude and get eyes on the battle. Atavistic fear whipped through our entangled souls as a dark shadow rose up from a nearby mountaintop. It split into smaller, individual shadows and swarmed our dragons. No, not just our dragons. *All* the dragons.

"What the hell are those things?" I whispered into the shocked silence.

"Wyverns!" Mayhem roared. "A full swarm."

A swarm was anywhere from fifty to one hundred wyverns. A perversion of dragons, the reptilian monsters were barely larger than griffins, but their narrow jaws were packed full of needle-sharp fangs, and the talons on their legs were deadly. And while they were more agile than dragons, they were stupid and barely controllable, and would attack anything in the air.

Sickening understanding slammed into me, twisting my stomach.

The Savinians had sacrificed their own dragons to get to ours.

"Send in the reserve wing," Colonel Harborne ordered. "Get me an accurate count, and for gods' sake, somebody roust the mountain griffins from the FOBs."

"Already relayed to Captain Franklin," the blue rider said in a deadly calm tone. "She's got the reserves on the move. Major Zeddemore relayed to Fort Arcadia. Mountain griffins are in the air along with a detachment of dragons. I need our griffins to get a count of the wyverns."

"Copy, wyvern count," Mayhem said as more Tennessan dragons shot into the sky to join the desperate battle. My breath caught as fear shot down my spine. One of them was a black, significantly smaller than Maximus.

Riven.

You'd better come back alive, Dimitri.

"Sixty-two wyverns," Mayhem said a few seconds later, but I could feel her leg bouncing beneath the table, belying her icy calm.

Shocked into action, I directed Felix to verify the number. The skies were darker now, but the moon balanced on the eastern horizon, full and bright enough to cast the battle in sharp relief for Felix as he worked. I barely felt the hot tears tracking down my face as yet another dragon fell screaming out of the sky, one wing gone and the other shredded beyond recognition. Training came to my rescue, and my voice rang out, just as cold, just as calm.

"Verified count."

Numbly, I wished Felix's eyes weren't quite so sharp, or that the night was moonless and dark. But we were the eyes. We had to watch as two more dragons were torn apart midair.

A dull burn took up residence between my shoulder blades, the closest analog I had to wings, as Felix climbed higher in tandem with Havok. They needed more altitude, to see, to track, to monitor. All the while I could feel my griffin's helpless rage. Claws flexed in and out, and a furious scream built in his chest as a ragged force of dragons broke away from the fight, flying as fast as tattered wings could carry them for Savinia.

"Savinian dragons have abandoned the fight." The fleeing dragons drew a small portion of the swarm with them. "Forty-four wyverns and dropping."

"Verified," Mayhem said, her voice unflinching as a red dragon fell, taking half a dozen wyverns with him, fighting the entire way down.

Felix tilted one wing low in a wide turn, and we lost sight of the battle again. As the flickering flames of the torchlit walls of Ashfall flashed into view, I remembered the original reason Colonel Harborne had wanted us to stay in the air—and it wasn't to count wyvern or bear witness to the terrible aerial battle. It was to monitor the steep hills and forests around the fort.

I nudged Felix to scan the ground, but nothing had changed in the past few minutes of inattention, and relief whispered through us. Until he wheeled again, bringing the sheer-sided cliffs into view. The same cliffs the fortress was nestled against. The same cliffs that were supposed to be unscalable . . . unless an enemy dragon snuck in under cover of a battle and dropped off a team of raiders on the heights.

Banshee should have spotted them. *We* should have spotted them.

"*Havok!*" Felix roared, drawing his wingmate's attention to the dark shadows creeping across the jagged rocks.

"Contact!" I shouted out loud. "Charlie quadrant, sector . . ."

I scrambled, trying to recall the chart that sectioned off Ashfall for just this purpose and coming up blank.

"*Two!*"

"*Two!*"

"Verified," Mayhem snarled.

"Roast them," Colonel Harborne said coldly.

"Relaying," the blue rider replied calmly. "Defense dragons armed and moving."

Gray wings beat the air as a pair of dragons launched from their eyrie. Felix circled high overhead, and we watched in shared triumph as the Savinian raider team *we'd* found abruptly reversed course. But there was no escape from those cliffs, and when the dragons dropped their firebombs, there was no escape from the flames.

Triumph turned to horror as we watched men burn alive. Enemies, yes, but still men.

"Contact!" Mayhem shouted. "Alpha quadrant, sector one."

More raiders, more flames, though this time Felix didn't have a close view. His flight path took him back around to the eastern side of the fort. We shuddered as one when the winds carried the scent of smoke and something burned, almost sweet to our nose. After a sharp scan of the rolling, thankfully empty, hills below his wings, he returned his gaze to the battle.

Horror gave way to fierce exhilaration.

"*Look!*" Felix said with a piercing shriek, completely ignoring the fact that where he looked, I looked. Mottled white-and-gray shapes arrowed into the black swarm, and wyverns began to fall in droves.

The Talons of the Dragon Corps had arrived in force.

More dragons joined the fray, and even the limited minds of the wyverns could grasp a losing battle. Keening cries erupted from reptilian throats, and a much-reduced shadow coalesced and flowed across the night sky, back to Savinia.

"The wyverns are retreating," I called out in a clear voice. I felt the entire room's focus shift to me, the weight of countless stares landing on my sightless face. Rolling my shoulders back, I kept my chin up and my spine straight. "The skies are ours."

"Verified," Mayhem said.

"Banshee concurs," Lieutenant Qualls said, his voice completely colorless once more.

Cheers erupted as Colonel Harborne raised his gravelly voice and ordered the rescue wing out. A small flight of six green dragons took off, finally released to find the injured and lost, escorted by a dedicated trio of reds to provide top cover. I barely noticed, too busy counting the battle-weary dragons flying home.

"Can Felix stay in the air?" Anderson asked, his voice barely audible above all those shouting, happy voices. The ones who had no idea how bad it was yet, the ones who had no idea why my eyes were burning, or why I could taste salt when I licked my lips. We'd lost so many. And I was so very afraid Dimitri might be among their number.

I wasn't done yelling at that asshole yet.

My gut tightened, and I distantly felt my nails digging into my palms. But I compartmentalized the dread and carefully considered my tired griffin. His wings and back burned with the effort of flying without the benefit of thermals, and his breathing was slightly more labored than I'd like.

"Felix?"

"I'm fine," he said firmly. He glanced across the mountain valley toward Havok, where the older griffin was flying without visible strain. *"If he can manage, so can I."*

"No heroics, please," I said as I sent him a boost of warm energy, as much as I could spare.

"I'm staying in the air." Resolve and gratitude filled my griffin's heart, and his breathing steadied along with his wingbeats. Again, he turned his head so we could see the dragons flying back toward Ashfall. His next words whispered across my mind. *"Until the last dragon comes home."*

"Lieutenant Tavros?" Anderson prompted me, slightly louder than before.

I sighed and nodded. "He'll stay in the air."

Time lost all meaning as Felix and I maintained overwatch along with Mayhem and Havok, griffin-sharp eyes alternatively scanning for movement in the hills below and unnatural dark shadows in the sky. We tried not to linger over the flame-blackened stones of the cliff, or the scorch marks near Ashfall's gate.

We found no sign of additional lurking raider teams, but tension and an awful awareness of the wounded dragons flying in kept us on edge long after we might have otherwise collapsed. At least an hour passed before the last of the dragons limped home, and then it was back to waiting, back to watching for the rescue wing. I wasn't sure how long it was before the last pair of greens flew in, a screaming red dragon carried in a net between them.

"Okay, Tavros, bring him down," Anderson said at last, his hand gripping my shoulder in reassurance.

"*Time to land, featherhead,*" I said with every bit of love and affection and pride I could muster through my exhausted haze. Felix dipped one wing low and spiraled down directly to the griffin eyrie, weariness in every twitch of his wings. "*Get something to eat, I'll be there as soon as I can.*"

I felt his acknowledgment and pulled myself back into my own mind—and I discovered *why* Anderson had felt the need to hold onto my shoulder. Exhaustion slammed into me so hard the room spun, and gray sparkles danced at the edges of my own, very tired eyes. Only my commander's grip on my shoulder kept me upright.

"I need water over here," Anderson snapped over his shoulder as I breathed through a wave of dizziness.

"She never got dinner," Mayhem said, her throaty voice ragged and raw. "Feed her."

A sharp shake of my head snapped my vision into focus. Mayhem sat next to me with her head in her hands, looking very nearly as wrecked as I felt.

She managed a smile for me. "That was a long time to be in your bonded's mind. Give yourself a few minutes to settle fully back into your own skin before you try to move."

"Yes, ma'am," I mumbled, painfully aware of all the conventional staff officers crowding the room. There were more than a few paying attention to us, and I remembered Mayhem's advice on sticking to expected customs and courtesies when we were on post. A vague scowl twisted my face as the blue rider leapt to his feet and strode out of the room, no worse for wear despite spending just as long in his bonded's mind. "How come he's fine?"

"Qualls has practice. Lots of practice." She shook her head, admiration and something very like aversion in her expression. "Blue riders are a strange breed. They spend more time in their dragon's minds than their own."

Even among riders, there were varying levels of *different*.

Anderson brought back canteens and a stack of ration bars. "Best I could do," he said apologetically. "Drink *slowly*, Tavros."

My hands shook so badly my first attempt spilled more water down my chin than into my mouth, but my second attempt went better. Mayhem recovered faster, and she left with Anderson to see to the other griffin riders. I sat quietly and watched the controlled chaos from the sidelines as I ate and drank. Eventually, my limbs steadied, and I felt less like I was trying to control a poorly-fitted puppet and more like myself.

The duracrete walls of the fortress were thick, but not so thick I couldn't hear the thunder of wings, the roars of enraged dragons... the screams of pain. Fort Ashfall had the largest medic detachment in the area, so all of the injured dragons and mountain griffins had returned here, regardless of which fort or FOB they'd flown in from.

I'd just finished my third ration bar when an agonized voice rose above the rest. The last time I'd heard a scream like that, it had been torn from Astra's throat when her rider, Elias, died. But that voice was human, driven to the edge of what anyone should endure, but still human. *Oh gods.*

Fear iced over my skin, and my canteen fell from nerveless fingers. I staggered to my feet and shoved my way through the staff officers, slipped past the guards, and ran outside into hell.

Wounded dragons were everywhere, being cared for by their riders and every medic we had at the fort. Riderless dragons crowded near the medical facility while they waited for their bondmates to be treated within. And that voice screamed again as if their soul had been torn in two. I was running for medical before I'd made the conscious decision to move.

I darted between two dragons, one gray, one green, and slammed into Zayne. He caught me, wrapped his arms tight around my waist and spun us around to dissipate my momentum, somehow keeping us both on our feet. His haggard expression sent a shock of terror through me, and I pushed back from him, gripping his arms and giving him a harried once over. No wounds, no blood, just the same terror I felt reflected back at me.

"Are you okay?" I gave him a sharp shake when he just stared at me. "Zayne! Are you okay?"

Twisting, I looked up at his bondmate. For once, the sight of the green dragon I was meant to bond with didn't fill me with a sense of longing—I was too busy scanning her smooth hide for injuries and feeling overwhelming relief when I found none. Cassia arched her neck and spared me a single glance, but her attention quickly returned elsewhere.

"I'm okay." A tremor ran through Zayne, and my gaze snapped back to his. "Dimitri..."

My knees buckled. Zayne didn't let me fall.

"He's alive!" His voice was a hoarse rasp from breathing in the smoke from the fires the misspent firebombs had scattered across the forest from up close. The scent clung heavily to his flying leathers. "In bad shape, but alive."

I couldn't breathe. I'd had the chance to fix things tonight, and I'd gotten it wrong, and now he might...he might...

"Damn it," I snarled, ignoring the fresh tears spilling down my cheeks. "Where is he?"

"They're working on him now."

I followed his gaze, and finally realized what, or rather *who* had captured Cassia's attention so thoroughly. Riven, curled up near the medical facility, wings tucked tight and head hanging low as a pair of medics worked to stitch his black hide back together. Great, gaping wounds carved down one side, but it was like he didn't even feel the pain. His black-ringed amber gaze was fixated on the medical facility, as if he could see through the duracrete if he just glared hard enough.

"He'll be okay," Zayne said, but I couldn't tell if he was speaking truth or desperate hope. "The wyverns nearly got them, but a mountain griffin saved them. Died doing it, and took three with him when he went." Slowly, he shook his head in raw admiration and genuine sorrow. "Brave, tough bastard severed in time. His rider... she's still holding on, but I think she's just waiting to say her goodbyes. We sent one of the Arcadia dragons back to get her boyfriend. Hell of a last request, but it was the least we could do."

My heart stopped. There were very few women bound to mountain griffins, and only two that I knew of at Fort Arcadia. My lips parted in horror, but I couldn't get the words out past the terror constricting my throat. All I could do was stare up at Zayne and silently plead with him to tell me what I wanted, *needed*, to know.

I could see the moment when the realization hit Zayne. The realization that as a griffin rider, I might know her, that she wasn't an abstract to me. Zayne's grip tightened on my arms to the point of pain, but I held onto him just as tight.

"Fuck, Harper! I'm an idiot."

"Where?" I managed to get out, my face contorting as I tried to hold back sobs. It might not be her. There was a chance. Felix roused in my mind, feeling my terror, but all of my focus was locked onto Zayne.

"Medical."

I tore free from his grip and ran.

The poor medic I'd waylaid when I'd burst inside directed me to the left of the open triage hall, where they'd drawn a set of curtains around a lone cot. The only courtesy they could give the rider after they'd finished treating her for shock. My hand shook badly, but I managed to pull the curtain aside far enough to slip inside.

To my shame, my first reaction when I saw that poor rider lying on the cot was *relief*.

The hair color was right, thick reddish-brown locks of hair, as messy as if she'd hacked it short with her knife, but that face was all wrong. The elfin features all twisted and drained of color.

My eyes burned as Felix surged forward and looked through them. He grew very still. And then I felt him lunge to his feet and run. I blinked my vision clear to adjust to his rapid withdrawal and shook my head in denial. And then the woman opened topaz eyes, so full of agony and loss, so *familiar*, that my heart screamed.

Felix ran faster.

"Bex," I whispered.

She blinked, and slowly, lethargically, as if it took monumental effort, lolled her head sideways. Her eyes found mine. I stumbled the two short steps needed and dropped to my knees next to her cot.

"Oh gods, Bex, I'm so damn sorry."

She smiled. How the hell could she smile?

"It's okay, Harpy." Her voice was a raw, thready whisper. "I'm not afraid to fall."

"*KATIE!*"

Reese tore through the curtain, stark terror on his face. Shaking, I forced myself to my feet and backed away from the cot to give him room. He ran past me as if he didn't even see me, as if all he could see was Bex. He threw himself down next to her and brushed her ragged hair out of her face with a trembling hand. She leaned her face against his hand and sighed.

"Waited for you."

"No, no, no, please don't leave me." Reese's voice broke. "Don't go. Please don't go."

Reese dropped his forehead to hers, still pleading, still begging a dead woman to choose to stay. She whispered something meant only for his ears. Reese shuddered, and his eyes, gods, his eyes.

"Merlin," Bex breathed out. She smiled, tremulous and beautiful, and her topaz eyes sparkled with happiness. And then she just . . . stopped. Stopped fighting, stopped breathing, stopped living. Everything that made her Bex was just *gone* as she followed her bonded into the dark.

Felix purred in my mind, and I leaned on his strength as I stumbled away from that cot, Reese's harsh sobs following me outside. I could barely see through my tear-blurred vision, but it didn't matter. I could always find my griffin. I stumbled right into him and buried my face in his feathers as his rumbling purr surrounded me, comforting me not at all.

Another griffin padded over to us, trilling a mournful cry, and Felix spread his wing over his clutchmate's back. I raised my tear-stained face and stroked my hand down Gage's neck. Between one shuddering sob and the next, Keaton and Tavi were there. Tavi shouldered in next to Gage's other side and pressed in tight, while I spun away from Felix and clung to my brother as much as he clung to me.

Time passed, and Reese stumbled outside. We stayed with him, refusing to let him be alone in his grief. Just like Felix and Tavi stayed with Gage.

Sometime during that endless night, the dragon riders lit a balefire at the highest point of their eyrie to honor the fallen. Everyone still awake took a moment to bow their heads in silent respect. We watched until the flames guttered out.

The next morning, Dimitri was finally stable enough for visitors. Since he was recovering from surgery, he actually merited a private room, not just some flimsy curtained-off area in the middle of triage. Zayne was sitting with him when I cautiously poked my head in the door, but he took one look at my red-rimmed eyes and ceded the chair to me.

"I've got to go anyway," he said when I protested. "We're heading out on recovery."

My gut tightened. That was the part of rescue I'd never looked forward to, but our fallen deserved to come home as much as the living. Wordlessly, I grasped Zayne's hand in support. He gave me a ghastly smile and shut the door behind him, leaving me alone with an unconscious Dimitri.

For long minutes, I just sat and watched him breathe. He was so damn pale and still. Just like Bex had been before the end. My eyes burned, but I had no tears left, so I reached out and smoothed a few wayward strands of hair from his forehead.

"Come back, asshole. I still haven't forgiven you. You're not allowed to die until I forgive you." I snorted a watery laugh. "Which means you're practically immortal, because I'm going to hold onto this grudge until the day I die, do you hear me?"

Dimitri stirred, and I held my breath.

"Harper?" His eyes opened, dramatic as ever though hazy with whatever they'd drugged him with. Relief whispered through me, and I smiled.

"Hey."

This time, my griffin didn't tease me for only managing a single word. He was too busy purring in the back of my mind.

"Am I still an asshole?" he mumbled, and I choked on another laugh.

"Yes."

"Good."

His eyes slipped closed, but he blindly reached out with one hand, the one that wasn't bandaged from shoulder to wrist. I gripped it tight, just like we used to when one of us was hurt or scared. I tried not to look at the thick bandages wrapping his torso, or how the bones seemed to stand out from his haggard face.

He was going to be *fine*. The medics said so. Zayne said so. I repeated it like a mantra, holding onto their reassurances as tightly as I held onto Dimitri's hand. Maybe if I said it enough times, I'd believe it too.

After a short eternity, Dimitri's eyes slid open again, a little sharper this time. A strange intensity flared in his gaze, and his bruised jaw set to that familiar stubborn angle.

"That griffin saved me, saved *Riven*." What little color was left in Dimitri's face drained away, and his voice, already hoarse, turned into a barely audible rasp. "I can still hear his rider screaming."

A haunted look grew in his eyes, and his head lolled on his pillow. Unerringly, he looked toward the back of medical, where his dragon waited outside, before he turned back to me.

"I couldn't live without Riven." For the first time since I'd bonded Felix, he looked at me without so much as a trace of pity in his gaze. "I'm starting to think griffin riders are braver than us."

He passed out again before I could tell him Bex hadn't been able to live without Merlin either.

CHAPTER 21

Within a few weeks, Dimitri and Riven were off the inactive list and flying missions again. Bonded healed quickly, especially when dragon healed enough to share energy with rider. I hadn't had the chance to talk with Dimitri since that day in medical, but we always seemed to just miss each other. Oz kept me busy on the trails, patrolling and learning the finer points of scouting, determined to teach me everything he'd learned from Nikos as quickly as possible. We even ran a few more messenger relays, and I spent far more time in Langston's irritable company than I wanted. Meanwhile, Dimitri and Riven were heavily utilized for waystation patrols while they healed, and then constantly deployed out to one of the FOBs when they were back in fighting shape.

Every rider stationed at Fort Ashfall and quite a few beyond it thought it was hilarious that we kept stopping by each other's eyries, looking for each other. Before I knew it, a betting pool had been started, though nobody was quite brave enough to tell me what exactly they were betting on. Keaton and Oz in particular ganged up on me, teasing me mercilessly about my dragon rider "friend" and keeping score of how many times they'd made me blush. Keaton was winning.

Every time I was on post, I watched for them. Every time they returned from a sortie, there were new wounds on the beautiful black hide, a growing collection of scars.

And then they didn't return. Shot down behind enemy lines and presumed dead. My heart screamed and shattered, but the war didn't care that my oldest friend was gone.

Zayne did.

It took him three days, but he pushed his sweep far enough north and east for Riven to mentally reach Cassia. All four came back with barely a scratch between them. Riven just had a sprained wing from some very desperate maneuvering, and Dimitri was suffering from dehydration and hunger after spending three long days hiding near the southern edge of the Smoke Mountains.

After that near miss, I was determined to talk with Dimitri. I needed to finally get things right between us, but he stopped dropping by the griffin eyrie, and I always seemed to just miss him. Unease twisted in my belly as I began to get the awful feeling he was avoiding me. It wasn't until I saw him actually turn on his heel and hurry away from me at the small lake that I realized he *was* avoiding me.

So I chased him down, and we promptly got into a shouting match on the lake shore. Awful things were said, and I ended up punching him in the face again. I wasn't sure what was worse. The fact that he let me, or the fact that he walked away without another word.

I stopped trying after that.

The heat of summer faded, replaced by the crisp air of fall, and Oz decided Felix and I were ready to head out on our first solo patrol. He spread out a small map on the scarred old table in the Griffin Corps Command Post and traced his finger along a familiar route.

"You're more than ready, Harpy. You've been on the Bristol run with me so many times now you could probably navigate it in your sleep."

My lips twitched into a fond, slightly sad smile. The only reason I was any good at land nav was because Elias had refused to give up on me back when I'd been fairly certain I was hopeless. Still...

"You're sure I'm ready?"

"Even if you weren't, Keira's going into heat. The last place she needs to be is out on the trail with a young male." Oz grinned and clapped me on the shoulder. "Just don't get ambushed by raiders and you'll be fine."

"Thanks for that." I scowled and rapped a knuckle on the wooden table for luck before I rolled up the map and tucked it in my travel pack.

"Oh, one more thing. You need to rendezvous with Sergeant Franks and his ranger team at Waystation Bravo-Four. They sent in a request for more arrows with Terrance."

I blinked. Captain Kat "Terror" Terrance had only been assigned to our detachment two weeks ago. Apparently, Colonel Harborne's complaints had finally resulted in us getting at least one more scout added to our ranks, though the entire fort had heard him sport bitching about the lack of mountain griffins.

"I didn't realize she'd been out on a patrol yet."

"Anderson took her out to familiarize her with the area. They came back with this." Oz handed me a bronze token with the ranger's crossed arrows and dagger emblem emblazoned on both sides. "Stop by the armory on your way out and the quartermaster will get you squared away."

Wrinkling my nose, I tucked the token in my pocket. My griffin was *not* going to be pleased.

I was right. Felix was not amused.

"*I am* not *a pack mule!*" He snapped his beak in protest as yet another roll of heavy-duty broadhead arrows was added to the seldom-used saddlebags attached to his harness. The quartermaster's assistant leaped back, eyes wide with fear, and I gave him a weak grin.

"He's just grumpy, don't worry about him." I shifted a glare to Felix. "*Behave.*"

"*Don't wanna.*"

Great, he was so irritated he'd regressed to a cub again. I stood by his head and waved for the assistant to finish loading the last of the arrows.

"*If it makes you feel better, I'll have to walk until we hand those off to the rangers.*"

"*It does* not *make me feel better!*"

He snapped his beak again, and the assistant jumped about a foot into the air, dropping one of the rolls. It rattled loudly as it rolled beneath Felix's belly. He craned his head, purple eyes gleaming with irritated mischief, and raised his paw. I snatched the leather tube before he could attempt to flatten it and jammed it into the saddlebag.

"Last one?" I asked the assistant brightly, but he was already scurrying back into the armory. The heavy steel door slammed shut a moment later. "Guess so."

Waystation Bravo-Four was the fourth waystation along the Bristol run. Felix was so irritated by the arrows, which faintly rattled no matter how well I packed them, that we made it in three days. Just like Oz trained us, I pulled the heavy saddlebags from his harness and waited while he scouted the waystation. When he called it clear, he did *not* come back to help me, and I ended up having to drag the saddlebags the last quarter mile.

Felix reclined under the shade of a tree crowned in brilliant red leaves, his tail lashing in smug amusement and his beak dropped in a griffin grin.

"Now who's the mule?"

Sweat ran down my spine despite the cool day, and my back ached from the awkward way I'd had to crouch to drag the bags. Growling under my breath, I dragged them under the shelter just in case the heavy clouds on the western horizon decided to dump rain on us tonight, and stretched my spine out with a relieved whimper.

"Keep laughing, featherhead. I hope you come up empty while hunting tonight!" When he gasped dramatically, I planted my hands on my hips and glared at him. "That's right. No fresh yummy game for you, just dried, tasteless, waystation jerky. Suffer!"

"Do you always talk to yourself, or are you shouting at your griffin?"

Startled, I whirled around, knife leaping to my hand almost of its own volition. Maddox stood just inside the waystation clearing, a smirk on his face and his hands up and empty. He glanced past me and grinned.

"Oooh, are those our arrows? Nice." Over his shoulder he called out, "Waystation clear!"

We spent the evening hanging out with the rangers, or rather, I did. Felix vanished to go hunting and, despite my earlier rant, I wished him luck. He really did hate the waystation jerky.

Sergeant Franks declared the night chilly enough and the area safe enough to warrant a fire. The creeping chill invading my extremities convinced me not to argue, and in short order the rangers had a small fire going, hot enough to warm cold fingers and toes, but sheltered enough the light wouldn't travel far.

Franks pulled out a set of throwing knives and, with a practiced flick of his wrist, sent one flying into a tree stump at the edge of the small circle of firelight. Another flick of his wrist, and a second knife hit next to the first, so close the blades chimed together.

He handed a set of throwing knives to the youngest ranger, Riley. "Give it a try, kid."

While the two rangers practiced, Maddox flung himself down next to me. "So, how've you been, griffin girl?"

"Living the dream, deer," I said with a wry smile. "You?"

"Well, my week was pretty boring, but my night's definitely looking up." That crooked grin made a reappearance. "Must be the company."

I stilled at the interested look on his face. It had been a long time since someone looked at me like that, and Maddox was definitely hot enough to catch my interest in return. Felix, dejected and on his way back from a failed hunt, perked up.

"Remember to shield this time!"

"One time! I forgot just one *time!"*

"One time was more than enough. Humans are so weird." Felix snickered. *"Oooh, I wanna see which ranger it is. I've got a bet going with Keira!"*

"If everyone could stop betting on my nonexistent love life, that would be great," I said with a grumble as he surged forward to look through my eyes.

Maddox stiffened as my eyes shone a little brighter. Subtly, he leaned away from me as the interest in his expression was replaced with wariness and a hint of revulsion. I felt Felix recoil, and he withdrew so quickly my vision blurred. My jaw tightened as I blinked my eyes clear.

"He was just curious."

"Yeah, sure." Maddox shifted a little further away so his leg no longer brushed against mine. "Does he get curious at *other* times?"

Embarrassment turned my face hot, but I kept my voice level, when what I really wanted to do was slap the disgust off his stupidly handsome face. "No, riders know how to shield from their bonded."

Felix crept out of the trees, his tail low and his ears flattened sideways with misery. Maddox's gaze tracked him as he padded over to the oak tree he'd sheltered under earlier that day. As Felix curled up at the base of the tree, Maddox shook his head.

"Yeah, no, sorry, griffin girl." He gave me a rueful shrug. "You're hot and all, but that's just too weird. I'm out."

And with that, he stood up and sat on the other side of the fire. Within seconds, he'd started up a lively, if one-sided conversation with the taciturn Buchanan, and had completely dismissed me. The rejection stung, but not nearly as much as the shame swirling through my griffin's mind. He laid his head on his front paws.

"I'm sorry, Harpy. I didn't mean to mess things up for you."

I shoved myself to my feet, ignored the furtive glance from the rangers on the other side of the fire, and stalked away from them. My hands curled into fists as my anger grew.

"You have nothing to apologize for. Screw him. Well, not literally, because that's apparently off the table. But screw him for being rude. His loss, because I am fucking awesome and you are fucking awesome, and if he doesn't want awesome, then he'll have to settle for less than awesome!"

My chest heaved for breath even though my rant had been mental rather than shouted like I wanted, and my nails bit into my palms. As I stomped over to Felix, his awful feeling of shame melted away into amusement, and he raised his head.

"That's a whole lot of awesome, Harpy."

I grinned and curled up with him, raising one hand to idly scratch behind his tufted ears until he purred. *"Damn right, it is."*

Loneliness soon crept in around the edges of my outrage though, no matter how hard I tried to pretend I wasn't. Felix heaved a mournful sigh, and I stroked my fingers through his feathers as we listened to the crackle of the fire and the murmur of the rangers' conversation.

My mind was drifting in that liminal space between waking and sleeping when Felix raised his head high. A pleased growl rumbled in his chest. Sleepily, I poked at his side.

"What are you so smug about?"

"You'll see."

His sharp gaze was fixed on the trail leading into the waystation, tail idly flicking back and forth as a growing impatience and joy filled his mind . . . but the feathered brat wouldn't tell me what he was waiting for. Nearly thirty minutes crawled past before there was the *snap* of a breaking branch, a deliberate rustle in the brush. The rangers abruptly fell silent. Hands crept for knives and bows, but a familiar gruff voice called out the current sign. Sergeant Franks relaxed, his gnarled hand releasing his heavy war bow, and shouted back the countersign.

A few seconds later, Keaton strode out of the shadows, Tavi prowling at his heels. With a happy roar, Felix leaped to his feet. Deprived of my pillow, I flopped gracelessly back onto the ground and laughed helplessly as my griffin tackled his brother with unbridled enthusiasm.

The griffins tumbled across the clearing, their playful roars and trills echoing off the trees and silencing the local wildlife. Keaton nodded at the rangers in passing as he ambled over to me and offered his hand. Grinning, I clasped his callused hand in mine, but instead of allowing him to pull me to my feet, I twisted and pulled him into the dirt with me.

"Bitch," he said with a wide grin as he pushed himself up onto his elbow.

"Jerk. What are you doing here?"

His grin faded as we sat up. "Felix called out for Tavi when we were passing through the next valley over."

"They can hear each other from *that* far away?" Shocked, I looked at our griffins, who were rolling across the grassy landing field and batting at each other with velvet paws, wicked claws well sheathed.

"Twins," Keaton said with a shrug, as if that were explanation enough, before his expression turned heavy with disapproval. "Felix said you were feeling alone. You should know better than that."

I grinned at his gruff concern, and laughed outright when Tavi got his back feet up against Felix's belly and launched him halfway across the landing field.

"So, what happened?" He arched a brow. "Get a little lonely on your first solo patrol?"

"Not exactly." Heat swept across my face, and I avoided looking at the rangers gathered around their fire. "My, uh, ego may have taken a bit of a hit tonight."

Keaton stared at me for a beat before he glanced over at the fire. His lips twitched. "I'm guessing it wasn't Franks who shot you down."

"Shut up." I shoved him, but I might as well have tried to knock over the supply bunker with my bare hands. Grumbling, I shifted so I could lean against his side and sighed as we watched our griffins play. "Thanks."

"Never alone, Harpy."

"I know," I said quietly. My stomach churned, and I finally brought up what had been bothering me for weeks. "Reese wasn't enough."

I swallowed hard and felt Keaton's gaze on the side of my face, but I didn't take mine off our griffins. He waited patiently, and I finally let out a slow breath.

"Merlin severed. Bex could've stayed, but she chose not to. Reese wasn't enough to keep her here, and she loved him, I know she did." I blinked against the familiar burn in my eyes and finally turned to Keaton. "What's the point of severing if we all just die anyway?"

"I think it's a last gift from our griffins," Keaton said slowly. "A chance to say goodbye, a chance to fight to live." He blew out a short breath. "It's more than dragon riders get."

"Dimitri—back when he was talking to me—said he thought griffin riders were braver than dragon riders." I shook my head and looked back at our bondmates. "I don't think *we're* the brave ones. They are."

Felix tried to tackle Tavi again, but his slightly older brother flattened himself to the grass, and Felix sailed right by with a miffed squawk. A grin pulled at my face and dispelled the melancholy.

"Insanely brave and utterly ridiculous."

"I heard that!" Felix shouted as he leaped to his feet, tail lashing and wings partially spread.

"Good, you were supposed to, you smug peacock!"

Keaton snorted a laugh—and the booming roar of a red dragon shattered what was left of the peaceful night. Our griffins snapped their heads up before they bounded out of the landing field, clearing the way for the massive red. Faint light from the fire played over the dragon, highlighting red hide and scales...and dozens of mostly healed claw and bite marks.

The dragon turned his head toward us, and I swallowed hard as the firelight revealed the narrow bite pattern of a wyvern perilously close to his jugular. He'd been swarmed, possibly in the same battle that had nearly cost me Dimitri, that *had* cost us Bex and Merlin. The injuries were well on their way to being scars, but a raw jagged tear running down the fragile membrane of one wing showed why this pair was still on messenger duty. Wings were slow to heal, and the great red might not be agile enough to return to the front lines just yet.

A brawny rider with captain's bars on the collar of his flying leathers rested one hand on his dragon's neck and tugged a messenger tube from his belt with the other. His fiery orange gaze, so like Bethany's, rested squarely on me. Recognition punched me in the gut.

"Lieutenant Tavros?" Captain Westbrook's harsh voice rang out as he held up the tube. "Priority message from Colonel Harborne."

He didn't dismount. *Still an ass, I see.*

Biting back an irritated growl, I pushed myself to my feet and strode over to the landing field. I froze midstride at a vicious hiss from the red, a stark reminder that no matter how much Nero looked like Jasper, he wasn't. His rider's mouth kicked up in a mean little smirk.

"Catch."

Westbrook tossed the message tube in an easy underhand—over my head. Keaton caught it with a dull *smack*, and pulled me back from the irritated red with a firm hand on my shoulder. Our griffins prowled forward and flanked us, a united front against the dragon rider prick. The rangers stood next to their fire, silent and watching. Keaton scowled at the message tube before glaring up at the dragon rider.

"Was this signed off by Major Anderson, *sir*?" Keaton demanded with the barest veneer of courtesy.

"How the hell should I know? We're just the messengers." Westbrook curled his lip, though whether at us or his current status was unclear. Probably both. As his gaze drifted past us to the rangers, his expression changed into something approaching respect. "Sergeant Franks."

"Captain Westbrook," the older ranger called back in a neutral tone.

Westbrook nodded farewell to Franks, ignored the rest of us, and leaned forward in the saddle. Without waiting for us to get clear, Nero crouched slightly and leaped for the stars, wings beating powerfully against the still night air. Snarling in one voice, our griffins snapped their wings out and shielded us from the blast of air and dirt.

The dragon's wingbeats quickly faded, and for a moment the only sound was the rumbling growl of our griffins and the crackle of the small fire. Riley broke the silence with a loud scoff.

"Wow, what an ass."

I grinned. "That's exactly what I thought the first time I met him."

Chuckles broke out as the rangers retook their previous seats, but Keaton's expression was tense as he tightened his grip on the tube.

"I don't like this. Since when do we get priority taskings from the *fort commander*?"

"Must be important if he skipped the chain of command," Franks called out. He tucked away the last of the throwing knives he'd been sharpening and gestured for Riley and Buchanan to make room for us. "Bring it here and let's see what she's got."

A few minutes later, we all stared at the terse message. What I had was the most dangerous tasking a griffin rider could get—a messenger relay at the border.

The tiny outpost at Brightburn, east of Bristol and just south of the Smoke Mountains, had raised an urgent signal flag requesting a messenger. The way was too rough for horses, too dangerous for dragons . . . and the griffin rider who had been dispatched was overdue on his return run.

"Fort Bramble hasn't had any contact from Brightburn in over twenty-four hours, and the rider hasn't passed through the fort." Keaton's hands tightened on the empty tube until it creaked in protest. "And they want you to find the rider and recover the message."

I stared at the name of the missing rider. *Not another friend.*

"*Friend is a stretch,*" Felix muttered, his ears flicking back and forth anxiously.

"*Fine, Bailey is your friend though, even if I'm pretty sure Langy still hates me.*"

"*According to Bailey, he's an equal opportunity hater.*"

"You're scouts, not trackers," Franks muttered in disgust. "What the hell is Harborne thinking? That rider could be anywhere between Brightburn and Fort Bramble. It's a fool's errand."

"No, it's not."

Mind racing, I yanked the map from my travel pack and spread it on the ground next to the fire. Maddox helpfully weighed down the corners with a handful of rocks.

"Thanks," I said absently as I studied the area around Brightburn. "Okay, so Langy and I were both trained by Elias back in the day—"

"You mean less than two years ago?" Keaton muttered, but I waved a dismissive hand.

"No time math, jerk. My *point* is, Elias helped both of us with land nav, and when we compared notes on our last relay together, we noticed we usually pick the same routes."

"Routes, as in plural?" Buchanan frowned. "Don't you just run point A to point B?"

"No," Keaton said as his eyes widened in understanding. "That's the primary route, but we're trained to pick two alternates—"

"And an 'oh shit' route," I finished triumphantly. I traced my finger along the map. "If I was Langy, and for whatever reason I couldn't travel the main trails to Fort Bramble, I'd go here, here . . . and if everything went to hell, *here.*"

Keaton considered the routes I'd traced and nodded.

"Agreed." A faint grin creased his face. "You want to check all of them, don't you?"

"Three routes, three teams." I lifted my chin and looked to Franks. "That is, if you're willing to help?"

The weatherworn ranger held my gaze for a long moment before he tapped the map without breaking eye contact. "Foot takes the closest route, you griff riders can flip for the other two."

Relief whispered through me, and I dipped my head in a grateful nod before I turned back to Keaton. "Tavi is faster," I said quietly.

He scowled. "You want me to take the furthest route while you take the dangerous one. It'll take us hours to get out there . . . we won't be able to back you up."

"I know." I drew in a deep breath and rolled up the map. "But it's the right call."

"We'll back her." Franks stood up as Riley smothered the fire. "If we get no joy on the first route, we'll assume the situation went tits up and meet you on your 'oh shit' route, Tavros. Happy hunting."

In seconds, the rangers had melted into the forest and were gone. A few minutes more, and I had Felix's bareback pad on, my bow strung, and a full quiver of our deadly little arrows. I secured everything else in the supply bunker. Either we'd be back for it after, or another griffin rider would.

"Ready?" Keaton asked, already in the saddle.

Felix nudged my side, and I slung myself over his back. His wings tucked in close, both securing and warming my legs against the chill night. My fingers brushed against the hilt of Callum's knife, and I nodded.

"Ready." Our gazes met for an instant, an eternity. "Be safe, brother."

"I'll see you back at Ashfall," he said without even a trace of doubt in his gruff voice, as if there was no other option. "Let's go."

Our griffins ran side by side down the trail for the first mile, their paws striking the hard ground in a synchronized beat. The night-dark forest flashed past, a shadowy blur only dimly lit by stars and a waning crescent moon. Too soon, the winding mountain valley spilled out into a wider valley, and the trail split. Tavi nudged his brother midstride before he veered for the northern path, while we took the center. I took one last look over my shoulder, but the night had swallowed them up. We were on our own.

Adrenaline and riding leathers could only do so much to keep me warm, and my ears soon burned from the rush of the cold air. Flexing with each bounding stride, I tucked myself as low as possible and ignored the discomfort. We had a long way to go.

Rolling hills grew to small mountains the further east we traveled, and if I turned my head just slightly north, I'd see the ancient Smoke Mountains blocking out the stars. I preferred not to look. Some smartass had written "Here there be monsters" on the planning room map. They weren't wrong.

Thankfully, it wasn't where we needed to go. We needed to go east and only a little north. The "oh shit" route I'd chosen wound through the hills, flirting with the Tennessan-Savinian border for klicks before it swung southwest toward Ashfall.

I hadn't told Keaton, but out of all of them, if I was Langston . . . this is the one I would've chosen. Alternate routes were for when weather interfered with your primary route. "Oh shit" routes were for when everything had gone to shit. An outpost gone dark and an overdue messenger meant everything had absolutely gone to shit. I just hoped I'd guessed correctly.

And that we weren't too late.

Hours went by, but Felix was running easy in that smooth lope he could keep up all night if he had to, and my ears had finally grown completely numb. I was just grateful I'd been able to convince him to inhale a few mouthfuls of waystation jerky before we'd left, even though he had complained bitterly with every distasteful bite.

We descended along winding trails toward the wide river valley that cradled the Wattspar River, but the further we ran, the more my doubt grew. I glanced up at the stars, trying to gauge the time of night, and decided we'd press on another hour before reassessing.

Luck and a trick of mountain acoustics was the only thing that saved us.

We were heading down a switchback trail that looped back and forth as it traversed the side of a steep hill when a distant clatter broke the relative quiet of deep night. Felix slowed before he abandoned the trail completely in favor of the sparse cover of the tangled brush and second growth trees, scraggly and thin but for the occasional ancient oak. Poor concealment was better than none, and we were dangerously close to the border. The clatter sounded again, this time without the echo distorting the familiar rhythmic beat, and there was a flicker of light where there should be none.

"Horses," I said urgently.

Somehow, I doubted it was Tennessan cavalry. Not this close to the border and so far from any of the forts. If it weren't for the echo, we might have ridden right into them. Felix halted abruptly, ears turning this way and that. His head titled, and he sidestepped, not nervously like a horse would have, but to get a better view of the valley below us. He clacked his beak softly.

"Torches. Moving in a wide line."

"It's a search party." A chill sank through my bones as I instinctively tightened my legs around Felix's sides. *"They're looking for Langy. If they're out here, we have to find them first."*

Agreement whispered through the bond. Felix padded quietly through the thick undergrowth down the hill and about as close to the search party as we could get without risking discovery. As it was, it would only take one person riding the wrong way . . .

Felix stiffened abruptly before he whirled on his back paws and ran a twisting path through the forest. The lights of the search party faded, and I realized with a rush of relief that we'd just gotten *behind* them.

"Well done, featherhead," I whispered, as if afraid the Savinians could hear mindspeech between entangled souls.

"Can't claim the credit," he replied just as quietly as he ghosted through the brush on soft paws. *"Bailey told me where to go."*

Triumph and relief surged through me as Felix eeled his way through a heavy thicket, brambles and thorny vines trying and failing to gain purchase on his fur and my leather. Unfortunately, my skin wasn't quite as tough, and I hissed in pain when a particularly enthusiastic bramble caught the side of my face, tearing a burning path across my cheek. I ducked my face down against Felix's neck where fur and feathers met to protect my eyes and trusted my bondmate to get us through.

A few steps, a few tugs on my hair, and we broke into the clear center—and found our missing messengers.

Langston's scowl was expected, almost comforting in its familiarity. Bailey's broken wing and front leg were decidedly not. I slipped off Felix's back so he could go to his clutchmate and stopped in front of mine. His muddy green eyes narrowed.

"You're bleeding, princess," he muttered.

"Bramble bit me." I dragged the back of my hand across my burning cheek. "Seriously, who gives a fuck? What the hell happened to Bailey?"

"Did our job too well, got too close. But we got the intel, got what we needed..."

It was dark. That was my only excuse for missing the dark bruises lining the side of his face, and the heavy wet patches on his leathers. Langston's gaze went unfocused for a second, and then he shook his head sharply and seemed to realize I was actually there.

"*Tavros.*" His lunge turned into a stumble, and I barely caught him. The bastard was far too big for me to actually hold up, but he managed to get his feet under him before we both went down. "Bleeding's bad. They have tracking hounds. I think they're dogs, might be broken things."

I held my wet hands up to the dim night sky and stared at the dark smears across my palms. "Langy, I hate to break it to you, but I think you're bleeding enough for the both of us."

A baying howl rose up, echoed by at least three more hounds. Langston was right, there was something very *wrong* in those cries, a dissonance that raised the small hairs on the back of the neck. It reminded me of the keening wails of the broken beasts that had invaded our training grounds at the academy.

"They found us again," he said hoarsely. He snapped his head around and met his bondmate's eyes. She dipped her head in a sharp nod. Langston spun back to me with a grim look I didn't like in the least, fisted his hand in my top, and jerked me close. "Listen and remember."

I stiffened at the seldom used phrase. It meant there was no written message, no messenger tube to carry and deliver. Just his words.

"The Savinians are coming for Fort Bramble. It anchors that whole line. If we lose it, the rest of the Bristol run will fall, and they'll be at

Ashfall's gates before spring. One of our rangers brought back word to Outpost Brightburn. They're planning a diversionary attack to draw our dragons away from the strike force until it's too late."

The broken hounds bayed again, closer this time. Hurriedly, he spat more details—troop types and numbers, weaponry, logistics support. My exhaustion fell away, and I used every trick I'd been taught to burn his words into my memory. Felix listened just as intently.

"You have to get them to deploy to Bramble, *not* the diversion."

The warm, orange flicker of torchlight played across the tangled forest, dim but growing steadily brighter. Langston's jaw ticked, and his fist tightened before it dropped away. Rage and terror fought for supremacy in his muddy green gaze as he looked at his bondmate. Bailey tilted her head and trilled softly. Terror won as Langston threw himself at his griffin, big hands cupping the sides of her face.

"If you sever, I'll still die at your side," he growled. "I'll just die pissed as hell."

Bailey closed her eyes for a second before she snapped them open, determination and love blazing so brightly, I wondered why I'd ever thought them muddy.

The broken hounds bayed again, so close I could pick out individual voices. Urgently, Felix leaped to my side, and I pulled myself across his back. Torchlight invaded our flimsy bramble shelter, and for the first time I saw how badly hurt Langston really was. *Oh gods . . .*

He bared his teeth in a bloody grin. "Get the dragon riders to Bramble, or this was all for nothing."

With a roar, griffin and rider launched into a shambling run and burst out of the thicket, drawing the searchers after them and leaving the way clear for us. I bit back my scream of protest, but Felix felt my dismay and echoed it with his own. Duty kept us silent and still in the thicket as we waited for the searchers to race past our hiding place, even as we felt like the worst sort of cowards.

A few minutes crawled past as the shouts and torchlight grew distant. The shadows deepened, and soon, dim moonlight was all that was left to light our way.

"Time to go, Harpy," Felix whispered, his ears flattened with misery. *"We can't waste their gift."*

"I know."

Before he could take so much as a single step, the thicket rustled.

My gut tightened at a wet, snuffling sound, and Felix tensed, his head slowly lowering as we stared at the thrashing clump of thorny brambles. What tumbled out into the small clearing wasn't a dog, though it might have been once. No fur, no external ears, limbs a little too askew, and nose far too large for its misshapen skull.

"At least it has eyes," I said somewhat hysterically.

The broken hound stilled, dragged in a deep, wet breath through its snout, and snapped its head toward me. My hand leapt up to my cheek, still burning, still bleeding. *Shit.*

CHAPTER 22

As the hound tilted its head back to howl, Felix lunged forward, claws out and beak open. My legs clamped down and I easily rode it out, because I'd felt what he was going to do *before* he did it. Felix darted his head low and snapped, but the broken hound flowed to the side, fast, so fast. A slash of wicked claws, another impossibly fast dodge.

"Don't let it howl!"

"Hold on then!"

Felix *moved*, slashing and snapping in a frenzy, and it took every bit of skill I had to stay in the saddle. The hound continued to evade, and in the distance, I could hear more rustling in the brush. *Double shit!*

My heart raced in my chest as I pulled my bow off my shoulder, set arrow to string, and waited for my shot. The hound stilled for a fraction of a second, and my bowstring sang. The arrow flew true, but the little broken thing threw its head back and bayed as it died.

"Run!"

We were so in sync in that moment, I wasn't sure which one of us thought it, but Felix put action to words and raced out of the thicket. Another hound burst out of the thick underbrush and raced after us, baying its stupid head off. Twisting in the saddle, I nocked another arrow. The hound raced through dappled moonlight and shadow, appearing and vanishing without warning as it jinked left and right erratically.

Gritting my teeth, I took the shot . . . and missed.

"Gods damn it!"

"You can do it, Harpy," Felix cried in encouragement as he bounded up the hill, intercepting the switchback trail we'd run down before.

The hound pursued, howling relentlessly, and more baying, dissonant cries rose up in answer, growing closer with every panicked beat of our hearts. We had to take this one out *now* before it brought the entire search party down on us. But the canopy closed overhead on the next turn, and I lost the little bit of moonlight I'd had—and lost sight of the hound.

"I can't see!"

Felix grunted and twisted the bond, pushing a tiny burst of energy toward me at the same time. The shadows vanished, and everything jumped into crystal clarity as if it were high noon instead of the dead of night. My eyes were no longer entirely human.

"Can't hold it long." Already, I could hear the strain in his voice.

He smoothed out his stride as much as possible, and I caught his rhythm as I nocked another arrow. The broken hound burst out of the brush and scampered up the trail, still erratic, still impossibly fast, but no longer hidden by shadows. My focus narrowed on the hound until it was the only thing I could see.

Nothing else existed.

A deep breath, a slow exhale. Three, two, one, *release.*

Thwack!

Between one stride and the next, the broken hound crumpled around the arrow lodged in its narrow chest and tumbled away. Relief sighed through my griffin, and my eyes snapped back to normal. We were halfway up the steep hill, halfway to escape, but riders on horseback were behind us now. Armed with torches, light spread across the hillside, pushing the concealing shadows back at a frightening pace.

Felix ran faster, pushing off with his hindlegs with everything he had on every stride, trying to stay ahead of the light. I felt the burn of his muscles, felt the acid bite of fatigue slowing him down. I was feeling it too, but nowhere near as bad. Another deep breath, and I pushed a warm ball of energy down the bond. Not enough to drain me, but enough to take the edge off his exhaustion.

Felix raised his head with a startled snort and practically flew up the trail. As we neared the crest, the thick underbrush rustled as we sprinted past. I twisted in the saddle and reached for an arrow, expecting another hound.

It wasn't.

"Archer!" I screamed. Felix immediately switched his headlong dash into a wild zigzag, trading speed for unpredictability.

It just wasn't enough.

A hard punch slammed into my lower back. I jerked forward, an involuntary cry spilling from my lips.

"Harpy!" Felix clamped his wings tighter around my lower legs and swerved, keeping my weight balanced over his spine. The arrow I'd just pulled from my quiver slipped from nerveless fingers, and my bow tumbled into the brush, immediately lost to sight.

"No!" I reached for it reflexively, and the pain hit.

Searing agony whited out my vision, and only Felix kept me from suffering the same fate as my lost bow. The deadly *hiss* of a second arrow flashed past, so close it felt as if I could reach out and grab it as it sailed by. Felix didn't give him the chance to shoot at us again.

He whipped around and rushed the lone archer with a mental scream of rage only I could hear. There was a panicked curse, the deadly *crunch* of breaking bones, a gurgling cry, and then he was running again.

"Harpy! Open your eyes."

When had I closed them?

I forced them open, forced myself to bury my hands in his feathers and grip tight with my legs, forced the pain into a dark corner of my mind. Felix helped me. He shielded me from the pain, but he could do nothing for the blood loss, or whatever damage the arrow was doing each time I flexed with his stride.

As we crested the steep hill, a griffin's scream rang out, full of the agony of a lost rider. An enraged roar quickly followed, the sound of a griffin with nothing left to lose doing her best to take her killers with her. *Give 'em hell, Bailey. Make them bleed, make them pay. And then go fly free with the other half of your soul . . .*

I swayed and shook my head sharply.

"Harpy!"

"I'm okay," I gasped, glancing over my shoulder. Cold fear shot through me. It was no slender hunting arrow that had punched through my riding leathers and into flesh and muscle and probably

bone. It was a heavy war arrow, like our rangers used...and the Savinian raiders. *"I'm okay."*

Liar. I wasn't okay, but I had to be long enough for us to get clear, long enough to hide, to send Felix ahead of me with our blood-bought warning.

The distant sounds of fighting abruptly faded away into an aching silence, but the horseback riders were still on our trail and gaining fast. The archer had cost us time, might cost us everything in the end, but we still had a chance thanks to the energy boost I'd already given Felix.

"Run, my love," I whispered, leaning over his neck. *"Run your heart out."*

Spurred on by terror, love, and pure determination, Felix ran as only a griffin could. On the flat, those horses would've outpaced us quickly, but in the steep, rocky, thickly forested hills? My bonded soon left them in his dust. He didn't slow his mad dash though. If anything, he ran faster, even when the shouts, and the baying, and the damnable torches had fallen away, leaving only the deep night behind.

"Felix...slow down." His muscles trembled and *burned* with fatigue, his heartbeat was a frantic pounding in his chest, and his breath was a harsh, ragged thing. *"Slow down, we're safe."*

"No, we're not. You're not, *I have to get you to help."*

Panic shivered along the edges of the bond, and I stroked his damp neck soothingly.

"No, you need to fly and warn Ashfall."

Rage and denial washed over me, and the comforting shield he'd placed between me and my pain wavered. I gasped, shuddered, and swayed, nearly slipping from his back before he slammed the shield back into place.

"Sorry!" Remorse drenched his voice, but so did stubborn determination. *"I'm not leaving you, Harpy."*

Trees and thick underbrush whipped past as he raced through a winding valley, his pace maybe a touch slower but no less panicked. Towering hills rose on both sides and the tangled canopy blocked most of the stars, but I remembered how the trees thinned along the next rise, remembered how the barriers fell away, leaving a griffin all the room in the world to spread his wings and fly.

We just had to make it to the next hilltop.

"I know you don't want to, but—"

Up ahead, the underbrush rustled and exploded with movement as someone lunged out of concealment. Despair swamped our entangled souls, but Felix snapped his beak, ready and willing to fight. The shadowy figure raised his arms high and shouted something. Something that sounded an awful lot like my name.

Felix abruptly slowed, his sharper eyes seeing what mine couldn't. *"Rangers, our rangers."*

He padded to a stop, sides heaving, as the rest of the ranger team stalked out of the trees. One of them stared at the ranger in the middle of the trail.

"Holy hell." Riley's voice squeaked. "That took some serious balls. I thought the griff was going to trample you."

"Shut up," Maddox snarled as he stalked down the trail toward us. "Something's wrong with Tavros. That's *not* how she normally rides."

I didn't realize how badly I was shaking or how cold I was until he rested his hand on my thigh, above where Felix's wings were keeping my lower legs tight to his warm sides. The heat from Maddox's hand burned through my leathers, and I breathed out a sharp exhale.

"Shit, griffin girl," he murmured, eyes narrowed as he examined the arrow in my blood-soaked back. "That's not good."

"What happened?" Franks asked as he ghosted up on Felix's other side, one weathered hand absently patting my griffin's neck. After I gave him a highly condensed report, he jerked his head at Buchanan. "Go! Check her backtrail and make sure they really did shake those Savinian bastards."

As the big ranger took off in a silent run, Franks extended his hand.

"Give me the message. I can run it in, while Mad and Riley stays with you."

"No, you'd take too long." I swayed, but Maddox steadied me. "Be too late to stop it . . . Felix will fly it in."

"No I won't," he growled.

"You have to." Drawing in a deep breath, I looked at Maddox. "Help me down?"

When he grasped my waist, Felix snarled and whipped his head around, snapping his beak inches from the ranger's throat. Maddox went very still, but he didn't let go, he just waited. He was braver than I'd thought.

"Felix, behave," I said out loud for the ranger's benefit. Instead of replying, he snapped his beak again, tufted ears angled back and purple eyes blazing with fury. "Felix!"

My griffin twisted his head around further and stared at me. The hurt in those eyes nearly gutted me, but it was his wordless, pleading cry that brought tears to my eyes. I didn't allow either to sway me from what we *both* knew was our duty.

"I'm sorry, but you either let him help me down, or I'll do it on my own. Which one do you think will hurt me more?" Felix sighed in misery and lowered his head. I stroked my hand along his damp neck and turned back to Maddox. "Okay."

I couldn't help it. I cried out when the ranger helped me off Felix's back. The arrow shifted, and the sharp shock of pain spilled over the mental shielding. My eyes went wide as gray sparks danced around the edges of my vision. *Can't pass out . . . can't die. I'll take Felix with me, take the* message *with me.*

"Don't worry, griffin girl, we've got you," Maddox said as he effortlessly supported my weight.

My fingers dug into his arms, but he didn't flinch as he helped me off the trail and into the brush. Felix stalked after us, tail lashing and wings flexing. Sitting down was almost as disastrous as dismounting, and for a short eternity all I could do was breathe through the pain.

At last, I looked up at my bonded, the other half of my soul.

"You need to go."

Felix shook his head, an entirely human gesture our griffins picked up from us, rage and denial and despair swirling in a toxic mess in his mind.

I lifted a shaking hand and stroked the side of his face. *"You have to. You said it yourself. We can't waste Langy and Bailey's gift. We have to do our job or a lot of people will die."*

"But you *could die."*

"So bring back help while you're at it, featherhead." I gave him an impish smile as I slumped against Maddox's shoulder. *"I'll just hang out here with the hot guy who rejected me until you're done."*

Felix let out a sound somewhere between trilling laugh and shuddering breath. He dropped his forehead to mine, closed his eyes for a brief instant, and spun away with a mournful cry. The *thud* of his paws was quickly swallowed up by the forest, but I felt it when he reached the clearing at the top of the trail, felt it when he spread his wings wide.

Felt it when he soared.

Franks' gruff voice pulled my attention back from the smooth flex of wings beating the still night air.

"She's still losing blood. We need to cut the arrow out and try to seal it up before she bleeds out on us."

"Yeah, but if you cut it out here, you could cut an artery and she could bleed out before we get her back to Ashfall," Maddox argued in a low voice.

"Either way is a risk," Franks said grimly as he clamped one hand on my shoulder.

I couldn't help my startled jerk. I could *feel* his other hand on the arrow shaft. My vision tunneled as agony stabbed deep into my lower back and spiraled around my spine, all acidic thorny tendrils.

Not yet . . . can't die yet. Can't let it be lost.

Desperately, I snapped my head around to Maddox and gasped out, "Listen and remember."

My voice came out thready, barely audible even to my ears because I couldn't *breathe* with Franks' hand on the arrow shaft, but Maddox heard me and tossed his hand up. "Franks, stop."

Franks didn't stop. His hand tightened on the arrow shaft, and I lost the ability to think.

"*Stop!*" Maddox roared. With an impatient growl, Franks reluctantly released the arrow. Maddox stared at his sergeant for a long moment before shifting his gaze back to mine. "What was that, Tavros?"

A deep breathe, a pain-filled exhale, and I tried again.

"Listen and *remember.*"

A hard expression settled on Maddox's face and he shifted to face me directly as Franks and Riley crowded close. "Go."

In a low, strained voice, I poured out every last, precious detail that Langston and Bailey had paid for with their lives. Maddox listened intently, and I held onto the grim look in his eyes, an anchor to hold myself to this world . . . because I could feel the dizziness of blood loss, could feel the dampness of my leathers, even though Riley had packed a cloth around the arrow shaft in an attempt to slow the bleeding. Felix tugged at my mind when I was done.

"Almost there!"

"I need time." I held up a shaking hand to Maddox, a silent request to wait a little longer. To my surprise, he wrapped his hand around mine, no sign of repugnance in his utterly normal eyes. Just an offer of comfort from one human to another.

"You'll have it," he replied, hard eyes shifting over to Franks. "As much as we can give you."

"Come fly with me," Felix said in a cajoling tone that did nothing to hide his barely controlled panic.

A shuddering breath, and I dropped down and down along the bond. Too much pain to worry about the nauseating stop, too much dizziness to worry about adjusting to his vision. I just slid into his mind and looked through his eyes.

"I'll always fly with you." A slight smile played on my lips as I felt the wind in his feathers. Felix roared his happiness and flew faster.

"Is she going into shock or something?" Riley muttered as my own eyes glazed over.

"No, you freaking twit," Maddox muttered back. "She's doing her job."

No longer constrained to the mountainous hills and winding valleys, Felix had flown a straight path back to Ashfall. The mountain valley was already in sight, but something was wrong. Light blazed bright along the sheltering hills and duracrete walls, men actively manned the anti-air defenses, and several dragons were already in the air, circling over the fort. As Felix drew closer, I could see more riders rushing to saddle their dragons, with Major Zeddemore's great black dragon perched at the top of the tallest eyrie, wings mantled as he roared.

"The diversion, has to be." Urgency thrummed through me. *"Hurry, Felix! We have to stop them!"*

Some trigger-happy soldier on one of the dragon lance ballistae swung the weapon toward Felix, but his partner shoved him away. His annoyed shout rushed past Felix's ears as he dove past.

"That's a *griffin*, you moron!"

Felix darted around the less agile dragons, an outraged shriek spilling from his open beak when one of them snapped at his trailing tail.

"Not so funny now, is it?" I asked as he whipped his tail out of reach.

Felix ignored my loopy giggles, flashed past the griffin eyrie, and glided straight for the brightly lit fortress. Two *very* startled guards threw themselves out of the way when Felix tucked his wings in at the last minute, touched down with a *thump* that reverberated through his joints, and charged through the open doors. Staff officers flattened themselves along the stone walls of the halls, shouts and calls for him to stop trailing in his wake as he skidded to a stop in front of the Ops Center.

Major Anderson snapped his head up as Felix squeezed himself through the human-sized doorway. He stood at the conference table next to Colonel Harborne, his eyes bloodshot and expression haggard. An unfortunately familiar red dragon rider stood at the fort commander's other shoulder, and Felix growled slightly as he stalked across the room. Crowded with staff officers, a handful of riders, and the fort commander's aides, the *click* of Felix's claws was sharp in the sudden silence as he flexed them with each agitated step.

If Colonel Harborne was fazed by the sight of an enraged griffin in his Ops Center, he didn't show it. He gestured sharply to Major Anderson, who stepped into Felix's path.

"Report," he said sharply. His eyes went slightly vague as Loki relayed. My lips moved in sync with Felix's words, mumbling along with him in a forest miles away from that brightly lit room. Anderson repeated everything out loud, his words slightly delayed, an echo that dropped into the silence like a firebomb and just as explosive.

Captain Westbrook scoffed loudly, cutting across the growing cacophony of the staff officers.

"Fort Arcadia requested backup—are we supposed to leave them to face the Savinians on the word of a griffin?" He turned to Colonel Harborne, his brow furrowed. "Sir, we have accurate intel on the forces moving toward Arcadia. Those numbers are too great for a simple diversion. The griffin rider is—" He cut himself off and quickly corrected himself. "The griffin rider's *intel* is wrong."

I scoffed just as loudly. *"Way to make your personal feelings about griffin riders obvious, ass."*

Gleefully, Felix relayed that to Anderson, and his lips twitched with a hint of mirth while a raging debate engulfed the staff officers. He dropped his voice low, his words only meant for us.

"Status of Langy and Bailey?"

Felix had only given them the dry facts, prioritizing the critical details over the personal loss.

"*Gone,*" we whispered together as unexpected grief stabbed my heart. I hadn't even *liked* Langston, but it still hurt. Anderson's expression darkened, and he spun away from Felix to face the fort commander.

"Sir, we lost two of our own tonight to get that intel to you. Lieutenant Langston was one of our best scouts and message runners. If he said they're coming for Fort Bramble, *believe it.*"

"Believe the word of a lieutenant barely a year out of the academy?" Captain Westbrook said incredulously. "Word that directly contradicts reports from *experienced* riders."

Experienced dragon riders, he meant.

"We are the eyes and ears of the Tennessan military," Anderson said coldly. "Ignore us at your peril, Captain Westbrook."

Colonel Harborne dropped his gaze to the map stretched out on the table. A faint smile creased his weathered face as he glanced back up. "What is the point of having scouts if we don't listen to them?"

The doors crashed open and Major Zeddemore strode into the room. The massive man seemed to take up what little room remained as he crashed to a halt next to Colonel Harborne.

"Sir, what's the delay? We're ready to launch, we're just waiting on your order."

"I'll tell you what the delay is," Captain Westbrook snapped before he snarled out a highly skewed version of events. Anderson countered, the staff officers joined in, and once again the room dissolved into chaos.

"Enough!" Harborne's battlefield roar cut across the raging debate. "Zeddemore, deploy your main force to Bramble. Get Banshee up on a surveillance flight to pinpoint that invasion force, send a single flight of reds to reinforce Arcadia, and keep the reserve wing here. Anderson, get a couple of griffs in the air over Ashfall in case this is another attempt to get raiders in close."

Overwhelming relief washed over me as everyone jumped to obey his orders. *We did it, Langy. It wasn't for nothing.*

I relaxed my death grip on Felix's mind, or maybe he relaxed his on mine, and everything got a little hazy. His crystal-clear vision blurred, dimmed, faded, until it felt like I was looking down a long tunnel.

Alarm surged. Not mine. Felix. He snapped his beak at Anderson before our detachment commander could rush out of the room.

"Help Harpy!"

The older rider stilled, his brilliant green gaze focused with unwavering intensity on Felix. "What do you mean, help Harpy?"

As Felix relayed through Loki, a dragon rider pushed his way through the crowd. Confusion weighted down my thoughts, all the more so because of the man's obvious concern. Did I know him? I thought I did, but I couldn't remember his name—not until I saw his green and gold eyes.

Zayne. How could I forget *Zayne*?

"Harper's hurt?" At Felix's emphatic nod, Zayne's jaw tightened. "Take me to her."

Felix raced outside. A rush of wings, a flash of green, and Cassia touched down. Longing spiraled through my soul as Zayne leaped into the saddle, and I was far too deep in Felix's mind to hide it from him.

"Sorry," I whispered, but there was no sense that Felix heard my miserable apology. Confusion and panic twisted through me. He should always be able to hear me. No matter how far apart we were. Never alone . . .

"Stay with me," Felix cried out frantically as he launched himself into the air, tired wings reaching for the distant stars.

Silly griffin, where would I go?

He didn't hear me. I couldn't see through his eyes any more, couldn't see anything at all, but I felt feathers and fur brush against my mind. He wrapped himself tightly around me, desperation and love burning bright as he fought to keep me with him.

I reached for him, but searing agony wrenched me fully back into my own mind before I could grab hold. I cried out at the loss, at the pain, at the sheer aching emptiness inside my head. Where was my griffin? I couldn't find him, couldn't *feel* him.

Felix!

Only silence answered.

"Sorry, Tavros," Franks said grimly. "Waited as long as we could."

My eyes flew open, and I blinked my blurred vision clear, struggling to adjust to the dark forest again. Maddox was still crouched in front of me, Riley to the side, but I couldn't see Franks. Then I realized why I couldn't see him.

My breathing sped up, faster and faster, as Franks grasped the arrow shaft again. Frightened and teetering on the edge of total panic,

I craned my neck, trying to see what he was doing, but Maddox gently gripped my jaw and forced my head back around.

"Just keep looking at me, griffin girl." Maddox wrapped his hand around mine again and squeezed tight, his expression grim as Riley grabbed my shoulders, holding me still. He nodded at Franks. "Go."

"Might want to brace yourself, lass," Franks warned in a low voice. *Snap!*

My scream tangled up with the thunder of wings as countless dragons flew overhead, and the distant shriek of an enraged griffin. *Felix!*

I reached for him, but red-tinged darkness swallowed me whole.

CHAPTER 23

A soothing purr rumbled through my soul, comforting, steadying, constant. My griffin would never leave me, never abandon me, never allow me to suffer alone. Every time I opened my eyes, I looked for him, but instead of purple I found amber eyes watching over me. The amber seemed to change, sometimes black-ringed and striking, other times solid and steady. Confusing snippets of quiet arguments drifted through my mind, but whenever I tried to hold onto the words, they floated away.

Once, I woke up panting and thrashing as I tried to escape the bone-deep *ache* twisting through my body. Cold sweat dampened my brow, and everything felt too bright, too loud. Blindly, I reached out— and a warm, callused hand gripped mine. A deep voice murmured to me, and the familiar rumble soothed me to sleep.

Another time, two voices talked quietly, not a hint of the former antagonism that had characterized the previous arguments floating in the haze of my memory.

"He's lost weight. He's feeding her energy?"

"Of course. All he's doing is eating and sleeping and giving everything he has to her. He's the only reason she's fighting off the infection."

"Thank fuck for him then."

The next time I woke, my mind was clear, but my body was so damn weak. It took a frightening amount of effort to turn my head, but it was worth it when I finally laid eyes on my griffin.

"Hey, featherhead," I said in a hoarse whisper.

Felix jerked his head up, wide purple eyes snapping open and latching onto my face with joyful intensity. I could *feel* his happiness. I could feel *him*.

"*Harpy! You're awake!*" He trilled a mocking laugh undercut with relief. "*Lazybones, took you long enough.*"

"Where..." Slowly, I turned my head and took in the plain walls, the narrow cot, the single window looking out onto a lake. I was in one of the private rooms in Fort Ashfall's medical facility. My smile faded as I remembered what happened and *why* I was in the infirmary. "Fort Bramble?"

"*Bramble stands. The dragons made it in time to save everyone.*"

Overwhelming relief whispered through my soul. We'd helped save people. Just like I'd always wanted, if not in the way I'd originally dreamed. Commandant Iverson's words echoed in my memory. *She'll never be the asset she should've been . . .*

Iverson had been wrong. And so had I. I'd made a difference *because* I shared a soul with a griffin, not in spite of it. Felix purred at the surge of pride and love I sent his way before he continued.

"*After the dragons wiped out the invasion force, the diversionary attack on Arcadia melted away at the first sign of resistance.*" He preened smugly. "*We're heroes.*"

"We were just doing our jobs," I said quietly. "Langy and Bailey were the heroes."

His ears drooped and he dipped his head in agreement. My brow furrowed in concern at the ragged state of his feathers and the way his ribs showed through his dull fur. He *had* lost weight. Felix felt my concern and purred soothingly.

"*Tavi and Keaton made sure I slept, and that dragon rider friend that you love to hate made sure I ate.*" He sighed in happiness. "*I was prepared to not like the guy, but he's the reason we bonded* and *he gave me all the cow I could eat!*"

Black-ringed amber eyes flashed in my memory, and my heart twisted in confusion.

"Dimitri was here?"

"*The only time Keaton left your side was if dragon boy was here.*" Felix tilted his head toward the small table on the other side of my cot. "*He left you a present.*"

Drawing in a deep breath, I slowly turned my head again—and gasped. It took a few tries to get my shaking hands to cooperate, but eventually I managed to pick up the small wooden carving. My lips curled into a small smile as I stroked a finger down its polished back. Everything from the half-spread wings, to the eyes, to the tail frozen midlash was a perfect likeness. Even the mischievous tilt to the head was perfect.

"He carved *you*," I said in astonishment and no little confusion. This must have taken Dimitri a long time, *months* even, but some of the marks were fresh, as if he'd just finished it . . . even though our last conversation had ended so badly.

"*Eh, I suppose dragon boy did all right. But it's not a cow. A cow would've been much better.*"

Felix carefully laid his head on the cot next to me, and I stroked my fingers through his feathers, breathing in his clean, spicy scent.

"You would've tried to eat it," I mumbled, weariness dragging my eyes closed again. I scooted closer to my griffin, hugged Dimitri's gift to my chest, and fell asleep to the sound of Felix purring in my ear.

"Harpy, when I told you not to get ambushed by raiders, that wasn't a challenge," Oz said in amused exasperation as we set out on my first patrol since I'd been cleared for active duty.

For once, he'd insisted on the lightweight scout saddles in an unnecessary burst of caution. Once Felix had regained his lost weight, he'd steadily fed me energy until my wound was completely healed less than two weeks from the time I was injured. Being bonded had its perks, and according to the medic who'd discharged me, surviving what would've killed an unbonded human was definitely one of them. I rode easily without a hint of pain and only a minor pull from scar tissue.

"You jinxed me! Even knocking on wood wasn't enough to save me." I shot him an amused grin. "It was totally your fault."

The only green left in the surrounding forest belonged to the evergreens. Everything else was an explosion of reds, oranges, yellows, and browns. The breeze carried a crisp bite, but the sun was warm overhead and the morning sky was a deep, aching blue.

Autumn at its most glorious.

"There's no such thing as jinxes," Oz muttered as we turned off the main trail and onto the offshoot that would carry us in a wide loop around Ashfall. Despite protesting that I was *fine*, Anderson had insisted on a short day patrol to "ease me back into things."

We rode the whole loop, found nothing of note, and made it back to the fort in time for lunch. I couldn't help my dejected glance toward the dragon eyries when we rode past. While I was recovering, Major Zeddemore and his great black dragon Maximus went missing on a patrol. No bodies delivered as gruesome gifts, no evidence of a fight. They were just gone. The day they were officially declared MIA, Mayhem didn't have her griffin burn off her alcohol, and she didn't speak to anyone for days.

To our detriment, Captain Westbrook had been brevet promoted to major and commander of Fort Ashfall's Dragon Corps detachment. Worse, he publicly blamed the scouts for failing to catch whatever was taking out dragons on what should be safe routes. Relations between dragon and griffin riders were at an all-time low, with the dragon riders under new orders not to fraternize outside of their ranks.

Anderson railed privately to Mayhem in his office loud enough we could hear him throughout the griffin command post, but his standing orders remained unchanged—we weren't allowed to start anything with the dragon riders, no matter what the provocation. He also spent hours closeted with the fort commander that week. Rumor had it he was urging for a closer working relationship between the Dragon Corps, Griffin Corps, and rangers, the three specialist branches of the military. Anderson came out of those meetings looking like a thundercloud, so we assumed things went poorly.

Except the last one that included both detachment commanders.

Anderson had come out of that one carrying an unmistakable air of triumph, while Major Westbrook had looked as if he wanted to stab somebody. The griffin rumor mill was churning, but Anderson would just smile when asked and mutter about small victories.

Kind of like making it through my first patrol back unscathed.

"Well, that was anticlimactic," I muttered as we trudged up the slope to the griffin eyrie, our griffins padding along at our sides.

"You think so?" Oz asked with a little smile as we crested the hilltop.

I stumbled to a halt and stared. Tables had been set up between two of the dorms, laden with food and drink, and bonfires had been built, all ready to light after the sun set. Best of all, every griffin and rider not out on patrol had gathered. Cheers rang out, and griffins trilled and roared. My gaze darted from face to beloved face as warmth grew in my chest.

"Surprise." Oz winked and hauled on my arm to get my feet moving again.

"Well?" Nikos called out impatiently.

"No trouble!" Oz shouted back. Now there were mingled cheers and groans, and riders exchanged money and flasks of the kind of alcohol that Oz acquired for us through mysterious means.

Keaton sauntered up and slung his arm over my shoulders.

"You look confused," he said with a straight face. "Let me help you out. This is a party. You remember parties, right?"

A slow grin spread across my face as Felix casually wove through the griffins, sneaking closer and closer to his brother's tail. He crouched, wiggled his hindquarters, and pounced with a silent cry. Tavi's ears didn't even twitch as he ducked. Felix sailed over his brother and plowed into Loki, his commander, who planted a massive paw on my griffin's chest and effortlessly pinned him. Heads tilted, griffins trilled mockingly, and they all decided Felix was "it" and started a massive game of tag across the eyrie.

"Yeah, I remember parties." I reached for the flask in Keaton's hand, but he pulled it away with a firm shake of his head.

"Nope, none for you."

"Oh, come on, I've got a clean bill of health." Unfortunately, Keaton was immune to pleading, and I traded puppy dog eyes for a scowl. "I can drink again, damn it!"

"The party is surprise number two. You need to get surprise number one before you start drinking."

My eyes narrowed. "What's surprise number one?"

Keaton's smug grin widened. "You'll see."

Anderson and Mayhem broke away from the riders swarming the tables, and I turned my ire on my detachment commander.

"Is this the reason for the short baby patrol?"

"We needed you out of the way to get everything set up, and we figured even *you* couldn't get into trouble on the Ashfall loop." Anderson arched a brow. "We sent Oz with you just to be on the safe side."

"There was a betting pool going on whether you'd manage to find trouble anyway," Mayhem added with a grin, which explained all the exchanges of money and alcohol.

"Harper doesn't find trouble, she attracts it," a familiar voice rumbled from behind me. "Like a magnet."

My shoulders stiffened, and I drew in a deep breath before I turned around. Dimitri gave me a crooked smile before he stiffened to attention and gave Anderson a crisp salute. "Lieutenant Thompson reporting as ordered, sir."

Anderson returned it sharply. "She's all yours."

Wait. What?

"Small victories, Tavros," Anderson added quietly.

"Have fun, Harpy." Mayhem winked and hooked her arm through Anderson's, dragging our commander back to the party. Slowly, I looked at Keaton.

"Dimitri's the surprise? That's a terrible surprise. No, that's a straight up declaration of war!" I gestured wildly and glared at him. "You throw me a party but don't let me drink, and now *he's* my surprise? What the hell, Keaton!"

"Wow. You done?" Keaton grinned at Dimitri because my brother was a *traitor*. "Been awhile since she's gotten this dramatic."

"I bring it out in her," Dimitri replied ruefully. "And no, Harper, I'm not the surprise."

He gestured for us to follow. Stubbornly, I planted my feet. Oz glanced over with a flask in hand and a shit-eating grin on his face.

"Hey, Harper! I've got good money on you two not kissing and making up until winter. Don't let me down!"

"Don't worry, love." I ignored the heat washing over my face and arched a brow. "I'm more likely to kiss *you*."

Nikos roared a laugh as Oz's face turned beet red, and I smirked as I finally allowed Keaton to pull me along behind him. We rounded the cluster of dorms to the back half of the wide hilltop, where the griffin's landing field was located along with one of the best views in the fort. Once again, my feet stumbled to a halt.

Sunlight sparkled off the lake, the random puddles from last night's rainstorm, and the black dragon taking up more than half the landing field, wings half extended as he lazily basked in the autumn sun.

"*That's* your surprise," Dimitri said quietly. A faint creak drew my gaze down. He'd nearly crushed his leather flying cap and goggles in his hands. "Major Anderson lobbied for you to get an incentive flight as reward for your actions in the Fort Bramble incursion."

My jaw dropped. Even dragon riders didn't fly whenever they wanted. They couldn't, not when attacks could come at any moment. Incentive flights for non–dragon riders, even griffin riders, were rare. And with the way things were going between the dragon and griffin riders . . . no wonder Westbrook had looked like he wanted to stab someone.

My stunned gaze shifted back to Riven. He was wearing a double saddle.

A shiver of intense longing rocked through me.

It had been so long.

"See you when you get back." Keaton waggled the flask and his eyebrows as he backed away. "Then the real party starts."

Once Keaton was gone, I reluctantly looked at Dimitri. Every nasty word we'd hurled at each other like weapons played in my memory, and my knuckles ached with the ghost of impact. We'd hurt each other so badly last time, but he'd still left me that painstakingly carved likeness of Felix. I didn't understand him, and it hurt because I used to know what he was thinking before he did.

"Why you?" I finally asked, my voice a hoarse rasp in my chest.

"Orders," he said with a shrug that was just a shade too casual. His gaze flicked up as a red dragon soared past, and a muscle in his jaw ticked, as if he'd rather be flying with his wingmate than me. I scowled, tempted to tell him to shove it, but . . . *flying*.

My bondmate grumbled in annoyance as he prowled around the side of the command post. His feathers were ruffled and his fur stuck up in odd places from wrestling with the other griffins, but there was nothing funny about the conflicted look in his purple gaze.

"I take you flying all the time."

"You do . . ." I reached up and patted his shoulder, my eyes fixed on Riven again. "But feeling the wind in your feathers isn't the same thing as feeling the wind on my own face."

"Yeah, I know," he replied with a trace of uncharacteristic bitterness. He stepped out from under my hand. *"You should go."*

I tore my gaze from the black dragon.

"Felix . . ."

His tail lashed, the wide fan of feathers on the end snapping out, and I let my hand fall to my side. He was the other half of my soul. While it was possible to hide things from him, I'd done a poor job of shielding my yearning for the sky lately. Orders or not, rare reward or not, I wasn't willing to hurt him.

I turned back to Dimitri to tell him shove his orders up his ass when Felix spoke again.

"You should go, but only if he stays low and slow so I can come too." My head snapped around, and I stared up at him with wide eyes. His tail settled as he felt my growing elation. *"I mean it, Harpy. Go fly. I think you need to."*

I threw my arms around his neck and buried my face in his feathers so Dimitri wouldn't see my tears. They weren't for him. Only when my eyes were dry did I pull away.

"I'll fly with you," I said haughtily, as if I were doing Dimitri a favor by agreeing instead of merely following orders. "But Felix is flying with us."

Dimitri strode over to Riven and slapped his shoulder playfully. "Riven says he won't leave your bird behind."

Felix trilled a mocking laugh at the mild insult, and I moved closer to Riven, studying him even as he arched his neck and studied me back. The young black dragon had grown since I'd last seen him up close, but he still wasn't even as big as a red, let alone a full-grown black. Scales that would eventually form armored plates had developed though, and one day soon he'd be nearly unstoppable on the battlefield. For now, he remained as agile as a gray, and about as large.

Before I could step up to his side, he swung his head down. I stilled, caught in his solemn black-ringed amber gaze. And then he nudged me in a pointed demand. A delighted smile spread across my face, and I gently rubbed his eye ridges.

"He likes you," Dimitri said softly before he stepped onto his dragon's helpfully extended elbow and leaped into the double saddle.

I'd be lying if I said the show of easy athleticism wasn't attractive. He grinned down at me and held out his hand. For just a moment, I forgot everything that had happened between us and just saw my old friend, all grown up and distractingly handsome.

With a deep breath, I stepped onto Riven's elbow and launched myself upward. Dimitri wrapped his hand around my wrist and easily pulled me into the trainee's seat in front of him. The warm smell of leather and dragon enveloped me, and something in my chest cracked a little.

A set of straps smacked into my lap. "You remember how to do this, hotshot?"

I shook off the melancholy and twisted to glare at him. "I think I can manage."

Just like when we were cadets, he saw right through my bravado. The man had more patience than the boy though, and he let me make a hash of the straps before he offered his help again. My shoulders slumped slightly as I admitted defeat. There was a trick to setting them so they tightly held the legs to the saddle without cutting off circulation, and I'd lost my touch after three years.

Dimitri leaned forward slightly, his warm breath tickling the back of my neck and his arms caging me in as he adjusted the straps to his liking. "Good?"

Unable to trust my voice—though I wasn't sure if it was due to overwhelming nostalgia or his very male proximity—I nodded. Felix cackled in my mind, and I shot him a glare.

"Shut it, bird brain."

Riven stood to his full height, but he didn't take off. I glanced back with a puzzled frown and was met with Dimitri's dramatic black-ringed amber eyes.

"I know you don't want to hear it, but I have to say it. All of it, just once. And if you want to hit me when I'm done, that's fine."

I tensed.

"I'm sorry, Harper, for everything." He held my gaze, his expression raw and vulnerable. "I'm sorry we switched your egg. I'm sorry we stole your wings." He drew in a deep breath. "And I'm sorry I *ever* made you think I pitied you."

"Didn't you?" I asked harshly.

He hesitated. "I know how much flying meant to you. I felt pity for that loss maybe, but never *you*. And yeah, I bought into all the academy bullshit about how dragon riders were so much better than griffin riders. I thought you got less than you deserved, but after a year out here . . ." He shook his head as he shifted his gaze to Felix. "There's nothing *less* about what you guys do."

Felix preened under Dimitri's admiration. *"He gives me cows and compliments. I approve."*

I rolled my eyes. *"You'd approve of anyone who did those things."*

"Yes."

"So . . . are you going to hit me again?" Dimitri asked, lips twitching in a suppressed smile.

"The day is young." I bit back a grin of my own. "Are you going to take me flying, asshole, or are you just going to sit there and look pretty?"

He treated me to a first-class leer. "You think I'm pretty, huh?"

"Talk less, fly more." My elbow shot back and caught him in the ribs. Dimitri just laughed and handed me a flying cap and goggles. My breath caught. They were *mine*. "Where did you get these?"

"Bethany. I thought you might like them back one day."

I twisted back around, not ready to face the genuine and entirely confusing affection in his gaze, and tugged on my old gear. It still fit. I tapped Dimitri's leg to signal I was ready, just like I would've as a dragon rider cadet. Old habits.

He tapped my leg back, and Riven loosed a roar that sounded of equal parts challenge and happiness as he bounded forward. His initial leap caught me off guard, but by the second I'd leaned forward into the proper position for takeoff. The edge of the field approached, and my heart pounded in excitement.

Massive legs bunched and pushed off as leathery wings spread wide and snapped downward. The ground fell away, and we soared.

The sun beat down on my shoulders, the wind was in my face, and I couldn't stop grinning. Everything was perfect. Riven had even kept to his word and stayed low so Felix could fly with us. The smaller griffin cavorted through the air, spiraling above and below us, flitting close to Riven's wings, and once even tweaking the dragon's tail. The young black ignored my bondmate's antics and flew smoothly, understanding that I was out of shape for this.

The time slipped past in a heartbeat. I never wanted to come down, but Felix abruptly beat his dappled wings against the air and pulled up in a hover.

"Harpy, we're getting too close to the border."

I leaned over and studied the ground beneath Riven's wings. He was right. The Wattspar River shimmered in the distance, and the Smoke Mountains were uncomfortably close. Our flight had started out west of Ashfall, but the winds must have pushed us northeast.

I reached back and tapped Dimitri's leg. "We need to turn back!"

The wind snatched away my words, but Dimitri heard and bellowed back, "Shit, you're right. Sorry, got lost in the wind for a bit."

I grinned. I knew exactly what he meant. As Riven tilted on one wing and executed a lazy turn back to the west, a glint from below caught my eye. I squinted, grateful for the goggles that protected my eyes, and tracked it as we continued our turn. There was something familiar about the color, but the thick trees blocked my view.

"Felix?"

I felt my bondmate look through my eyes, felt his surge of alarm. The words burst from my throat at the same time his shriek pierced the air.

"Dragon lance!"

Tension thrummed through Riven in response to my scream, and his wings cracked down hard to roll out of his turn. Instead of reaching for altitude, he dropped to gain speed, and my legs clamped tight to compensate. Without prompting from Dimitri, I flattened myself as much as possible to cut down on drag.

Riven roared in fury, and I dug my fingers into the front of the saddle as the world tilted sideways. Despite holding on with everything I had, I slid out of position. As I hung halfway out of the saddle, my wide eyes caught the flash of sunlight on sharpened metal as the dragon lance whipped past, missing us by bare meters despite our desperate maneuvering.

Somebody down there knew how to shoot down dragons.

Dimitri's hand dug into the back of my leathers and he wrenched me back into place.

"Check your straps," he roared over the thunder of Riven's wings.

I hurriedly jerked at the straps and flattened myself against the saddle once more, flexing my thighs tight as the great dragon fought for speed.

"Incoming!"

Before I could warn them, another dragon lance arced up, and Riven had to flare his wings to avoid the hit. The maneuver saved our lives but killed our airspeed. It also threw me back into Dimitri, and he roughly shoved me back into position again. Damn it, I had to do better than ride like a sack of potatoes. Especially when we were the last place a dragon rider wanted to be—low, slow, and squarely in the "shoot me, fuck me" zone.

I kept most of my focus on moving with Riven, but sent a trickle of awareness to Felix, asking, always asking to see with his eyes. And just like always, he let me in.

Everything leaped into sharp relief.

While I briefly struggled with the typical disorientation, Felix dropped lower, wings tilted as he cut sideways at a sharp angle. My heart jumped into my throat as arrows sleeted up from the trees in response.

"Be careful!"

He trilled a sharp laugh. *"Always am."*

"No, you're not! You're the opposite *of careful!"*

"Multiple emplacements, north, south, and east." Felix's voice turned brisk as he zipped across the treetops.

Red, orange, and yellow leaves flashed past in a colorful blur, rolling hills undulating beneath his outstretched wings. Glints of metal resolved into anti-air artillery and men in Savinian uniforms or dark leathers. Artillery troops and raiders, on *our* side of the border.

"They're dug in like ticks, like they were just waiting for a dragon to draw near—" His ears caught a distinctive buzz, like a pissed-off beehive. The sharp taste of fear cut through his reckless amusement. *"They've got flechette rounds!"*

"Flechettes," I screamed over my shoulder.

The tiny metal projectiles wouldn't pierce leathery hide, but they'd tear right through delicate membranes—and feathers. Vicious curses spilled from Dimitri, barely audible over the rush of wind, and Riven threw his whole body into gaining altitude.

I pulled out of Felix's mind and focused on riding. My muscles *burned* with the effort of staying with the black dragon. In the next instant, a flash of phantom pain ripped through my shoulder.

"Felix!"

"Just a stupid arrow. I'm fine."

The tearing, burning agony with each beat of his wings said otherwise. Fear gripped my heart, and I did something stupid—I fed him my energy. Terror made me sloppy, and I gave him too much. My grip on the saddle weakened, and I was flung against the straps at Riven's next sharp turn.

"That's enough, Harpy! It was a through and through. I'm good."

A wave of love and affection accompanied the stinging words, and I cut off the flow. As if to prove he was fine, my idiot griffin soared up in front of us, his wings spread wide as he angled southwest. The glint of a river beckoned just beyond him. Entangled as we were at the moment, I didn't need him to spell it out.

"The river," I howled back to Dimitri.

A third dragon lance shot up from almost beneath us. Riven didn't flare this time. He pulled up and arched back, until his nose pointed straight up and beyond. My stomach flipped along with the ground and sky, and the straps groaned as my full weight stressed them. In the next instant, he rolled upright facing the opposite direction.

A perfect Immelmann turn. It just wasn't enough.

The dragon lance grazed his wing. He skewed violently to the right, flinging me against the straps again, and I heard the sound every dragon rider feared—tearing leather.

Riven beat his wings frantically to regain lost altitude, his whole body surging upward like a bucking horse. Dimitri rode it easily, but I couldn't find the rhythm, and my straps finally gave way with a chilling *snap*.

My thighs strained to hold my place in the saddle, to keep my feet tucked into the divots that served as stirrups, but while I remembered what to do, my muscles couldn't deliver. I slipped sideways. Fear froze the breath in my lungs as the ground swung into view, so very far below.

"Hold on!" Dimitri stretched out his hand. His fingertips brushed my arm, and relief shot through me. Too soon. The high-pitched *buzz* of another flechette burst ripped through the sky. Riven banked sharply to the left to avoid losing a wing, and Dimitri's hand brushed past my arm without gaining purchase as I was flung from the saddle.

"Harper!" Dimitri roared.

I bounced once against the dragon's leathery side, and then I was free-falling. A terrified scream ripped out of my throat and was torn away by the wind.

"I've got you, Harpy!"

Felix swept beneath me, rolled over onto his back, and snatched me right out of the air. His forelegs wrapped around my torso and tugged me tight against his chest. When he flipped again, my stomach flipped with him.

"If you puke on me, I swear I'll drop you in the river."

His tone was playful, but I could sense his intense focus as he used every bit of skill he possessed to get us safely to the ground. His wings beat hard, pain flaring higher with each downstroke, and he shot for the western bank. We lost altitude with every strained wingbeat, but my bondmate was all heart, and I silently urged him on.

The water flashed by bare meters under my feet.

"You know, on second thought . . ." Smug amusement mixed with Felix's fierce determination. *"Dropping you in the river is the best idea I've had all day."*

"What? Don't you dare, you featherbrained—"

Felix let go, and I plunged into the water before I could even draw breath to scream.

Rivers in the middle of autumn are cold. Rivers that originate somewhere up in the Smoke Mountains are *very* cold, and I shivered uncontrollably as I followed Felix through the dense underbrush. My riding leathers were already beginning to chafe, but there was no time to dry off, no time to do more than use my wet undershirt to bind the bleeding hole in Felix's wing.

He'd been right, it was a simple through and through, but I wasn't going to let him leave a blood trail. A shiver that had nothing to do with the cold raced down my spine. The Savinians might have more of those broken hounds.

Bad enough we were leaving a trail of trampled vegetation a blind child could follow, but we had little choice. After he'd dropped me into the river, my sharp-eyed bondmate had spotted Riven going down somewhere ahead of us, southwest of the river and well within Tennessan borders. Not that it mattered. We were long miles away from Ashfall and any help, Felix was grounded, and our enemies were only separated from us by one little river—so we'd traded stealth for speed.

We had to find them first.

Desperation and fear tightened its grip. We couldn't let Dimitri fall into Savinian hands. Sunset eyes and chain-scarred legs flashed in my memory. A dragon would do anything for his bondmate. My gaze briefly rested on Felix. Just like a griffin would.

A baying, dissonant howl rose up behind us. Distant, possibly still on the wrong side of the river, but that would change. The Savinians had brought a dragon down, they weren't going to let him slip through their fingers easily. Urgency thrummed through our entangled souls as we broke into a run.

"You jinxed us!" Felix snapped as he ducked beneath an evergreen, allowing the sappy branches to slide over his fur.

"It doesn't count if I didn't say it out loud!" An evergreen branch sprang back and smacked me in the face, but I just followed his example and bulled straight through, bringing the sharp scent of pine with me.

"Tell that to the hound!"

My breath rasped in my throat, and my ribs ached with each ragged inhale. Felix hadn't been gentle when he'd caught me, and my torso would be black and blue before the end of the day. It wasn't the sharp stab of broken bones though, so I pushed aside the discomfort and kept running.

A few minutes of hard slogging later, we lucked out and hit a narrow deer trail. No words were needed. I sprinted with everything I had and caught up to Felix. I got one hand on his neck, then the other. I leaped, he swerved under me, and I pulled myself onto his back without him missing a stride. He dashed down the trail, putting several klicks behind us until we could no longer hear the hound.

Abruptly, Felix slowed, his sharp eyes scanning the dense forest. A thick carpet of dead and dying leaves blanketed the ground, and saplings and broadleaf plants competed for sunlight, filling the spaces between older trees. Small shafts of golden light speared down through the brightly colored canopy, leaving the forest in dappled sun and shadow.

My hand drifted to the hilt of my knife as I searched for threats, finding none. Felix's tufted ears perked straight up and his soft trill sang with triumph.

"Found them!"

He tightened his wings on my legs, gathered himself, and leaped as far off the game trail as possible to leave a break in our scent trail. He bulled his way through another drooping evergreen, and I ignored the itchy scrape of pine needles over my skin in favor of looking for black dragon hide. A few steps later, we broke into a newly made clearing.

Sunlight flooded through the broken canopy, shining on several freshly downed trees, one black dragon, and one dragon rider, sitting next to his dragon with his head in his hands. Riven rested his head next to his rider, emitting a low rumble that sounded suspiciously similar to a griffin's purr. I swept a hard glance over them both. Neither looked critically injured.

Relief hit me so hard I swayed on Felix's back and let out a sound somewhere between a sigh and a sob. Dimitri's head snapped up. Red-rimmed eyes latched onto my face, and he mouthed my name before he shot to his feet.

"*Harper!*"

He crossed the clearing in a heartbeat, almost before I'd slid off Felix's back, and swept me up into a hard hug. I didn't hesitate to hug him back. His arms tightened around my bruised ribs as he pulled me closer, and I hissed in discomfort. Immediately, he stepped back, hands on my upper arms as he ran a sharp gaze over my body.

"You're hurt?"

"Getting snatched out of the air by a desperate griffin isn't exactly a gentle experience," I explained wryly. Felix grumbled in annoyance, and I sent him a wave of affection and gratitude. "Not that I'm complaining."

"Better than the alternative," Dimitri murmured in agreement before he let out a shuddering breath. "I thought you were dead, hotshot."

"I think I used up all my luck on that one," I whispered, hearing the rip of tearing leather in my memory again. My heart skipped a beat as he gently touched the side of my face, but he pulled away as his expression darkened.

"I thought I could keep you safe, and I almost got you killed instead." Drawing in a deep breath, Dimitri turned to my griffin. "Most *dragons* couldn't have made that catch. Not at that altitude. You're amazing, Felix."

Felix's tufted ears shot straight up and he trilled in delight. "*You hear that? I'm* amazing."

"*Yes, you are,*" I said fondly. My gaze shifted to the young black as he cautiously stretched his left wing. "How's Riven?"

"Wrenched his wing, same one as the last time we were shot down.

He's not flying anywhere." Dimitri grimaced and turned back to his bondmate. "And he hurt his front right leg taking out one of those trees on his way down. I don't think it's broken, but I don't think he can make it far on foot either."

I eyed the awkward way Riven held his right leg and blew out a short breath. On only three legs, there was no way he'd outrun the raiders, let alone the hound.

"Damn. Felix isn't flying anywhere either."

Distant shouts echoed through the trees, and Dimitri clenched his jaw. His eyes darted to mine, indecision and unexpected rage swirling in their depths.

"Harper," he said with an edge of desperation, but Riven jerked his head up, a low growl spilling from his jaws. Dimitri briefly squeezed his eyes shut and nodded at his dragon. I gave them both as reassuring a smile as I could manage.

"It'll be okay. Felix and I've got this. We'll draw them off and go for help. You two displace half a klick to the west." I arched a brow at Riven. "Just try not to leave a massive trail, big guy." The black snorted, but sounded amused rather than annoyed. I'd take it.

That dissonant baying howl rose up again, closer this time. Another howl quickly followed. I shuddered, Dimitri paled, and Riven gave me an excellent view of every one of his sharp fangs as he dropped his jaw in a rippling snarl.

"Great, now there's two of them." Felix flexed his claws, shredding the ground foliage. *"Somehow you double jinxed us. Bad Harpy!"*

"Oh, shut it, featherhead."

"What the hell was that?" Dimitri demanded in a near-soundless whisper.

"Broken things," I whispered back. Dimitri took in the barely suppressed horror in my expression and shook his head sharply.

"No." His dragon grumbled again, but he shot his bondmate a fierce glare. "No. I can't let you do this, Harper."

"You know the Dragon Down protocols as well as I do. You said you didn't think we were less." I lifted my chin and held his stare. "Prove it."

"Damn it," he muttered after a tense silence, his shoulders slumping. I'd never seen my old friend look so defeated. I reached out and touched his hand. He curled his fingers around mine before he abruptly pulled away. I ignored the stab of hurt and smirked at Felix.

"Lure and ditch?"

Eagerness suffused the bond and buried the unease. Felix crouched slightly and nodded, tail lashing.

"Lure and ditch."

My gaze strayed to the bloody shirt clumsily wrapped around his wing.

"And we know just how to lure them, don't we?" The hounds bayed again, closer still, and I whirled back to Dimitri. "Go! Hide if you can, evade if you can't. We'll bring back help, I promise."

With a strained grunt, Riven heaved himself up and slid out of the clearing, moving exceptionally well for his size and injuries. I barely heard the dried leaves rustle beneath his talons.

Dimitri reluctantly followed, but he glanced back once, expression anguished. "I'm sorry, Harper."

And then they were gone, swallowed by the tangled autumn forest. Unease twisted in my belly, but there was no time to examine it. Felix and I quickly retraced our steps to the deer path, again leaping from the brush to the bare ground to break the scent trail.

The shouts and calls of the raiders were closer now. The only reason they'd make that much noise was if they were hoping to flush us out. A hard grin stretched my lips. They were putting so much effort into it, it'd be a shame not to give them what they wanted.

Felix stopped in the middle of the trail, tail lashing with his impatience to run. I slid off his back, gently unwrapped the bloody shirt, and examined the arrow wound. It had mostly stopped bleeding, but I needed it all the way stopped. I gripped Felix's shoulder to steady myself, drew in a deep breath, and pushed a small amount of energy along the bond.

Not small enough. My knees hit the dirt, my vision blurred, and a wave of dizziness threatened to drown me.

"Harpy!"

"Had...to be...done," I managed, head hanging low as I panted through the worst of it. The world steadied, and I pushed myself back to my feet with more than a little help from a very irritated griffin. Quickly, I reexamined his wound before I met his narrowed gaze and held up the bloody shirt. *"Luring is easy. If we want the ditch to work, we need one source of blood, not two."*

His ears flicked in reluctant acknowledgement, and he even more reluctantly held his tail still as I tied the bloody shirt around the end, flattening his fan of feathers. The second I was done, he whipped his tail out of my hand and took a few experimental steps. The bloody shirt dragged along the path behind him. *Perfect.*

My shoulders stiffened as the hounds bayed, close enough I swear I could hear the wet snuffling. I could definitely hear the trample of boots through tangled underbrush.

"Time to go."

"You think?"

As I pulled myself onto his back, I glanced over my shoulder, scanning the thick foliage for the raiders. A flash of brown drew my gaze. I hunched low over Felix's feathered neck and tightened my legs around his sides. *Come and get us, assholes.*

We raced down the path, leaving a blood trail behind us, luring the hounds and the raiders away from Dimitri and Riven. It worked a little too perfectly, and we found ourselves running full speed toward Ashfall with a pack of enemies on our heels. But Felix could easily outrun a human in the open, let alone through a tangled forest, and it soon became more of a challenge to stay just far enough ahead to lure them without losing them.

The first time we got enough distance on the hounds, Felix scaled a tree and got eyes on our pursuers. We counted twelve raiders. Interestingly, this time the broken hounds were leashed rather than allowed to run freely. Long miles passed beneath Felix's paws before we judged we'd lured them far enough.

Ditching worked just as perfectly as luring had. We left the bloody shirt behind, and Felix carried us up into the trees, leaping between several ancient oaks to thoroughly break our trail before descending to the ground again. My legs ached from gripping so tightly, and my ribs were screaming, but it was worth the cost.

As the sounds of pursuit faded into the normal chirping, rustling sounds of a daytime forest, Felix drew to a stop. I flexed my shoulders, trying to shake the unease gripping my soul. As the minutes ticked past and more nothing happened—no baying hounds, no shouting raiders—the feeling only grew worse.

"Are you thinking what I'm thinking?"

"Too easy," he agreed with a soft clack of his beak. *"We're good, but not even Bailey could shake those broken things, and she was better."*

I slid off his back, pressing one hand to my abused ribs as my boots hit the ground, and watched my bondmate scale the nearest towering oak. Confusion and concern spun through his mind, and he tugged on mine. I followed the tug, fell into his mind, and looked through his eyes.

My jaw dropped, shock easily pushing aside my usual disorientation. I could buy the raiders frantically searching for the lost trail. I could even buy the raiders figuring out they'd been lured from the downed dragon and turning back to search for them. But for the raiders to turn around and casually walk away as if they were on a pleasant afternoon hike?

"Something's not right, Harpy."

I fell back into my own mind, and my eyes narrowed. *"Agreed. We need to get back to Ashfall. Now."*

After we made it through the gates, Felix charged straight to the Dragon Corps Command Post. Without slowing, he shouldered open the doors and burst into the ready room with his wings mantled. High ceilinged and big enough to echo when empty, the ready room was where dragon riders sitting alert duty waited for any emergencies. A planning table with an identical map to the one in our command post dominated the center, with scattered couches and chairs littering the rest of the space. Half a dozen riders loitered within, five of them involved in some kind of card game at one end of the table.

Felix roared for attention, and the dragon riders snapped their heads around.

"Dragon down," I said into the harsh silence. Words no rider wanted to say, but were guaranteed to kick everyone into a rapid response. Cards were dropped and riders leaped to their feet. To my dismay, the duty officer in command was Major Westbrook, who glared at me as if I'd personally shot down one of his dragons. I tightened my grip on Felix's neck. *"Call Loki, we need backup."*

Fortunately, I had some already. Zayne pushed his way forward, the tiny slip of a woman Oz had once flirted with at his side. The Search and Rescue green dragon riders on duty that day.

"Where?" Zayne barked. His pale face said he knew exactly who I'd been flying with. I slipped off Felix's back and staggered on shaking legs over to the map, Felix subtly guiding my hand as I tapped the last known location. His geographical awareness had always been better than mine. My voice was steady as I reported everything.

"I knew it was a mistake to give a griffin rider an incentive flight," Westbrook muttered, hard gaze fixed on my face instead of anywhere useful—like the map where I'd just marked the artillery emplacements. Zayne clenched his jaw, but his wingmate rapped the table pointedly, her low contralto cutting through the noise.

"Those emplacements are nowhere near our normal flight lanes. Even straying too close to the border, Lieutenant Thompson couldn't have anticipated Savinian artillery that far inside our territory."

Westbrook reluctantly shifted his glare to the map—and the doors burst open again.

"Damn it, Tavros. How the *hell* did you find trouble on an incentive flight?"

Relief swamped me as Major Anderson swept into the ready room, Mayhem at his heels. Both of them looked a little rough around the edges, and I was willing to bet their griffins had just helped them burn off whatever they'd drank at the party. Mayhem passed me two ration bars and a canteen without comment as a medic led Felix outside to examine his wing.

I gave my commander a strained smile.

"It's a gift."

"More like a curse," he muttered as he stepped up to the table and faced off against the new dragon detachment commander. Felix had relayed to Loki while I reported, so he was already up to speed on the situation. "What's the plan?"

"We'll send the greens in with a carry net to pick up Lieutenant Thompson and his dragon," Westbrook said dismissively before he gestured to the artillery emplacements. "Meanwhile, the rest of us will take those out."

As the dragon riders gathered around the map, planning approach vectors and armament in a rapid-fire assessment, my gaze landed on Zayne. The unease swirling in my gut twisted into nausea at the thought of the greens going in alone.

"No!" I pushed my way up next to Anderson and locked eyes with Westbrook as I tapped at the map. "We need the greens back here, and a pair of reds here and here—"

"One little incentive flight doesn't make you a *dragon* rider again, Lieutenant Tavros," Westbrook said scathingly.

For just an instant, I faltered at the vicious reminder of what I'd lost. Then a voice like iron floated up in my memory.

Hold on to that fire.

My spine stiffened.

"No sir, I'm a *griffin* rider. We are the eyes and ears of the Tennessan military and you will *listen* when we speak." Dead silence fell over the ready room, but I didn't dare back down. "Something is very wrong, and if we send the greens in without top cover, we'll lose them."

"Harpy," Mayhem murmured into the quiet. "Are you sure?"

I thought of the raiders' odd behavior, anti-air artillery emplacements where no dragons typically flew, and how utterly careless it was for an experienced rider like Dimitri to get that close to the border. Vague suspicions coalesced into sharp-edged certainty.

"It's a trap," I said, my voice ringing with conviction. I swallowed hard. "The only question is whether Dimitri—Lieutenant Thompson is bait, or a willing participant. And I know how to find out." I tapped the map again. "Drop me and Felix off here first."

Anderson took one look at my grim face and nodded before he turned back to Westbrook. "Lieutenant Nikos and Erra can scout the artillery emplacements and make sure there aren't any surprises waiting for your dragons."

Major Westbrook ground his teeth so hard I could hear it from across the table. His hands flexed as if he were contemplating strangling me, but one of his riders coughed pointedly, and he regained control.

"You'd better be right about this, Tavros."

"I hope I'm wrong, sir," I said, my shoulders hunching in misery despite everything I could do to keep them straight. "But I don't think I am."

A friendly gray dropped Felix and me exactly where I'd asked, and then we did what we'd been trained to do—we scouted. When I couldn't get close enough to Dimitri and Riven, Felix went on alone, slipping through the forest like a ghost. After he'd found a good perch, he let me see through his eyes.

And my heart shattered.

An hour later, Dimitri looked up as I walked into the small clearing, a natural one this time rather than dragon made. Two green dragons slithered through the underbrush and flanked me.

"Harper!" He forced a smile but his gaze jerked away from the greens and their riders, as if he couldn't bear to look at them. He could barely look *me* in the eye. "I'm ... glad you're back with help. The raiders kept us moving."

"Did they?" I asked coldly.

I'd watched through my griffin's eyes as Dimitri betrayed ... everyone. Rather than eager, he'd been stoic when he coordinated with the Savinians, as impassive as Keaton at his worst. Rage and pain roared through me as he looked at me with that same impassive expression—if he was a traitor and a villain, he should've at least had the decency to act like one. It would make this so much easier.

My heart was bleeding out, but I didn't let a hint of my inner turmoil touch my expression.

"We know, Dimitri."

He froze. His jaw tightened as he took in the bloodstained maws of the green dragons. Once Felix had relayed the Savinian raider teams' positions, it had been a simple matter for the dragons to ambush the ambushers.

"How?" he finally asked in a careful voice. But I knew him. I could see the shadows growing in his eyes.

Felix growled low in my mind. *"Relay my words for me, love."*

"Dragons are all flash and look at me, look at me. Griffins, though?"

I pointed to my griffin, hidden in the expansive canopy of an ancient oak. Comfortably stretched out across a thick branch high above, Felix's dappled coloring blended with the rough bark perfectly. His tail slowly moved back and forth, the feathers on the end fanning in and out.

"Griffins are *sneaky.*"

Riven lunged to his perfectly healthy legs and flexed his perfectly healthy wings, but the thunder of more wings overhead announced the arrival of the reds. He lurched to the side, but the two greens had carefully positioned themselves to cut off the easy escape routes. Dimitri held up his hand, and his dragon reluctantly stilled, though his tail lashed back and forth. Felix didn't even notice. His predatory gaze was focused on Dimitri, poised to attack if my oldest friend so much as twitched in my direction.

"*Why?*" The word burst out of me without permission. "What could they *possibly* have offered you?"

Dimitri glared up at Major Westbrook as he descended on his massive red. Slowly, his hands clenched into fists before he looked back at me, his expression impassive once more.

"I have nothing to say."

That, apparently, was the last straw for Zayne. Cassia surged forward a step, a rumbling growl rippling through the air.

"Are you kidding me right now?" Zayne roared. "You betray everything, *everyone*, and you have nothing to say? Since when? You never shut up!"

Dimitri's gaze locked onto Zayne as the red dragons landed one by one, flanking Riven and effectively taking dragon and rider prisoner.

"I have *nothing to say.*"

Zayne went very still, but I glared at Dimitri as I flashed back to eavesdropping outside of Iverson's office. A bitter laugh escaped my fragile control. He'd had nothing to say on the day he'd ruined my life either. Why should the day he ruined his be any different?

My nails bit into my palms, and I took a stomping step closer to Dimitri. I couldn't breathe, could barely think. All I knew was I wanted to make him hurt like he'd hurt me.

Westbrook's dragon whipped his head around and hissed. I froze midstep, not so lost to rage that I was stupid enough to ignore the vicious red's warning. Felix leaped out of his perch and landed between us, something between a purr and a growl rumbling in his chest. Westbrook gave me that same smug smile, but there was something ugly in his gaze. He hadn't liked it when I'd contradicted him, and I had a feeling he'd liked it less when I'd been proven right.

He'd make me pay for it.

I don't know if Zayne asked, or if Cassia did it on her own, but the green dragon eased forward and broke Nero's line of sight. Together, we watched in silence as our friend was escorted out of that sun-drenched clearing, leaving us to make our own way home.

CHAPTER 24

Fort Ashfall was in an uproar. It wasn't every day that one of the precious dragon riders was declared a traitor, and there were more than a few who celebrated Dimitri's fall from grace.

Felix and I dragged ourselves back to the eyrie, but Anderson had done us the kindness of spreading the word so we didn't get mobbed. Keaton didn't say anything. He just waited for me to get my griffin settled with Tavi, dragged me up to our favorite roof, and passed over a full flask. I drank myself stupid, but not a single tear fell. I was far too angry for that. Keaton carried me back to my room, tucked me into bed, and left.

My blurred gaze landed on the carved griffin, and what was left of my heart cracked in two. One tear finally broke past the dam, then another, and another, until it was an unstoppable flood. I curled into a ball and sobbed myself to sleep.

Late the next morning, Zayne ambushed me in the griffin dining hall. My elbows rested on the scarred table, aching head in my hands and a cup of coffee I hadn't been able to stomach cooling in front of me. Keaton had slid over a plate of dry toast without comment or censure, but I'd only been able to nibble a corner before my stomach rebelled.

"I need to talk to you," Zayne hissed. He was downright twitchy, nervous eyes darting all over the place like he was afraid Savinian raiders were going to pop out of the woodwork. "Outside, by the lake."

I didn't have it in me to fight him.

"I'm going too." Keaton shoved to his feet and glared at me. "Every time I leave you alone, bad things happen."

I didn't have it in me to fight him either. He also wasn't wrong. Felix snickered in my mind, *loudly*, and my head pounded harder. He was getting his own breakfast from the griffin livestock pens with Tavi and had been remarkably quiet until now.

"Ow," I said pointedly. *"You're supposed to be supportive and loving when I'm miserable."*

"I do love you, Harpy," Felix said with a much quieter snicker. Red-tinged hunger stained his thoughts, but a flash of predatory delight brightened them. *"Oooh, and this chicken!"*

"You're a chicken," I shot back fondly before I refused a second offer to help my hangover. I didn't know how to tell him I wanted the misery as a distraction from the pain. *"Eat first. You burned a lot yesterday, and I don't want to strain you."*

There was a caress of fur and feathers in my mind before he withdrew. Zayne was practically vibrating with impatience at the door, and I sighed as I followed him out into the painfully bright day with Keaton stalking along at my heels. If the weather had any sense of justice, it would be gloomy and overcast, but it was just as beautiful as yesterday. The breeze stirred the copper strands of hair that had escaped my regulation braid, and a few colorful leaves tumbled past, bringing the musky-sweet scent of autumn with them.

I hated everything.

By the time we reached the lake, sparkling in the late morning sunlight, I was stomping hard enough to give my headache a headache—because I knew *exactly* what Zayne wanted to talk about. I was too hungover for this, and too heartsore, but Zayne was frantic, pacing back and forth along the shore, short hair sticking up in ragged tufts. He spun back around, his green-and-gold gaze locked onto my face like Keaton didn't even exist in that moment.

"We have to help Dimitri."

"Dimitri *betrayed* us," I spat out, ignoring the stab of pain in my chest. Maybe if I said it enough times I'd finally believe it. "I saw it with my own eyes... or through Felix's, which is the same damn thing. I *saw* him coordinating with those Savinian bastards to ambush you. There's no getting around it, no gray areas here, no *puzzle* for you to solve. He. Betrayed. Us."

"Us, or you?" Zayne asked quietly, brows raised. My hands curled into fists, but Keaton caught my arm before I could do more than shift my weight.

"Maybe listen to him before you break his face." Keaton gave me a slight grin, nothing of amusement in it. "When he's done talking, *then* you can break his face."

"Oh, so long as I have your permission," I said tightly. I tore out of his loose grip and turned my glare on Zayne, furious and hurting. "Dimitri *used* me, and he used the Dragon Down protocols to manipulate me into bringing back help. The duty roster is always posted. He knew who I'd bring back. What do you think General Serrano's son would be worth to the Savinians?"

"Come on, Harper, you know something's not right. Dimitri? A traitor? Never. I don't believe it, and neither do you." Zayne stepped closer, sunlight sparkling off the lake at his back, giving him an odd halo. "Do you really think he sabotaged your straps?"

I hesitated before I crossed my arms. "No, if only because I wouldn't be able to bring back help."

Now Zayne's hands tightened into fists, and he bared his teeth in a snarl.

"Gods damn it, Harper, would you quit being such a stubborn brat?" His roar echoed off the water, and a couple of soldiers walking on the far side paused to stare at us.

"She won't," Keaton muttered. Zayne ignored him.

"If you really think he would *ever* try to kill you, walk away now. I'll save him without your help."

Zayne shook his head in disappointment when I said nothing and backed off a step. I didn't move. My jaw clenched, and I abruptly sat down on the lakeshore, my arms still very much crossed. Zayne grinned, bright as the damn sun making my eyes ache, and I scowled up at him.

"I'm not saying he needs saving, I'm just . . . saying he wouldn't have messed with my straps." I sighed when his grin didn't dim in the slightest, uncrossed my arms, and rolled one hand dramatically. "Fine, Zayne. Dazzle me with your brilliance."

"When has Dimitri not tried to charm his way out of trouble?" Apparently, that was rhetorical, because Zayne didn't pause for an answer. "The only time he's had nothing to say was the day you won that damn argument with him in our third year, and the day Iverson tore us a new one for messing with your egg. Dimitri didn't say a *word*, but somehow, he came out of that mess assigned the first black dragon egg in years. It didn't make sense, and it bothered me."

"Of course it did," I sighed, rubbing my aching temples and trying to wrestle my temper under control. "Dog with a bone."

"The argument was easy to understand. You backed him into a corner until he had no choice but to admit you were right." He gave me a fleeting smile. "It was epic. But then there was Iverson's office. I know you were eavesdropping that day. I know you heard us. Cal tried to blame it on your supposed incompetence. Because he was a dick. I blamed ignorance." An embarrassed flush swept up his high cheekbones. "I didn't know the griffin eggs were due to hatch that day, and I *should've* thought to check that. Dimitri said nothing. How many times did you get us into trouble and Dimitri talked us right back out of it? Even when it would've been easier to get just himself out of trouble, he protected *all* of us. All of us, Harper, *always*. But the one time, the *one time*, we really needed him to talk . . . he didn't. Why?"

Apparently, that *wasn't* a rhetorical question, because he finally fell silent and waited for me to answer. The longer he waited, the more my gut tightened.

"I don't know!" I finally burst out, frustrated because I'd never known.

I shoved myself back to my feet, thoroughly fed up with everything. I wanted to go back to bed. I wanted to hide under the damn covers and pretend yesterday never happened. I wanted . . .

I let out a shuddering breath. "Damn you. Why didn't he?"

"It took me a little bit to figure out, but I finally got it. The only thing he could've done was blame *you*. For your arguments, for your pranks, for every time you two took your competitive bullshit too far." Zayne stared at me, waiting for me to say what we both knew. My vision blurred with unshed tears.

"And he wouldn't have done it. Not in a million years would he have thrown me under the dragon with Iverson." I closed my eyes. "Any more than he would've cut my straps."

Damn it. How much of my anger at Dimitri had been for the pity in his eyes, and how much for his silence in Iverson's office that day? Felix brushed against my mind, steadfast support without judgment.

"Dimitri never told me what he did to earn the black dragon egg, but I know he went back to Iverson on his own," Zayne said quietly. "I know he came out of that meeting convinced Iverson was kicking him out. I *know* whatever he did that day, it was to protect us. And I guarantee you that's exactly what he's doing now."

My eyes flew open as hope ignited, burning away some of the pain, if not my hangover. Zayne's intensity was catching, because when he'd solved a puzzle, when he was *right*, he made you feel it. He stared at me, fierce conviction burning in his gaze.

"Dimitri isn't a traitor. He told us yesterday, in the only way he could, because the only time that bastard has nothing to say is when he's been backed into a corner." He raised his brows. "Or when he's protecting us. Protecting *you*. Don't you want to know which it is this time?"

I hesitated again, because if Zayne was wrong, if we found out Dimitri really was a traitor after getting my hopes up . . . it would break me.

"Isn't it better to know?" Felix asked, gently pushing energy my way, burning up the last of my hangover. I whispered gratitude before I snorted a laugh.

"You just want him to be innocent so he can give you more cows."

"No! Okay, yes, but it's not just that. He saved me, saved us when I was a cub. He sat with you when you were sick from that stupid arrow." An echo of fear and relief flashed in his mind. *"And you didn't see his face when your straps broke. I did. You can't fake that kind of terror, Harpy. I think Zayne is right. And so do you."*

"Damn it." I scrubbed my face and opened eyes that no longer ached. "It's not like we can go ask him. They're not letting anyone in the brig."

Zayne gave me a sly grin. "And you would only know that if you'd tried to talk to him."

Keaton smirked. "I wondered where you'd disappeared to this morning before breakfast."

"I'm not done yelling at that asshole yet," I muttered.

"Lucky for all of us, my father was the fort commander before he made general, and I spent some time out here as a teenager before the border moved closer. I know the back way into the brig, and if we're really lucky, they're not guarding it." He glanced at Keaton. "You up for a little misdirection?"

A slow smile spread across my brother's face. "What did you have in mind?"

If it weren't for all the prison cells, Fort Ashfall's brig would be a pleasant place, especially in the summer. Located beneath the fortress and constructed from the same duracrete, the underground level was dry and cool. Supposedly, there were two more levels beneath this one devoted entirely to food storage.

Zayne's back way into the brig involved sneaking into the guard commander's closet and through a false panel in the back, climbing down a surprisingly sturdy ladder, and crawling through a small, spiderweb-choked passage. I made Zayne go first.

We exited the passage through a panel and into another supply closet. The panel swung closed on silent hinges, but Zayne spun around, pulled his boot off, and jammed it into the rapidly closing gap before it could seal shut.

"Can't let it close or we'll never get it open again," he said in a reasonable approximation of the low-but-clear voice griffin riders were trained in.

I nodded silently and eased open the closet door. The first thing I heard was Keaton, arguing with the guards, and the rumbling growl of a highly irritated griffin. Or at least, Tavi was doing a great job of acting like he was irritated. I exchanged a quick grin with Zayne and slipped out of the closet.

The brig was laid out with a double row of cells lining the stone walls, with a wide aisle down the center. Our little closet was at the end of the aisle, with an empty guard station and a set of stairs at the other. Keaton's voice echoed down the stairs, with the quieter responses of the guards drifting down. The smokeless torches at this end were unlit, and we emerged into shadows.

I ghosted down the aisle, passing empty cell after empty cell, and paused just outside of the pool of light cast by the torches near the guard station. My head tilted as I listened to the ongoing argument, but it sounded like Keaton had them completely distracted. I stepped into the light as Zayne trailed along behind me, doing an admirable job of moving silently despite having only one boot on.

Dimitri was in the first cell to the right, sitting on the bench with his head in his hands and his shoulders slumped. Déjà vu hit hard.

He'd looked much the same sitting next to his dragon in that clearing. I drifted to a halt in front of his cell. Anger and pain and hope swirled in a toxic mess as I stared at him.

Today had given me emotional whiplash and it wasn't even noon.

Time was slipping away though, and I ruthlessly compartmentalized everything before I cleared my throat.

"Hey, asshole."

Dimitri's head snapped up. I tilted my head toward Zayne, lingering at the edge of the torchlight.

"He thinks you're not really a traitor." My voice turned ice cold. "Convince me."

Dimitri lunged to his feet and strode up to the bars, desperate hope burning in his dramatic amber eyes. His voice was a hoarse rasp, barely audible over the increasingly loud argument upstairs.

"Cal's alive."

Shock held me immobile as goosebumps washed over my skin. Out of every possible explanation I'd imagined, that hadn't even made the list. A harsh exhale traveled down the aisle, and I glanced back at Zayne. Apparently, that hadn't made his list either.

"Impossible," I whispered, even as I desperately wished it were true. "They threw back his body."

"No," he snapped. "They threw back a mutilated corpse wearing Cal's uniform. It wasn't him."

"How could you *possibly* know that?" My hand dropped to the hilt of Callum's knife, and my knuckles turned white from the strength of my grip. Dimitri wrapped his hands around the bars, and I didn't feel a trace of fear that he might reach through and hurt me. It was as impossible as Callum being alive.

"We saw Artemis. When we were shot down near the Smoke Mountains. We *saw* her." His eyes narrowed, some of that inner darkness peering out at me. "She wasn't the only dragon we saw chained."

Horrible understanding sucker-punched me in the gut. "You found a POW camp."

He dipped his chin in a slow nod, never once breaking eye contact. Anger roared through me like a flash fire.

"Why didn't you *say something*, you freaking moron! And what the hell does any of that have to do with yesterday's shitshow!"

"Keep your voice down," Zayne hissed.

I gritted my teeth and stared at Dimitri. His voice dropped into an angry growl.

"I reported it. The instant I got into debriefing, I reported what we saw to my wing leader, *Captain* Westbrook." Bitterness flashed across his face. "He held a knife to my throat and told me I had two options. Keep my mouth shut and follow *his* orders, or he'd kill . . ."

His gaze skipped away from mine. Pure helpless rage twisted his expression, and his hands tightened on the metal bars. An awful certainty grew in my belly, twisting and sliding through my soul. Felix flexed mental claws and growled.

"Me? Why *me*?"

"He figured out you were important to me," Dimitri replied in a low voice. He finally looked up, and I couldn't breathe, completely ensnared by the look in his eyes.

"Knew it," Zayne muttered gleefully. I cheerfully could've murdered him in that moment, because Dimitri broke eye contact to smirk at him.

"I knew you'd figure it out if anyone could, brother. You always were persistent when it came to inconsistencies."

Zayne held up a middle finger, thought about it for a second, then held up both.

"Next time, tip me off sooner, dumbass. I could've helped you out of this mess." Zayne leaned against the bars of an empty cell and arched a brow. "General's son, remember? Got to be good for more than just sneaking into brigs."

"Westbrook was watching me too closely. He isn't the only traitor in our ranks. There's more dragon riders, maybe a griffin rider. Probably someone in the conventional command staff." Helpless rage twisted his expression again as he looked back at me. "That messenger relay you were sent on wasn't ordered by Harborne. I . . . I made the mistake of trying to tell Major Zeddemore, but I couldn't get near him. Then you were sent on that relay as a warning, and the major disappeared on what should've been a simple patrol. I couldn't risk telling anyone after that."

Oh gods.

Remorse swamped what was left of my anger. Dimitri had been trapped ever since he'd been rescued, and I'd been fucking clueless.

Now his avoidance and the awful things he'd said made sense. He'd been trying to drive me away, to *protect* me. Just like he always had.

"Westbrook couldn't kill me because Riven is too valuable. There was no way he'd ever get Zeddemore under his control, but me? He had me by the balls, and through me his own personal black dragon. So he decided to use your incentive flight as a way to punish me and use you." His grip tightened on the bars so much they groaned in protest. "Your straps breaking was just an accident."

"You sure about that?" a familiar voice asked. I spun around as a Savinian sergeant limped out of the shadows of the cell across the aisle. His face was scruffier, but otherwise he looked no worse for wear. "There's a standing kill order on all griffin riders. Might not have been Westbrook who ordered the sabotage, but I doubt it was an accident."

I shot Zayne an exasperated glance. "Did you know Sergeant Aral was in here?"

"Uh, no," he said sheepishly. "And since when do you personally know Savinian POWs?"

"I was there when he was captured," I said with a casual shrug. I froze at an alarmed squawk from Felix.

"Tavi says hurry. The guards sent for the watch commander."

"We're out of time," I hissed to Zayne.

"So . . . did I convince you?" Dimitri asked me quietly as he held up his hand through the bars. I held his gaze and allowed my lips to curve up in a slight smile. My fingers had just brushed his when an angry bellow echoed down the stairs. His face paled. "Westbrook."

I spun toward Zayne, who had already hustled back to the closet. There was no way I could escape, but Zayne could. Since I wasn't directly under Westbrook's command, better him than me anyway.

"*Go!*" Boots pounded down the stairs, and I desperately waved Zayne away when he hesitated. "We can't have you grounded by him. Get out!"

The closet door *snicked* shut, and Dimitri darted back to his bench and dropped his head in his hands. Sergeant Aral leaned against the bars as if he were anticipating entertainment. I imagined being locked in the brig was boring, so I might as well put on a good show.

"Gods, you are the *worst* excuse for a rider I've ever seen," I snarled as I wrapped my hands around the bars of Dimitri's cell. The boots reached the guard station, but I kept my focus on Dimitri and ignored them as if lost to rage. "It's not enough you stole my wings, not enough you ruined my future—you had to drag me into your filthy schemes and nearly got me, got my *griffin* killed!"

I kept yelling at him, and Dimitri just sat with his shoulders slumped, head bowed and unresponsive—until a broad hand gripped my shoulder and roughly spun me around. Dimitri shot to his feet with a silent snarl, hands balled into fists. Fear rolled down my spine in an icy wave at the furious expression on Westbrook's face. Behind him, a pair of guards and the watch commander, a middle-aged captain with a face like a bulldog, hovered by the guard station, looking highly amused.

"How long has she been cursing out the poor bastard?" one of the guards muttered to Aral.

"Not long," he said with a rough chuckle. For whatever reason, the Savinian sergeant was playing along. Possibly because I'd helped treat his leg, possibly because I'd managed to entertain him. He grinned. "You missed the part where she implied he's a dickless wonder who has to pay for—"

"Gentlemen," Westbrook said over his shoulder in a pleasant tone. "Could you give me the room? I need to have a little counseling session with my rider."

Shit.

The guards retreated before I could tell them I wasn't *his* rider. Or beg them to stay. As soon as their footsteps had faded to silence, Westbrook tightened his grip on my shoulder to the point of pain. I'd have finger-shaped bruises by tonight . . . assuming I survived. Felix felt my fear, but neither entrance to the brig was sized for a griffin. He couldn't reach me down here.

"What did he say to you?" Westbrook asked, still in that pleasant tone. I wasn't fooled. He wasn't doing a very good job of hiding the ugliness lying beneath, if he was trying at all. I lifted my chin and held his gaze.

"Nothing." I awkwardly shrugged the shoulder he wasn't bruising to shit. "Suits me. I don't really give a damn about any of his excuses. The word of a traitor is worthless."

"Sir. The word of a traitor is worthless, *sir.*"

"Sir," I repeated quietly. Technically correct, and if it got me out of that brig, I'd call him sir at the end of every damn sentence. "No disrespect intended, sir."

He smiled, but there was nothing nice about it.

"Ah, but you're disrespecting my orders, Lieutenant Tavros. My orders were for nobody to talk with this traitor, but here you are. Good little griffin riders follow orders." He leaned closer until his sour breath washed over my face. "Or they get sent out on messenger runs they don't come back from."

Felix snarled in my mind, but I begged him to calm down, to wait. The situation was still salvageable—but then Westbrook's hand clamped down hard, and I couldn't hold back my gasp of pain.

"Are we clear, little griffin rider?"

Dimitri's restraint snapped.

"Let go of her," Dimitri said through gritted teeth, his eyes flashing bright with the presence of his dragon.

"Ah, the traitor speaks," Westbrook said maliciously.

"I will," he said with all the softness of a bared blade. "If you hurt her, I will."

It was a threat, one I wasn't supposed to understand, but Westbrook just barked a laugh.

"I could kill her right now and there isn't a damn thing you could do to stop me, boy." That smug little smile of his made a reappearance. "A tragic accident. Got a little too close to the Savinian raider and he strangled her. I tried to save her."

My eyes widened and I jerked out of his hold. I made it three steps toward the stairs before Westbrook grabbed me by the back of the neck and slammed me against the bars of Sergeant Aral's cell. I struggled wildly, desperately, as Dimitri roared in rage, but Westbrook was twice my size and easily pinned me against the unforgiving metal. One broad hand pinned my wrists above my head, while the other wrapped around my throat and squeezed.

"Tell me you're going to keep your mouth shut, Thompson," he said casually over his shoulder. The bastard wasn't even out of breath. "Or I'll snap her neck."

A booming roar reached us, audible even though we were separated by the length of the fort valley and layers of duracrete.

Riven.

"Kill her, and I'll make sure everyone knows what really happened down here," Dimitri said with the quite intensity of a vow.

"Who's going to believe you? How did she put it..." Westbrook's gaze drifted back to mine. "The word of a traitor is worthless."

Dimitri rattled the bars of his cage with a snarl of pure fury, trying to draw Westbrook's attention back to himself.

"I still have friends, Westbrook. They would listen."

"You mean the Serrano boy?" Westbrook barked a laugh. "I handed Zeddemore and his great beast over to the Savinians. You think I can't handle one little green and her rider? Decide now, Thompson."

His hand tightened. I kicked out wildly, but he blocked with his thigh, rendering my attack mostly ineffective. A pained grunt was his only reaction. I couldn't break his grip, couldn't breathe. My vision began to tunnel. I found Dimitri's enraged gaze over Westbrook's shoulder and held on to it. Panic flashed in his eyes before he closed them in defeat.

"I'll stay quiet." The words sounded as if they'd been dragged through hell before clawing their way out of his throat, all sharp edges and broken glass.

"That's better," Westbrook said.

He eased off on the pressure, and I drew in one ragged breath after another. Felix decided he was done waiting and surged forward. My eyes burned and watered as they adjusted to the weight of his soul, but Westbrook *smiled*.

"Hello, little griffin. I want you to listen very carefully. If you relay any of this, I will know. *My* little griffin friend will tell me, and I will make your rider suffer before I kill her. Do you understand?"

His grip loosened enough for me to speak. Felix raged, but I felt his understanding and reluctant compliance. We were as trapped as Dimitri.

"He understands." A hand skimmed along my side down to my belt ... where Callum's blade hung. I coughed to cover the sound of metal sliding free and hoped to hell I wasn't about to take a knife to the back. "Now let me go, *sir*. You've made your point. I shouldn't have disobeyed your orders."

I had to pretend Dimitri hadn't told me the truth, had to pretend that I thought Westbrook was just being a power-hungry dick, instead of a treacherous bastard.

"Maybe I should just kill you," he murmured as he tightend his hand around my throat again. "You've been an irritating little thorn since you showed up."

So much for pretending.

"Kill her and you lose your leverage," Dimitri said, face bone white beneath the flickering light cast by the torches.

Westbrook tilted his head, but there was nothing of the griffin in the predatory movement. "Maybe it would be worth it."

"Maybe *you* should listen to the lady and let her go," Sergeant Aral said mildly. Westbrook froze, his gaze snapping down to where Aral held my knife against his inner thigh. He tapped the blade once. "Or your dragon rider won't be the only dickless wonder down here."

Carefully, Westbrook released my throat and backed away from the blade, smile still frozen in place. My heart pounded in my ears. I had an honorable Savinian at my back, a traitorous Tennessan at my front, and an enraged griffin in my head.

"Everything okay down there?" the guard commander called down the stairs, shattering the tense silence. I took my chance.

"Everything's fine," I called back, hoping the rasp on my voice wasn't obvious. I lifted my chin and didn't look away from Westbrook. "Isn't it, sir?"

"You've got fire, little griffin rider." Westbrook abruptly laughed. "I remember you, you know. The dragon rider cadet who *almost* matched my checkride score. So much potential wasted on a griffin." His frozen smile finally melted away. "Make sure you say goodbye to your friend before you go. He won't be down here much longer."

Panic surged. He was going to kill Dimitri. I knew it as surely as I knew Felix wanted to kill Westbrook.

"And remember what I said." His gaze locked onto my own, still burning bright with Felix's soul. "One word from either of you, and I'll make sure you suffer."

A tremor ran through me, but I remained motionless as Westbrook spun on one heel and stalked up the stairs. As soon as he was out of sight, I stepped away from the cell bars and spun around. Sergeant Aral flipped my knife, caught it by the blade without looking, and extended it to me, hilt first. Cautiously, I took it back, the knife a reassuring weight in my shaking hand.

"Why?"

He'd taken a big risk to help me. Tennessan honored the POW treaty with Savinia, but Westbrook had no honor. And that bastard might not be in charge of the brig, but he'd just proved he could gain unsupervised access with a mere word to the guard commander.

"My sister was a griffin rider," he said almost idly as he limped back to his bench. His voice drifted out of the shadows, a melancholy whisper. "You remind me of her."

Was. Oh. I swallowed against the ache in my throat and turned back to Dimitri.

"We need to get you out of here."

"No," he shook his head, that familiar stubborn set to his jaw. "You need to get the hell out of Ashfall and find Major Zeddemore. Riven can tell Cassia where to go. If we're lucky, he's at the same POW camp as Cal. He's the only one we can trust to set things right."

Dimitri was right. Zeddemore could fix everything. He was also a moron if he thought I was leaving him here.

"Why not both?" I asked with a smirk.

I marched out of the brig with my shoulders back and my chin up. If Westbrook was watching, let him see I wasn't afraid. The fact that I was terrified was irrelevant. Time was slipping through my fingers with every controlled breath I took, and my mental breakdown would have to wait. Ruthlessly, I compartmentalized everything I didn't need and marched past the guards at the fortress entrance and into the brilliant sun of a gorgeous autumn day. There was no sign of Westbrook, but I could feel eyes, real or not, watching me. I bared my teeth in a humorless grin. *Let them watch.*

Felix waited just beyond the guards, wings mantled and tail lashing in pent-up aggression. I jerked my head and he fell in beside me as I stalked away from the fortress.

"That was close."

"Too close," he said as a growl rumbled in his chest. Red didn't tinge his mindspeech, it *drenched* it. His claws flexed. *"Going to kill him. He touched you, he dies."*

He sent a warm pulse of energy, and the ache in my throat diminished.

"What's going on?" Keaton and Tavi fell in on my other side, matching us stride for stride. Tavi's tail lashed in annoyance. "And why has Felix suddenly gone silent?"

I held up a hand for him to wait until we reached our predesignated rally point—the storage bunkers at the rear of the valley. As soon as we were safely out of sight, I told them everything. Fury burned in their amber eyes before I was even partway through. Zayne joined us before I finished, cobwebs in his hair and a matching fury in his eyes.

"We need help, but we can't go to the command staff, because *somebody* over there signed off on that messenger relay order for Harper," Zayne said as a distant expression flitted over his face. "Can't go to the other dragon riders because I have no idea who to trust anymore."

"We can't go to our commander or the other griffin riders for the same reason," Keaton added with a frustrated growl. "And I'm due to go out on patrol again this afternoon."

I huffed a soft laugh, because I suddenly knew *exactly* who we could trust. Felix didn't stop scanning the sky for a certain red dragon, but he did clack his beak in quiet agreement as he nudged his brother. Tavi tilted his head. His tail stopped lashing.

"With Nikos, right?" At Keaton's nod, I grinned, a real one this time. "Perfect. Tell him everything. He isn't our traitor, I'd bet my life on it."

"You're betting all our lives," Zayne muttered, his gaze still distant as his sharp mind chewed away at our myriad assortment of problems.

"But I'm willing to bet she's right," Keaton said. "Nikos hates everything the Savinians are, and he's been involved with at least one POW raid that I know of, probably more. We couldn't ask for better help. I'll make sure to grab extra gear for you before we go, and I'll brief him as soon as we're out of griffin hearing range."

He glanced up at the sun, gauging the time, and grimaced. It was past time for him to go, and we both knew it. I pulled him into a hard hug.

"Go. We'll meet you at Waystation Bravo-Two tonight." After we'd done what we needed to here. Keaton rested one hand on Tavi's shoulder and gave me a little side-eye.

"You're going to cause trouble before you leave, aren't you?"

"Oh, I'm going to cause *all* the trouble." I winked, he groaned, and then they were gone. My smile faded as I turned to Zayne. "Please tell me you have a plan for breaking out Dimitri."

"Oh, I figured that out hours ago. It's Riven I'll need your help with." His gaze sharpened as a disbelieving grin spread across his face. "Harper . . . Dimitri isn't a traitor, and Cal is *alive*."

Hope was a heady thing. Dangerous when false, but when it was true... A wild, joyful laugh escaped me, and I gripped Zayne by the shoulders.

"Dimitri isn't a traitor, and Cal is alive!" I didn't need to say the words to believe them. I just wanted to. I gave Zayne a fierce grin. "Let's go save our friends."

CHAPTER 25

We made it to Waystation Bravo-Two near midnight, the gold autumn moon casting a soft glow on black and green dragon wings as we circled high overhead. Tawny feathers caught the moonlight as Felix dropped like a stooping hawk, sweeping past the landing field, sharp gaze scouting for hidden dangers. Joy seeped through our bond, and I knew he'd spotted Tavi and Keaton. A muffled squawk drifted up, and I rolled my eyes as my griffin tackled his brother.

I reached back and tapped Zayne's leg. "Clear."

In short order, both Riven and Cassia landed. I slid down Cassia's side and gave her a grateful pat, too high on our escape to dwell on the fact that I'd just flown with my intended bondmate for the first and possibly only time. The dragons quickly abandoned the open landing field for the sheltering cover of the trees surrounding the waystation, though Riven was a little too eager and knocked one young pine over.

Muffling a laugh at Cassia's exasperated hiss, I led Zayne and a haggard Dimitri over to Keaton, keeping watch from the cold firepit. My amusement faded when he was the *only* one waiting for us.

"Where's Nikos?" Tension tightened my gut. If I'd bet wrong . . . but Keaton grinned.

"He said he knew where to find more help." Keaton passed me a loaded travel pack, my compact recurve bow, and two full quivers of our deadly little arrows. Then he surprised me by gesturing to two more travel packs, bows, and quivers. "Wasn't sure if Zayne would be able to secure supplies, but I figured our bows were similar enough to yours to be useful."

Dimitri accepted the supplies and weapons with a tired but grateful nod, while Zayne, ever curious, snatched one of the bows. He examined it, strung it, and snapped off a shot at another defenseless pine tree before nodding in satisfaction.

"They'll do. Thanks." Zayne cast a worried glance at the stars visible through the canopy. "How long did Nikos say he'd be?"

Keaton shrugged. "As long as it takes."

"We can't stay close to Ashfall for long, we . . . weren't exactly subtle when we left," Zayne added with a sideways glance at me. I scowled.

"It was *your* plan, genius. You can't get mad at me for exceeding expectations."

"Yes, we can," Dimitri muttered as he slumped down against the nearest tree, leaning his head back against the smooth bark and slitting his eyes mostly closed. I planted my hands on my hips and shifted my scowl to him.

"You needed a distraction to get Riven out, I gave you one."

"Harpy." Keaton bit back a grin. "What, exactly, did you do?"

I waved a hand. "Nothing much, just a harmless prank."

Zayne stared. "You got every griffin on base to drop live chickens on the dragon eyries, using both dragons and riders as target practice."

I smirked at the memory of all those ruffled feathers. And I wasn't thinking of the chickens.

"Don't forget the pigs we released in the dragon rider dining hall and dorms," I said gleefully.

Keaton dropped his face into his hands. Muffled laugher escaped in explosive little snorts. My grin widened.

"We labeled them too—pig one, two, four, and five." My head tilted. "I wonder how long they'll look for number three before they figure out there *isn't* one?"

Keaton finally got control of his laughter and was side-eyeing me much like Zayne had. "What about the griffin traitor?"

"What about them?" I gave him a sly grin. "We didn't *tell* the others it was a distraction to break out Riven. Felix and I just suggested a prank. With the way things have been going with the dragon riders lately, everyone jumped at the chance for a little friendly payback."

Keaton sighed. "Well, whoever our traitor is, I'm sure they've figured it out by now."

My shoulders slumped as the high dissipated, leaving only cold reality in its wake.

"I don't think it matters right now. Dimitri is an escaped prisoner, and Zayne and I are technically AWOL. That's if we haven't already been declared outright deserters." My gaze settled heavily on Keaton. "If you and Nikos come with us, you'll be deserters too. Dereliction of duty is the least of the charges they can level on you both if we fail."

Keaton advanced on me with a growl. "Stubborn bitch. Of course we're going with you. Even if Zeddemore isn't at that camp, your friend is, and that'll be one hell of a testimony all on its own."

Dimitri grunted something not quite a laugh.

"He's right. Cal vanished the same way Zeddemore did. It's got Westbrook's stink all over it. Even if they don't believe Cal, they'll listen to Artemis." He allowed his eyes to drift all the way closed. "We'll wait as long as we can for Nikos and his help to get here, but we need to move before dawn."

Felix and Tavi slunk out of the shadows, feathers and fur ruffled from their play fighting but their eyes sharp.

"We'll keep watch," Felix said firmly. *"Rest."*

Three hours later, in the dead of the night, Tavi let out a warning trill, waking everyone. By the time we'd rolled to our feet, Nikos trotted into the waystation on Erra, tired but triumphant with four rangers in tow. Sergeant Franks huffed a laugh when he saw me standing next to Keaton.

"Should've known you were involved, Tavros. Seems like anytime there's trouble, there you are."

"I could say the same about you guys." I grinned at the older ranger. Things had just gone from desperate to doable.

"This is our territory, griffin girl." Maddox winked as he adjusted the heavy war bow on his shoulder. "We're the only rangers out in this quadrant."

Nikos slid off Erra's back and dropped to the ground. I dipped my head in silent gratitude, and the older lieutenant returned the gesture, expression hard as his gaze shifted from me to the dragon riders.

"Is this all of us?"

Riven lifted his head and rumbled quietly from the trees. A moment later, Cassia eeled her way out of the thick brush, her hide changing and blending with the surrounding foliage as she moved.

Riley startled, one hand dropping to his dagger before he blew out a sharp breath.

"Shit," he squeaked. "I didn't even know that one was there."

"Green," Franks said by way of explanation. There was no doubt the more experienced ranger *had* known she was there. "Now, somebody show me where this POW camp is."

Zayne pulled out a map, while Keaton lit one of the waystation lanterns, keeping the flame just high enough for us to see without becoming a beacon in the night. Franks' brow furrowed as he studied the area marked out by Dimitri.

"This isn't Savinian territory. It's in the Smoke Mountains." He glanced at Nikos. "Isn't this near where we were tracking broken beasts a few months back?"

Nikos' gaze sharpened. "You're right."

"Remember the waterfall?" Franks smiled. "Good staging area. Thick enough canopy to shelter the dragons from sight, running water, and enough clearance over the river for dragon wings."

Nikos nodded. "It's perfect."

Relief smoothed the sharp edges of my anxiety. We didn't just have help, we had *competent* help.

Both Franks and Nikos had more experience than the rest of us combined, and Nikos technically outranked all of us, even if there was no rank between lieutenants. I was happy to let the burden rest on their shoulders, so long as the rest of us could do our part to help. Dimitri, who'd been carrying everything alone for so long, looked like he might collapse without the weight.

Before I could so much as shift toward him, Felix sidled up and offered him a furry shoulder. Dimitri blinked in surprise before he sighed and leaned on my griffin, but it was nothing compared to my shock.

Felix chuffed softly in amusement. *"Cows and compliments, remember?"*

He didn't fool me for a second. He knew Dimitri was as important to me as I was to him. I sent my griffin a wave of love and gratitude before I returned my attention to Nikos, who was planning our next steps with ruthless efficiency. He pinned Zayne with a direct stare.

"Can your dragons get all of us there before sunrise? It'll be close with two trips."

For caution's sake, neither rider had unsaddled their dragon when we'd arrived, and both wore double saddles. Riven was also large enough to carry a third rider behind the saddle, so long as we used a spare set of straps to secure him, which we'd brought. We hadn't known to account for the rangers, but Zayne laughed.

"We don't need two trips." He leaped from Cassia's extended elbow to the saddle, where he unstrapped a leather bundle and held it up with a triumphant grin. "I thought these might come in handy."

I stared at the carry harnesses. "You're a genius."

Maddox groaned. "Aw, man, I hate those things. Always feel like bait dangling on a hook."

While the rangers strapped on their harnesses, Dimitri got Nikos secured behind Riven's saddle. He slid down his dragon's side and walked over to me with confidence in every stride. I knew him though, and I caught the uncertainty hiding behind his dramatic eyes. He held out his hand, and I pretended I couldn't see how he crushed his flight cap with the other.

"Would you fly with us again, Harper? Riven says he won't let you fall." Dimitri's uncertainty melted away, replaced by raw determination. "*I* won't let you fall."

A shiver of remembered fear ran down my spine, but...you couldn't fly if you were afraid to fall.

I took his hand.

We made it to Franks' staging area just as the sun crested the horizon, golden streaks of light spearing across the red and orange sky. Dragons and griffins alike flew low over the treetops, descending one after the other over the fast-moving mountain river and landing on the shore. I slid off Riven's back and slowly scanned my surroundings.

The Smoke Mountains rose all around us, mist hovering near the peaks and valleys, curling around the trees. The sunlight was hazy and strange, and the forest rang with the calls of birds and animals I'd never heard before. The river itself seemed almost normal, but there was an odd sheen to the waterfall, an iridescence only glimpsed from the corner of my eye, and liquid-fast shapes darted beneath the surface of the water. Fish. Probably.

At Nikos' urging, we moved deeper into the trees until the river was out of sight, getting the dragons fully under cover. Both dragons and griffins were exhausted from the long flight, and I flexed my shoulders, trying to soothe an ache that wasn't mine. Felix mimicked the motion, stretching out sore wings as he padded under the sheltering canopy.

A shriek rang out somewhere deep in the tangled forest, and my hand dropped to Callum's knife.

"What the hell was that?" I whispered.

"Howler," Maddox said calmly as he unstrapped his carry harness and rolled it into a neat bundle. "It's like a big squirrel. Loud but mostly harmless."

A melodic cry answered it, sweet and high-pitched, rising and falling like a song. Now *his* hand dropped to his dagger.

"And that?" Keaton asked in the low voice of a griffin scout.

"Kirin," Maddox replied nearly soundlessly. The melodic cry repeated, further away, and his shoulders relaxed. "Think really big, single-horned carnivorous deer with the personality of a copper dragon."

"Just remember everything in these mountains not only *wants* to eat you, but is capable of eating you, and you'll be fine." Franks gestured sharply at his ranger team. "Standard perimeter sweep, and don't forget to check the cave behind the waterfall. There was a broken beast hiding back there last time, and I don't feel like getting eaten today."

The three rangers vanished into the undergrowth, but Franks paused long enough to address the rest of us.

"Stay here and get some rest. We've bought ourselves time to scout and plan. No need to act hasty and get ourselves caught, understand?"

Nikos snorted, his eyes bloodshot but alert. "This ain't my first rodeo, Franks. We'll settle in."

Franks disappeared into the forest without a whisper of sound to betray his passage.

"Can either of your dragons reach the ones in the POW camp?" Nikos asked. Both riders shook their heads.

"Too far," Dimitri said tiredly as Riven sprawled out in the shade of the biggest oak I'd ever seen. Cassia nudged her rider fondly before she slid between the trees, Erra stalking along behind her.

"She's hungry," Zayne said in weary explanation as he collapsed next to Dimitri, who had already passed out against his dragon's side.

Two sleepless nights in a row had caught up to him. But I wasn't tired, and I didn't want to settle in. I wanted to *move*.

And I wasn't the only one.

Keaton and I exchanged a glance as Felix and Tavi flanked us, tails lashing, wing-sore but restless. We turned to Nikos, and he sighed.

"You two want to be hasty, don't you?" He shrugged as he settled with his back to a tree where he could keep an eye on everything. "Don't be stupid, but get me a layout of that POW camp before nightfall."

We grinned, but Zayne leaned forward. "I could go with you. Seeing it with my own eyes could help me devise a better plan."

I gestured for Keaton to get ready and crouched in front of Zayne. "You can't move like we can. We'll bring back all the details you need."

Before I could rise, Dimitri's eyes slit open, the shadows underneath so deep they looked like bruises. "Be careful, hotshot," he mumbled.

A flippant response balanced on the tip of my tongue until I noticed his genuine concern. "We'll be careful. This is what we do."

As the dragon flew, we weren't all that far from the POW camp. On foot, it took us hours to wind our way through the mountains. We rode our griffins and had our bows out and strung, arrows in hand. We weren't just in unfamiliar territory, we were in the damn Smoke Mountains, where monsters dwelled. Griffin ears twitched nonstop, and tension knotted our shoulders until we were strung tight as our bows. Too many strange noises, too much mist that wasn't mist obscuring our sight lines. We rode through a patch, and it left no moisture on our skin and an odd taste coating the back of our throats. We avoided the mists after that.

Fortunately, Dimitri had marked the location true on the map, and getting from point A to point B was basic land nav, even with the minor detours we made along the way. By midmorning, we'd gotten as close to the POW camp as we dared and stopped just inside the upper tree line of a particularly craggy mountain. A frigid breeze dried the sweat on our faces, whistling through the jagged spines of rock that pierced the achingly blue sky above. We dismounted and low crawled to a ledge overlooking the narrow valley stretched out below us.

The POW camp was located in the dead center, nothing but open ground all around it with layers of singe marks, as if they'd burned out any vegetation repeatedly. We were so high up the details were lost to human eyes, but our griffins could see just fine.

A tug, a fond invitation, and I dropped into Felix's mind. No hurry this time, no desperation. I gave my belly a moment to settle, gave my mind a moment to accept the increased visual input, and then looked through my griffin's eyes.

High, smooth gray walls enclosed a massive rectangular stockade. Rolls of concertina wire were gathered along the base, and deep score marks scarred the walls from the ground to almost twenty feet up. Claw marks.

Cold fear shot through me. *"Are those walls duracrete?"*

"Shit . . . yeah, I think so." The ledge was narrow enough we were pressed against one another, and I felt the tension bunching Keaton's muscles. *"Even dragons can't do that."*

"Broken beasts can," Felix relayed in Tavi's slightly deeper tone.

Felix turned his attention to the top of the walls, where anti-air ballistae were placed at regular intervals, manned by pairs of Savinian regulars. A massive gate, large enough for most dragons, was set in the south wall, sealed shut and heavily guarded. Within the stockade were the faint outlines of buildings long gone, a wooden barracks built against the southeast corner, so new sap still seeped in places, and dragons. Fourteen of them, including the unmistakable shining black armored hide of Maximus, chained in the very center.

All of the dragons were chained around their legs, but they must have feared Maximus the most, because they'd thrown additional chains across his back, and he wore a thick collar around his neck with two more chains, keeping his head close to the ground. His yellow eyes were focused with unwavering intensity on a tiny building near the rear of the stockade.

Felix sharped his gaze on that building, and everything leapt into even greater clarity. Shattered remnants of duracrete outlined a large square around the oddly sloped rectangular structure. There was a heavy steel door at the tall, narrow end, manned by alert guards with a pair of ballistae armed with dragon lances set on either side, both aimed at Maximus. Felix tilted his head, the change in our perspective just enough for the odd construction to make sense. Whatever building had originally been there was long gone, but the *stairs* remained.

Dread sank through my gut like a stone. The riders were imprisoned underground, where the dragons couldn't reach them. Not even the griffins could fit through that door. We'd have to free the riders ourselves.

"Looks like a pre-War facility the Savinians found and repurposed," Keaton said grimly. At Tavi's urging, Felix shifted his gaze slightly to the right, where a small, square panel was inset next to the door. Just like the hatchery and library back at the academy. *"Going to be tough to get past that."*

Confusion twisted through me before I remembered—Keaton had never been inside the dragon crèche, possibly not even the library on the dragon rider campus. He didn't know how those doors worked. Or rather, how they *didn't*. I grinned.

"Without the magic to power those little panels, there's no way to engage the locks manually. The best they can do is bar them from the inside."

"And the griffins could probably break it down."

"Exactly."

Felix relaxed his eyes, returning to a less focused view as he scanned the rest of the facility. Excitement surged as he tugged on my mind. There was a small postern gate in the north wall maybe thirty meters behind the underground entrance. It was big enough for the griffins, but still barred, if not as heavily guarded as the main gate. As barren as the valley was, there was no way a dragon could get a rider over the wall to open the gate for the rest of us. Not even Cassia with a green's ability to blend in—but griffins are sneaky.

Matching excitement rose as I nudged Felix, and he looked up and up, to the towering mountain rising behind the stockade.

"Do you think we could make it over the wall?"

"Definitely." Felix traced my proposed glide path, calculating the angle and distance to the battlements over the gate, before his gaze caught on the wicked glint of sunlight on dragon lances and flechette artillery rounds. His confidence wavered. *"Assuming they don't turn us into a pincushion midair."*

"We'd need a good distraction," I said thoughtfully as we looked at the barracks again. *"Firebombs would be nice to have right about now, but I bet you Riven could flatten that whole structure and cause a nice bit of chaos if Cassia provides top cover."*

Felix hummed in agreement, his beak clacking softly.

"Seen enough?" Keaton asked long minutes later. Felix and I took one last look at the captured dragons, noting any injuries that might hinder their escape. Horror twisted through my soul at the number of scars littering hide and cutting through scales, at the way their ribs showed, at the dullness of their eyes. My jaw tightened. The sooner we got them out, the better.

"Yeah, even Zayne should be happy—"

A wailing roar echoed off the mountains. We all hugged the rocky ledge and went motionless, barely daring to breathe. Another wailing roar answered it.

Coppers.

Four of the spiky assholes. They flew into the valley at a lower altitude than our ledge, thank fuck, and circled over the stockade. One landed and perched on the southern wall over the gate.

"Standard patrol, you think?" Keaton asked. The copper's rider dismounted and spoke with a guard, probably the commander. It didn't look like the guard was speaking much. The other three circled over the stockade, and their wailing roars held a mocking edge as they glared down at the chained dragons below. *"Or delivering new orders?"*

The rider hopped back into the saddle and his dragon took off, arrowing back the way they'd come. With a final derisive, spine-rattling roar, the other three coppers formed up on their flight leader and were gone. I drew in the first deep breath I'd taken in far too long.

"If it's a regular patrol, we'll have to account for them—" Maximus flexed his wings irritably before folding them tightly across his back, revealing the lithe gray dragon chained behind him. There were *fifteen* dragons, not fourteen. I froze, utterly, completely. *"Artemis."*

Hot tears tracked down my cheeks at the undeniable proof that Callum was still alive. It wasn't that I hadn't believed Dimitri, I *had*, but so many weeks had passed since he'd seen her.

Hold on, just hold on a little longer. We're coming for you.

On our way back to camp, we passed Riley on a narrow game trail. The young ranger gave us a friendly grin as he slipped past with a small bow in hand.

"Franks asked me to do a little hunting. I'll try to bring back enough for your griffs too." He spun back around. "Oh, and Maddox and Buchanan are out on deep perimeter sweep. Franks saw signs of broken beasts, so be careful."

With that, he was gone, vanishing into the undergrowth nearly as silently as the other rangers.

"He didn't seem all that concerned," Keaton remarked in amusement. Tavi clacked his beak and trilled a quiet laugh.

"Nope." Felix gathered himself to leap over a fallen giant of the forest. My thighs tightened around his sides almost on autopilot, and I leaned forward slightly as we soared over the half-rotted trunk. "Think Riley's ever *seen* a broken beast?"

Tavi chose to jump onto the trunk instead of clearing it, and prowled along the top for a few paces, tail idly flicking back and forth. Keaton grinned down at me.

"No. Want to wager on whether or not his voice shoots up an octave again?"

I snorted as they leaped down and paced alongside us once more. "No bet."

As we rode through dappled sunlight and shade, the quiet roar of the waterfall steadily grew louder. As the strange, sparkling waters finally came into view, the ear-piercing shriek of a howler rang out from almost directly overhead. None of us so much as twitched. We'd heard it so many times this morning we'd become numb to it. I glanced up into the tangled canopy in time to catch a glimpse of something large, brown, and fluffy racing along the branches. It shrieked again, a warning cry. Again, Felix and I ignored it.

Tavi didn't.

The slightly older griffin paused, one foot in the air, tufted ears perked forward. Felix jerked to a halt a step later. Keaton and I set arrow to string and snapped our bows up, scanning the thick undergrowth for threats.

"Damn it, I should've known teasing Riley would jinx us," I muttered.

"It's not a broken beast," Felix relayed for Tavi. A second later, we heard what Tavi had—a muffled, enraged shout. I lurched forward, one hand digging into Felix's feathered neck.

"Dimitri!"

Keaton latched onto my arm. *"We send the griffins forward. Brush is too thick around our camp for us to move silently, but they can."*

Reluctantly, I slid off Felix's back and joined Keaton on the ground when all I wanted to do was charge forward. Our griffins eyed the tangled undergrowth, then the canopy. A chuff of agreement, and they scaled one of the massive oaks, claws sinking deep and tails lashing as they climbed. Within seconds they were out of sight, hidden by bright foliage and tangled branches.

Keaton and I eased deeper into the brush, away from the game trail we'd used. Barely a minute passed before alarm raced along the bond. Keaton stiffened, and his eyes glazed over. Felix tugged, and I let him pull me into his mind, faster than I could drop on my own. Panic shivered through me.

Savinians had found our camp.

Dimitri was on his knees, arms held behind his back by one soldier and a knife held to his throat by another. Blood sheeted down the thin skin of his neck, and one side of his jaw was red and swollen. A deep, rumbling growl spilled from Riven's maw, but with his rider's life threatened, he remained motionless beneath the ancient oak that Felix had hidden himself in. Zayne was also on his knees, but his head hung slack, and it was clear the only thing holding him up was the soldier gripping his arms. Nikos knelt beside him, fury contorting his features, burning gaze fixed not on the Savinian soldiers, but on *Franks*.

Franks, who wasn't bound or restrained. Franks, who was casually talking with a Savinian officer. Franks, who we'd trusted without question or reservation . . . but who was always nearby when something went wrong, going all the way back to the broken beasts unleashed on the academy training grounds.

My nails dug into my palms as rage ricocheted through the bond, my thoughts perfectly in sync with my griffin's. We wanted nothing more than to drop out of that tree and rip out his throat, but we couldn't. Not without risking everyone. Now I understood Dimitri's helpless rage, and I desperately wished I didn't.

"I'm going to kill you, Franks," Nikos said with a guttural snarl, straining against the soldier holding him down and getting exactly nowhere. Like most griffin riders, he wasn't a large man, and the soldier had him beat in size and leverage.

Franks ignored him in favor of rummaging in the leather pouch the officer had tossed him. There was the faint *clink* of metal on metal, the glint of sunlight on gold, before the old ranger tightened the drawstrings with a frown.

"You're short, my friend."

The officer, who was rather short, gestured to his three captives. "The bounty is for live dragon riders, I paid for live dragon riders."

"You only gave me enough for two," Franks growled. The officer snorted and eyed Nikos' riding leathers pointedly, just different enough from flying leathers to be obvious.

"Which is exactly what you gave me. Two dragon riders. There's no bounty for live griffin riders."

"So there isn't." Franks sighed and met Nikos' enraged eyes. "Sorry, lad, I tried."

He flicked one hand. A flash of silver sliced through the air, and a throwing knife sank into Nikos' chest. He gurgled, spasmed, and slumped in the soldier's hold. The soldier let him fall with a grimace.

Somewhere deep in the forest, a griffin screamed.

No! I clamped a hand over my mouth to muffle my own cry.

"There's a bounty for dead griffin riders," Franks said calmly, as if he hadn't just murdered Nikos in cold blood.

The Savinian officer barked a laugh and tossed over a gold coin. Just one. Fury and grief spiraled through our entangled souls as Felix's claws sank deeper into the branch. A single gold coin was all our lives were worth to them.

"Always a pleasure doing business with you, Franks." He tilted his head toward Zayne. "Any idea where his dragon is?"

"I wouldn't worry about it. You know she'll come running with just a little pressure applied to the rider." Franks gave Dimitri a little salute, a glimmer of respect in his eyes. "You bought the green a little time by knocking him unconscious, but that's all you accomplished. Still, that took balls, lad."

Dimitri said nothing.

He'd been backed into a corner again.

"I've got my men out looking for the other griffin riders," the officer said to Franks before he tossed him a second gold coin. "Consider this a finder's fee."

Franks caught it as easily as the first. "Heh. Maybe I'll actually be able to retire before I die of old age—"

His head snapped around.

"Franks? What's going on?" Riley's voice shot up an octave as he dropped the deer he'd dragged back and raised his hunting bow. His wide eyes darted across the camp, taking everything in, before latching onto his sergeant's face, silently begging for an explanation.

"Aw, damn it, kid." Franks sighed. "You weren't supposed to be back so soon."

Another flick of his hand, another flash of silver, and the young ranger gagged, clawing desperately at his throat, tearing the throwing knife free. Blood cascaded down his pale skin, and he fell to his knees, his terrified gaze never leaving Franks. The older ranger looked away.

Felix and I didn't look away. We were the eyes. We would bear witness. We watched Riley die and raged that we could do nothing to save him. To save any of them.

Keaton squeezed my hand hard, a silent signal to return, and I yanked myself back into my own mind. His eyes were hard as he panned his gaze around the trees. Rustling in the brush from one direction, footsteps from those not quite as practiced in stealth from several others—a net, steadily tightening around us. Nowhere to hide, and no time to get to our griffins. A bolt of terror raced down my spine at a wet, snuffling sound from the rustling brush.

"Broken hounds!" I cried out, both a warning to Felix and a request for relay.

I jerked Keaton into a silent run toward the water. It was our only chance to escape.

Keaton followed my lead and didn't hesitate to slide into the river with me, right at the base of the waterfall. Icy cold water pounded down on us, and my boots slipped on a slick rock hidden by the churning waves. Before I could get swept away, Keaton grabbed my arm and tugged me toward the opposite bank, but we froze at a muffled shout.

They were already across the river.

Keaton's frantic gaze landed on the waterfall, and he dragged me through the deluge and into the tiny, water-carved cave behind it.

It was a horrible idea, but it was our only option.

We treaded water in a deep pool, our feet not even brushing against the bottom. Enough dim light filtered through the iridescent waterfall to highlight a narrow shelf of rock running along the left side. There was nothing else to the cave, just jagged rocks above and dark water below. Something slithered past my thigh, and I thrashed my leg, clamping my jaw shut on a shriek.

A dissonant baying howl, cut off almost as soon as it began, reached us through the water, along with the distorted voices of men. Not so distorted that we couldn't understand them.

"The dogs caught their scent, sir, but they lost it at the water. Think they crossed?"

"Or went downstream. I'll send a squad in both directions. You two check behind the waterfall."

Eyes wide, I locked gazes with Keaton. He took an exaggerated deep breath, I copied him, and we ducked under the water. Full lungs wanted to float, but we swam to the bottom of the pool, maybe seven feet deep at the most, and gripped slime-slicked rocks to hold ourselves down.

Long seconds crawled past before Keaton tapped my arm and pointed up. Above us, shadowy figures peered down into the pool. Common soldiers didn't have griffin eyes. They couldn't see us through the dark, churning waters, but we were trapped. Surfacing while they were up there was a death sentence. Our only chance was to outlast them, but I couldn't hold my breath forever, or even as long as Keaton could. My lungs began to burn, but those damn shadowy shapes lingered. One lazily poked a staff, or maybe a spear, into the water, getting nowhere near us.

Desperately, I looked at Keaton, his face bare inches from my own. Gray sparks danced at the edges of my vision and my body jerked, desperate for the air I was denying it. His eyes widened in dismay, and one hand reached for mine. Felix relayed for us, fear tightening his voice.

"Hold on, they're almost gone."

"Can't. Can't. Can't."

I tried, I really did, but my body overruled my mind. It didn't care that we were surrounded by water, it only cared that I wasn't giving it what it needed to survive. My mouth opened. Water poured in and I choked, mere feet away from air, from life.

Felix howled within my mind. *"They're gone, they're gone!"*

"I've got you!" Keaton lunged forward, one arm wrapping around my waist as he pushed off the slick bottom of the pool with a powerful kick. Felix screamed at me to hold on. The surface of the pool shimmered overhead, close enough to touch, but my vision tunneled to a pinpoint.

Everything went dark.

I came back to Keaton cursing viciously and pressing on my chest, hard enough to hurt, hard enough to expel the water from my lungs. I rolled over onto my side, hugging the clammy rocks and sucking in air between coughing up water and worse. When I was done, I rolled back over and stared up at the rocky ceiling, murmuring silent reassurances to Felix. My eyes watered, my throat burned, and my ribs *ached*, but I could breathe.

Keaton leaned over me. Water dripped from his face onto mine.

"Never do that to me again," he whispered harshly, eyes burning bright with rage. I tried to speak, couldn't, and he hauled me up into his arms and hugged me hard enough my bones creaked. "Stupid bitch. Stupid stubborn bitch. Too stubborn to die, you hear me?"

"Can't . . . breathe," I croaked.

He stilled. Then he pulled back and glared at me.

"Too soon?" I gave him a shaky smile. He closed his eyes and his shoulders sagged.

"I hate you, Harpy."

"Love you too, brother." I shoved wet strands of hair out of my face and enjoyed the simple act of breathing for a moment. Keaton's amber gaze was fixed on my face, traces of fear lingering in his eyes. No time for that, because then I'd have to acknowledge my own, and I could only compartmentalize so much. I rolled my shoulders back. "Are the Savinians gone?"

He nodded, the fear vanishing behind his impassive mask. "Tavi watched them go. They took Dimitri and Zayne, and Riven followed. We need to do something about Franks."

My lip curled. "I know."

Felix startled and yanked me into his mind without warning. My recently abused stomach protested the hard landing, and everything seemed blurry and out of focus. Felix curled around my mind with a whisper of apology, and the camp snapped into sharp clarity.

Franks stood with his back to Riley, scrubbing his face with a weary slump to his shoulders. But that wasn't where Felix was focused. It was on Nikos, rising up on one knee, Riley's short hunting bow in hand, deadly little arrow nocked. He drew the string back, grim determination in the set of his jaw and rage burning in his eyes.

"Hey, Franks!" he ground out. "You missed."

Franks spun around, one hand darting for a throwing knife on his belt, but Nikos was faster and his aim fucking perfect. An arrow sprouted from Franks' eye as if by magic, buried up to the fletching. The treacherous ranger dropped without a sound.

The bow slipped from Nikos' shaking hands. His head bowed as he pressed one hand against his blood-drenched chest and braced the other against the ground. His ragged breaths were the loudest noise in that clearing. I yanked myself back to my own head. Keaton was already on his feet, and he pulled me into a headlong run back to camp.

In the few minutes it took us to get there, Nikos had fallen unconscious. Franks might have missed his heart, but the knife was lodged deep in his chest, and the pinkish foam around the edges warned of a lung puncture. We had to get the knife out and seal it up, quickly.

Our griffins paced around us, tails lashing, wings rustling, as we worked to save his life. Their heads snapped up in unison, purple and amber eyes focused with predatory intensity on the trees. Maddox and Buchanan stepped into sight moments later. They both halted abruptly, taking in their dead companions, the wounded Nikos, and the missing dragon riders.

And then Maddox noticed the arrow in Franks' eye. A griffin scout arrow.

"What . . . what the actual fuck happened?" he roared, rage overriding discipline and making his voice far too loud for our precarious situation.

"Franks was a gods damned traitor is what happened," Keaton growled, bloody hands pressed tight to Nikos' chest, keeping pressure on the wound. I bit back a groan. Of all the times for him to lose his temper, he had to pick now.

Angry denials rang out, fists were clenched, tensions rose. Hurriedly, I got the knife wound cleaned and tightly bandaged before I rose to my feet. We were balanced on a razor's edge, and I glanced around the camp, desperately looking for a way to tip the balance in our favor. My gaze landed on a leather pouch, half hidden under Franks' body.

"Check the pouch! The Savinian officer paid Franks."

Snarling, Maddox stomped over, snatched the pouch, ripped it open—and froze. He shook his head as he stared at the gold coins, stamped with the crest of the Lord of Savinia.

"Not possible," he whispered.

"Mad, this was Franks'." Buchanan had knelt beside Riley and held up a bloody throwing knife. The big ranger gently closed Riley's eyes before he stood up and stared at Franks, his expression terrible. "Tell us everything."

By the time we'd brought them up to speed, a distressed green dragon had returned, a limp griffin draped over her back. Erra was nearly unconscious, giving everything she had to keep Nikos alive, but she woke up enough to slide off Cassia's back and curl up around her rider. A low whine escaped the green dragon's jaws, and I looked up at her.

"We're going to get him back." My nails dug into my palms. "We're going to get them all back."

Maddox jerked his head up from where he sat next to Franks in the dirt, his eyes burning with fury and barely suppressed pain.

"You're insane," he said flatly. "This was risky enough before, but we're down to four fighters, two griffins, and one riderless dragon who won't fight!"

"Can't, not won't." My shoulders rolled back and I held his gaze. "It's all right if you want to turn back. I won't blame you. But I *can't*."

"Why?" he demanded.

Keaton snorted and ticked off the reasons on his fingers. "AWOL, dereliction, desertion, and let's not forget Westbrook will probably kill her if she goes back without Major Zeddemore."

"There's that," I agreed as my jaw tightened. "And that camp has all three of my boys. I'm not leaving without them. They're morons, but they're *mine*."

"Do you have a plan?" Buchanan asked as he examined his heavy war bow with a critical eye, not bothering to glance up.

"Yeah, break out the riders."

"That's not a plan, that's a goal." Maddox shot to his feet and paced from one end of our little camp to the other, his face alternatively sunlit and shadowed. Every time he passed Franks' body, his stride faltered. "And even if you break out the riders, so what? The dragons are still chained."

"Those chains can't hold the dragons, they're just there to make the guards feel better." I glanced up and sidestepped until I could judge the angle of the sun. So much had happened and it was barely past noon. We had some time before dark, but not much, not with the days growing ever shorter. "They're only really chained by their riders. Break out the riders and the dragons will do the rest."

A melodic cry rang out from the west, a faster song than before, dark with warning and anger. Another kirin answered, before both were silenced by the keening wail of a broken beast. The whole forest seemed to hold its breath. Even the howlers shut up. We all froze, except for Buchanan, who snapped his bow up, hard eyes scanning the thick trees. The keening wail didn't repeat, and gradually the strange things that lived in the canopy resumed their normal racket.

Maddox's shoulders relaxed and he looked at his fellow ranger, picking up the thread of the conversation. "She's crazy."

"She's right," Buchanan said quietly as he slung his bow over his shoulder. "Was on the last POW camp raid with Nikos and . . . Franks. Small team, but we got the riders loose and then all *hell* broke loose." He gave our griffins a considering look. "Can they get that postern gate open?"

"Not exactly." I drew in a deep breath and very carefully didn't look at Keaton. "But I can."

A beat of silence, then a vicious curse in his gruff voice. Reluctantly, I glanced at Keaton and winced. He looked seconds away from murdering me, or having his griffin sit on me—and Tavi looked as if he were seriously considering it.

"Tavi and I can't make the glide. I'm too heavy." Keaton frowned down at me, that same fear peeking out from behind his impassive mask. "You'll be on your own."

"Only until I get that gate open," I shot back with an impish smile. He looked up as if praying for patience. Or a new sister.

Felix snapped at Tavi irritably, but the other griffin narrowed amber eyes and snapped back. Felix sighed and relayed.

"My brother can be overconfident, but never when it comes to your safety. If he thinks you can do it, I believe him." Tavi paced forward and stared into my eyes. *"Do you?"*

"Yes," I said without hesitation, nothing but confidence in my bondmate's abilities—and my own. Lifting a hand, I waited for permission. Always more reserved than his twin, Tavi dipped his beak in a nod. I stroked my fingers through his feathers before I wrapped my arms around his neck and whispered into his tufted ear. "We won't fail."

Tavi nuzzled me, stepped back, and looked at his bondmate. Keaton's hands tightened into fists and he let out a slow, controlled breath before he nodded agreement.

"If Harpy can get the gate open, the griffins can bust open the door to the underground facility. Then they distract while we free the riders. It could work." He fixed Maddox with a fierce stare. "Are you in or out?"

The silence stretched to the breaking point before the ranger blew out a breath.

"Yeah, I guess we're all fucking crazy. But I'm not doing it for you riders." Maddox flexed his jaw and looked at Riley. "I'm doing it for him."

"He died for this, got to see it through now," Buchanan said in agreement. "But what about him?"

The big ranger nodded at Nikos, lying so damn pale and still against his griffin. The thick bandage wrapped around his chest was already bloodstained. If we didn't get him to a medic, we were going to lose him. My gaze flicked to Erra, her reddish-brown feathers already dull. Lose *both* of them.

A low growl rumbled in the green dragon's chest, her attention fixed over the eastern horizon, where her rider had been taken. Her wings rustled, stretched, flexed. My breath caught, and my gaze snapped from those glorious wings to Nikos. I darted in front of Cassia with my hands up and she snarled. My gut tightened, reminded that even greens could be vicious, but I held my ground.

"Can you wait?" I asked her desperately. "I know Zayne will call for you when he wakes. They won't give him a choice. But right now we need your help."

Cassia hesitated. Tilted her head in silent question. I pointed at Nikos.

"Can you fly them to . . ." I trailed off and looked at the rangers.

"Bristol's the closest place with a medic on staff," Buchanan said.

"Can you take them? They'll die without your help." I held my breath until she dipped her head, and I went dizzy with relief. "Thank you."

Working quickly, we got both griffin and rider secured to her saddle, though it took a little ingenuity to properly strap Erra down. The green dragon stood to her full height and stretched out her wings again in preparation to take off—and an idea that had been churning in the back of my mind snapped into crystal clarity. Nausea rose up along with guilt.

Forgive me, Zayne.

"Cassia!" I called out, speaking her name, the name I'd picked out for her, out loud for the first time. She looked down at me with Zayne's beautiful green and gold eyes. "When he calls for you, ask him if he can hold out until nightfall."

She growled, long and low, but I held her gaze.

"I know it's not fair to ask it of him, or you, but we need every advantage we can get if we're going to save them."

After a short eternity, she dipped her head in a nod.

"If he hasn't called you by full dark, go to him. When you're close enough, I need you give the POW dragons a message." I glanced at the others with a sharp grin. "I've got an idea that might make this a little less crazy."

CHAPTER 26

A cold wind whipped strands of my hair into my eyes and ruffled Felix's feathers. Overhead, the first stars of the evening shone bright, while twilight's gloom hung over the valley below, all dusky blues and purples and deepening shadows.

The wind gusted harder, and I shivered. We'd had to climb high to get the glide path Felix wanted, and there was no shelter to be had up here. Below, so far below I didn't really want to think about it, Keaton, Tavi, and the rangers were in position, as close to the postern gate as they could get without breaking cover and crossing into the burned zone around the stockade walls. The POW camp looked like a child's toy from up here, and I shuddered from more than the cold. One mistake...

Resolve stiffened my spine. We were fucking amazing at gliding. We could do it. Dimitri, and Zayne, and Callum, and everyone else held prisoner down there was counting on us.

We were just waiting for the cover of darkness—and one last, vital player.

Time crawled past, but we waited patiently, flexing muscles and stretching wings to stay limber and warm. Waiting was good. Waiting meant the Savinians hadn't broken Zayne, hadn't forced Cassia to return before we were ready. Relief whispered through me as true night blanketed the valley. *Well done, Zayne.*

I just hoped defiance hadn't cost him too much. He'd always been the most outwardly mild of the four of us, but he had a buried stubborn streak that rivaled my own.

Torches were lit along the walls and within the stockade, pushing back the dark. I leaned forward and buried cold fingers in Felix's feathers, sniffling as the wind froze my nose and the tips of my ears. My legs were warm at least, pressed between my griffin's warm sides and warmer wings. He wore only a bareback pad. No stirrups to steady my feet, no saddle to grip . . . but we weren't stupid. We'd taken the last set of straps from Cassia's saddle before she left, and I was as secured to his back as possible. I brushed frozen hands along the straps for the dozenth time, feeling the ghost of Dimitri's arms around me as I adjusted them to hold my legs a little tighter without cutting off circulation.

Felix's head snapped up as an echoing roar shattered the quiet night. That was our warning call. His claws extended, scraping against the rocky slope, and his tail lashed in growing anticipation. My heart pounded a frantic rhythm in my chest, but my breath was steady as I checked my weapons one last time—bow and sealed quiver of arrows securely strapped to my back, and Callum's knife strapped to my hip.

A second echoing roar, and Felix's wings unfurled, cold air kissing my legs. My thighs flexed, tightened, and I rested my hands on either side of his neck.

Cassia roared a third time as she slowly approached from the south, drawing every Savinian eye—and then every last dragon chained to the ground lifted their heads and roared.

"*Go!*"

No room for fear, no time for second thoughts. Felix bounded down the slope and counted down his strides.

"*Three, two, one, and go!*"

Felix gave a mighty leap with his back legs and launched us into open air, his wings stretched as wide as possible. Despite everything, joy still spiraled up within my soul as I felt the wind on my face, a joy that was echoed by my bondmate. Feathers twitched and flight muscles made a thousand tiny adjustments as he glided away from the mountain, toward the POW camp, the walls growing larger with every steady breath we took.

No thermals stirred the cold air, but there were plenty of wind gusts curling around the mountain, threatening to blow us off course. Thank fuck for the flight straps, because in the next instant a sharp gust of wind knocked Felix sideways. My heart leaped into my throat, but I kept my legs tight and my gaze resolutely fixed between his tufted ears and not on the ground, so very far below.

I wasn't going to fall. We were going to make it.

Grunting with effort, Felix beat his wings hard and righted himself. The battlements rushed up with frightening speed, but I had faith in my bondmate. He was all heart, and he wasn't going to let us fail. Wings flared and beat hard, slowing us to something survivable.

He slammed down onto the wall in the shadows between two anti-air emplacements. An involuntary grunt escaped my clenched jaw at the bone-rattling impact, but fierce triumph thrummed through our entangled souls. Neither pair of Savinian soldiers had noticed us, too caught up in leaning over the inner wall, staring at the dragons as they roared and thrashed their wings and generally made a spectacle of themselves. Only Maximus held himself calm and quiet.

Letting out a shuddering breath, I forced cold-numbed fingers to cooperate. Thick leather straps loosened, and I slid off Felix's back, thighs shaking from gripping his sides so tight. I pulled my bow off my back, nocked an arrow, and put a little tension on the string. Together, we crept along the battlement toward the stairs at the center of the wall, hidden only by shadows. Felix kept a wary eye on the artillery team behind us, while I watched the one on the other side of the stairs.

Despite the racket the dragons were making, something gave us away. A scrape of a claw, the rattle of an arrow. It didn't matter. One of the guards glanced over his shoulder and saw us. His warning cry was lost beneath a booming roar—Riven, I think. He spun around, and my arrow sank into his throat. His cry choked off as blood trickled from his mouth, soaked the front of his uniform. For an instant, I saw Riley in his young, terrified face. I hardened my heart against soft brown eyes and snapped off another shot with steady hands, taking out the second guard, while Felix silently savaged the other set.

The guards at the corner emplacements heard and saw nothing.

Felix prowled back on velvet paws, blood dripping from his beak. I slung myself over his back, he spread his wings, and we ignored the stairs in favor of a controlled fall to the ground, choosing speed over stealth. It was only a matter of time before the other guards noticed their slaughtered brothers.

Bounding forward, we charged the postern gate. Two guards stared at us in shock and no little terror. I gripped with my thighs and raised my bow. One guard pivoted a stand-mounted, single-man ballista toward us, torchlight glinting off the wicked bolt. Not a dragon lance, but more than big enough to take out human or griffin.

My arrow took him through the heart. The other fell beneath Felix's claws. I slid off his back, hurriedly slinging my bow over my shoulder before I extinguished the torches, giving us the barest amount of concealment. The heavy waft of smoke stung my eyes, but I blinked them clear and turned to the gate. If it had just been barred, Felix or Tavi could've handled it, but it was bolted, top, bottom, and two across the middle. Thick bars, meant to keep out broken beasts, but still too small for griffin beak or claw to manipulate.

Tension bunched my shoulders as I worked. It felt as if I had a target square on my back. Felix crouched low behind me, watching for the first signs of discovery. Three bolts slid back easily, but the forth was rusted, and I couldn't rotate it far enough to slide it free. Hissing in frustration and rising panic, I wiggled the bolt. Flakes of rust rained down, but it wouldn't budge.

My teeth gritted. *"You can't out-stubborn me you stupid piece of shit metal, now* move!*"*

Felix sniggered and relayed my words because he was a pest. Without warning, the bolt rotated fully, and I slammed it back and opened the gate on a sigh of relief. Maddox and Buchanan slipped through, then Tavi, with Keaton bringing up the rear. He arched a brow.

"Were you talking to the door?"

"Shut up."

Tavi stopped next to Felix and absently nuzzled him. Felix leaned against his brother in a brief embrace without taking his eyes off the nearest guards. The two rangers hesitated in the shadows long enough to scan the stockade interior—distracted guards, rioting dragons, Cassia circling overhead and bellowing her head off—before they stepped clear of the wall. A quick glance at the guards we'd already killed, and they raised their heavy bows and snapped off shots at the guards at the northwest corner emplacement. Without waiting to see them fall, they spun and shot the guards at the northeast corner. We couldn't leave them alive. They'd spot us the moment we moved away from the postern gate.

The last guard fell off the wall with a shrill scream. Maddox pulled back on his bow to its full extension, muscles straining, before he released. His impressive shot took out the one guard midway down the wall who'd noticed.

A griffin rider's compact recurve bow couldn't reach that far down the wall, but the guards manning the ballistae on either side of the underground entrance were well within range. A steady draw, a tickle of fletching against cheek, a half breath exhaled—and release. My arrow took one guard in the side of the neck, tearing through arteries. I'd been aiming for center mass, but the unfortunate guard had ducked at the wrong moment and died choking on his own blood. Keaton's hit between the partner's shoulder blades, sinking deep. They were only wearing black uniforms, not leather armor. Stupid. At this range, leather could've protected against our arrows. We sidestepped until the other ballista crew was in view, and we shot them too.

No time for remorse as they fell. Right now, they could only be targets. Later . . . later there would be time for horror and regret.

The rangers snapped off a final pair of arrows, and then we were running for the underground entrance, in full view of the entire stockade. There was no cover to be had, not even the cover of darkness. Too many torches, too many guards. Not even the dragons could keep us from being spotted, but we'd known we would be and had planned for it.

Felix and Tavi launched themselves into the sky with piercing shrieks. They were fast, and agile, and if they couldn't be sneaky, they could be deadly. They tore through the nearest guards and did everything they could to draw all the attention to themselves. As I followed Keaton around the side of the sloped building, a pair of guards charged us. I ducked beneath the wild swing of a guard's fist, but it clipped the side of my head and my ears rang.

Buchanan came up behind me and dropped him with a single blow between the eyes, while Keaton throat-punched the second. Maddox slid up behind them and slit both guards' throats without even blinking.

I shook my head sharply to clear it and shoved against the door. It rattled in the frame but didn't open.

"*Felix!*"

My griffin twisted midair and dove straight for the door. He landed without sacrificing much in the way of speed, snapped his wings closed, lowered one shoulder, and rammed the door. A sharp snap, and it swung inward, revealing a shattered wooden beam lying on a metal floor.

Not even ironwood could withstand a determined griffin.

I flexed my shoulder against the shock of ghost pain, because that was going to leave one hell of a mark, and gave Felix a grateful pat before he charged back into the fight. I pushed the door fully open and found a set of ancient metal stairs leading down into the dark. Before I could step through, an arrow hissed through the air from behind me and sliced through the outside of my upper arm. Another ricocheted off the metal door, and I ducked, clamping my hand to my bicep with a hiss of pain. Blood seeped through my fingers, and Felix roared in rage as he tore apart the unfortunate guard who'd dared target his bondmate.

Buchanan grabbed my shoulder and dragged me inside, Keaton close behind.

Maddox stopped just inside the door, where he was protected on three sides but not easily forced back.

"I'll hold here." He snapped off a shot with his heavy war bow. Without pause, he smoothly drew another arrow and fired at a charging guard. The arrow took him through the heart and he tumbled, tripping another guard. Hard green eyes darted back to us. "*Go!*"

Buchanan tapped his fist to his chest in solemn salute and descended the ancient metal stairs. Before I could follow, Keaton touched my shoulder with a silent frown. Wincing, I flexed my injured arm, but while it burned like fire, I could still use it. I raised my bow in silent answer.

As I descended the stairs, I glanced back once at Maddox, standing tall as he kept up a steady rate of fire. Another step down and he was lost to sight. We crept down the stairs, leather boots quiet on rusting metal, bows up and arrows nocked. Smooth metal walls closed in around us as we descended down the narrow shaft, and the air grew cooler but not stagnant. The stairs turned at a landing and turned again before we reached the end of them.

Cautiously, we pulled open an unbarred metal door at the bottom. It swung open on silent, recently oiled hinges. A long metal hallway stretched out before us, metal doors lining either side, small glass panels inset at eye level. Lighting was built into the ceiling, but no magic powered them. Instead, smokeless torches like the ones in Ashfall''s brig lit the hall, pools of light and shadow stretching into infinity.

I exchanged a shocked glance with Keaton and saw the recognition in his eyes. This place . . . it was like the hatchery. Moving silently, I strode to the first door, rose onto my tiptoes, and peered inside. I barely suppressed my gasp. Sand instead of floor, fragments of shells, and the bones of something long dead that was very much neither griffin or dragon. I shuddered and dropped back onto my heels, letting Keaton look. He quickly glanced away, expression tight.

Angry shouts, thick with rolling Savinian accents, echoed down the hallway, too distorted by distance to make out the words. Other voices with the sharper consonants of Tennessan accents shouted back. It sounded like the riders were kicking up as much of a fuss as their dragons, and a predatory grin pulled at my lips.

That's it, guys. Keep them distracted just a little longer.

We cleared each room as we ghosted down the hall, but they were all empty, full of nothing but sand, shattered shells, and twisted skeletal remains that hurt the eye to look at. Midway down, hallways branched off to the left and right. Buchanan and Keaton shared a hard glance and simultaneously swung around the corners, bows up and arrows nocked, but the hallways were empty. We kept moving.

The shouting grew louder as we edged closer to the door at the end of the hall. If the layout was the same, our people were held in the largest room in the hatchery—the dragon crèche. There was even another square panel next to it, as inert as every other one I'd seen.

Guards shouted again, and dragon riders jeered and shit talked, voices ragged with rage and desperation. One sharp-edged, beloved voice rose above the rest, and fierce joy flooded my soul. Callum had always had a mouth on him, had always been able to get under people's skin. The tone of the guards' shouting changed from frustration to threatening. Metal clanged and that sharp-edged voice cut off midword in an explosion of breath audible over the cacophony. A *thud* followed, and I was done waiting.

A hard push, and the door swung inward on silent hinges. The cavernous room had been divided in two by jury-rigged metal bars, with the rear half full of enraged dragon riders. The guards were shoving several riders back from the gate as they slammed it shut and locked it. Callum had been dragged out and thrown to the ground. He was curled up, protecting his belly, agony twisting his angular face. A guard stood over him with a heavy cudgel raised high for another blow.

My bow snapped up, but I was no faster than Keaton. Our arrows slammed into the guard's back in near unison. Half a dozen guards spun around. They were well trained, and didn't let the surprise of our attack slow their response. Our only saving grace was none of them were armed with bows.

Buchanan dropped one with a well-placed arrow, Keaton a second. My injured arm spasmed as I pulled back on the string, and my shot went wide and hit the third guard in the shoulder. He snarled and kept coming. Before I could snap off another shot, he lowered his uninjured shoulder and rammed into me. The air whooshed from my lungs, but I managed to turn my tumble across the sand into a roll and regained my feet. With a broken bow dangling in two pieces from my hand.

"Son of a *bitch*!"

I threw my useless bow into the guard's furious face and darted out of reach, frantic gaze searching for help and finding none. Keaton was locked in struggle with a guard half again his size, and Buchanan was fighting two. Sand slipped beneath my boots, slowing my run just enough for the guard to grab my arm over the bleeding gash and yank me against his chest.

Vision whited out from the pain, I made a blind grab for my knife, but his arms pinned mine before I could reach it. Panic beat its wings, threatening my control, but I didn't let it win—I leaned on Reese's training. A bootheel to his toes, a snap of my head back to try to break his nose, a sharp twist of my hips to try to throw him off balance.

Nothing worked.

The guard was bigger than me, stronger than me, and just as well trained if not better. I couldn't even get any leverage on him. He easily kept me restrained with one arm while his other came up in a bar across my neck.

"I'm going to have fun breaking you, rider freak," he said, his voice rasping in my ear.

Snarling, I twisted toward his elbow and nearly slipped free before his arm tightened. Pressure built around my throat, and I swung a fist down between his legs. He gasped, high-pitched and miserable, and I reached for my knife again. My fingers brushed the hilt but I still couldn't quite reach. So I reached for the arrow in his shoulder instead—and yanked it free. Blood sprayed, but the guard's grip didn't loosen. If anything, he gripped my neck tighter. The bloody arrow slipped from my weakened fingers before I could stab him with it.

"Help!" I gasped out with the last of my breath. My gaze locked with Keaton's, but he couldn't break away from his own fight. Worse, I'd distracted him. His opponent cracked him across the face and he went down hard. The guard restraining me barked a laugh.

"Nobody's going to help you, freak."

"Wanna bet?" a cold voice grated out.

They'd forgotten about Callum.

He appeared at my side, and I twisted my hip toward him. He slid his knife from my belt sheath and slammed it into the side of the guard's neck, twisting the blade viciously before ripping it free. I jerked away from the guard's limp hold, mostly avoiding the blood spray. Callum didn't stop, ghosting up behind one of Buchanan's opponents and stabbing him in the kidney. As the guard arched back in agony, the big ranger slashed a dagger through his throat.

Keaton had since gotten the upper hand on his opponent, and I was unarmed. So I did the only thing left to me—I ran for the keys still grasped in a dead guard's hand, ripped them free, and unlocked the gate. Freeing over a dozen pissed off riders, including Major Zeddemore, who was still the largest man I'd ever met. He was first through the gate, and he grabbed the guard fighting Keaton and tossed him against the metal wall. Bones cracked, and the guard collapsed in a heap on the sand. He didn't move again. Buchanan and Callum had already killed the last.

I sagged against the bars. We'd done it.

As Major Zeddemore snapped out swift orders, Callum sauntered over to me. He was painfully emaciated, and he'd collected new scars during his captivity, but his arrogance seemed intact.

"You're overachieving again, Harper." Callum smirked, his fever-bright gaze holding my own. And then his cocky mask cracked, and he swallowed hard. "I apologize."

The breath rushed out of me. "I forgive you."

"I know you do." He held up his bloody blade, the torchlight reflecting off a savage grin. "You kept it."

"Of course I did, it's good steel." My gaze darted around the room, searching for two faces and not finding them. "Where's Dimitri and Zayne?"

"Interrogation," a deep, rumbling voice replied. I snapped my head up to look at Major Zeddemore. The man looked a little rough around the edges, but if he carried any wounds, they weren't visible.

"We need to get them." Anxiety and fear for Dimitri, for *Zayne*, swirled deep in my belly. I didn't know what we'd find, but we had to find them *now*.

"We will." Zeddemore held up a massive hand in a request for patience I didn't have. "All part of the plan."

"Plan? What plan?" I snarled, seconds away from losing it.

White teeth flashed against dark skin, though there was little humor in Zeddemore's smile.

"Did you think we were sitting on our asses, just waiting for rescue, little griffin rider?" Somehow, he made the term sound endearing rather than patronizing. "Everyone else is racing for the surface. As soon as there's no chance of them being trapped underground again, their dragons can act."

Already, the room had cleared, leaving only the two dragon riders, Keaton, Buchanan, and me. I kept my eyes up, refusing to look at the dead guards. If I looked at the one who'd wanted to break me, I'd start kicking his corpse and never stop.

"They need to run faster," Keaton said grimly. Blood ran down the side of his bruised face, but his eyes were clear. "Our griffins are holding the door alone."

Alarm raced through me, but Buchanan closed his eyes on a heartfelt "Damn it."

"*Felix?*"

"*Hurry.*" Sorrow rode his whisper, and he sent me a flash of memory—Maddox, slumped in the doorway, two crossbow bolts in his chest, trying and failing to nock one last arrow. His heavy bow slipped from his fingers, and his eyes glazed over in death. Felix and Tavi took his place guarding the door. I shook free of the memory with an angry cry.

Maddox was gone. He'd never call me "griffin girl" again. I blinked back unshed tears. Later, I promised myself, later.

"If your riders are going to do something, do it now before we're dead too!" I raged, flinging one arm toward Keaton.

Acid-bright fatigue burned into Felix's muscles, his great heart racing as his lungs struggled for breath. Tavi couldn't be much better off. Terror for our griffins made me reckless. I sent Felix a burst of energy, and glared at Zeddemore as I swayed. Callum gripped my arm, but his feverish gaze was locked to his commander, impatience in every line of his emaciated frame.

Anger tightened Zeddemore's expression, but it wasn't directed at me. His eyes glazed over, and tension stiffened his shoulders, as if he were the one chained, not his dragon. Seconds ticked past at an agonizing crawl—and then a hard grin stretched across his face.

"They've got the door. Maximus, *go.*"

The enormous black dragon's deep roar sounded for the first time. Even as far underground as we were, the bellowing basso cry vibrated my damn *soul.* The rest of the dragons answered his call to battle, their roars echoing down the stairs and bouncing off the metal walls.

They'd only ever been chained by their riders, and their riders were free.

Savage delight flared bright in Felix's mind as Maximus broke the chains that bound him. Gleefully, he yanked me into his mind so I could see, giving me zero time to adjust. Callum growled in annoyance as my knees buckled, but he kept me from collapsing. My vision snapped into focus. Felix and Tavi were circling high above the walls as the dragons cut loose on the stockade.

My jaw dropped.

Maximus was a freaking *tank.* In the seconds it took the other dragons to snap their chains, he'd flattened the barracks—and any soldiers unfortunate enough to still be inside. Not to be outdone, the lone red dragon ripped the six-foot anchor spikes out of the ground instead of breaking the chains. He proceeded to use the chains as a flail, ripping through men and weapons alike. The rest of the dragons attacked the guards and the anti-air artillery.

But the Savinians didn't run. They fought savagely. Several artillery crews fired, and dragon lances flashed through the air. One struck a gray through the chest, and my heart stopped as she collapsed in a spray of blood. *Not Artemis, please.*

Callum's grip didn't waver. Relief and guilt mixed. Relief that it wasn't Artemis, guilt that a dragon and rider had died and I'd felt *relief.*

Another dragon twisted and took a lance to the shoulder, but he ripped it out with a terrible roar and tore the artillery crew to bloody shreds. The balance shifted to the ex-prisoners, and the guards hovered on the edge of breaking.

And then wailing roars cut through the cacophony of battle.

Felix snapped his head around as the guards rallied. The coppers had returned. For an instant, the Tennessan dragons, underfed and injured, faltered. Then Maximus took to the skies with another earth-shattering roar. Felix and Tavi skittered out of the way as the great black dragon tore into a copper, blood and worse raining down on the stockade. More dragons shot into the air, and now the battle raged above and below.

My view skewed sideways as Felix dropped one wing low and slipped out of the path of a stray dragon lance. Terror iced over my heart.

"Be careful!"

"Always am!" he shot back with a reckless amusement tempered by determination.

Major Zeddemore's grim voice pulled me back to myself before I could chastise my griffin further.

"Now, let's go get my riders back." He picked up the heavy cudgel that had been used on Callum, spun it once, and strode out of the room, massive shoulders scraping the doorframe. Buchanan stalked after him, bow up and ready.

I nodded to Callum and pulled free of his grip, as steady as I was going to get after giving too much to Felix. Keaton's glazed over eyes snapped back to awareness as he pulled himself from Tavi's mind. He briefly pressed his shoulder to mine before he followed Zeddemore. Callum hesitated only long enough to liberate a pair of daggers from the dead guards, then passed me his knife back. I wrapped my fingers around the hilt, the knife a comforting, familiar weight in my hand.

As we trotted down the hall, chaotic flashes from the battle slipped from Felix's mind into mine. Dragon lances flashing across the night sky, the soldiers below not caring what they hit. A copper and a gray tangled up, claws slashing and jaws snapping as they fell together, wings shredded by an indiscriminate flechette round. Another copper tumbling from the sky, headless, Riven roaring in savage triumph.

Zeddemore turned right midway down the main hallway, long strides just shy of a run. No torches lined the cross corridor, and the far end was lost to shadow. Keaton grabbed a torch from the wall and passed it to me, unable to carry it and use his bow. I held it high and chased back the dark as Zeddemore stopped in front of a door a third of the way down. He glanced at Buchanan, and the big ranger nodded his readiness. The door was thrown open, the men swept through, weapons ready . . . but only silence followed.

"Clear!" Zeddemore called out after a few seconds.

I shoved past Callum and Keaton, heart pounding in fear and anticipation at what we'd find. My feet stumbled to a halt a few steps inside.

They'd been left in darkness. Bound and bloodied.

And *alive.*

Relief hit me so hard I bent over and nearly singed myself on the damn torch. Keaton snatched it out of my hand with an irritated growl, but his grip was gentle as he pulled me upright. Both men had been beaten, but Zayne was in far worse shape. He was also stupid proud of himself if his smug grin was anything to go by. He winked at me as Zeddemore cut him loose, or maybe he blinked. It was hard to tell with one of his eyes swollen shut.

"Who's the stubborn one now, Harper?" he said in a hoarse voice, as if he'd been screaming, or maybe cursing his tormentors.

"Definitely you," I said before I shifted my gaze to Dimitri, who was battered and bruised, dried blood on his chin from a split lip. I grinned. "Hey, asshole."

"Hey, hotshot." He smiled, even though it must have hurt, and looked at me as if I were the only person in the room. "Took you long enough."

Buchanan cut him free, and Dimitri rolled his shoulders with a sigh of relief. Slowly, he stood up, as if testing whether he *could.* The ranger went to steady him, but Dimitri waved him off.

Another flash from the battle leaked from my griffin. A rider scrambling across the stockade to his fallen dragon, blood pouring from the gray's shoulder where he'd torn a lance free. Felix diving, slamming claws first into the guard who'd raised a bow to shoot the rider in the back. The rider never even noticed as Felix sprang back into the air, blood dripping from beak and claws.

"Time to go," Zeddemore barked as he half carried Zayne. One of his knees wasn't bending properly.

I stepped aside to let Buchanan take lead—and arched my back as a scream ripped from my throat. Agony tore through my shoulder blade. One hand clawed at my perfectly healthy shoulder as fire ate into muscle and bone, while the other reached for something I couldn't touch.

My griffin.

"Harper!" Dimitri lunged forward, steadied me when I would've fallen, but he wasn't who I needed right now. My wild gaze darted past him to Keaton.

"It's not me, it's not me!" A sobbing cry, a desperate plea. "*Felix!*"

Keaton's face went bone white, terror obliterating his impassive expression before his eyes glazed over.

I reached for my bonded. A bolt had torn through feather and muscle, punched a hole straight through his dappled wing. He faltered midair and fell out of the sky. Agony spiraled higher as he slammed into the ground, the sharp *snap* of breaking bone stabbing into my thigh. I screamed our pain. I could have shielded, but I didn't want the distance. I wanted my griffin.

Everything ceased to matter but him. I dropped the endless drop into his mind, screamed his name, looked through his eyes.

My brave griffin tried to push me back out. He couldn't sever the bond as easily if I was at his end of it. I didn't let him. If we were going to go, we were going to go together. Torchlight flickered on metal, and we stared at the dragon lance that would be the death of us. Regret and pain and love, so much love, flared bright in our minds. Bright as flame and just as fragile.

"*Love you, Harpy,*" he whispered as the soldier smashed a fist on the release.

"*Love—*" Something slammed into us.

But it wasn't the dragon lance.

It was Tavi.

We howled our denial, our grief, our *rage* as we tumbled across the unforgiving ground. Tavi collapsed, the dragon lance meant for us buried in his side.

Felix roared in soul-rending agony and crawled to his brother. He ignored the green dragon who savaged the artillery crew before she stood over the griffins protectively. He ignored the pain in his shattered wing, his broken leg. He ignored everything but his brother.

Felix nuzzled him, purring desperately, but Tavi sighed and didn't breathe again. Amber eyes full of protective love never looked away from Felix as that insanely brave griffin stilled, as he *died*.

Screaming, I yanked myself back into my own head. Just like Felix, I ignored everything around me. I only had eyes for Keaton, for my brother . . . who screamed like his soul had just been torn in two. Because it had.

Tavi had severed.

I tore out of Dimitri's arms and slammed into Keaton, wrapped my arms around him as if I could keep him here by the strength of my grip alone. Together, we sank to the cold metal floor. His screams broke me. Hot tears poured down my face, and I couldn't breathe.

And then he stopped screaming.

"No, no, *no!*" I cupped the sides of his face, stared into his dying eyes, his bleeding soul. "Don't go, please don't go. Keaton, *please.*"

"Ty," he whispered, voice a ragged ruin. "He called me Ty."

My heart shredded. *Oh gods.*

"I can't hear him, Harpy. But I know where to go to hear him again."

"Please no." My throat tightened, threatened to cut off my words when I needed them most. "Please don't leave me."

I wrapped myself around him tighter, trying to hold his shattered pieces together. It wasn't enough. *I* wasn't enough.

"Harpy . . ." His face contorted in agony, eyes burning bright with unshed tears. He closed his eyes, and they spilled over, burning tracks of sorrow and grief cutting down his face. "I *can't.*"

"Never alone," I said desperately. "You *promised.*"

Keaton's eyes flew open and rage stirred in the dull amber. "You told me once that you would've followed Felix. How can you ask me to stay when you wouldn't?"

"You told me once that it was a chance to fight to live, so *fight*, damn you!" I raged back, pressing my forehead to his. "I don't think I can do this without you, brother."

His eyes closed again, breath shuddering, soul bleeding out. In the back of my mind, Felix mourned, heartbroken and screaming in pain. I held tight to both of them. My heart was already shredded, but if Keaton followed Tavi . . . it would shatter.

"I know I can't make you stay." My voice dropped to a tear-soaked whisper as I held up my hand. "But if you do, you'll never be alone."

A promise, a vow, a heartfelt plea. It was all I had to offer him, but the choice was his. Because our griffins loved us enough, were brave enough, to give us that choice.

An eternity passed while I waited for him to decide. Cold metal seeped through my riding leathers. Weight shifted and voices murmured as Callum, Dimitri, and Buchanan kept watch over us. I was vaguely aware that Zeddemore had carried Zayne out, that he'd left to help with the cleanup. That the fighting was over. That we'd *won*.

None of it mattered. I'd wait forever if that's what it took.

Keaton finally opened his eyes. Met my gaze. And took my hand.

"Never alone."

CHAPTER 27

The weather turned to shit as it so often did in the fall, gloomy and rainy, a perfect match to the shitstorm that erupted when we returned to Fort Ashfall with Major Zeddemore and the surviving POWs. Westbrook didn't even try to pretend innocence. He fled over the Savinian border and took the names of his coconspirators with him. We'd have to clean house before Ashfall would feel safe—and with Westbrook still out there somewhere, I'd never feel safe beyond the fort walls again. On the other hand, no patrols were safe anymore, so a little extra paranoia wasn't necessarily a bad thing.

The medics did what they could for the POWs. Many had been in Savinian hands for a long time and would be a long time recovering, but they would recover. So would Nikos. The tough bastard was still in bad shape, but he'd been brought back from Bristol, along with Erra.

Felix had gotten lucky. The bolt had done considerable damage to his wing, but nothing that wouldn't heal. Two of the rescued dragons weren't so lucky. They might never fly properly again. Artemis was one of them.

Three dragons and riders died fighting for their freedom. And one irreplaceable griffin.

A week passed, and the weather improved. Seven days of rain and gray skies turned to bright sunshine, an achingly blue sky, and a breeze that was almost warm. I sat on the grassy slope of the griffin eyrie with Felix stretched out at my side and the fort valley spread out below us. The horses were out in the fields for the first time in days, sunlight sparkled off the lake, conventional soldiers ran through a practice drill, and dragons soared overhead.

Felix and I were just enjoying my freedom.

Our desperate rescue of the POWs had been exactly that—desperate and unauthorized. The days of interrogation we'd endured on our return had been less than pleasant, but necessary to sort everything out. Major Zeddemore had ensured the charges against all of us were dropped, but Anderson had still torn a strip off my hide. He'd stopped yelling when I told him about our possible griffin rider traitor. I made sure Zeddemore and Harborne knew too. Just in case.

Unofficially, we were praised. Officially, we were reprimanded and most definitely not rewarded with things like drunken parties or incentive flights. I didn't care.

Nikos had been right. We didn't do it for the civilians, and we sure as shit didn't do it for the reward. If we did, we'd be no better than Franks, taking money from whoever was willing to line our pockets. I gazed down at the medical facility where Artemis stretched out her shredded wings, Riven curled around her protectively, and smiled.

We did it for each other.

My smile faded as I dropped my eyes to the gold chevron in my hand. Turning it over and over, letting my thoughts wander where they wanted.

We'd lost so many people. Some to betrayal, like Riley. Others to the Savinians, like Maddox . . . and Tavi. Sorrow and pride twined in my soul. Tavi hadn't hesitated to give his life for Felix. I'd be grateful for his sacrifice for the rest of our days, and grateful he'd given Keaton the chance to live.

Insanely brave griffin.

Felix sighed mournfully. The ache in his broken leg had faded away, and the brace had been removed this morning. Griffins healed fast when their bondmate did nothing but answer questions, stuff themselves with questionable chow hall food, and feed them energy for a week straight. The medics had even cleared him for short flights, but he had no interest in stretching his wings. His head laid on his paws, and his eyes were dull. I stroked his shoulder and wished I had the ability to purr for him.

"Ear scritches will do, love," he murmured with a faint edge of amusement. A slight smile pulled at my lips, and I complied, burying

my fingers in his feathers and breathing in his scent, all sun-warmed cinnamon and *home*. Footsteps approached, and Felix's tufted ears perked up, just a little.

"A cow would be even better," he added as Dimitri sat next to me. I rolled my eyes at my griffin before turning to Dimitri.

"Hey, asshole."

"Hey, hotshot." He paused. Leaned away with a teasing grin. "Am I allowed to call you that again?"

"Haven't punched you for it yet, have I?"

"The day is young," he said with a quiet laugh. Sunlight glinted off gold, and he glanced at my hand. "What's that?"

I showed him the cadet rank Commandant Pulaski had given me before tucking it away.

"Just something I'm trying to hold onto." I leaned back on my hands and tilted my face toward him. "I see they finally let you loose."

He flexed his shoulders, trying to shed the tension from long days in interrogation. I could relate, but his had been far worse, and I'd barely seen him since our somewhat triumphant return.

"Yeah, I told them everything I knew, everything I guessed. I just hope it's enough." His expression hardened. "I think the Savinians are desperate, Harper. Desperate to push into our territory, desperate to eliminate our griffins, desperate for more dragons. That's what they wanted out of that POW camp. Not captured fighters like before. Breeders."

My lips parted in understanding. It had never been about Zayne, the general's son, at all. It had been about Cassia.

"That's why they wanted the greens…"

"Any females, really. And reds, so they can breed more of those nasty coppers. I think they just had Maximus there because they didn't have anywhere else to put him."

His eyes unfocused for a moment, but I couldn't tell if he was talking to his dragon, or if he was lost in thought. I took the time to study his face. One side of his jaw was still a sickly yellow and green. His split lip had healed, but the dark shadows under his eyes had barely faded, and he carried a haunted look I didn't like.

"You look like you've barely slept since we got back. What are you doing out here, Dimitri?"

"Getting some sun, obviously," he said with a straight face. I elbowed him gently, conscious of his still-healing ribs, and his smile broke free. "Riven told me you were out here. Thought you might like some company. More company."

His smile faltered as he looked at Felix.

"I'm sorry about Tavi."

Tufted ears flicked back and forth, and a feathered tail twitched, but Felix dipped his head in a gracious nod. If anything, though, Dimitri's haunted look deepened.

"That wasn't your fault," I said with a frown.

"I know." He turned his face away, bruised jaw flexing. "But I messed everything up, Harper. Everything I did was to try to protect you from Westbrook. But then Franks betrayed us, and the Savinians were looking for you and Keaton . . . and they would've killed you, because they have no use for griffins."

He shook his head as that helpless rage twisted his expression.

"And there was nothing I could do to protect you then."

"Oh, really? And whose idea was it to knock out Zayne?"

Zayne had already told me everything, but I needed Dimitri to say it, needed to banish the shadows in his amber eyes.

"It was the only thing I could think of to keep Cassia free," he said with a dismissive shrug, as if fighting back against the Savinians long enough to strike Zayne hadn't nearly gotten him killed. He still wouldn't look at me.

"If you hadn't done that, we never would've been able to pull off that rescue. Not without Cassia coordinating." I brushed my fingers against the side of his neck, where his throat had almost been cut. "Your back was to the wall, and you still found a way to protect us. To protect *me*. Just like you always do."

His closed his eyes and let out a shuddering breath. A rueful smile twisted his lips as he finally turned to face me again.

"I tried to protect you, Harper, but you saved me." His gaze shifted to Riven as the black dragon curled a little tighter around Artemis. "Saved us."

Felix lifted his head and clacked his beak decisively. I smiled.

"He says you saved us first."

A faint frown marred Dimitri's brow, but then understanding dawned, banishing the last of the shadows. He rolled to his feet, knelt in front of Felix, and lifted his hand. "Can I?"

Felix nudged his hand pointedly in answer. Dimitri chuckled and scratched behind his tufted ears. A purr rumbled in my griffin's chest as his eyes drifted shut.

"They're fucking blind if they can't see your value," he said quietly. Black-ringed amber eyes shifted to me, including me in the compliment.

"Now all I need is a cow," Felix said with a small trill. *"Tell him about the cow!"*

Laughter burst out of me, and my heart felt a little lighter. Dimitri obediently scratched Felix's ears and promised to get him a cow. It was nice. No, not nice. It was amazing. All the old anger and tension was gone. I had my oldest friend back. It only took three damn years.

"How's Keaton?" he asked, breaking the silence as he retook his spot next to me. My shoulders tensed.

"Still fighting," I said hoarsely. "How's Cal?"

"Malnourished, scarred inside and out, and very angry. But there's hope for Artemis' wings, and it's helped him, I think. They'll need to go back to the academy. The medics said only the Mavens know how to regrow membrane when it's been shredded that badly, but the rest of her wing structure is sound."

"Long trip," I said, thinking about how Cassia and another green had flown her back to Ashfall in a carry net. Because of course Zayne had thought to bring a carry net.

"They'll do it in stages." Dimitri ran a hand through his short, dark hair. "Think Keaton will want to go back to the academy and bond another griffin?"

I forced a shrug, but my shoulders refused to relax. Keaton was still fighting, but he was barely talking, barely eating, barely *living*.

"Most griffin riders who survive severing can't go through with it, though leadership 'encourages' it strongly." A tremor shook my frame, and my gaze locked onto the medical facility, where Keaton was resting. "If he could though . . . it'd be another reason for him to fight."

Fear for my brother strangled the breath in my lungs, and my eyes burned. I'd cried too much this week. I didn't want to cry again. Dimitri held up his hand. Waiting. I let out a shaking breath and held on to him for dear life. For my brother's life.

Eventually, I regained control of myself. He didn't let go.

"One good thing came from this mess," he said with a smirk that meant nothing but trouble. "Zeddemore and Anderson finally got approval from Harborne for a joint team. I'm tapped for it, so is Zayne." His gaze shifted to mine. "I heard you're getting tapped for it, too. I fucking hope so. We're kind of a mess without you."

I snorted. "You guys did fine without me."

He stared. "Cal ended up a POW, Zayne was captured and tortured, and I got blackmailed into betraying everyone. Meanwhile, in your first six months on active duty you prevented a raid on Ashfall, stopped a major incursion at Bramble, and liberated an entire POW camp of dragon riders."

I blinked a few times before I shook my head. "I didn't do any of that on my own, remember?"

"Who said you had to?" He raised his brows. "Come on, Harper, you know you want on that team with us."

I fought back a smile.

"Yeah, I guess you guys did mess things up pretty bad without me." My teasing smile broke free as I looked up at him. "And here I thought I was just the trouble magnet."

"You were always more than that, Harper." His warm, callused fingers tightened on mine. "Zayne was the strategist. Callum could fight like a demon. I was the charismatic bastard who could talk our way out of all the trouble you got us into, but you . . . you were our fire."

I stilled, completely ensnared by the intense look in his eyes.

Felix snickered in my mind.

"I'll think about it," I said somewhat breathlessly. Felix laughed out loud this time, and I shoved his furry shoulder before smiling at Dimitri. "Working with my brothers wouldn't be the worst thing ever."

"Harper . . ." Dimitri used his grip on my hand to tug me closer, and his voice dropped low, without even a hint of teasing. "I never said I wanted to be your *brother*."

"What does that mean?"

As I frowned in confusion, Dimitri reached out and tucked a loose strand of hair behind my ear. My breath caught as his fingers trailed down my cheek, as his heated gaze dropped just a touch lower than my eyes. A shiver of breathless anticipation held me frozen in place.

"Dimitri?"

His low laugh curled around me and did all sorts of interesting things to my insides. I wanted him to do it again. Instead, he stood up and gave me a crooked grin.

"You're smart, Harper. You'll figure it out."

And then the damn man walked away.

"No, I won't!" I bellowed after him in exasperation. "Dimitri! Come back here! What does that mean?"

He just laughed again, a bright sound full of amusement this time. He didn't even look back as he strolled down the grassy slope. All the things I wanted to shout at him tangled up, and I ended up just glaring in frustrated silence.

Felix nudged my side and snickered. *"I see we've regressed to nonverbal status."*

"Shut up."

A smile pulled at my lips as I watched my oldest friend walk away from me again. Because it wasn't for good, not this time. I still needed to yell at him more.

And maybe think about what he wanted to be if it wasn't my brother...

An echoing roar pulled my gaze to the sky. A green dragon soared over the valley, wings stretched wide to catch the wind. Cassia and Zayne. Their first flight together since we got back. Zayne's knee had finally healed enough to handle the strain. I watched them soar together and smiled through the longing. I knew what it was like to fly on her back now.

It was enough.

Felix tilted his head. Gradually, the bond tightened. He was shielding from me. I ripped my gaze off the beautiful green dragon and frowned at him in concern. He'd never shielded like that, not even during the worst of his grief for Tavi. I reached for him, buried my fingers in his feathers, curled myself around his mind.

"Felix?"

"Do you ever regret it..." His voice was very small and he wouldn't look at me. *"Regret me?"*

Three years bonded together, and he'd never once asked me outright—and I'd never reassured him. I was a *terrible* bondmate. Remorse threatened to drown me.

I'd never wanted him to feel a moment's doubt or guilt that I'd bonded him instead of a dragon. So I'd hidden things from him to try to protect him. Instead, I'd only succeeding in hurting him and undermining his confidence, his *faith*, in me and our bond.

"*Never.*" I dropped my shielding and let him in. Without reservation or holding back. I let him see *everything*.

My sorrow over losing my original dream. My longing to fly, to feel the wind on my face. My pride in my new life, in *him*, in the incredible things we'd accomplished together. My unconditional *love* for him.

And yes, my regret—for ever hurting the other half of my soul.

Tentatively, Felix dropped his own shielding and let me back in. I'd never doubted his love for me. I'd never doubted the joy he felt when he pulled me into his mind and took me flying, when he let me feel the wind on his feathers, see the sky through his eyes. I'd even caught flashes of his guilt and sorrow that he couldn't give me more than that.

With a mournful sigh, he relaxed the last of his shielding and let me see what he'd buried deep, so deep I'd never known it was there. A terrible guilt he'd carried since he was a cub.

Guilt that he wasn't, could never be, what I'd wanted—a dragon.

The last time guilt had sliced into him, sharper than the sharpest knife, I'd failed to find the right words. This time, I stroked my hands along his downy cheeks, stared into his purple eyes, and told him what I should've told him every damn day.

"*You are insanely brave, and utterly ridiculous, and* mine," I said fiercely. "*My griffin. And I wouldn't trade you for all the dragons in the world.*"

Felix stilled, so deep within my mind there was no room for him to doubt my words. The black stain of guilt slowly melted away, replaced by the crystal clarity of belief. The wound wasn't gone, but it would heal. *We* would heal.

My griffin pressed his forehead to mine. "*Love you, Harpy.*"

"*Love you, featherhead. And I will* always *love flying with you.*"

Felix leaped to his feet, tail lashing with excitement. His wings rustled as he stretched them wide. And for the first time since Tavi died, he bounded into the air and took flight.

"*Come fly with me, then, love.*"

I dropped the endless drop into his mind and felt the wind on his feathers. Joy flooded my heart, tangled with his, and rebounded until our entangled souls sang with it. His wings flared wide as he caught a thermal, and we soared ever higher.

Together, always together.

My wild laughter rang out across the hill, and his roar shook the skies.

ACKNOWLEDGMENTS

This novel and its insanely brave, utterly ridiculous griffins wouldn't exist if it weren't for the amazing people at Baen. Huge thanks to Toni, Griffin, Jason, Leah, David A., Marla, Joy, and everyone on staff who helped make this dream a reality. A special acknowledgment to the annual Baen Fantasy Adventure Award Contest. My story, "Fall From Grace," was a 2023 finalist, and it's from that story that this novel took flight.

To Marisa Wolf and Kacey Ezell—cheerleaders, badasses, sisters in every way that matters. This story wouldn't be what it is without your feedback and endless support. Love you both so damn much.

To Jason Cordova, griffins champion extraordinaire! I'm not sure you understand how much your feedback and boundless enthusiasm for this project has meant to me. So here you go—you are the bestest champion of griffins EVER!!

To Howard Andrew Jones . . . I can never thank you enough for the mentorship you provided. Your encouragement and genuine enjoyment of the novel was nothing short of amazing. Thank you so much for your support and friendship. It means the world to me.

A big thank you to Bill Fawcett for dedicating so much of his time to reading the story and providing incredibly insightful critiques. I still have a document specifically for your feedback, because I know it'll be useful for all of my future projects!

To everyone who bawled their eyes out at *that* scene—you can thank Chuck Gannon and an epic night of plotting at a bar. Thank you so much for your insightful input, Chuck! You're downright diabolical and I love it!

Casey Moores and Nick Steverson. My Obi-Wan and my Evil Twin. You guys are awesome and I owe you both so much.

To Jon Osborne, AKA our feral bachelor—thank you for allowing me to tuckerize you. As so often happens, your character grew into someone vital to my story. Harper wouldn't have made it without Oz.

All the thanks to Chris Kennedy at Chris Kennedy Publishing. I wouldn't be where I'm at today if it wasn't for you. Best "Boss" ever. And thanks to all the kickass Cantina authors and editors, you guys are amazing!

Finally, last but never least, so much gratitude to my incredible husband and my monsters...I mean, my kids. There's no way I could've done any of this without Dan's support on this crazy writing adventure. My kids have been just as supportive, and are always so excited when I have a book release. Probably because it means a trip to the bakery for reward cupcakes! Love you all to pieces.